I0822315

BEYOND POWER

SPECTRAL SERIES BOOK 1

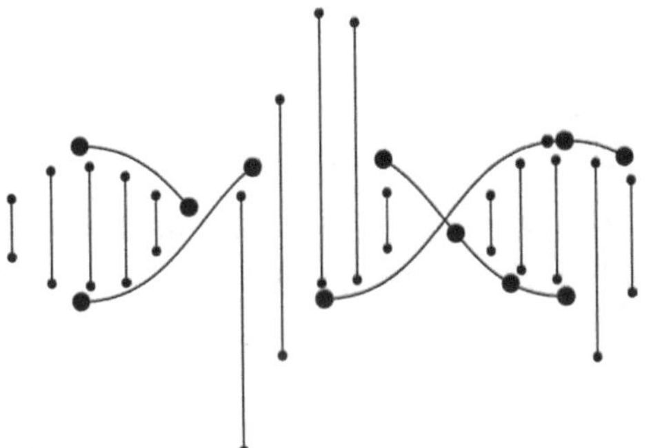

MISCELLEANA TSALIKIS

Originally published as *Beyond Power* by Lina Hart.
Revised and republished as *Beyond Power* under Miscelleana Tsalikis.

Cover design by Christonikos Tsalikis (OutsideTheBox.nyc), based on an initial concept by Sheer Genius (99designs).

Publishing services by Paper Raven Books LLC.

Printed in the United States of America.

First Edition, 2023

Second Edition, 2025

Paperback ISBN: 979-8-9881061-0-4

Hardback ISBN:

DEDICATION

To my husband, the beautiful method to my madness, the magic in my dreams, the love of my life.

For my Anamastasia, every word was written for you, my lover of books, my sparkle, my gift.

AUTHOR'S NOTE

All time-hopping and character-shuffling novels need a map...

The reading order of Beyond Power is like a shuffled deck of cards, bringing you around twists and turns as it weaves together an intricate tapestry of characters and events that will keep you guessing until the very end.

But, the only place I want you to get lost are amongst the pages.

The following chronological timeline will guide you through my labyrinthine maze without leading you astray. Find the full map here or every chapter holds your place for you.

May you enjoy the adventure.

With creativity and inspiration,

Miscelleana

TIMELINE

2101
SEPT
CH 5
2104
OCT
CH 1
CH 3
CH 7
NOV
CH 11
DEC
CH 14
CH 18
CH 4
CH 2
CH 9
CH 12
CH 8
CH 17
CH 13
CH 16

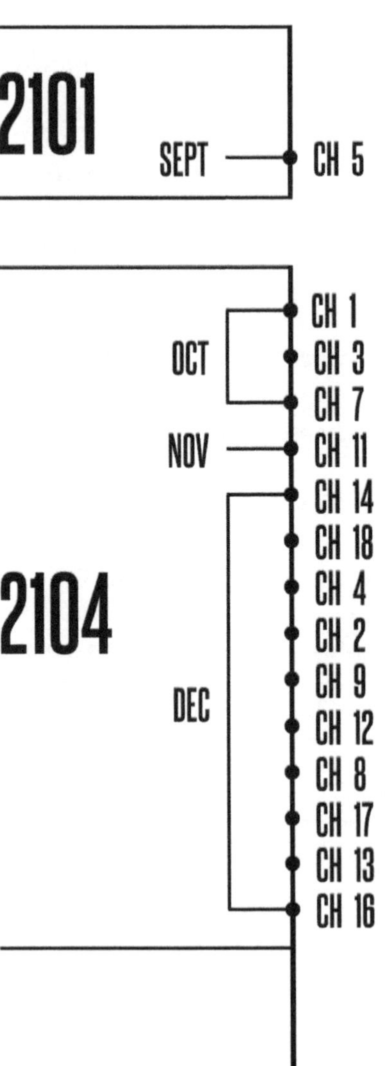

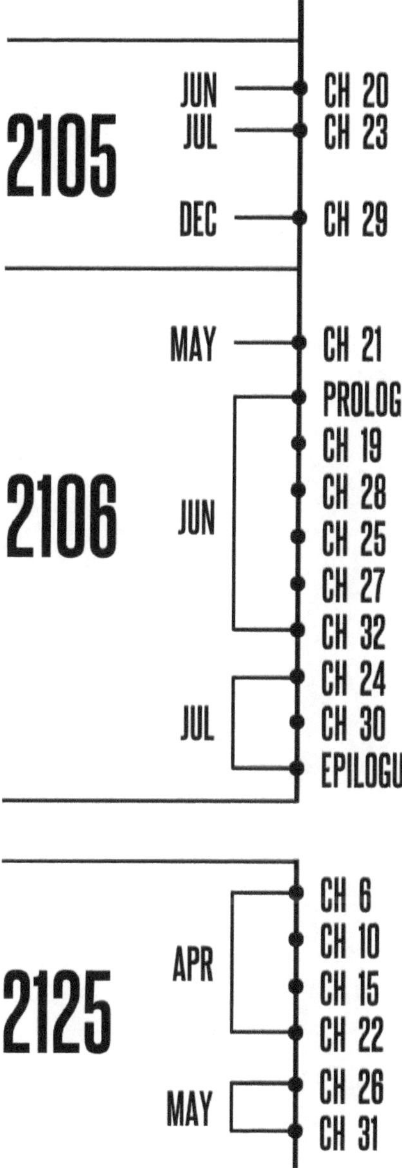
2105
JUN
CH 20
JUL
CH 23
DEC
CH 29
2106
MAY
CH 21
JUN
PROLOGUE
CH 19
CH 28
CH 25
CH 27
CH 32
JUL
CH 24
CH 30
EPILOGUE
2125
APR
CH 6
CH 10
CH 15
CH 22
MAY
CH 26
CH 31

BONUS CONTENT INCLUDED

Don't stop at the last page—dive into an exclusive sneak peek of Book 2 "Beyond Ruin: Origins" at the end of this book.

PROLOGUE

JUNE 17, 2106
Leeya

The pain was excruciating.

A silver light traveled from the top of my head down through my spine and swirled around me. I was ripped open from the inside, like a light needed to burst from my chest. Somehow, my body contained a fire hot enough to consume me. It was unbearable.

I kept screaming as it coursed through me.

As I gritted my teeth, holding myself together, fighting to keep myself in one piece, the pain started to subside. Slow at first, it eventually quieted to nothing.

Pulling my hands away from the side of my face, I slowly opened my eyes, blinking them in the light shining through the window, tears wet on my cheeks.

I looked around the living room in the small apartment and tried to regulate my erratic breathing. As I opened my mouth to call for my dad, a bright light took over my mind. It was white at first—blinding white—and then it changed to a bright black, like all the energy of the world sat in one place inside of me.

Images started crashing into my mind.

I was flooded with pictures of life, people, places— everything and everywhere. I saw images of men, women, and children doing everyday, spectacular things, yelling, laughing, screaming, crying, playing, living their lives. Lovers. Children. Loners. Families. It was everything all at once.

Everyone.

My mind felt as though it disconnected and floated in its own space. I was just the vessel, and it was the existence.

Purple strings of light, power, and energy left my body in waves in every direction. Small specks of light the same color swirled outward. It was terrifying and beautiful. I tried to focus on the energy leaving my body, but the images…

…the images changed.

All of those people, every one of them, started screaming. In pain.

Just as I had.

Billions of people screamed. The entire world screamed at the same time.

And then—it just stopped.

Green smoke escaped their lips as I felt every single one of them die. I felt loss spread out from within me, twisting and seeping into every fiber of my being. The black light pulsed in my mind and crashed around me.

They disappeared in a second. Their energy exploding into everything, everywhere.

All I could do was cover my mouth to stifle my own screams from ringing out and echoing into forever.

PART ONE

CHAPTER 1

OCTOBER 2104
Angelia

"Yeah? Well, fuck you, too." I held up my comm screen and slid the white button to the left, disconnecting the call.

That's one way to get the final say in an argument. Of course, the problem was that the service representative probably heard that line multiple times today and could give two shits. But really, did anyone who dropped an F-bomb mean to actually offend the other person? It's really just a personal vindication to the person saying it.

This time around, I wasn't getting a new specglass tablet because apparently I'd used up my accidental coverage too many times already. But, by the Gods, it felt good to drop an explosion of bad language and hang up. Somehow it made me feel like I won.

I dropped my comm on the table a little too aggressively and winced—my coverage was up on it too. My victorious revelation was short-lived, and I slumped back on my plush yellow couch—last year's birthday present to myself—dropping my head back. I glared at the clockglass. The screen's bright blue numbers glared back at me.

02:57 p.m.

Shit. I'm late.

This would be my 134th time being late, and I cared as much this time as I did the previous 133 shifts of tardiness. Today specifically, I might have cared less.

Today was a day to be home and stare at a wall or listen to music. Today was something my mom would call a day for mourning, which it was. I wanted to sit around and miss my mom. That's what today was for. It wasn't a day for working, but I supposed I should get myself together and go to work, even if my job wasn't exactly in jeopardy. It's not like they could find someone else as versed in tech-mechanics, at least not someone without a graduate degree who didn't want to be at the top of the food chain and manage a team. I just wanted payment for services rendered.

That would be the one and only reason that this was my 134th, and not my second, late arrival. Any big-box store would have locked me out by now. TechHalo needed me. I needed them. It was a happy symbiotic relationship—for now.

Thankfully, my hair was already pulled to the side and braided down to my waist, so a change of clothes was all I needed. Rather, I should put ON actual clothes, and it would be an improvement.

I laughed at the thought of Noreen's face if I walked into TechHalo naked. It was almost tempting to see the shock on her face, but riding my hover bike *au naturel* in this fall air would be unbearable, even with the weather regulators doing their jobs.

"Sorry, Noreen. Not today."

Besides, now I needed some extra cash to buy a new nexscreen for my specglass tablet. I'd be able to install it easily enough. My extra room—more like a workspace spider-webbed in cables and overrun with tools—had all I needed to perform the very delicate surgery. I could do it by touch—another reason why TechHalo kept me around.

I watched the bright blue numbers tick by three more times.

FINE. I'll get dressed. Stop rushing me.

Pushing myself up, I huffed down the hallway to my bedroom at the end. Even in my emotional, gloomy state, I still traced my finger along the wall-to-wall bookshelves that lined both sides of the corridor. The bookshelves made my hallway much narrower, but it always felt like walking through a library every time I moved between them. I went through as one person and came out another—more calm, centered—on the other side.

When I stepped into my room, I glanced at my unmade bed. My black comforter hung off the edge of the bed along with my grey sheets. I kicked them in my sleep, and then I left them there on the floor—as usual.

Every day, it was a personal protest against my legs, who obviously didn't receive the memo about how I hated making beds. It was a Cold War standstill. I wouldn't pick them up, and my legs wouldn't stop kicking them off during my nightly nightmares.

I am definitely winning this battle.

I rolled my eyes at myself, stepping over the pile of dirty clothes strategically placed in front of my laundry hamper. Judging by the height of my leg as I stepped over the pile, I needed to wash it all soon.

Opening the door to my closet, I smiled at the one area of my room always organized. My shirts hung chromatically from white to black with all my grays in the middle. I grabbed a scoop-neck shirt two shades darker than white and a pair of worn, black, low-rider cargo pants. Every pair of pants I owned featured at least two giant cargo pockets. It was a mandatory requirement of all purchases or a deal breaker. I never knew when I would find discarded bolts or random wire. I'd never been able to turn down a lone wire that needed a new home. Now in a cream-colored bralette with matching hipsters, I pulled the almost-but-not quite white shirt over my head. After freeing my braid from the neck hole, I stretched the sleeves down my arms until they rested comfortably at my knuckles before stepping into my pants. A quick buckle and a tie later, and I was ready.

Oh, shoes. Yeah, those are probably needed.

I grabbed my black boots, pulling them on without socks.

The clockglass was green in my bedroom and now showed 03:09 p.m.

Okay, okay. I'm going.

Traveling back down the hallway, I entered my workroom, found the 456 lined screw casing I needed for work, then walked to the front door. I grabbed my messenger backpack, my tan overcoat, and IDfob from their respective hooks.

A small chime signaled as I reached for the door knob. I looked at the screen beside my doorway.

"Are you coming into work today?"

"Nikola, reply 'I am on my way.'" A different chime rang out, signaling the message was sent. I stepped out the door. Before closing it, I said, "Nikola, shut off the lights."

I turned away from my door, which was the end of the apartment hallway on this floor and walked toward the elevators on the other end. Before I took my first step, the screen panels built into the walls came to life. The panels didn't reach from floor to ceiling or show a beautiful landscape for the season. Those luxury walls were for the penthouses and expensive condos. Here, we viewed the always lovely and entertaining ads that wanted to sell us useless shit we didn't need.

Today's ad that followed me down the hallway was for a new toilet paper dispenser that supposedly made it easier to get "extra clean."

I rolled my eyes as I pressed down, learning that "Oh wait! There's more!"

Why is there always more? Who needs two free toilet paper dispensers?

By the time the elevator doors opened and closed behind me, I knew the phone number by heart. I vowed right then to do everything in my power to forget the number, but I knew it was ingrained for at least the rest of the elevator ride. Thankfully, the screen inside the elevator had been broken for a long time. Otherwise, instead of enjoying a silent forty-five seconds down—if no one needed the elevator in between stories—I would hear the phone number at least another seven times.

I held my backpack between my knees—I saw my mom do this a hundred times—and glanced at my reflection as I zipped up my jacket. Just the usual blue-eyed, pale, freckle-faced, full-lipped girl I'd seen a million times. I winked at myself.

"Let's do this day."

The elevator stopped on the ground floor, and the doors opened with the usual clunk. A quick walk across the lobby, and Phase 1 was officially complete: Exit the building. Now to get to my hover bike and ride across town.

The parking structure for my building was next door. It'd been over two decades since cars parked alongside curbs. There was just no room. My mom talked about seeing the streets lined nose to butt down the line, row after row, street after street. I couldn't imagine that way of life. Now, streets had to empty for the few remaining motorized vehicles and low-level hovercrafts like my bike. The streets in the sky, though, didn't follow the same rules.

It had taken years to simply add the sensors needed to create the skyways now traveled by tens of thousands of people a day. The problem was hover cars cost money, as well as the permits to buy the sensors and the licenses to drive them—although I thought "fly them" was more accurate. To make up for the buildings converted into storage facilities, cities simply made the many apartment structures reacher higher into the sky. The cities rebuilt the apartments, converted buildings into parking garages, and THEN built the skyways. It had all been done in twenty years, which always blew my mind. But I guessed, when a country was trying to heal itself, anything was possible.

I walked to the black pedestal in front of the oversized garage door. The screen on the podium was black, sleeping as it waited for its next customer. I pushed my comm into my bigger utility pocket before placing my right hand on the screen. It bleeped to life.

I removed my hand as my name displayed on the screen.

Angelia M. Solis

Grabbing my IDfob from my front pocket, I waved it over the screen. Another series of bleeps and then—

Approved.

The screen went black again.

I stepped back as I heard gears and metal moving behind the transport door. A minute later, the doors opened and revealed my blue hover bike.

I walked over to the craft, running my fingers along the grip of the handlebars. "Hello and good afternoon, Miss Earhart."

I grabbed the matching blue helmet from the back of the bike and put it on, clasping the sides together under my chin. After sitting down and situating my boots and bag, I tucked my braid into my jacket.

I ran the IDfob over the three-by-three screen between the handles and waited as the bike woke up. Chimes rang out as the systems turned on one by one. The screen flashed green three times before the countdown began.

10…9…8…

…at 7, a humming began…

…6…5…

…at 4, the light booster started…

…3…2…1…

At zero, the power engaged. I braced myself a fraction before zero, and a soft hum pulsed through the battery as I took off out the door and into the soft traffic of the below.

There were mostly hover bikes and hover cycles on the streets. With the majority of the traffic now above us all, it made it calmer and by far quieter on the roads. Although slower traveling by bike, it made it easier to cross one side of the city to the other—less weaving, less traffic, less stress. I enjoyed being on the roads. I relished the smell of bakeries as I zipped past, the swaying branches on the trees on a windy day, the hum of the hover bike, and the thrumming in my ears as I flew past one building after another.

New Eastland was one of the biggest cities on the east coast. That title used to be held by New York City decades ago, before my lifetime. My mom remembered it well because she came to NYC shortly after the Social War started. She was around eight or so, but she remembered the tall buildings, the blinking lights, and so much poverty. There were also so many gangs and districts. New Eastland was run by factions for years until the government took it back. My mom used to talk about the way the sky disappeared and could make a newcomer feel lost or, worse, drowning in industry. For all its negatives, my mom had always been in awe of the giant, never-sleeping city—so much life, color, and secrets.

Too much fighting was centralized in the capital-sized city. It became the battleground more than once throughout the Social War. One faction took it over and then another. It was a pivotal spot for the war on equality versus society. After fifteen years, no one won the fight, but we destroyed cities along the way before creating new ones from the ashes. New Eastland was one of those cities. Boston became New Bostland. Chicago became New Lakes. Los Angeles was forever lost with most of the seaside towns of the west coast when a cataclysmic tsunami came through. It destroyed the Pacific Coast Highway from the top of San Francisco, which managed to keep its name, down to San Diego, which had been officially part of Old Mexico now for about forty years.

My father loved history and always brought home books with new pictures for me to read. I learned about the strangest customs of the world. Considering it was only fifty years before I was born, it shouldn't have been so different. But then again, the difference between 1950 and 2000 was one of the most shocking transformations that I read about over the years.

I stopped at a red light and sat back on my bike, glancing up at the soaring cars above my head. I didn't remember a world where the sky was quiet and the ground was buzzing. What a difference it must have been. Although the idea of traffic made me queasy, so I was happy it didn't exist anymore. The cost might have been too great with so many lost in the Social War across our country, but who was I to judge the history of the men and women before me?

I shook my head. *See what happens when it's an emotional day? I get lost in the emotional ramifications of the world on a short trip to work.*

The light turned green, and I sped off, hoping to stop the emotional thoughts from invading my mind. It took another fifteen minutes to reach TechHalo. As I turned around the corner to park in the employee area in the back, I saw a woman in too-high heels struggling to push a large mall cart from her hover car to the store. Inside the cart was a CleanBot with one arm missing. That would be a two-hour job for me, but Noreen would charge the woman in unconventional heels four.

I used my fob to open the employee parking doors and left my helmet on the bike before walking out and waving my fob again to shut the doors. I checked my comm for the time as I walked toward the building.

3:41 p.m.

Not bad. Only forty-one minutes late.

A rumbling in the distance diverted my eyes from my comm to the sky as I walked through the parking lot to the front of the strip mall. The lane for hover cars coming to land crossed over the building and ended to my left. Looking past the multi-crossing lanes in the sky, dark clouds rolled in. Hopefully, tonight would be nice and rainy. Those were the best kind of days. The rain always made me calm. The sound of falling water patting leaves on their way down to the earth. The air feeling moist and thick with a living breath. The smell of water covering the old pavement. Rain made everything fresh.

I gave the sky a brief smile as if to say thank you before rounding the corner, crossing the glass-front entrance, and walking through the door, a *whoosh* echoing behind me.

Mrs. Heels was at the counter speaking to Noreen.

"—and then water was everywhere! I had to change my clothes for work, and I don't have time for this. So how long until you can fix it? I need it back, like yesterday."

I rolled my eyes. Everyone always needed it done *like yesterday.*

"I will have my technician take a look and call you in the next two hours. Then we can give you an estimate."

I felt the heat coming from Noreen's eyes as I passed the counter, crossing into the back of the store where we kept the machines that needed repairs. Rather, this was my workshop. Noreen wouldn't know the difference between a number twenty-two gauge yellow hook-up wire and a DFR analog sensor cable if someone paid her.

I rolled my eyes as I heard Mrs. Heels ask Noreen to move her to the front of the line. Noreen replied, "Of course. You will be our number-one priority." I shook my head as I sat down next to the other four "number-one priorities" that I had to work on first.

I could run this business by myself. I mean, I did at this point, anyway. I just didn't pay the rent for the building. I'd thought a few times of owning my business, but let's just leave that kind of stress to people like Noreen.

I pulled out my black box of smaller tools to finish working on a Triple Stage Drone XL that a young college student brought in two days ago. He flew it into a tree, and the two-foot-wide flying robot lost two of its top propellers. Lucky for him, I had the 456 casing he needed. I'd just order a new one on Noreen's dime and bring that one home.

I heard the door open and close behind me. I didn't turn around. "Hi, Noreen."

"Seriously? Didn't we JUST have a conversation YESTERDAY

about you NOT being late TODAY?" Noreen was always one for emphasis.

I turned to see her overly tanned face and angry eyes glaring at me. "We did. And I tried. I really did. I started getting ready before my shift—just not as before my shift as I should have."

"Lia, please." She pressed her hands together in front of her face, closing her eyes for a second. "I don't want to have this conversation every day."

My lips raised on one side, "Then don't. Accept me for my tardiness. You'd be a much happier person."

I watched as she consciously took a deep breath before speaking. She's not one for sarcasm. She practically shoved the next words out of her mouth. "Can you just make it into your shifts ON TIME?"

I pretended to consider for a minute as I watched her fake tan skin flush red. "I'm sorry. I'll stay an extra hour and work through lunch today to make up for it. Okay?"

She threw her hands in the air. "Fine. Do whatever you want. I need to finish counting the connectors and headers. Can you take the new robot from the front and check it?"

I crossed one arm across my chest, making a fist over my heart. "Yes, my queen."

Noreen rolled her eyes and stalked out of the room, leaving me to my work.

I looked around at my neatly organized shelves lined with dozens of bins side by side, filled with wires, bolts, and instruction manuals. I sighed a slow and calm sigh and moved quickly to roll the newest robot into "my" back room and place it next to the other priorities.

"Hello, my beautiful friends. Let's get you all finished today, shall we?"

I removed my wireless buds from my bag and placed one in each ear. Reaching for my comm, I decided on a softer playlist and selected "Cello Chill" once I was in my music world.

As the sultry sound of a cello rose into and through my mind, I closed my eyes for a moment, taking a deep breath. About thirty seconds later, I finished my short meditation of preparation and grabbed my pair of black gloves. Tight and thin silicone gloves with grips along the fingertips helped me work with precision. It was like wearing another skin. I modified them one day and added a paper-thin magnet—that I found left by a trash can one day and lived in my cargo pocket until it was needed—in between the flat silicone layers on the left glove. It helped if I needed small screws nearby without needing to keep them in a small dish.

The cello dropped into a deep thrum. I smiled, reaching for the first drone on my list.

Five hours later, I reattached the panel to an Apple glasstop as my last and final project of the night.

Noreen had poked her head in about an hour before to check in that I was actually "going to stay LONGER like we had discussed." I told her I was, and for once, she seemed impressed and not irritated with my answer.

Taking off the last small screw from the top of my hand, I finished closing the panel and realized as my eyes adjusted with a blur that I was officially done for the day. I normally worked three to five hours at a time without a break and at a high level of focus. My concentration didn't break until these gloves came off, and right now, I wanted to eat and take off these clothes. I had half of a breakfast sandwich waiting for me at home from yesterday's dinner, and I could already taste the bacon.

I put both my comm and my headphones into my bag, removed my gloves, and put them back in their place next to my small black tools in the top drawer. I left the computer on the table to make sure it was the first thing I touched tomorrow and put my bag on my back. That was when it started. I heard the heavy weight of the drops falling onto the roof.

Clap. Clap. Clap. Clap. Rapid-fire succession, over and again.

The smile spread across my face. I was so glad that I didn't miss the rain tonight. Now to enjoy it.

I walked to the front of the store, shutting the lights off as I went. Each one made a chunky sound and eclipsed the room to almost complete darkness by the time I reached the entrance. The rain became louder as I walked through the door, waving my IDfob—with access to the entire building—to lock up.

A torrential downpour raged before me. My smile was wide across my face. *How beautiful could it get?*

I decided that I'd sit and wait until the rain subsided, not for any reason but to watch it fall. I knew I could mount my hover bike—get drenched—and watch it from my apartment balcony, but after such a long day, I just wanted to sit and watch. But my stomach didn't agree with me and started an argument, which I quickly settled as I told it we'd get pizza from the restaurant next door.

The pizzeria wasn't usually busy this late at night. There was one young person sitting in the corner with his glasstop open, eating a piece of pizza with his left hand while typing on a floating keyboard with his right. I walked up to the counter as the smell of pepperoni filled my nose. Looking at the various options, I decided on my usual childhood favorite.

"Can I have a slice of Stalk and Roni, please?"

Hal, the sweet old man behind the counter, had already been reaching for the broccoli usually reserved for salads. He smirked at my attempts to consider another choice. I thanked him when it came out of the oven, took a giant whiff of its delicious aroma, and turned to take it outside with me.

As I walked out the door, another patron walked in. I couldn't see his eyes with the hood hung low over his face, but I saw him smile at me as he walked by. I smiled back.

The rain was in full fall now. It was hard to see more than five feet in front of where I stood. I leaned against the wall between the pizzeria and TechHalo, under the awning, and enjoyed my greasy pizza until the rain stopped and turned into drizzles. I just finished my slice when the pouring ended.

Nice timing, clouds.

I threw out my trash and started walking toward the back of the mall, passing in front of my store. The awning stopped at the end of my building. I looked up as I passed from under its protection, the soft sprinkles falling on my face, misting my cheeks.

I stopped walking and closed my eyes for a moment, reveling in the chill of each hazy drop on my skin. I inhaled the crisp air, blinking back the mist on my eyelashes. I stood like that for a couple minutes, just feeling the world in its natural, calm, cool state.

Man, I love the rain.

When I finally came to myself, back to where I was, I continued walking. The best part about it being so late was walking through the general parking areas—empty of any hover cars or other crafts—at a diagonal and chugging straight through dozens of puddles. It was like a landmine field in front of me. My eyes widened. This was going to be fun.

Before I could cross through the field of puddles, I had to cross a small pond about ten feet by ten feet, created perfectly by a flaw and a dip in the concrete. It was massive compared to the others around me, and considering its size, it must have been deeper than the other ones too.

I scanned the area. All was quiet. I was all alone.

And I jumped with two feet as hard as I could into the giant puddle.

I laughed as the water splashed up to my face, drenching my whole front. I smiled as I leaped through the giant puddle, picking up speed as I hopscotched through the mini lakes surrounding the giant one. I laughed hard enough to feel the beginning of a stitch in my side by the time I jumped across the last puddle to the pedestal waiting for my command. My braid dripped. My shirt stuck against my skin. My pants were sopping wet. I couldn't be happier.

Rain, rain. Always rain. Come again another day.

I stood, soaked, face up to the sky, smiling.

"Happy birthday, Mom. I wish you were here."

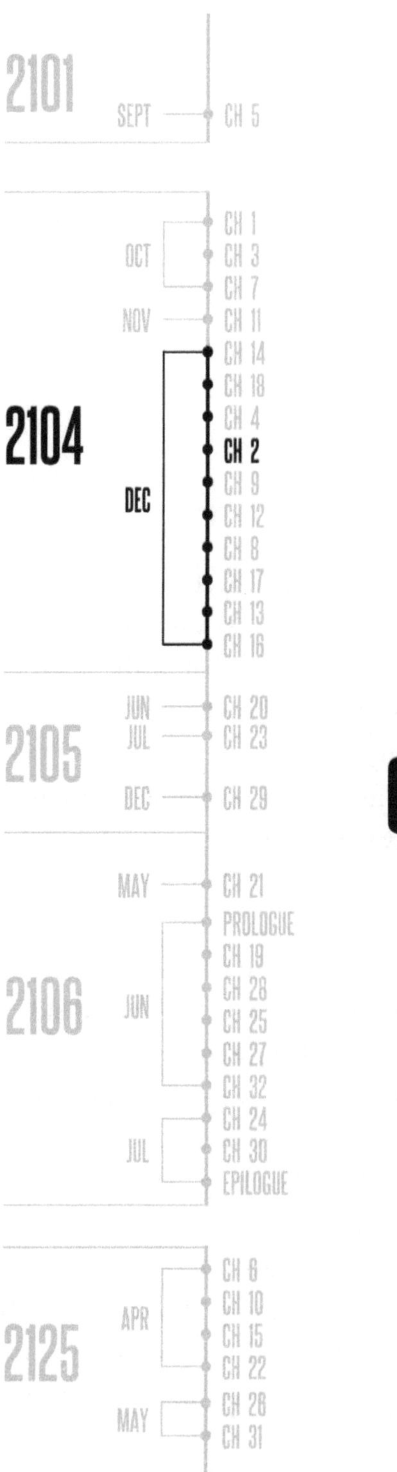

CHAPTER 2

DECEMBER 2104
Dr. Atlas

The bald man in blue screamed first. I thought he would be the first. I could always tell which Testers were the weakest. It's almost laughable to call them that. They were below the poorest class of our citizens, closer to roaches, if I could be honest. But at least now they could serve a purpose—my purpose.

I watched as the man in blue suddenly stopped screaming. Trails of green smoke traveled up from his open, dead eyes.

I looked at the other two. One was a woman in orange, and the other man—boy, really—in white. The woman's eyes were squeezed tight, and her fists clenched against her restraints. She was trying her hardest not to scream as her face jerked side to side. Her long, hooped earrings made little jingling sounds as she twitched.

Or at least I was sure they were. I couldn't hear them, just as I couldn't hear the man in blue scream before he died. I stood on one side of a glass room while the three newest Testers were inside, strapped to their chairs, screaming—or trying not to scream—and they were doing it silently to my ears.

I watched the woman in orange shudder as her body calmed and her tense strain relaxed. I leaned forward, hoping.

Looking at the screen next to me, I watched as her heart

flatlined.

Damn.

That left the boy in white. The young ones seemed to last longer, but only seconds passed before he too went still along with the others, green smoke swirling around his face. He hadn't made any sound.

Why is this so difficult?

I squeezed the bridge of my nose.

Could ONE just live so I can see what frequency I need? So I can see what made them different? SOMEthing needs to work. SOMEone has to live.

I took a deep breath and cleared my throat. I needed some wine. "Dr. Logan?" I looked to my left at my young, bright assistant.

"Yes, Dr. Atlas?"

"Walk with me."

I strode past her, my hands clasped behind my back as I walked, without waiting for her response. My long black lab coat swayed in time with my steps, and I heard her heels click toward me in the quiet hallway.

The walls were white. The floor was white. The ceiling sections were white. And I was a stark contrast, wearing all black. I always liked it that way, like I was the opposite of everything I created here. Somehow, the contrast gave me a power against the walls. I held this power over the forty-four other researchers who lived here, not counting the eighteen Testers housed in their rooms at the other end of the facility.

New Testers came in every week, ready and willing to let us do this with the chance of something better. This was batch number thirty-two, and it had yet to happen. I tried tiny changes in frequency, but I wondered if I was making them too minute and should make an abrupt change.

I heard a soft clearing of the throat as I realized that the young Dr. Logan Fay was still walking beside me. "Give me the details."

Dr. Logan seemed to come to life, looking down at her specglass tablet, resting on top of her clipboard.

"It will take the rest of today to receive the final details, but from the preliminary results, it seems these three Testers were able to endure the electromagnetic radiation better than any before them. Each one held on longer than the previous thirty-one Tester groups. These three were also younger than the others, more specifically the third Tester in this batch. Unfortunately, as with the previous groups, the ionization damaged tissue and broke apart their DNA, which created irreparable damage and ultimately death to the three Testers."

I considered this as we walked down the long corridor. Without realizing it, I directed us toward the other Testers, as my mind was normally there with them. I needed just one of them. One would at least give me a place to start.

But with ninety-six failures, the universe told me ninety-six times that I was wrong. I didn't like being wrong, and I didn't like being reminded over and over again that I was failing.

If I could find just one pattern, one Tester, one PERSON, who had the gene I needed, then I could compare it to the original. Then we could find a correlation. Finally, I would have proof that the original was not just a fluke, that it could happen again. I could create more like the original.

More like me.

But there were two originals. I was only one.

Haileen.

She was the one other. She was always the one, always my other.

What a pair we were—so young, fresh, and honest to a fault with each other. I worshipped her mind as much as her body, and she found she couldn't concentrate when I was around. We gravitated to each other the moment our eyes met so many years ago—decades now—in our doctorate degree years.

Her blonde hair had been longer then and wild around her shoulders. She wore a simple summer dress covering just enough to be modest, and yet it showed enough to make you want to see more. She had a red cup in her hand, but I never saw her take one sip of it. She was like a bright candle at the other end of the room when I came through the door, and she was all I saw for the rest of the night.

She finally saw me staring after about ten minutes. At that point, my friend of two months—*oh, what was his name? Something with a G*—had already left my side to chase after someone. I was unimportant and, at the moment, lost in watching her movements.

The first time I saw her reach up and, without thought, push a loose strand of her wild hair behind her ear, I remember how my heart tingled. It was a gesture so small, so insignificant, but in the moment, it was everything. A second later, she looked up and saw me staring. My God, if she didn't just smile at me, not flinch at catching a stranger's eyes blazing into hers, but a calm, meek, wonderful, gorgeous smile that I sank into and prayed that I'd get to see every day.

She placed her hand on her friend's arm and excused herself, and that's when I learned about her strength of will. I knew then she was a woman who went after what she wanted, and I was shocked to see I was what she wanted.

I was never one to shy away from girls, but so help me if my stomach wasn't doing flips when she walked up to me and said a simple, elegant, "Hi."

I managed a smile through my overpowered heart and said, "Hello," back to her smiling face.

We were inseparable from that moment. No one seemed surprised when we moved in together a month later. No one seemed surprised when one of us was invited somewhere and we both showed up. It was as if the universe itself accepted that we were two halves of the same whole.

Two stars aligned on different paths until we collided and

created our own neutron star, traveling the same way. My Haileen—my stronger-than-me, better-than-me, deserved-the-world, better-half of me.

I shook my head, realizing Dr. Logan was still talking statistics, and I refocused on the door at the end of the hallway.

"—so once we have more information, I hope to find the correlation between the two."

I nodded, unsure what she described, but moved the conversation along. "When are you holding another seminar to bring more Testers? With only eighteen left, we can only test six more groups for Project Evolution. I want to head full force into the next round."

I want to find one. I only need one.

We reached the door, and I placed my hand on the keypad. The door bleeped a short pattern before automatically opening.

"The newest group arrived this morning, making the new total fifty-one Testers. I'm starting their psych evaluations tomorrow. By Friday, we can add the new group into the Tester schedule. I have the next three seminars set up already, once a week for three weeks. Hopefully, these—"

"Set up more. We need more."

I knew Logan well enough to know she was up to the strenuous task. "Okay, I'll schedule more."

"Do what you must," was all I said as we walked through the door into a short hallway that turned left and then right. She said nothing else but started writing notes onto her clipboard. Her pen flew across the page.

Of the hundreds who already crossed into our facility, for whatever reason, they were trying to save the world with one gene therapy session at a time. We learned more. They left with what we promised.

But there was another group of our Testers being tested for more. More than finding a cure for our natural world's disasters. They were being tested for evolution itself. But they never—to date—had gone home with anything but a black box as a companion.

Another access door opened after scanning my palm, and we walked into a wide corridor. The entire right side was floor-to-ceiling glass. We called this room the Observatory. Beyond the glass was a large room the size of an airplane hangar, where small glass partitions divided the space. All the areas connected to a long glass hallway down the middle of the space that led to a common room. There was a kitchen, a large dining table, and another space for entertainment, which was stocked with projectionTVs, gaming systems, VR stations, and other technology to keep the Testers busy. There were multiple couches and chairs and other comfortable spaces. There were even a few beds in the back corner, in case someone didn't want to return to their room for a rest.

I walked along the side with Logan and saw some sleeping, some reading, some watching the projectionTV, some eating. "Do we know who we are testing next?"

Logan flipped a page as we walked toward the end of the observatory, where a group of Testers sat at the kitchen table. One sat on the table. As we got closer, every head turned to look at us.

I bristled. I shot the man of twenty-something a look, glaring at his folded legs and boots on the table. His hair was as black as my clothes, but his eyes were a striking green in contrast. There was a black bird tattooed across his neck. One wing trailed under the bend of his right jawbone, and the other wing disappeared around his neck.

He looked up at me, and I held his gaze. We stared at each other for a time before he unfolded himself from the table and walked slowly to the glass wall in front of me. He never took his eyes off me. When his nose practically touched the glass, he flipped me off, smiling. Then, he looked at Logan and winked.

"Evening, Doc."

I saw the young doctor become very focused on her clipboard

before the man turned and walked back to the table.

Logan cleared her throat and pointed to a man sitting nearby. "He's one." She paused and scanned the room. She pointed to a woman sitting at the table and continued, "Plus the redhead over there and a man in his thirties. I don't see him in the room."

I kept my eyes on the green-eyed rebel, wondering what happened in a man's life to bring them on a path to stand here, before me, behind glass, waiting to be experimented on for the promise of something that might never come.

Then I remembered Haileen—her young and beautiful sense of life at the same age as this Tester before me—and just for a moment, I was sad for the life and energy being lost every time. I saw her eyes, lifeless and shocked.

I would find one other like me, and I would find out why I was the way I was. I would find a way to change the world.

There was no other option.

2101
SEPT
CH 5
2104
OCT
CH 1
CH 3
CH 7
NOV
CH 11
CH 14
CH 18
CH 4
CH 2
DEC
CH 9
CH 12
CH 8
CH 17
CH 13
CH 16
2105
JUN
CH 20
JUL
CH 23
DEC
CH 29
2106
MAY
CH 21
PROLOGUE
CH 19
JUN
CH 28
CH 25
CH 27
CH 32
CH 24
JUL
CH 30
EPILOGUE
2125
CH 6
CH 10
APR
CH 15
CH 22
MAY
CH 26
CH 31

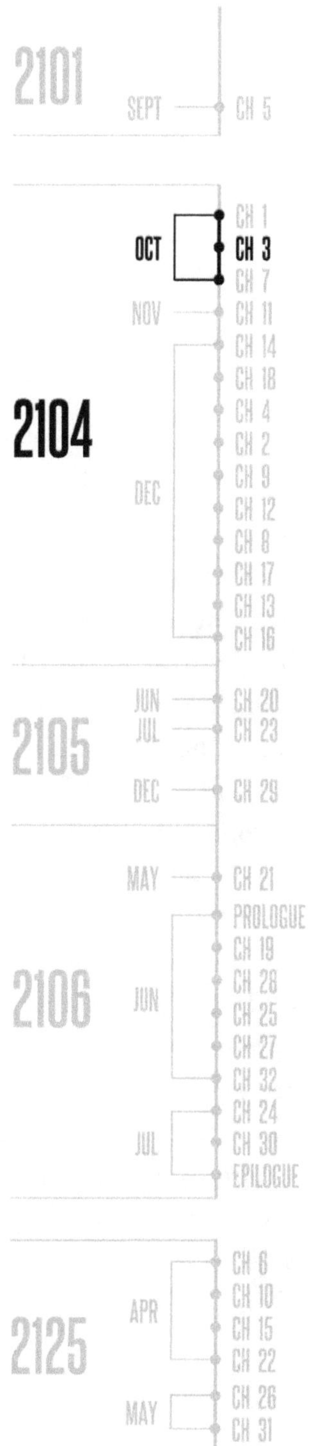

CHAPTER 3

OCTOBER 2104
Rylan

Larry, Curly, and Moe walked at a slow and steady pace between the two hover Audis parked in the front roundabout. If the luxury black cars were not occupying the three-car garage, I could only imagine what was. Moe put his hand up in a fist, and Larry and Curly obediently stopped. With a quick head flick to Larry, Moe let him know it was his turn to take the lead.

Nodding so slightly that anyone less trained would miss it, Larry took off toward the front door. He glanced up at the rotating camera above the peaked front entrance. Of course, I already turned off the cameras well before they even touched the bricked driveway.

"Have a little faith, boys," I said as I watched the Three Stooges travel through the night from five miles away.

Larry reached into his large cargo pocket on his right side and pulled out a long rectangular fob with a small screen attached by a wire. My duplication software had already analyzed and created the needed code and sent the sequence of numbers to the upgraded fob.

"Now all you have to do is..."

Larry waved the fob in front of the door, and the door unlocked.

"Perfect."

After a thumbs up from Larry, Curly and Moe followed the same path to the front door. Together, they slipped in one at a time.

I typed a quick code into my keyboard, and my screen's view changed to the interior of the Audi-lover's house.

Moe put up a fist as they entered the foyer, and they all went still. He opened the panel on his wrist-tech and studied the downloaded blueprint, confirming the layout. It all matched, of course, because I didn't make mistakes. With two fingers, he gestured to Curly, the smallest of the three, and with only a smile as a response, Curly was off.

Following Curly through the front hallway, I watched him round the left side of the double staircase in the large entry hall. He looked up briefly at the massive glass chandelier hanging perfectly centered in the room before climbing the stairs. I didn't see his feet as they fluttered up the steps, with his back to the wall. Curly didn't need a blueprint on his wrist to tell him where to go. He had memorized the blueprint weeks before and could have walked through with his eyes closed.

I switched my camera view back to Moe and Larry as they moved through the entryway to the left, under the double staircase balcony to a set of white double doors. They opened the door without a click and moved in. The two stocky men made their way around the study's couches to the desk on the opposite end of the room. A large picture framed the wall, offset by two bookshelves on both sides. Larry took out his fob again and ran it like a scan over the books until there was a soft click from behind. He glanced at Moe before grabbing the set of books and swinging the façade open, revealing a small safe with a screen mounted to the right of the latch. Moe glanced back over his shoulder and gave the camera a thumbs up.

"Thanks, Moe. Now back to Curly," I said as I typed code to switch back to the stealthier stooge.

Curly rounded a corner when I found him. After turning

down another hallway adorned with large, framed paintings, he crossed through a formal lounge to an ornate double door. My instruments registered no sound as he opened the door and went inside. The master bedroom was dark, except for a blue light pulsing on the nightstand. It sat next to an oversized, lavish four-poster bed that stood at the center of the wall on the far side of the door. There were two figures in the bed.

Opening his back pocket, Curly pulled out two small metal cylinders, both about an inch in length. Pressing down on the tops of both, the cylinders started to pulse red like a heartbeat until they both went to a solid green. I watched as he stood at the foot of the bed, preparing.

This was where I always held my breath. I never understood how he did it. He crouched down, both arms out to the side, shoulder height for a heartbeat of five, before he leaped, somersaulting in the air, and landed between the two figures. Both jolted under the covers, but as always, Curly was too fast. He pressed the heads of the cylinders to their cheeks. Before they could see him or even understand what was going on, they were both back asleep. This time, they wouldn't wake up easily.

"Nicely done as always, Curly."

He rolled off the bed and crossed over to the mister's side of the bed, and from under his vest, he pulled out a scanner with a glowing orange screen. Taking the man's right hand, he placed it on the face of the scanner, settling it in an angled position.

My computer beeped beside me as the images were sent for verification. Little circles popped up in multiple places, marking the important parts of the man's prints. We needed at least an 85 percent match, or we had to scan it again.

The computer chimed: *"91 percent, Rylan."*

"Thank you, Lessa." I looked back at the screen with Curly while I typed across the projected keyboard. "Man, he's good." I pressed the large mic icon on my screen. "Confirmed. You're a go."

Curly nodded, and my fingers flew across the keyboard to switch camera views. I typed in the next code and sent the image to the waiting graphing machine on Larry's wrist. The screen that was attached to the cream-colored silicone glove clicked orange as it received my instructions. With the final details of the fingerprints loaded, the glove started to turn red. After three minutes, the light on the glove clicked green. The tiny indentations of the newly created fingerprints on the glove tips were ready to be used.

Larry placed his right fingertips onto the waiting screen in the safe without his palm touching. The screen turned on, and a bright light blinked as it scanned the prints for accuracy.

"You won't even nod at 91 percent," I half laughed, waiting for the light to blink green.

When it did, I got a thumbs up from Moe. I made a silent, shaking fist of excitement before my fingers started flying across the keyboard again, preparing for the next step.

I glanced back at the screen as Larry stepped to the side, and Moe opened the now-unlocked door. Twisting the knob, the small door opened to reveal a stack of papers. Moe grabbed the pages and started flipping through them, looking for the page we needed. When he found it, he placed the other pages back inside the lockbox and gave me another thumbs up. Larry already had the camera scanner in his hand when Moe turned to him, holding the page flat out on his two palms. Larry scanned the documents with random symbols across it, and I received the image on my screen.

Ten codes were written on the page in shaky handwriting. Different symbols and special characters were penned across the lines by hand, which was rarely ever seen anymore. To most, it would look like gibberish, but to me, it was better than gold. I opened my Cryptonotes program and entered the Micronote passwords.

The only way to use someone's Cryptonotes account was to have their passwords, which were always handwritten. Most kept their Micronote passwords in their safes, locked away from people like Larry, Curly, Moe, and myself.

But I knew how to find them. I knew how to find who had a Cryptonote account and where they hid their passwords. I had also created multiple programs to shut down surveillance cameras and duplicate key fob frequencies.

And yet my gift of technology and programming wasn't enough, not in this world of high-tech educations and Ivy League apprenticeships. No, that was saved for those with money. Or in our case, Cryptonotes.

Larry, Curly, Moe, and I had traveled across the country for the past six months, hitting house after house—although most were more mansion than house. Every time we took, I split it three ways. At least, they thought I did. I had a fourth account. I called it my Get Away account.

The three of them were in this for their cliché future of sandy beaches and drinks by the beach. I always agreed with wanting to buy an island somewhere—if there were any left—and rot away into old age with women and luxury. But it wasn't what I actually wanted.

I wanted a high-tech education. I wanted an Ivy League apprenticeship. I wanted to run my own tech company with an educational background that couldn't be ignored. No one could brush me off then. What I could do with a computer wouldn't be chalked up to accidental genius. I wanted to live and breathe computers, and this was the only way to get the cash, the currency, the Cryptonotes to do it. I'd never bankrupt anyone. I just shaved a bit off the top that translated into a lot of bits for us to put away.

We had a figure in mind, and once we reached it, we'd stop. This was the third-to-the-last stop for us. Only a couple more, and I would disappear. I couldn't wait. I would never have to see Larry, Curly, or Moe again. I'd never have to hear their borrowed fantasies of life, watch Curly terrify someone again before knocking them unconscious, or steal and be dishonest. I didn't want this life. My parents didn't raise me to do these things. But they did raise me to be resilient.

And here I am—two houses away from freedom.

I typed my final code into the computer and watched the numbers drop on one side of the screen, increasing into one larger number on the other. I threw my hands in the air in a silent celebration as the number hit the third-to-last goal amount.

I spoke into the comm. "We are a go, gentlemen. I repeat, we are a go. Three minutes. Mark."

I watched as the two men high-fived before putting the room back the way it was. I switched the screen to see Curly walking out of the master bedroom and closing the door behind him. At two minutes, I typed in my final code for the day, which would reset all the cameras back to their normal programming and wipe all code and information from our newest job. Once I hit enter, I got out of my chair and moved to the front of my full-sized, black technology van to start my three-hour trek to the closest main city. Even in the sky, it took time. Larry, Curly, and Moe had their own hover transportation, and we had a rendezvous point in five days. We kept space and time between us after every job. They traveled south, and I headed north.

The two-minute warning, alerted with a series of beeps, sounded behind me. I smiled and turned up the audio player before activating the boosters. The Neoteric Beats' latest song filled the silence of the van as I navigated to the nearest skytrack. A few lefts and a right and fifteen minutes later, I was in a line ready to join the main highway toward New Eastland.

I hadn't been there in years. I was fourteen when I came to see the new skylanes launched, just over eight years ago. My parents were tech lovers. Anything new was exciting and worth a trip from our home in Ann Arbor, Michigan. They wanted to be where life was changing, and the University of Michigan was the founder of the mini solar panel. One panel, a two-by-two inch square, powered a city block. The mechanics behind it were astounding. One of my favorite projects in school involved the mini solar panel. Technically, the one I created was modeled five years before the university perfected it, but it didn't matter without an Ivy League education.

Only two more houses.

The long line finally shortened, and I was next. I entered the mouth of the wide, clear tunnel and waited for the green light.

When it pinged, I disengaged my hover band and turned on my thrusters. A slight roar came from the thrusters pressing into the gravel before I released the van up and through the tube. Everything in the skytracks was monitored perfectly. With millions of little sensors on buildings and the cars themselves, there was no way to accidentally do anything but fly to your destination. They facilitated a much simpler way to travel, especially when I was tired. All that thieving always made me exhausted.

It wasn't the hyper focus. It was the BS—the lies, the nonsense. *Just two more houses.*

I turned up the music and started singing the next track at the top of my lungs. Happier days were coming.

The next day I rolled out of bed when the sun had already set a while ago. I had found myself a little hotel off the main road right before entering the city. It was like the last stop before you got lost in the tall skyscrapers and parking garages. I hadn't wanted to drive into the city only to drive back out again, so I opted to stay here and sleep. And I did, for eighteen hours.

Food. I needed food. And a bank to transfer my secret money. More specifically, a mall that had both would be ideal. I sat up in my tan-colored bed and looked around the tan-colored room. Everything blended from one tan piece to another.

"Computer, lights."

The old-model AI beeped behind the television before the lamps blinked on from either side of the bed. Now the room was a bright tan.

"Computer, find me a strip mall with food and a Bank of Enterprise in the same area."

"There is a Bank of Enterprise 4.7 miles northeast. There is a Pizza Plaza, a Great Burger, and a Mandarin Chinese restaurant within 0.1 miles of its vicinity. Would you like the directions sent to your comm?"

I yawned into the air. "Yes."

"Sent."

Well, that was done. Now, I needed to shower and join the living. I had another three days with nowhere to go. *Why not get lost?*

"Computer, play the latest track from Ivy Comp League."

"Automatic music is not included in your room. Would you like to upgrade?"

I shook my head. Even in a world of conveniences and AI, we still needed to pay for simple pleasures like music streaming.

"Yes."

"Upgrading."

A few seconds later, 'Soundlocked' sang out from the room. I took a deep breath, rolling my head from side to side and loosening my neck. I stood up and grabbed my towel from the table. After a quick shower, new clothes, IDfob and glasstop in hand, I was finally out the door to eat.

It only took a couple of minutes to reach the nearest skytrack, and above the city I flew.

The paths of the skytracks were much higher in the city, with more impressive views. Tall skyscrapers were stacked next to smaller, shorter buildings, like piano keys down every block. Every few minutes, the computer navigation instructed me to turn left, right, or continue, and 4.7 miles later, I could see the pizzeria from the sky. My stomach rumbled in excitement.

When it was my turn, I dropped down the skytrack entrance into the parking lot. Once I reached a safe distance, I reengaged my hover, cutting off my thrusters, before finding a spot near the entrance. The rain fell steadily, and I needed to be close to connect into the Bank of Enterprise mainframe.

I activated my tinted front window before reaching for my glasstop, sitting like a guest in my van's passenger seat. Grabbing both sides of the glass handles, I pulled the screen out, placing my hand on the surface to gain access. I clicked the button to trigger the keyboard and began typing my usual code into the projected keys to gain access to the bank's transfer system. I didn't want a trail of proof if I could help it, even if the defense systems were easily controlled by a hacker newbie.

After transferring the three-way amounts into our various accounts, I transferred the remaining balance into my Get Away fund. It was already twice the amount of our "team" accounts. I reminded myself that I never took from our pot. I always gave us exactly what we planned together, every time.

I just took extra without them knowing. I looked at it like a finder's fee. This was my plan. Besides, not one of them could program, so I ignored the twang of guilt.

I was in and out of the transfer grid in less than five minutes. I laughed, "Ivy League education, huh?" Typing across the glass with flying fingers, I exited my program and erased my session. "Now, let's eat."

Closing my screen, I locked the front panel with my thumbprint before putting it into a compartment on the front dash. That's when I realized it was pouring outside—torrentially.

I grabbed my Neoteric Beats sweatshirt from the back and pulled it over my head before stepping out of the van and moving under the awning. I managed to move before I got drenched, but my sweatshirt was now two different colors. I looked up into the large window in front of the pizzeria. I could smell the pepperoni from here. My stomach could too. Pepperoni and broccoli were on my mind, and my mouth couldn't wait.

I blinked twice as a girl about my age came walking toward the door with a slice of pepperoni and broccoli in her hand. I'd never seen anyone order like that anymore. It was a secret menu item that most pizzerias didn't list. You had to special request it by name—Stalk and Roni. I couldn't help but smile, and I just happened to catch her smiling back from under my hood.

What a beautiful smile.

She walked out behind me as I continued up to the counter. "Evening. What can I get for you?"

I pulled my hood down. "I'll actually have what she's having—a Stalk and Roni, please."

The man smiled. "Coming right up."

I moved closer to the wall on the left side of the restaurant and looked out the window in front. Big droplets of rain crashed on the roof and everywhere else it touched. That was when I saw the girl leaning against the wall, watching the rain while she ate. I couldn't see her face and found myself moving closer to the window until I could see her profile.

A beautiful profile to go with a beautiful smile.

When the cook called me over, I kept my eyes on her until I couldn't anymore, breaking my view just long enough to grab my slice, say thank you, and resume my spot by the window.

She looked so calm, taking a bite one at a time. She ate on purpose like she had nowhere to go, nowhere to be. It was just her, the rain, and a good slice of pizza. What it must feel like to be free like that. I always felt like I was running—away from the life I didn't want, toward the life I did. I was running away from the chaos I caused, from my own repercussions—always running. To be able to stop and enjoy the rain seemed like a dream.

The rain slowed to a mist as she finished her slice and tossed out her trash, her long braid swaying as she walked. I didn't want her to leave yet. I enjoyed her silent, calm company.

I watched as she walked to the end of the awning, and instead of pulling up the hood on the back of her coat, she stepped out into the misty rain.

She just stood there, lifting her face into the streaming mist and closing her eyes.

My heart skipped a beat. Everything disappeared. I only saw her. The tilt of her chin. The faint silver line of mist settling on the top of her head. The soft upward curve of her lips. But it was the expression on her face that captivated me the most. It was like nothing else in the world existed, save for this one moment.

I'd never seen anyone—anything—so beautiful.

When she finally started walking away, I wanted to follow. I needed to follow.

I threw my half-eaten pizza into the trash as I stepped out the front door of the restaurant. I saw her rounding the corner at the end of the walkway toward the back parking lot. All I could do was follow after her, entranced as the mist swirled around my face.

When I reached the corner, I slowed and peeked around the wall. I jolted slightly when I saw her closer than I thought she would be. She stood still in front of a puddle, just staring at it. Then she looked around, side to side. I pulled back so she wouldn't see me. Heart pounding, I held my breath and peered around the corner again, hoping she wasn't staring back.

But she was too preoccupied with dozens of puddles.

She jumped from one to the next, laughing every time the water splashed her in the face. The water flew all around her—through the air, on her pants, in her hair.

I was mesmerized by her energy, by her unapologetic love of life.

My eyes followed her as she jumped again and again until she made it across the parking lot. She stood on the concrete with a smile I could see from over a hundred yards away. She beamed with every part of her, and my heart softened.

I had been many things in this life of mine: a thief, a programmer, a hacker, an—occasional—delinquent, a son, a loner, a lover of computers, a seeker of knowledge, a code breaker. I had never been a believer in love. It was just a fantasy, a wild tale told by those gullible enough to believe.

But this. What I was feeling. It enveloped every part of me. It overshadowed what I was, what I wanted, and made me into something else. It changed me. I looked at this girl, smiling, soaked, and radiant. For the first time in my life, I was a believer.

And I was in love.

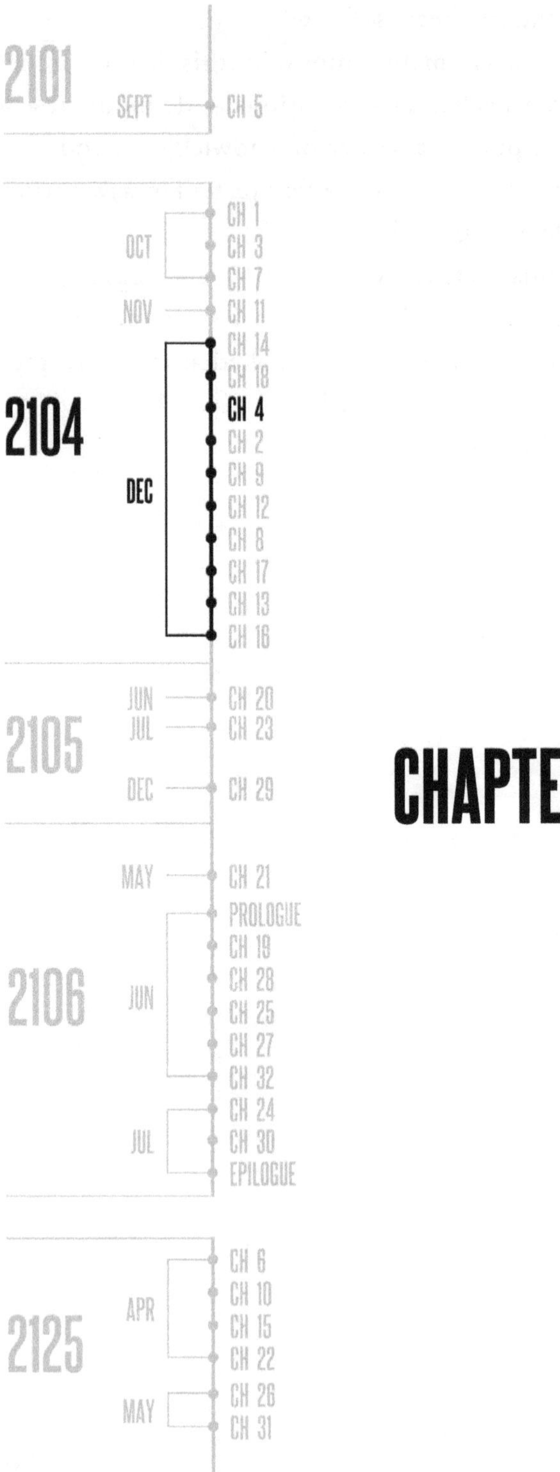

CHAPTER 4

DECEMBER 2104
Raven

I took a deep drag off my cigarette. It was a real cigarette, not those imitation won't-kill-you cigarettes but real, honest-to-earth tobacco and nicotine. I let the smoke flow out of my nose for a few seconds before blowing the rest out through my lips. I felt the instant reaction in my body.

The buzz. The high. It tasted so good.

If nothing else, I was glad I came today for this. I'd listen to anyone talk for an hour for a real cigarette, but I was getting annoyed at the sound of this guy's voice. He'd only droned on for five minutes, but I was already done listening to him. There was, however, a rather good-looking redhead standing next to him. Maybe she should take a turn.

As if on cue, the guy turned to his hazel-eyed partner and introduced the girl with the clipboard—with actual paper attached—as Dr. Logan. Somehow she became even sexier than her short wavy red hair had originally conveyed now that the word *Doctor* was in front of her name. I stared at her and the freckles across her nose while she recited the words from her part of the presentation, although I was more focused on the movement of her lips than the words coming out of her mouth.

How is this little thing a doctor of anything?

I thought it was cliché of her to wear a white lab coat. Was that actually a thing? It hugged her hips nicely, though, as did the grey tweed pants that ended at her ankles. The double straps on her three-inch black heels were not lost on me. She was like a dream incarnate.

I focused back on her lips and some of her words.

"It is imperative for us to understand the repercussions and effects the H-Serum may have on multiple levels of DNA. This is why we are seeking volunteers such as yourselves to help us navigate through this portion of our trials."

I took another deep drag as someone shouted from inside the crowd of fifty or so. "Can we make this easier?" The crowd parted and looked back to see who interrupted the person with the PhD. "Enough of the science babble. You are really just glorifying us becoming guinea pigs for your tests. Am I wrong?"

More than half of my fellow visitors nodded their heads, most of whom wore ripped and tattered clothes and had tattoos telling their own rough stories. More than that, they all came from the same world I did—the world of the forgotten or the ignored. Most looked as though they'd do anything for a break.

The doc picked from the right crowd all right.

When she didn't offer an answer in return, the kid continued. "What's in it for us? You test this H-Serum on us and get answers to your science questions. So what do we get?"

Doc folded her hands behind her back and held her clipboard with her left hand, making her chest push forward—I wasn't unhappy about it.

"During your stay at our facility, you will have your own shared living quarters, a soft bed, hot showers, ample food, and entertainment, and when you walk out of our doors, you'll walk out with 5,000 credits in whatever form you wish."

Now there were murmurs and whispers. Everyone liked the

sound of that, including me.

She continued, "For those of you who wish to participate in our program, we will be back here in three days. Please have your affairs in order. On your way out, there are black duffle bags. Whether you choose to return or not, they are yours to keep, but if you should decide to return, all of your essentials need to fit within it. You cannot bring anything beyond the duffle bag, as space is limited." She shifted from one heel to the other, gazing back into the crowd. "Does that answer your question, sir?"

I smiled. I liked the doc more and more.

Three days later—after twenty people in front of me—it was my turn to sign on the dotted line. I stood in front of the lovely redheaded doctor and could smell her flowery perfume. *I love when a girl takes care of herself.*

"Where do I sign, Doc?" I clutched the duffle in one hand, my leather jacket lying across it.

Doc looked up from her glasstop. "Let's start with your name."

"Sure, as long as you promise to remember it when I get you out of that coat." I winked. She didn't flinch. "Name?"

"Oh, cold. All right. I can play cold. Although I'm much better at keeping lovely things such as yourself warm."

She raised an eyebrow. "Name?"

I threw my hand up in mock defeat. "Raven."

She looked up at me. "Your real name?"

"Doc, I haven't used my real name in twenty years."

"I need your real name if you're going to join our trial."

I leaned closer to her. "If I tell you my real name, will you tell me yours?" I winked.

Doc shook her head and typed on her glasstop. "Raven Smith it is."

I couldn't help but smile. *She has some fire, this one.*

She didn't look up with her next question, but I saw the

faintest smile on her lips. “Date of birth?”

“The twenty-fifth of February, 2079.”

For the next five minutes, I answered all of her questions from where I was born to how many tattoos I had—just one—to the medications I took and the drugs I currently enjoyed.

“At this exact moment, none, but I can think of a few we could enjoy together.” Her fingers crossed the screen before she turned it around with a line for me to sign my life away. Using my index finger, I signed just Raven. “You don’t by any chance count as part of our entertainment, do you?”

She turned the glass back around. “Thank you, Mr. Smith. Please take your duffle bag and follow the hallway behind me to the transportation to our facility.”

“Breaking my heart over here, Doc.” She fixed her eyes on mine. “Okay, okay. Yes, ma’am. Down the hallway.” I started to walk away but paused for a moment. “By the way, you should just lead with what you are going to give us.” She looked up from her glasstop.

“I’m sorry?”

I tilted my head toward the line of another dozen people behind me. “These kinds of people don’t care about the rest of it. They don’t want to cure diseases. They don’t want to save the world. They only want what they can get out of it. Your cute looks keep us focused on all the science nonsense, but we can only stare at those gorgeous lips for so long.”

A smile tugged at the side of her mouth before she pointed over her shoulder. “That way, please.”

I winked again and tossed my jacket over my shoulder. “Your wish is my command, Doc.”

The ride to the facility was uneventful. Ten of us at a time had piled into black hover vans. I would have preferred the heat off, but hot or not, I decided to sleep while I could. It was a three-and-a-half hour drive from New Eastland up north to wherever the driver said, so I pulled my hood over my head and was happily sleeping within forty-five seconds, my leather jacket balled up behind my head.

I opened my eyes as the van slowed down. I heard the crunch of dried leaves under the tires before I saw the bare trees around us. The heater clicked off, and everyone started to wake up.

The building beside us looked like a solid block of cement with two small slits for windows along the top. I couldn't see any other windows anywhere. There was one door, one doorknob, and a giant number one in a metal cutout above the door. I started to feel a pang of regret. *Will someone hear us if we scream?* I somehow doubted it.

The door to my van swung open. There were two people closer than me to the door, but I took their hesitation as an opportunity and got out first. Dipping under the roof of the van, I felt my necklace fall out of my shirt.

As everyone else started filing out, I grabbed the silver wing pendant and dropped the chain back into my shirt before I put on my leather jacket over my sweatshirt, needing some protection from the cool air. Thankfully, this was as cool as it got in this region. Although I would only admit to myself that I missed the snow.

I heard the opening of a door, just one of the many to our new "home." The boring man from the speech came out first, followed by my favorite doctor—wearing her black, double-strap heels no less.

My eyes were on her as another five probably-doctors exited in white lab coats. Even in her heels, Doc was three or so inches shorter than everyone else. I hadn't noticed before. She stood in front of the six, towered over by all, but she held the power. Her expression gave me no doubt.

Her eyes caught mine as she scanned the crowd. I winked before she continued down the line.

Once all the new guinea pigs were out with their bags in tow, the tall one got everyone's attention with a whistle. Looking up from her ever-present clipboard, Doc spoke. "Thank you all for coming. We appreciate you all taking the time to join our program…"

A whisper came from my left, drowning out her next words. "Well, she's the hottest doctor I've ever seen."

I glanced to my left and saw a guy about my age, deep-set eyes, outgrown beard, and a cocky smile. *My kind of crowd.* I leaned closer and whispered, "I didn't know we were getting teased while we're here."

The guy smiled. "No kidding. And in black heels? Come on."

I reached my hand across my chest. "I'm Raven."

His tattooed hand shook mine. "Sloan."

At least there was one person here that seemed tolerable. Who knew how long we'd be here.

Doc finished her speech a few minutes later and looked like an airplane marshaller pointing to where we needed to go, with her damn clipboard flying around.

I glanced around at everyone as we separated. Of the thirty-something of us, men and women, none carried beauty even close to the doc, but some weren't bad either.

Sloan and I were in the same group and walked to the other side of the barely windowed building to its brother around the corner. Judging by the long row of windowless buildings, this was a rather large family.

Although her lips were more of a focal point for my attention, I listened to exactly what we'd be doing next. I never was a fan of being in the dark. First was a nice wash for toxins, followed by time in a decontamination chamber for a bit, and topped off with some medical procedures that involved a lot of blood giving. Considering my stomach was already growling, I wished food had been added into this particular list of to-dos. But the doc assured us food would be available after we settled in our rooms. Sloan and I walked by six stoic buildings until we made it to the one with a metal "seven" above its boring door.

"This is us," Sloan said as the number came into view. He leaned closer to me. "Is it too late to change our minds?"

The door under the seven opened, and a six-foot bulk of a man wearing an all-black uniform stepped out. No gun was needed on his hip to tell us he was the security detail. I stared at the looming man. "I think the answer is yes, it's definitely too late."

Our group—the Sevens, as Sloan and I coined us in the few minutes we were in the building—was led into a stone room with multiple baths built into the floor. Transparent glass separated each of the baths. It seemed like a waste of glass to me. If we were all going to see each other naked, what did it matter?

One by one, our names were called out, with a number for our assigned bath stall. The numbers were also built into the floor. I found my lucky nine and waited. Once everyone stood beside their baths, we were instructed to undress and put all of our belongings into the bags next to the bath holes so they could be decontaminated while we went through the process.

A kid younger than me raised his hand, "Are you going THROUGH our things?"

The black-haired doctor checking off names with his specglass tablet answered, "If there is something you don't want us to find, we'll probably find it. If you brought an item that violates our code, it will be confiscated. If it doesn't violate the terms of you being here, it will remain in your bag. Everything you brought is yours and will be returned to you at some point."

The kid didn't say anything, but his twisted expression and lips pressed together were enough.

The doctor pushed up his glasses at the bridge of his nose.

"Any other questions about your personal items?" Everyone else shook their heads. "Good. Please get into your baths. Once you hear the bell ring, it will be time to remove yourself from the bath and move on to the next phase of decontamination. Is that clear for everyone?"

I nodded with everyone else.

"Good." He looked off to the side toward a blackened window. "Turn on the walls."

I turned to look at Sloan, who was two baths away, but in an instant, the once-transparent walls turned an opaque white.

Now that makes way more sense.

I looked down into the bath. A wax-like substance floated in the water. I figured now or never. I striped down, put my stuff into the bag, and stood staring into the dark water. I tested it with my toe. *Yup, definitely some kind of wax.*

I knelt down and slowly got in. The water wrapped around me like a warm, oversized towel fresh out of the dryer.

That hour was better than the cigarette.

The next two after that were not.

I was poked, tapped, prodded, looked over, turned over, stuck with needles, given cups to pee in, dressed and undressed, blinded with sharp lights, and squeezed by machines. Guinea pig was right.

When all the lovely tests finished, I was finally released to go to my room, which I prayed was stocked with food and a bed. That's all I wanted.

I felt like I could sleep for a week as I walked down the corridor to my new home. There were three other people walking with me. They all looked as beat as I did. It felt like we were walking down a hallway in a hospital. Everything was white—the floors, ceiling, walls, doors. If I was sleeping in a hospital-type room, I would be pissed.

But I'll be pissed off tomorrow, after food, after sleep.

A young doctor walked us to the double doors at the end of the hospital corridor and paused at the door to enter a code. I glanced down the other hallway to an even larger double door. I watched as a doctor leaned in for an eye scan.

"What's down that hallway?" I asked our guide, who tried to enter her code a second time.

Flustered, she glared in my direction. "That's the classified wing. You won't have access to that area." She turned back to the code screen.

Interesting. I took a quick breath and leaned to the girl to my left, whispering, "Hopefully, the intern knows where we are going."

She glanced over at me with beautiful brown eyes before looking back at the white coat, still struggling with the access screen, and smiled. "What makes you think she's an intern?"

The door beeped at her error a fourth time. I watched as an older guy in our group shifted from foot to foot. I brought my attention back to her brown eyes.

"Aside from not knowing the code?" I raised my eyebrow and crossed my arms across my chest, gesturing toward the door. "No specglass. All the real doctors have tablets. This one is left to bring us low-lees to our rooms."

The girl smiled again. "Low-lees?"

I smiled back. "You know, instead of peons. Low end of the spectrum. I never liked peons. There are too many awful connotations."

She raised an eyebrow. "Well, you can be a low-lee or a peon all you want. I just want to get through this and get out of here."

"I agree with you." As she glanced back at the intern, I glanced over her body—curvy and strong. I wasn't planning on spending too many lonely nights here, so I needed to find someone who wouldn't mind keeping me company. I lowered my voice on the sixth denial beep of the door. "Hopefully, this isn't like college, and boys have to sneak into the girls' side of the dorm."

Her eyes found mine. "Well, maybe girls can find their own way to the boys' side, if that's the case." Her lips parted before she smiled again.

I opened my mouth to answer, but the door beeped a new sound, higher and happier.

"Oh, finally," the intern said as the door started to open. "Sorry about that. The code was changed. Through here, please."

I gestured to let my new friend go first, and she nodded her thanks. I heard the door beep and click behind us—I guess that was the way out—and tried not to feel like a prisoner.

Double doors at the end of the corridor opened up to a more homey environment. The walls changed to a slate, grayish-blue color, and our feet transitioned to a wooden floor. Landscape pictures hung from the walls. A small table here, a fake plant there, and this hallway felt like we stepped into an apartment building on the East New Haven side of town. Halfway down, we saw doors set close in pairs.

We passed about ten doors before we came across three that were already open. A woman in a white uniform exited one of the rooms with a cart. Half-used toiletries cluttered the top, along with some magazines, a smart watch, a picture of a bald man hugging some beautiful blonde, other random items, and a bag of trash underneath with rumpled clothes and worn shoes. Hanging over the side of the cart were a leather jacket and a navy sweatshirt.

One guy in our group asked, "Why are you throwing away perfectly good things? Did someone break a rule or something?"

I watched the intern's face twist with confusion. She took a quick breath and replied, "Some of your fellow—uh—roommates leave occasionally, rather—um—abruptly, and we need to clear the rooms for new Testers."

My eyebrows raised. *Testers?* I looked back at the cart, grabbed the watch, and held it up. "Why would someone leave something like this? These aren't exactly everyday items."

She looked almost cute with her deer-in-the-headlights expression. "I— uh—" She hesitated as she tried to find the right words. It was painful.

I moved closer to her. My sleeve brushed hers, and I lowered my voice, changing the subject. "So can we take these, then, if they are just going into the trash?"

Miss Intern looked nervous, shifting her eyes to the side. "I don't know if—I don't know if that's okay."

I leaned in, my lips close to her ear. "If we do things they don't know about, it can't be a problem, right?"

Her face flushed. It took her a moment, but she slowly shook her head. "No. I don't think it's a problem."

I winked. "You're my angel. Thank you." I clasped the watch onto my wrist as the young guy grabbed the magazines and Brown Eyes swiped the leather jacket.

The woman in white, and the rest of our group, remained silent. Their eyes darted around and watched the situation unfold.

Miss Intern cleared her throat. "Okay. Let's keep going."

Brown Eyes held back a moment and whispered to me once the others walked a bit ahead. "Nice move."

I gave her my half smile. "Thanks. It never hurts to ask." I looked her over. "You look smoking in that jacket. It suits you."

She ran her hands over the front of the jacket. "Thanks to you. Funny, I've always wanted one but never wanted to spend the credits."

"Well, now you can enjoy it for every occasion." I touched the leather collar. "I wonder what else we can get away with in this place."

She smiled at me from under her lashes. "I'm sure a lot, with you around." She tucked her black hair behind her ear. "I'm Della."

"Nice to officially meet you." I reached out my hand. "I'm Raven."

My mind fast-forwarded through the next thirty minutes while Miss Intern showed us the different rooms in our new apartment complex. At least, they made it seem exactly like an apartment complex, complete with a laundry room, a gym with a pool, a community garden, another media room, and another living room area with even more technology. I guess being bored was out of the question.

Then, I saw it—a giant, fully stocked, eat-whenever-I-want kitchen. Once we were finally left to our own devices, I practically sprinted back to it. There were a few other people in the giant room separated by some of those glass doors we saw at the baths. I ignored them all while I stocked my plate with everything that looked delicious. I took my plate to some couches in the corner and ate until I couldn't eat anymore. When I finished, I planned to return to my room, but I saw Della walk by. I watched her grab some food and make her way over to the kitchen table.

I decided I'd work on the possibility of not being lonely while I was here. I rinsed my plate and put it in the dishwasher before walking over to the group.

"So it looks like we had the same plan. I think I ate more than I have in a week."

She looked up from her bite of grilled chicken and smiled. "Hey. Yeah, no kidding. I may go back for another serving."

"They may have to keep the fridge stocked more than they think."

"Totally agreed." She took another bite of chicken while I sat next to her. My shoulder almost bumped hers, but she didn't move away.

I gestured to the room. "It seems like this is where we'll spend most of our time. Although that pool was a perk I wasn't expecting." I leaned closer. "I wonder if skinny-dipping is allowed."

She grinned through her next bite. "I think someone should definitely test that out, you know, for the rest of us to know."

I lowered my voice. "I agree. Someone should. Maybe in about an hour? It's a good time to test out the waters."

I watched as she licked a drop of dressing off her finger before she answered. "Sounds like we should know what we can get away with in this place soon enough."

Smirking, I glanced up as a group walked into the kitchen. I recognized Sloan, but the other four I hadn't seen yet.

Sloan caught my eye and nodded as he walked with the others to the kitchen. Della ate her salad, and we talked about random things—sometimes whispered under our breath—until Sloan and his group approached the table.

"What the fuck did we get ourselves into?" he blurted as he walked over.

"You're telling me. We're rats in a damn maze." I motioned to the glass walls.

Sloan looked down at Della, a greedy smile spreading on his face. "Della, this is Sloan. Sloan, Della." I looked at the others. "Hey, guys. I'm Raven."

"Ritch."

"Hanna."

"Mack."

"Laurea."

I smiled at Laurea. She now became the third best-looking girl I'd seen, but Della was winning by far. I stood and leaned on the edge of the table to make room for the newcomers.

Fifteen minutes later, everyone finished eating and laughed as we shared our sordid pasts. I now sat on the table, telling a story of how I circumvented security at a marina. All eyes were pinned on me, until Mack—who seemed captivated by my stories—turned toward the back wall, shifting all of our attention to the two figures walking out of the door on the other side of the glass. One of them had my favorite wavy, red hair and black heels.

The tall doctor next to her must have been some kind of big deal. He was the first and only person I saw wearing all black, for starters. But it was more about the look on his face. You could tell he was the king of the castle. It's the only time I saw a little fluster on our lovely doctor's face.

Interesting.

My companions started commenting about the duo, but I kept my eyes on them until they came to a stop across from us. Dr. Black's eyes bore into mine, and his expression of smugness turned to disgust.

Who the hell was this guy? The king AND an asshole.

I got up from my seat and walked toward the glass. My eyes blazed into his. When I was close enough to touch him—if not for the glass between us—I flipped him off, just to make it clear his feelings were mutual.

I glanced at the doc. The horror on her face made her look so cute I could hardly take it. I winked at her.

"Evening, Doc." She looked down at her clipboard. I gave Dr. Black one more glance before walking back to the table, and I leaned over Della. "I'll be at the pool in half an hour."

Her eyes caught mine as she smiled.

I waved to the group. "See you guys later. I'm going to go relax, away from prying eyes."

As I moved toward the side door, I peeked over my shoulder one more time at the man in black and the woman in black heels beside him.

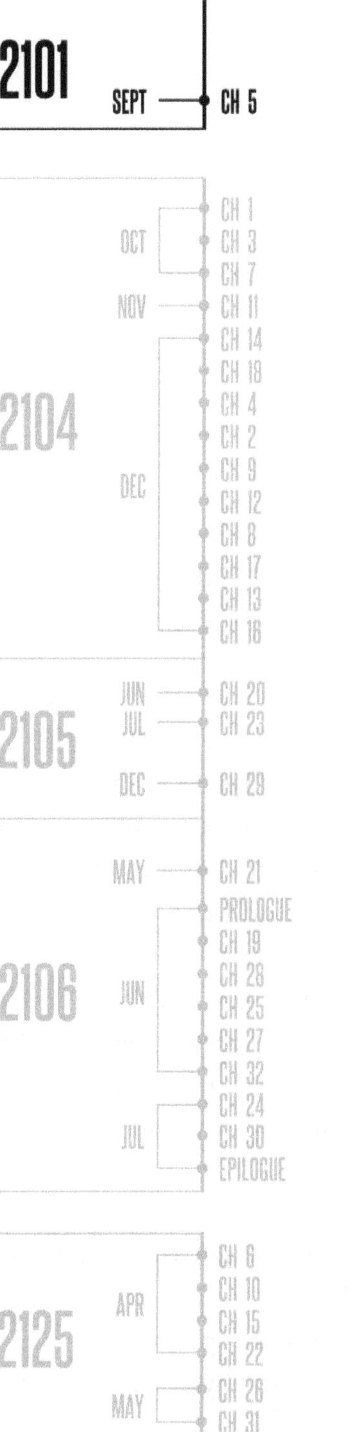

CHAPTER 5

SEPTEMBER 2101
Dr. Logan

I counted down from 100. I hit eighty-seven for the second time and suspected that I would run through it another four to eight times. Staring at nothing, I breathed slowly as the numbers flowed from my mind to my lips.

I'd been counting up and down to 100 while I waited since I was in elementary school, when I'd hit a girl who called me a nerd for loving numbers because no one loved numbers. But I did, and at the time, I counted up and down to 100 almost a full eleven times before my father arrived at the office. I needed a distraction from the overwhelming anxiety in my stomach.

My father had come in angry and ready to kill whichever child hurt his little girl. I still remembered the look of shock on his face when the principal told him that it was the other girl who was hurt because his daughter punched her right in the face without a second thought.

Then he laughed. Oh, that laugh made me love my father even more than I did already. His laugh said it was impossible that I did such a thing. Only when he looked over at me and saw the expression on my face did he realize it was true.

He made his apologies, and I was sent home for the day. In

the hover on the way home, he hadn't said anything at first. I glanced over at him a few times, and he just looked like we were driving, as if I hadn't just been suspended for the day. But after two up-and-down 100s, he spoke.

"Don't ever let anyone make you feel like what you love to do is not worthy. If you love it, it's worthy." And that was all he ever said on the matter.

That moment made me push myself even deeper into everything I loved, and I loved numbers. I loved math. I loved making numbers do extraordinary things—yield incredible results. I loved languages too and had wished I could learn them all. And science—the universe to the atoms and the body. How the body healed itself was one of the most fascinating processes of them all. The list kept going.

That day changed me because I no longer hesitated. I only drove myself forward into what I wanted, and right now, I wanted this job.

An opening at the Atlas Institute working on NOMO was an extraordinary opportunity. Alongside Dr. Atlas himself? That was a dream.

I started counting faster for a moment before pausing to breathe and continued at a slower pace. Since my medical residency, I had read every paper, article, and companion dissertation from a new student affiliated with the NOMO Project. I absorbed everything public from the Atlas Institute and anything theorized by anyone else. I knew everything there was to know, and although I never prayed, today I thought I might start.

The basics of the theory were how to use ionizing radiation more efficiently by not only destroying the malignant cells but by merging the penetrating power of gamma radiation specifically to reach DNA. Basically, the NOMO Project wanted to change the DNA of someone with cancer to make it so they wouldn't have the gene to begin with. No cancer gene meant no cancer. They wanted to change the core of a person, the very fabric of their makeup, to ensure the cancer not only disappeared but wouldn't return or materialize in any generations following.

The reach was not limited to only that specific genetic disease. The applications made my head spin.

I looked around Dr. Atlas's office. Every corner of the room displayed success. One wall was covered with licenses and diplomas. Awards accompanied many of them. Another wall displayed a dozen holoprints, each one projecting images of honorable mentions on the wall from different prestigious online sites such as The New York Times. The many articles blended with pictures of Dr. Atlas and celebrated scientists in his field of genetics and others.

His desk was surprisingly clear of clutter, sleek, and modern. Only the techscreen sat in the middle with a tablet next to it. In fact, the whole office was sparse of any personal effects, except for one item. I saw one photograph, at an angle, of him standing beside a woman with wavy blonde hair. They looked so young together.

I wonder if that's—

The door opened behind me, cutting off my thoughts as I reached my third round of counting. I took a deep, quiet breath as the man himself walked past me.

You are made for this job. Don't forget it.

Dr. Atlas sat behind his desk and placed his palm on the screen on the tabletop. The screen brightened, and the lighting in the room dimmed automatically. After a short blue light, Dr. Atlas typed into the glass. A 3D rendering of a gene came to life in front of me in green and red.

I almost flinched when Dr. Atlas finally spoke. "What disease is this?"

Without hesitation, I replied, "Turner syndrome."

His fingers typed. "This one?" The image changed with red glowing in different areas of the gene.

I counted the rows from the top to the red and answered,

"Spina bifida."

Another command entered. "And this one?"

The red areas changed again. It was a rare disease, evident by the damage it caused. But which of the many? I counted and reviewed the breaks from top to bottom. It was the bottom that gave it away.

"It's nothing."

Dr. Atlas raised an eyebrow. "I'm sorry?"

I straightened my back. "It's not a genetic disorder. It's fake. There is no disease that looks like that."

"Why do you say that?"

I pointed to the bottom of the gene. "The termination sequence is wrong. The mRNA won't encounter another termination, so it will continue to mutate. That's not a complete gene for a living human."

Dr. Atlas smiled. "Well, Dr. Fay—"

"Dr. Logan."

He raised his eyebrows. "Okay, Dr. Logan. I have interviewed thirty-six candidates for this position. Out of them all, you are the first who didn't fumble and make something up for that last example. Every single one of them thought they saw something they didn't, because I must have been giving them something. Therefore, it had to BE something. You saw it for what it really is. I must say that I am impressed."

I concealed my raging joy and simply said, "Thank you, Dr. Atlas. Your praise means more than you know."

He stared at me a moment while I tried to hold his gaze and breathe at the same time. He swiped four fingers across the techglass. The lights on the ceiling turned back on.

"Tell me about yourself, Dr. Logan."

"I attended Stanford University on a full—"

"No, no." Dr. Atlas waved his hand, dismissing my words. "Tell me about YOU. Why genetics? There are dozens of medical fields. Why did YOU decide to follow this route that put you here in front of me?"

His direct tone stopped my defenses from flying up, but it was his eyes that asked for raw honesty. A well of emotions flooded my chest, and I looked down at my hands for only a brief moment before I answered. "My father. He was diagnosed with lung cancer when I was fifteen. It was stage three." I took a small breath. "I lost him three days after my seventeenth birthday. That was the same day I abandoned my dream of being a mathematician and changing the world with numbers. I decided I wanted to go into medicine and change the world so no one would have to lose someone they loved to a disease like cancer."

It took all of my strength to hold back the tears brimming in my eyes. I hadn't expected the interview to venture into my personal history, but I was honest to my core. That's the best I could do.

Dr. Atlas seemed to look through me for a moment. His face reflected the pain in my own voice. But it didn't last before he collected himself. Standing from his chair, his eyes brightened.

"Come with me, Dr. Logan. Let me show you how you're going to help me change the world."

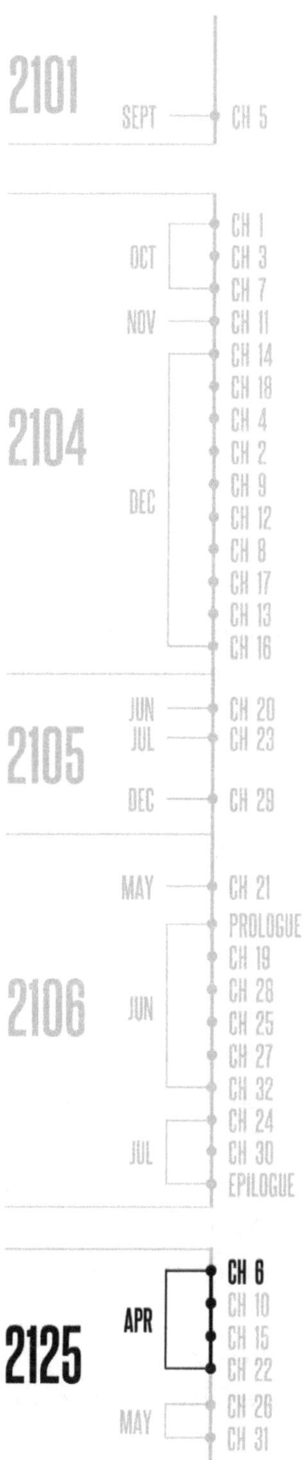

CHAPTER 6

APRIL 2125
Marina

"Shit."

I close the door to the second store I checked today.

"It's just a little coupler. I mean, it's not even an inch in diameter. Come on."

It doesn't usually take this many tries to find something I need, especially in a city like this one. The first two shops—TechHalo and TecSpec—are my usuals. I normally move my way through them first, but interestingly, they don't have the gear couplers I need to repair my solar panels.

"Shit." I kick at a few pieces of rubble on the sidewalk, or what is left of one. I pull out my comm from my pocket. Since there is no Internet to connect to or any calls to make, at this point, it's just a paperweight. But it's good for storing information. Right now, I need a map.

Swiping through the directory of businesses from 2106, I search for another tech store. M&M Technologies is a bit farther away. I've seen that one on the map a few times but never needed to visit.

"Until now. Okay, let's go already."

Climbing back in my hover van, I drive for about ten

minutes. It would probably surprise people to know how fast they could have traveled from one side of the city to the other if not for skylane restrictions and other regulations. I park my van in the front against the curb and shut down the engaged engine. The store name letters M&M TECHNOLOGIES are yellow, although the LOGIES is broken. Only the frame for the letters remains.

Rubbing the dust off the store-front glass in a circle just big enough for my eyes, I see rows of tech bins. The shelves are reflecting in a mirror along the left wall, making the room seem almost endless from my angle.

"Well, if I don't find them in here, I quit."

Although I know I won't stop looking. I need every ounce of energy my solar panels pull in, so having a whole section down will not last for the long haul.

Damn couplers.

I check the door to see if it's locked—which it is, as most are, interestingly enough. I'd rather not rust my parts, if at all possible, so I try to open the door without damaging it.

The weather isn't regulated like it used to be. Winters in New Eastland had once turned to spring earlier and kept away days of snow. But now, the earth has reclaimed its natural order, and it snows here. Who knows what I'll need to repair over my lifetime.

Or need to build.

I grab my toolkit from my bag, disengage the pressure lock on the inside, and swing open the door. The dust hits me as I walk in, my feet kicking up a layer into the air. The enclosed room feels thick from the years of stagnant air in the room, and the silence is deafening—as most stores are now. A long, open walkway runs down the middle of the room, ending at a large double door, with dozens of shelves on either side.

"Wow. How have I not been here before?" I think it's odd that Mom and I never came here. I considered. It is farther out of the way than the others. I shrug. *Well, I found it now.*

I put the toolkit away and look around. To my right is a pile of water bottles.

"I'll be taking you with me." I reach down to open the bag, and the plastic rips easier than expected, spilling the bottles. *That works too.* I take one to drink and scan the right side of the room before looking to my left, and I almost jolt. That wasn't a mirror I saw through the window. It's an entire other section of the store.

There are more than thirty rows of parts, wires, and tools sorted into perfectly organized bins with labels.

"It is perfect in here. Well done, owner of M&M. You were one of the few who knew what people like me needed. All right, gear couplers, where are you?" I drink the rest of the water in the bottle, placing the empty bottle down, and begin my hunt. I search row after row until I finally find them on the last shelf on the left side of the store—on the top shelf, too high to reach. And I have no ladder.

UGH.

"Well, I guess we're climbing up then." Warning bells go off in my mind. I huff. "Okay, let's understand the gravity of the situation. If I don't have these gear couplers, I don't fix my solar panels. If I don't fix my solar panels, then eventually, the automation in the greenhouse stops. Food dies. I die. All right?" It's dramatic, but it also happens to be true. "So, up I go."

I set one foot on the bottom metal shelf to test its durability. It seems fine. Shifting my weight off the floor, I lift my other foot to the next shelf and wait. Will it hold me? Yes, it does.

I breathe out. "Okay, keep going."

I make it up another two shelves before I hear the metal buckle. I hold my breath, hoping that I can make it, until, suddenly, everything tilts, and I fall backward.

The dozens of plastic bins crash to the floor. Wires and parts fly everywhere. Thankfully, I don't fall backward as I somehow manage to land on my feet, stopping the unit with my hands above me. The only thing that saved me? A corner of the shelving unit hitting the wall.

And what's worse? I'm stuck.

I curse myself. What the hell was I thinking? I only come into the city twice a month, and already, this trip is one of my least favorites.

I cringe as the metal of the shelving unit squeaks in movement. "Yes, thank you. I appreciate your feedback."

I consider my predicament. I'm about to be crushed by metal and am not entirely sure how to get out. If Mom was here, she'd take care of it easily. But today is not the day to wish for impossible things.

"Okay. So. Let's talk it out, right? Because when you're angry, you're dumb. Let's be honest and review the situation." I look up.

"A very tall, very heavy shelving unit is at a thirty-five-degree angle above your head and is teetering by one corner. There's a wall on one side and another shelving unit on the other. My already tired arms are balancing the unit and keeping it from falling more, barely. Thankfully, that one corner caught the wall behind me on the way down or I'd be more than stuck—I'd be broken. But also as the shelves fell, they knocked down a smaller shelving unit, preventing me from getting out of my current, stupid, squished space."

I push against the shelving unit. Nothing happens.

"Breathe, Marina. Breathe. You can do this. Where is the leverage?" I slowly twist my head to see to the other side, but the shelf squeaks again in protest. I take a deep breath.

"Come on. Stay with me, shelf. Stay with me."

I can see the angle that the shelf will take if my arms give out. It will snap my femur in half. I am no healer, and being at least four hours from home by hover is not an ideal situation for me or my leg.

"Let's not think about the repercussions of that actually happening. How about that? Thanks, Marina."

I shake my head. "Think. Think." I feel the energy stir in me. An idea comes to me in a flash—the water bottles in the front of the shop. There was one pack of twenty-four—actually, twenty-three, since I drank one. The bag is already opened. Maybe they would be enough.

"I don't know if I can reach that far." I feel the muscles in my arms weaken. "Well, if you don't try now, there won't be any energy to try later."

I close my eyes and take a deep breath. Hold it. Let it out. Calming myself down as deeply as I can, I repeat this three more times.

I pull into my mind. I see a white light getting brighter and brighter. When the light almost blinds me, I send my power, thin white tendrils of light, outward from my body like floating spiderwebs. With small particles of light circling the threads of energy, I push them through the room toward the water.

My power touches different solid objects, but they all create a dark solid grey void in my mind. I find the edges of the bottles as I push deeper into my energy. Little droplets of sweat bead on my forehead while I pinch my eyes together, pushing even more.

It feels like my fingertips touch the edge of the water, cool and soft. I call the energy of the water to me. The closest bottle rocks toward me an inch before falling back.

I call the water again. This time, one bottle starts to roll. Then the other ones follow. After a minute of pushing and pulling, all twenty-three bottles roll toward me and stop at my feet.

I open my eyes, taking shallow breaths and hoping I have enough energy to finish what I must. "You can do this. You just need to get the bottles open." I look around. "How the hell do I do that?" My arms are cemented in place. If I move an inch, I won't be able to keep the shelf from falling.

"I need my hands. There's no other way to do it. Yeah? How long do you think you can hold it with your back?" A vision of my back giving out comes to my mind, but I stifle the doubts. "No, no. You can do this. Let out as much water as you can, as fast as you can.

Don't think. Just do it."

I take a deep breath, holding my light nearby for when I need it. "Okay, go."

I twist my body to the left and listen as the shelf groans. I hold tight to nothing but faith that it won't fall as I shift my weight lower to counterbalance the shelf with my back, leaning over and supporting the unit without my hands. The weight pushes down on my legs, but I breathe steadily as I stretch my hand out to the first bottle. It rolls to me, standing up on end, and I practically snap open the lid and throw the bottle down. As the water rushes out, I already have the next bottle in my hand.

Ten bottles. Just open ten bottles.

I remind myself to breathe, even as I try to hold my breath and not move an inch. When I grab for the tenth bottle, a dull twinge in my back strengthens. My legs start shaking.

Closing my eyes, I call my light—it comes faster and brighter. My whole body trembles as I reach out with my light to find the water. White tendrils come out of my hands as my energy touches the water once more. The water starts merging into two solid puddles, one larger than the other. I spin the water into a vortex until it stands like a staff off the ground to the height of my bent-over body. The white light in my mind swirls, changing colors into a softer blue. The light blue tendrils and specks move outward, touching the water and freezing the vortex into a solid staff of ice.

I reach out my hand, and the solid staff slides to me. I quickly position the ice staff at my shoulder, just under the shelf, and reach down to call the second puddle of the water. It slithers up and around the ice staff like a snake, working its way to the top. As if stacking brick on brick, the water reaches the top. Ounce by ounce, I freeze the remaining water to push up and take some of the weight off my back. Blood rushes to my sore back. Relief hits me, but I can't enjoy it for too long. I can't hit the staff on my way out from under the metal shelf.

Let's just hope you hold.

Despite my tiring leg muscles, I dip even lower, testing the weight of the shelving unit on the ice. It doesn't move. I dip even lower and completely release the shelves from my back before dropping to my knees and crawling out. Once I clear the metal unit a few feet away, I flop to the floor and lie flat on my back. The tension slowly leaves my body as I regulate my breathing.

On my third breath in, I hear the ice crack, water dripping in the humid air, and before I let it out, the shelf crashes to the floor—with any items that didn't fall the first time—where I was pinned moments before.

I swell with gratitude for that corner. My eye catches a bag beside my shoulder. It's a bag of gear couplers.

"Well. Thank you very much."

I drop the first of two water bottle packs into the open trunk of my hover van. The other thirteen single bottles that came to save me lie in the front seat. They deserve an extra perk.

I wipe my forehead. I didn't bring my hat with me today, but at least I pulled my hair back in a braid. It falls to my waist normally, but I hardly notice it.

I found everything on my list in only a couple of hours—not including the time I spent with my friend, the shelving unit. So, that was pretty good time. I might make it home before the sun sets so I can unload in the light—a bonus for the day.

After I add a second pack of water to the trunk, I rip one from the bag and sit down on the curb. Of the four shops I hit, I found all of the new blades and tools I needed. Earlier stores had a ton of canned goods in rather good condition. But can I just say? Every time I see a can of peas, I get sad I've never tasted them. They look like beautiful little balls of deliciousness. Unfortunately, those weren't in the sets of seeds my mom brought with her when she planted our garden.

I don't normally eat the food in the cans I find. I store them for emergencies. My mom always said it was better to have it and not need it than need it and not have it. So there are a few items I've accumulated just in case.

Thankfully, my fully functioning greenhouse produces plenty of food constantly. The weather is mostly predictable now since it stabilized and the sky stopped falling. I was very young when the satellites fell from the sky, with no one to maintain them.

I look up the street at the rusted satellite I passed on the way here. Half of the body is stuck in the ground, with debris cluttered around the base. I can tell it was an Earth Observation Satellite because of the long solar arrays on both sides of its skeletal framework.

Over 10,000 artificial satellites crashed to earth the year before I turned one. It came as a huge surprise when one fell the year I turned five. My mom explained that all the satellites should have fallen by then. But tell that to the one that dropped right in front of me and my mom.

That day, we were out in our garden. The sun was setting, and we just finished cleaning up for the day when I saw a light in the sky. I never saw an airplane—or anything else for that matter—in the sky before, so to actually see something was an amazing surprise. It wasn't until I heard my mom screaming for me to move that I became scared and ran with her holding my hand.

It crashed less than thirty feet from us. Debris ricocheted off the ground when it hit, sharp aluminum flying. It left a deep hole.

I rub the top of my left wrist where a piece had hit me. I don't remember the cut itself, but I remember the stitches. Thankfully, that's all that happened. Well, that and the fact that we had to move part of our garden. The satellite landed in our tomatoes.

I still shake my head in wonder after thirteen years.

I drink more from my water bottle. Gazing around the rest of the street, I realize how easily I forget the pain of not knowing what this world even was at one point. The Event happened eighteen years and nine days ago. I wasn't there, but I'll never forget. Every year—just like I did a little over a week ago—I light candles and sit outside. Somehow, it feels right, even if there's still so much I'll never understand.

Many of the roads cracked as plant life grew and forced a way through even the smallest of fissures. Building exteriors are largely intact, although most of the windows are broken. What is left of wildlife makes homes wherever they want. I spend a lot of time wondering what it would have been like to live in a place with flying cars, appointments to keep, jobs to work, children to raise, and playgrounds to play in. Mostly, though, I wonder what it was like to live in a place with people—hundreds of real people. With so many of them, you could just reach out and hug someone if you wanted to. Everyone would be there for each other, and we'd help the world grow and be amazing. You could just sit and talk to them about the wonders of the world or do nothing and just sit beside them.

But even in a world with no people, I know that life wasn't blissful for everyone. Most trudged along in their own worlds, wishing for more but never achieving it. There are databases upon databases of mentors, gurus, and advisors telling people to do what they want to be happy.

I never understood why that needed to be taught. Of course that's all we want. But what do I know? I am looking into a world I never knew, never lived in, never touched. My mom did her best to teach me all the beautiful—all the good—facets of life. She wanted to honor the memory of the billions we lost, the billions she always said she lost.

I take a deep breath as the memory of my mom's pain floods back to me.

I stand up, the dust kicking from under my feet. "Stop. Stop. This is not the time. You want to think about Mom? You can, but not here. We need to focus and get home before the sun sets."

I take a couple more long breaths and let my eyes wander, trying to compose myself before I fall too deeply into my memory. That's when I realize I definitely stayed too long.

Dozens of small specks of light that constantly float around start to gravitate and accumulate by me. It always happens when I sit somewhere for too long. These too have been here since the Event.

After 10.9 billion people were killed, the pinpricks of light were all that remained. I used to pretend that the lights were the people that were no longer here. I'd play with them, talk to them, name them. The faster ones were Maddies. The slower ones were Saddies, and the ones that jumped around were Addies. Besides, they were all I had to talk to, except for Mom.

Now, I hardly even notice them, unless they group around me like this. A speck bounces around my face like a fly.

"All right, Addie. It's time to go home. I got it. I'm leaving. Let me just mark my street first. Is that okay?" The speck bobs a few times before I finish off my water bottle and throw the container in the back of the trunk, closing the door.

Planetrees line this street on both sides. Growing for almost twenty years unchecked, the branches sprout in every direction, some in broken windows in the buildings beside them. I smile at the trees. They are my favorite city tree. My mom and I uprooted five of them from the city when I was about ten, and we planted them in a circle on the side of our garden. It made my mom feel more at home.

I check the trees to my left and right to see which are the taller ones on both sides and then walk away from the van, moving to the middle of what was once an intersection. I close my eyes and root my feet, drawing into my energy. I take a deep breath in, hold it, and let it out slowly three times before I pull deeper into my mind. The white light brightens before it changes to a darker shade of green. I reach out my power to find the two trees I visualize in my mind. I find their energy, deep and old, and raise my hands at diagonals toward them. Green tendrils and specks of light leave my hands, floating toward the trees. The earth energy and my own blend together to create a tight bond before I pull my hands together, palms open, in front of me.

I feel the two largest branches of both the left and right tree grow in thickness and length as they reach toward the middle of the intersection to find each other. When the branches from either side touch, the energy crosses between the two trees, and I feel them both grow stronger. The branches twist, turn, and wrap around each other before the tips find their way up and out of the embrace, creating an X above the street.

I take one more deep breath and lower my hands. Opening my eyes, I admire my new marking. I've been here, and there are still more supplies. Satisfied, I turn around, walk to the driver's door of the hover, and pause, taking one more look at the street of ruin.

"Take care. I'll be back in a few weeks."

Closing the door, I settle in my seat for the four-hour drive home. The sun, just overhead, makes everything look bright and fresh, even in its disheveled state. I reach over and turn on the audio player, select shuffle, and let the music build as the engine beeps through its two-minute series.

Activating the booster, I turn the music louder. The Neoteric Beats dance through my ears as I drive away from the old New Eastland.

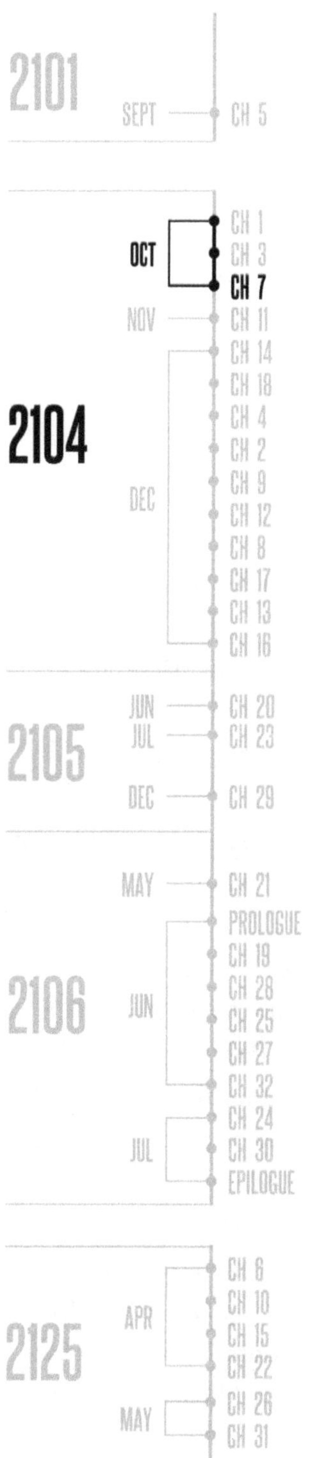

CHAPTER 7

OCTOBER 2104
Angelia

I reached out my fingers to trace the uneven spines of the dozens of books on this particular shelf in the science fiction section. I was by far a bigger sci-fi and fantasy nut than anything else. There was nothing like disappearing into another century of the future, meeting an alien that sang instead of talked, or saving the universe with magical powers.

New sci-fi books dropped monthly, and I never missed opening day. Combing these shelves was my one true joy every thirty days.

Noreen always gave me the day off. She knew I just wouldn't come in if she scheduled me. She tried that once, and the five CraftBots scheduled for repair that day sat around, beeping. Noreen called me at wit's end by the second hour of hearing the sound echo through the store. I had been nice enough to shut them down, but I still came back to my bookshop. And now we had an understanding, our perfect symbiotic relationship at work again.

The bookstore was cleverly named The Last Review. 144 years ago, it wasn't the only bookstore or the last of anything—until now.

The Last Review became popular back before tablets even existed. Was that even possible? Sadly, the need for real paper—touch and feel—books dropped as tablets integrated more into everyday life. Once schools realized they could load a tablet with all the books that students needed, from their pre-K workbooks to their senior economics textbooks, actual printed books became almost obsolete, except to people like me, and people like my mom. She taught me the simple and yet immense joys of books.

How the cover of a book really could give you a glimpse into the quality—judge away. How opening a brand-new book for the first time was a moment to enjoy. How the smell of a book was one of the most amazing scents in existence. How you should never use a metal bookmark as it will only rip your pages. How a book could open any window into another adventure. How you could escape into the worlds of the page if the real world wasn't where you wanted to be.

I wondered how long this place would stay in business. How much longer could they keep printing books for nerds like me who wanted to touch the coarse paper, the wrinkled spines, the glossy covers? Not all authors were fortunate to line these shelves, only the ones that the owners truly loved.

That was the other amazing fact about The Last Review. They printed books on demand in their small warehouse in the back. People ordered books online and then picked them up after they were printed and ready. It was actually pretty genius, printing on demand.

My mom used to tell me that when books were published, companies would print thousands of books and send them everywhere—department stores, grocery stores, airports. The idea of walking into a building and seeing wall-to-wall books quite honestly amazed me. It made me jealous to have missed out on such a beautiful sight.

I breathed in the smell of paper and ink and smiled. I loved Sci-book release day.

Two hours later, I lounged at my favorite coffee shop in the city, The Dark Roast, twenty minutes away from my apartment by hover—thirty minutes from The Last Review. The drive along the river was always spectacular, even on cloudy days like today.

I sat outside in the crisp air with my white, favorite, cracked cup of coffee, foam still on top, and my new Sci-book—Fates Unexpected—in hand. I'd already read three chapters and drunk two cups from my favorite barista, who brought me a new one whenever I finished. I was hooked by the first couple of pages. The heroine was strong-willed and already a powerhouse. She was definitely my kind of character. As I turned another page, a sudden torrential downpour lasted about ninety seconds. I stopped reading and enjoyed the rainfall cascade off the awning, sipping from my cup with two hands. Once the sky cleared up again, I stayed another hour before Bren—my barista and owner of The Dark Roast—approached my table.

I looked up at him from behind my book. "Noooo, I don't want to stop. Come on, five more minutes? I want to see what happens in this chapter."

Bren smiled and shook his head. "No. It is 9:30, which means you already had an extra thirty. So go. I want to go home."

I dramatically rolled my eyes, grabbed my coffee cup and saucer, and handed them to him. "Fine. Thank you for all of your delicious coffee. What do I owe you?"

He took the cup. "Too much. Now go home."

"You love me, Bren."

"Yes, yes I do. Now go."

I saved my place with my favorite bookmark, pausing for only a second to read the words "The Universe Belongs to Those Who Read" before putting the book into my backpack.

I bounced up to kiss Bren on the cheek. "I'll see you in a few days."

"Yeah, yeah. Bye."

I laughed as I walked backward away from him, keeping my body facing him. "Goodnight!"

He waved over his head as he walked through the open door leading into his shop.

As I turned to walk forward, I fought the urge to sit down on the bench nearby and keep reading. I wanted to get home before it possibly rained again.

I rode slower than usual on my ride home, enjoying the wet pavement and new-city smell. I parked and closed the gate, walking the few feet back to my building. I traveled up the elevator—did I need a new couch that came with a sound system built into its walls?—and down the hallway to my door. As my key fob beeped with my return announced, the fresh new sound of rain falling greeted me. I dropped my bag on my couch and walked toward my room, running my fingers along my books as I went. I stripped down to nothing and paused.

For once, I put my damp clothes in the bathroom to dry, instead of plopping them on top of my leaning tower of laundry.

Tonight's choice of comfy PJs consisted of my favorite Moonstruck black sweatpants and a t-shirt with flowers and the words "No Rain, No Flowers." I liked my t-shirts oversized and comfortable, and this one suited me perfectly.

Stepping into my bite-sized kitchen, featuring a half fridge, a stove with two burners, and a sink, I heated the other half of my breakfast burrito—eggs, bacon, cheese and potatoes—for thirty seconds. I leaned against the counter, waiting. I couldn't complain, though. I had a dishwasher. Granted, it was small and held about five dishes at a time, but I wasn't hosting any grand parties any time soon.

My nightly routine waited for me as I sat at my tiny dining room table in my yellowed chair. The next piece of paper in my flip-book of multi-colored sheets was a pale orange color tonight and had the same twenty-one lines as the rest. I looked into my coffee-cup-slash-pen-holder and selected a dark blue pen.

I bit into my burrito before I started to write.

Dear Mom,

The newest Sci-book came out today! Man, I love the last Thursday of the month. I think you'd really like this one. The main character is even more headstrong than me, if you can believe it. The two main characters just started their journey together across a very different world. It's a new author I haven't heard of before, but I am definitely looking into more of her work.

Best part of the day? While I was reading at The Dark Roast, it started pouring. It was amazing. I just sat and listened. Remember when we went to visit Theadora when I was about ten? Dad had to work, so we went just the two of us. I was so excited to get you all to myself on that trip. It rained every single day, for the entire three days we were there. Rain. Rain. Rain. And it was one of my most favorite trips we ever took.

I miss you the most when it rains.

I took a soft breath before signing,

Love Always and Everly, Your Lia

I ripped the page out of the notepad and stood. I grabbed my lighter with flowers on it and took the sheet of paper with me to my small—but existent—balcony. It could only hold a chair and a potted plant, but it fit me fine. The vines from my plant, happily covering the balcony's bars, made for a fairytale balcony for my prince below, calling up to me with a song.

The rain fell in huge drops again by the time I walked outside. I looked out across the narrow courtyard and watched the heavy rain glisten on the few replanted trees. I glanced at the note in my hand and read it one more time. When I was done, I held it out away from my face one last time before lighting the edge of a corner. I turned the note to its side as the flame engulfed my words. Once the fire hit "Love Always," I released the flaming paper and watched the wind gust and blew it into the rainy night.

"I miss you, Mom."

I smiled as the rain poured harder.

Rylan

I am not a stalker.

I probably repeated this to myself about a hundred times throughout the day, and yet that's exactly what I was doing.

She picked up her giant coffee and took a sip, and I smiled, wondering what the coffee tasted like, what the flavor was that she liked the most. Did she like creamer, or oat milk, or milk and sugar? Maybe she loved it black.

I am not a stalker.

For the past five days, I followed the pizza shop girl. I watched her drive to work, visit a bookstore, drink her coffee, and ride her hover bike.

What the hell is wrong with me?

I also asked myself that a thousand times. I felt crazy, to be totally honest, like someone came into my head and stole my body. I got back in my van about a dozen times to leave, go back to my room, grab my glasstop, and actually drive to meet Larry, Curly, and Moe. They had already sent me messages, wondering where I was, if there was a problem, when I was meeting them. The farthest I ever got was the end of the driveway at the hotel before I reversed and parked again.

I couldn't do it.

Every time I thought about leaving this bright light of a girl, my stomach twisted and knotted. I couldn't handle it.

But what was I doing? Was I just going to follow her around forever? How much longer was I going to ignore the Stooges? I couldn't answer any of these questions, nor could I decide what else I wanted to do. This was all I wanted to do right now. I just wanted to eat, sleep, and watch her.

Hey, bro, here's an idea. Why the hell don't you TALK to her?

I shook my head. What the hell would I even say to her?

Hi, there. I've been stalking you for days. I am in love with you, and I can't seem to continue my life without you.

Sure, all of that sounded totally normal. She wouldn't possibly run away in the opposite direction, would she?

I huffed out a deep breath and looked up through my open window. Pizza Girl arrived home a few minutes ago, and now I waited for my favorite part of her night routine—watching her light paper on fire on her balcony. I wondered what she burned. Why she burned. Was she burning to remember? Or burning to forget?

A few minutes later, the rain pelted down so hard, I couldn't see through my windows. I closed up the van and got out, leaning under some awning behind a pole, hoping she couldn't see me from where I watched.

I saw the back door open and her head come through. Two minutes later, a small, orange flame lit up her face. She stood closer to the edge of the balcony than the past few nights, and I could see her expression for the first time.

My heart ached at the pain in her eyes and the longing in her face. Now I knew. She burned because of loss.

And you are intruding on her moments.

I instantly felt sick to my stomach. I couldn't keep doing this. It was not fair to her and her memories. I needed to stop.

Moving slowly, I walked around my van and climbed in, sitting still, hand on the wheel. *She deserves more than this, more than you. You're just a hacker—a thief. What the hell can you offer her?*

I didn't know the answer, but I was tired of running, tired of being scared, of everything.

I was going to go talk to her tomorrow at work. *Oh yeah? And what are you going to say?* I shook my head and raised my eyebrows. *I'm going to start with "Hi."*

But first, I have an old alias to activate—one that just so happens to live in New Eastland.

Angelia

I heard a soft voice say, "Excuse me," as I searched through the box for the screw I needed.

"One second," I said loud enough for my voice to carry from the back, trying to grab a tiny screw with my fingers. It slipped three times. "Shit," I muttered under my breath. My aggravation grew at the stupid inanimate object that wouldn't listen.

I decided to retrieve my mini magnetic telescoping tool when I heard an object slide across the counter. I remembered the soft voice. "I'll be right there." I took off my gloves and placed them gently beside the open tablet panel, careful not to knock any small pieces to the floor.

I put my wireless buds in my cargo pocket as I walked out from the back.

I saw a glasstop on the counter, but no human. "Um, hello?"

A pair of silver eyes popped up from under the counter, followed by a beautiful smile. I actually jolted from the impact of that smile.

"Hi."

I stupidly stared at his gorgeous face for a second too long and finally found my voice. "Hi. What can I help you with?"

He pointed at his glasstop. "My beautiful paperweight. It stopped working a long time ago, but I finally decided that if I'm not getting it fixed, I'm tossing it out."

"Oh, no, don't do that. Even if it's dead, there are so many great parts inside that can be salvaged." His smile grew. Long hair curled at his forehead. I ignored his beach boy face and tried to focus. "When did it stop working?"

"About a week ago. I was just working on it like usual, and the bottom touch stopped responding. I restarted and tried to reset it. After a while, I had to factory restart, which just broke my heart. No joke. I literally cried."

I let out a short laugh. "Oh, well, then I'm so sorry for your loss."

He laughed back. "Thanks. I'm still getting over it." He beamed at me. "So, what do you think? Touch screen sensor or motherboard meltdown? Please don't let it be a meltdown. I can't take two critical hits."

I shook my head, smiling, as I took the glasstop from the table, searching under the counter for where I could connect it. "I didn't know there were too many of us left in this techie world of ours."

He looked at me, confusion sparkling in his bright eyes. "Us?"

"Yeah, people who love technology but also *understand* it, instead of wandering through life using all the sparkly techie toys and not having a clue what actually goes into each one of our conveniences." I found the port and plugged the cord from my end into his glasstop. A tingle ran down my spine as I looked back up into his silver eyes. "You seem to be the software kind of techie."

His smile beamed bigger. "You got it. I live and breathe it, actually. This lovely girl right here was my tester for all my programs. Kind of a glasstop down at the moment."

I raised my eyebrows. "Really?" I watched as the backlight came on and text scrolled across the screen. "Do you think code in your software interfered with the signals or its regular processing?"

"Not a chance." He shook his head but then considered for a

moment. "No. No, the program I was testing wasn't for any hardware construction."

"Oh, good, because us hardware techs hate when you software techs ruin all our hard work."

He shook his head. "Don't you hardware techs know that you guys wouldn't even be able to use your tech without us software geeks? I mean, who creates the programs to run your robots?"

"And who creates the robots to house your programs?"

We both stared at each other for a second before we started laughing. "Spoken like a true hardware tech," he quipped.

"Only a software tech would say that."

He raised his hands in mock defeat. "All right, all right. You win. Besides, you're the one holding my glasstop, so I should probably be nice."

I was reading the code flashing on the screen. "Good idea." We both went silent as I typed in a few commands. A few screens later, I looked back up. He was staring at me. The same jolt went through me when his eyes locked on mine.

"Not saying anything, but it seems you have a little software tech in you too," he said, gesturing to me.

I rolled my eyes. "Stop trying to bring me to the dark side. I need to know at least some software to fix the hundreds of robots, tablets, and glasstops that come through here every month."

He smirked. "Oh, so you're saying software is—"

"I thought you were going to be nice to the hardware techie holding your equipment." I held up the glasstop.

He threw his hands in the air. "Fine. Fine. Hardware can be superior for the rest of this conversation. But that's it."

I smiled, putting the glass top back down, and checked the next few screens of code. "Okay, so the good news is that software doesn't seem to be the issue." I glanced up at him expecting a comment, but he stayed silent, looking innocently offended that I anticipated a retort. "Bad news is I'm not sure exactly which hardware part it is. I need to see what's going on inside." I raised an eyebrow at him. "Are you going to survive if I take her apart?"

He dropped his open palm onto his chest. "I'll do what I must."

I laughed. "Okay, drama queen, I'll be gentle. I promise. When do you need her back?"

He shook his head. "Whenever is good for you. I'm not in a rush."

I thought for a moment. "Okay, I have a full day today and tomorrow, but I can get in there tomorrow morning at least and see if I can figure it out before I jump into everything else."

He smiled while I tried to ignore the butterflies in my stomach.

"Okay, great," he said.

I turned to the screen to my right. Placing my palm on the glass, the screen projected to life in front of me, lighting up the space around us with white light. "Okay, let me just grab some information from you, and I'll call you tomorrow when I know more."

"Sounds good."

I typed a few commands and got to the right screen. "Go ahead and scan your IDfob." He scanned it, and the computer beeped, accepting the information. His image and other personal information popped up. "Jaeden Lowe? From downtown, it looks like."

He nodded. "Guilty."

"Great." I typed in a few more notes of what I needed to do before swiping the computer screen to save and close. The projection stopped. I turn back to him. His eyes were still fixed on me. "Okay, so, I'll call you tomorrow, Software Tech Jaeden."

He shifted to one side. "Great. Thank you, Hardware Tech—uh?"

I smiled. "Angelia."

"Angelia." He repeated, his voice soft for a moment. He

smiled, his expression shifting. "Well, thank you, Hardware Tech Angelia. It was amazing meeting you today, and I'll leave you to all your hardware techie stuff."

I laughed. "Don't break any more glasstops before tomorrow, okay?"

"Ouch." Both of us laughed. But he didn't move.

A moment of silence passed between us before he finally spoke. "Okay, I'll wait to hear from you, then. Thanks again, Angelia." He turned and walked out of the store.

I was left sitting there, staring at the space he no longer occupied. I replayed our conversation in my mind.

Damn. Gorgeous and smart? Too bad he's a software tech. I laughed at myself as I unplugged his glasstop. "It's you and me, little lady. Let's see what's bothering you."

As I turned to walk toward the back, I heard footsteps behind me. I turned to Jaeden's beautiful silver eyes.

"Hi."

I smiled at him. My face was starting to hurt. "Hi." He grinned and ran his hand through his hair but said nothing. I dramatically looked around the room. "Didn't we just do this?"

He laughed nervously. "Yeah, we did. Um—" He glanced around the room for a second before coming back to my eyes. "Look, I know I just met you, and you just met me, and I'm sure you don't hang out with software guys, but I'd love to take you out for coffee or something, if—uh—you want to."

Again, I was lost in his smile and could only stare back. I found my voice somewhere between my stomach and my chest. "I'd love to."

His smile grew and lit up his face. "Yeah? Great. I know a really great coffee spot. Not many people go there, but it's one of my favorites. It's about half an hour from here. It's called The Dark Roast."

My eyes widened in shock. "You know The Dark Roast?"

"Do you?"

"It's my favorite coffee place! That's crazy you even know it. We may be the only two people who do."

Laughing, he replied, "Okay, well, it shouldn't be hard to find it, then." He took a breath. "When do you—"

"I'm off late tonight. I close down at nine, and Bren doesn't like staying open past nine unless I ask him nicely."

"You know the owner?"

I nodded. "I do. He was a good friend of my dad's. He's kind of an uncle-figure to me." I consider my schedule. "How about tomorrow afternoon at 1:30? I'm only working a half day."

"A half day? I thought you said you had a full day today and tomorrow?"

"I did, but now I have a coffee date." I smiled at him from under my lashes, and his face mirrored my own.

"Well, Angelia—"

"You can call me Lia. Everyone else does."

He considered for a moment. "I think I like Angelia better. It's a very beautiful name."

I tried not to blush under his gaze. "Thank you."

"No, thank you." Too many seconds passed before he broke our gaze and started walking backwards. "Okay, I'm actually going this time. I'll see you tomorrow, Angelia."

"See you tomorrow."

I seemed to float on air to the back room. What a day, and it wasn't even 11 a.m.

Rylan

I walked out the door of TechHalo and tried to breathe on my walk back to my van.

She said yes. Holy shit, she said yes!

As I sat in my front seat, I realized too many things at once. It took me some time to recoup and focus on what I needed to do.

First, I needed my glasstop. I pulled it over from the passenger seat and situated it on my lap. Less than a minute later, I connected on a secure line currently bouncing somewhere over the Middle East. I typed out four sentences in a message to the Stooges. "My plans changed. I'm not coming back. Your accounts are waiting for you at Culver Bank under your aliases. Take care."

Ten minutes later, their funds were in the Culver Bank database with years of records to support the validity of their accounts. Now that I needed access to my credits, I transferred my two accounts to the Bank of Enterprise in front of me, the bank I stopped at when I first saw Angelia.

Angelia.

I shook my head. *Focus. You have a lot to do in twenty-four hours. Like, where the hell are you going to buy a car? I'm sure a hacker van is not what she's expecting. Better yet, where are you going to park the van because you—Jaeden—apparently live downtown?*

I looked up suddenly. *Did I just officially move to New Eastland?*

An image of Angelia laughing answered my question. I refocused my attention on where to buy a car.

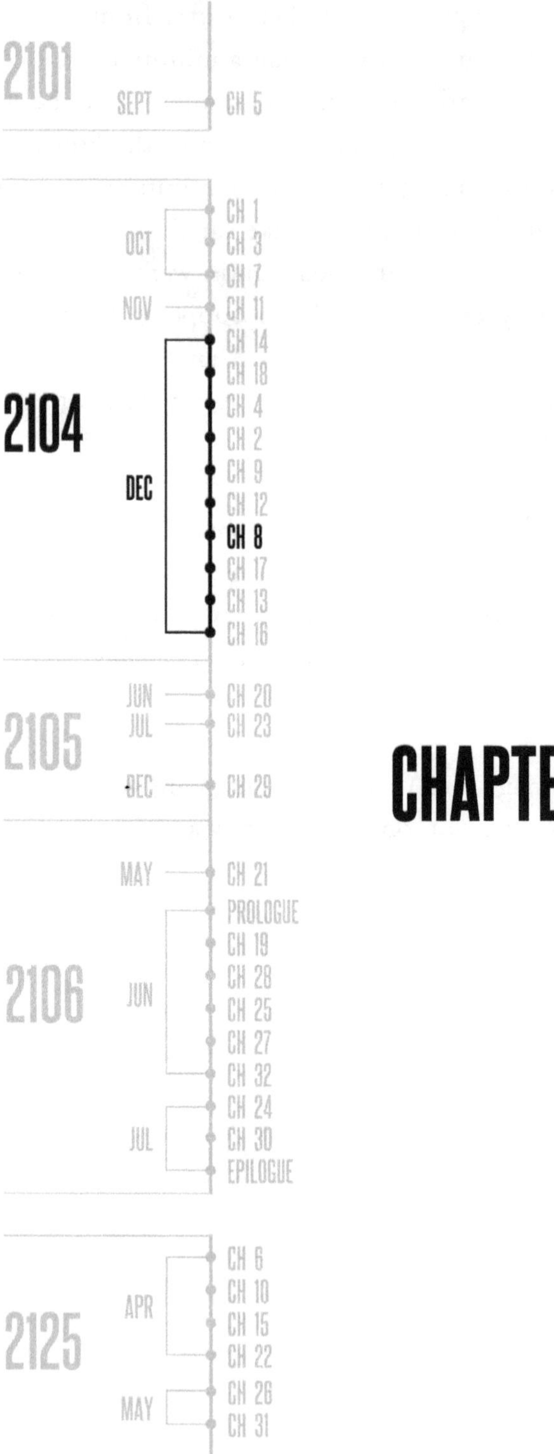

CHAPTER 8

DECEMBER 2104
Dr. Atlas

A light *ting* shattered the silence in my room. For the past three minutes and forty-two seconds, I steeped my tea in the perfect 208 degrees Fahrenheit water that I poured into my favorite cup. The timer marked the end of my wait. I removed the glass infuser from my cup, letting the excess tea drip down for a moment before placing the long tube on a nearby napkin.

I breathed in the aroma of my Earl Grey tea as the moist tea leaves sloshed to one side. I was more than grateful that some suppliers still made real tea, not the fake best-selling flavor of the year. I honestly couldn't stand the pseudo-tea brands. I was so glad Haileen never knew such brands existed. She would have lost it. She was more of a tea snob than me.

I took my first sip and closed my eyes as the warmth raced across my tongue and down my throat. I relished this moment. I enjoyed my tea for another five minutes before I heard a light knock on my front door.

Placing my cup back in its saucer, I leaned back in my chair. "Mendel, unlock the door."

"Yes, Dr. Atlas."

The front door swooshed open as I waited for my guest to

approach my sitting room, or rather what had become my sitting room. All of the spaces for the staff who lived at the Institute changed many times over the years. It had only been me living on this compound for a number of years.

A man in an all-white uniform and a black chef's hat came around the corner, pushing a cart covered with fruits, pastries, and my usual breakfast choice—eggs Benedict.

"Good morning, sir."

I smiled. "Good morning, Guillaume. How are you?"

The older man looked at me. I noticed bags under his eyes and a deep set of lines on his forehead. I saw the shake in his hands as he set the crystal bowl of peaches and pears on the table in front of me.

"I feel like shit."

I raised my eyebrows. "Indeed." I leaned forward, reaching for his wrist, but he shook me off. "Guillaume?" I kept my hand out toward him. The old man shook his head, grabbing another bowl of grapes and apples to place in front of me. "Please don't be stubborn. You know I'll win anyway."

Guillaume threw his hands in the air and extended his hand. "Fine. Just hurry up so I can get back to work. I have more trays to deliver."

I raised one eyebrow at him but said nothing as I took his wrist in my right hand. I closed my eyes.

My mind filled with a red light as I felt my energy flow through me, through him. It took me a moment to find what I searched for—the darkness in his chest. *It is deeper and, my God, a lot bigger than the last time.*

I opened my eyes and looked into his, my face brimming with emotion. He dropped his gaze before pulling away, reaching for the platter with my eggs Benedict, hands shaking more than before. "Guillaume?"

He held up a hand, his back turned to me. "Just give me a

second." The man's shoulders shook, and I waited patiently, letting his moment pass. When he was done, he turned to me with my platter and a plate with a small pastry. He cleared his throat. "Can you actually eat all of the food I bring you? Because out of everyone, you and Miss Logan are the most wasteful." He placed them both down onto the table.

I admired his strength. "I am sorry to deplete any resources we don't have. I'll do my best."

"Thank you. Now, I'm going to go because you've kept me long enough."

I gave him a faint smile, my eyes saying more than words. He returned the gesture with a short nod and walked out of the room.

I ate my breakfast in a few bites, too preoccupied by Guillaume to enjoy it today. His cancer was the entire reason this project—this facility, these *Testers*—were needed. Haileen and I wanted to stop anyone from having to endure what he felt, what his family no doubt felt.

When I met Haileen, and sparks flew, I couldn't even consider it a coincidence when I discovered she was working on her PhD in physics, like I was. She was at Stanford, at the time, and I attended Harvard. It wasn't until after her father died—of cancer—that she moved across the country to join me in my small studio apartment, transferring schools for the fall. Without a discussion, we dropped our original plans and started working on our doctoral dissertation together that September. We wanted to find a way to end cancer and all genetic diseases before anyone else experienced the pain of losing someone they loved.

We both had such passion then. There was so much we wanted to give back to the world. Haileen wanted to change the world, and she knew, together, we could do it. She was such a beautiful force when we presented to benefactors and donors. We needed more than a small amount of funding for this type of project, and with her spirit and unwavering belief in our mission, we received every penny we—she—ever asked for.

After a year, we found this space, hired the research assistants, and stocked the equipment before we started our build. My studio had pages and pages of plans, blueprints, lists, tasks, and information tacked to the walls. It all waited for us to finally move into our research labs permanently.

In between the calls, research, planning, and building, Haileen and I couldn't keep our hands off each other. It was an insatiable thirst that we never could satisfy. I felt like I was floating whenever I was around her and knew the world was a better place with her in it.

When we finally cut the ribbon on the new facility—the one I sat in now—we made love on her new desk for hours until we fell asleep from exhaustion. The world was ours for the taking, and we were going to change it. We knew it.

I sighed, putting my tea cup back down, and rubbed the bridge of my nose with my middle finger.

Another knock on my door brought me out of my thoughts. I glanced at the clockglass to my left—8:00 a.m.

And there it was. My morning calm was done. It was time to work. "Mendel, open the front door, please."

"Yes, Dr. Atlas."

"Good morning, Dr. Logan," I greeted as she walked around the corner.

"Good morning, sir," she replied, standing by the table waiting for an invitation to sit—like she did every morning. I gestured for her to take a seat. As she took out her clipboard, filled with more paper than usual, I noticed, I piled my small platters to the side, leaving just the pastry—her favorite, a blueberry scone.

When she was ready, I sat back, and she spoke. "How was your trip to Montreal?"

I waved my hand. "It was uneventful, the usual drivel. I truly detest taking time from our work here to speak in front of droves of people who neither care nor understand the level of work we do. But," I shrugged, "the funding we receive from those *RoboCon* events more than pays for itself. I would prefer someone else do them, but they want me as the face of the Atlas Institute. So that's what they get."

"I heard the esoskeleton did well."

I raised my eyebrows, nodding. "Yes, it's impressive work. I was surprised myself at the fluidity of the connection of nanotech and tissue." I threw one hand in the air. "But it's not the point. Is the technology going to change lives? Yes. But it's just another Band-Aid on what we are trying to accomplish. Humans already have the ability to heal themselves. There just has to be a way to tap into it." I looked at her puzzled face, quietly staring back at me. "My apologies for a rant so early this morning. There's so much more to talk about. How about we start?" I picked up my teacup once more and took a sip.

After a quick breath, she began. "I finished meeting with all of the new Testers, all thirty-three of them. Of the thirty-three, ten of them don't have the gene sequence we are looking for and need to be dismissed. That process started at the end of the day yesterday. They should all be gone by today." She glanced down at her clipboard. "We have two tests scheduled for today, one at 1300 hours and one at 1700. The first is testing a new level of gamma radiation, combined with different levels of ionizing radiation—our constant—and the second is testing the frequency of both." She flipped back a few pages into her clipboard. "That gives us a total of fifty-one Testers on site and ready to go, with another batch of between forty or fifty coming in tomorrow. Our next seminar is next week on Monday, so hopefully that brings us an even bigger group with the higher incentives."

I nodded, thinking how it didn't matter what we offered. No one had received anything to date—nothing but their last rites. It made me angry. There was so much life lost, so much waste. I squeezed the cup in my hand. I was trying to save the world and make it stronger, better, and I couldn't do it without casualties. Not that many of these Testers weren't better off. I thought of the Tester from a week ago, sitting on my table without any manners. I ground my teeth and felt the cup crack in my hands before I felt the stab of pain.

"Dr. Atlas!"

Blood dripped down my wrist from the glass shard embedded in my palm. Before I could stop her, Logan jumped up and ran to the bathroom down the hallway—she'd been here enough times to know—and returned with a towel in her hand.

The towel, however, was unnecessary. We both knew it. The puncture wound had already closed after a red light wrapped around my arm, healed before she even came back to my chair. I pressed the towel onto my uninjured hand, wiping away the blood. The expression on her face portrayed shock and awe in equal measure. "Thank you, Logan. I'm truly sorry for scaring you. My emotions can get the better of me sometimes. Can you please continue?"

She didn't speak right away, only continued to look at me. Finally, she composed herself. "I was saying that the new tests today look promising. We've pushed the limits further for both radiations, but I feel that the energy-saving additives are beginning to stabilize the energy wavelengths. I believe if we can get them to stabilize under a 0.5, it won't be lethal. We could finally have live results."

I admired her enthusiasm, which was one of the reasons I hired her. Plus, she knew the pain of losing someone, and that was a strong driving force. I needed someone with the drive, the motivation, and the passion to do what they must for the results we needed. She was very much like my Haileen.

"Excellent. Thank you, Dr. Logan. It seems everything is going to plan. I appreciate your efforts." I rewarded her with a smile. "What are the ages of today's Testers?"

Pages flipped. "Test one has twenty-two, fifty-one, and thirty-four. The second test has twenty-five, thirty-nine, and forty-one."

I considered for a moment. "The tattooed fellow—the one with the black raven across his neck? How old is he?" I ignored the image of his boots on my table.

Without hesitation, she replied, "Ra—Mr. Smith. Yes. He's twenty-five."

I raised an eyebrow. "Yes, Mr. Smith. How fitting. Is he one of the ten that needs to be moved out of Project E?"

She shook her head. "No. He's—I finished his evaluation yesterday. He's suitable for our project."

I nodded. "Good. Where does he fall in line for testing?"

She held my eyes for just a moment before answering. "Uh—he's scheduled for…" she flipped a few pages, finger dragging down the page, "the end of the month."

I waved my hand. "I think we need to round off test one with similar ages because we are testing the gamma radiation AND the ionizing radiation. Can you please replace the fifty-one-year-old with this Mr. Smith?"

She stared at me for a long moment. As I was about to repeat the question, she blinked a few times. "Yes, of course, sir. Let me change the Testers and swap them in the system. I'll go prepare for the test that's in a few hours."

I met her eyes. "Don't say a few when you can be precise. It's a doctor's prerogative to always be direct and precise."

She took a short breath. "I'll go prepare for the test that's in four hours and thirty-six minutes." She smiled weakly.

"Perfect. I'll see you then."

She stood. "Will you get it looked at, at least?"

I smiled softly at her. "I'll consider it." She shook her head but didn't press. "Oh, Dr. Logan. Don't forget your pastry. Guillaume told me this morning that he wants to make sure we both enjoy what he brings us."

"Well, I wouldn't want to upset Guillaume." I saw a slight

shake in her hand as she picked up the pastry. She nodded her thank you before turning and walking away.

I heard the door close, and I leaned forward, dropping the towel on the table. I started to feel lost, as if we were never going to achieve our desired results, as if none of this loss mattered. It took two seconds for me to condemn a man to death, and yet I kept doing it without any regret. Knowing I was already too late for Guillaume crushed the positive spirits I usually carried with me. I felt so close to the answer, and yet I was just as far as I was when we started to build our machine.

It had taken two more years of experiments after we opened our facility to figure out the best way to build our machine. We called it NOMO, which stood for the simple and specific saying—NO MORE. No more cancer. No more loss. It was always our pride and joy—everything we knew we were supposed to create together.

Two more years after that, we were granted our doctorates and more funding than we needed. However, we hadn't even gotten NOMO to work yet. Sure, the amount of research and findings thus far carried their own worth, but it was discouraging.

But Haileen wouldn't give up. She knew it would work and never wavered. After another stressful, sleepless five years, we were finally ready to test NOMO. We started with the mouse and worked up to primates. We refined test after test, each working better than the last. Another half a decade passed before we could consistently find and destroy exact DNA strands with whatever code we wanted.

Yet another five years, and we received approval to start testing on humans. The genomes of primates to humans were similar in many ways, but the fundamental differences were where we needed to focus to ensure we accomplished our endgame of changing the world.

The day we finally conducted our first human test was the beginning of the end. *And yet… Here I am, still trying to bring her vision to life.*

She deserved it. She gave twenty years and everything she was for the Atlas Institute and for NOMO. I was going to make it work. It didn't matter how many we lost along the way. Mr. Smith was just another casualty to teach us how to move forward. The machine was going to work. I wasn't giving up.

Five hours and twenty-three minutes later, I stood behind the glass as three Testers and two doctors walked into the room. Mr. Smith was among them. I narrowed my eyes on Mr. Smith and tried to ignore the smug smile on his face. Two of the men seemed to know each other. One with a longer beard laughed at something Mr. Smith said. The other man in a white t-shirt looked terrified.

I ignored my guilt as I watched staff members strap the three men into their chairs. I could see the tattooed Tester talking to the tech, but the doctor was trained well. He ignored him.

Dr. Logan stood beside me, still and staring. She seemed more on edge about this test than the others, not surprising as this was round thirty-four. Every time we got closer, but every time we lost life. I thought it was perhaps starting to weigh on her.

I glanced over and saw her squeezing her clipboard. "Dr. Logan?"

She snapped her gaze up at me. "Yes, Doctor?"

I decided not to push and simply said, "Are we ready?"

She cleared her throat and spoke out loud. "Stations A through C, confirm." Through unseen speakers, voices answered back.

"Station A, confirmed."

"Station B, confirmed."

"Station C, confirmed."

Dr. Logan glanced at me, and I nodded. "Stations D through G, confirm."

Each station responded in kind. I looked into the chamber. Mr. Smith checked out his surroundings and talked to the other Testers. They all laughed. He turned to the glass and saw me standing in front of him. He winked.

At that moment, I felt my heart soften, but I held steady. This was always the hard part. *Remember why you started. Her name was Haileen.* "Proceed, Dr. Logan." I saw her take a long, deep breath as if to steady herself before she spoke.

"All stations, we are confirmed. Set the sequence."

The lights in the Tester's room dimmed. A long series of beeps echoed through the panels as the different stations completed their task.

G was last. G sent out the gamma radiation. That's when I held my breath.

A slight warning bell chimed. Myself, Dr. Logan, and the other four techs put on our safety glasses. A second warning bell sounded, and a few seconds later, the third and final went off.

A bright light filled the room on the other side of the glass. The room went completely white for ten seconds before it stopped. I took off my glasses and stared at the three Testers.

Now we waited.

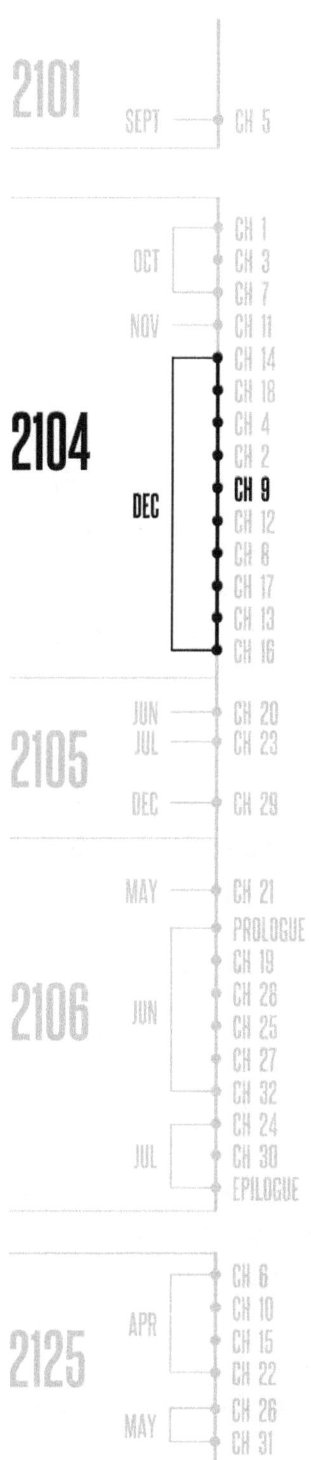

CHAPTER 9

DECEMBER 2104
Raven

I was led into an unoccupied room and told to sit wherever I wanted before being left alone to stare at the surrounding walls. I peered around the room. It looked like a shrink's room.

This is going to be a fun morning.

Although small, the lavish space had a great layout. There was a large window on the opposite side of the door that opened to a small, fabricated courtyard, complete with a waterfall. *Very fancy.* The inside of the office was simple with furniture in the middle of the room—a white couch to my left, a white chair to my right, and a round, metal coffee table with a cage-like base between them.

Not my style, but nice.

Two smaller side tables in the same shape sat beside the couch and chair. On the left was a larger version of the coffee table with random knickknacks and a few stacks of papers. The right side of the room housed wall-to-wall bookshelves lined with books. Apparently, my new shrink was an avid reader. But there were only two pictures on the wall. One was a black-and-white photograph of a misty tree line. The other held every vibrant color—a pink field of flowers capped with a sunset fading from blue to pink to yellow. It was the brightest spot in the room. I gazed at the interesting contrasts. I wondered what the shrink would say about herself. Yes, herself. No guy would have that bright picture in the room.

Having to choose between the two options, I decided to stand. I wandered over to the bookshelves and tilted my head to read the titles—medical, medicine, genetics, cancer, radiation. They definitely weren't topics of my interest, but considering this place, it made total sense.

At the edge of a long white shelf, a book stood out among the others. It was smaller than the giant textbooks, and it had prominent creases along the spine. I walked to the edge and put my finger on it. I was sure there were cameras, although you would think a shrink wouldn't record in here. I shrugged, too curious.

As I pulled the spine down, I heard the door open. Without turning around, I said, "This is quite a collection. Did you actually read all of these?" I turned to face my shrink and smiled. "Well, if it isn't my favorite doctor. You're a shrink, too?"

"Good morning, Mr. Smith—" I made a short laugh. She raised an eyebrow at me. "Yes. I not only have my PhD in genetics but also psychology."

I walked toward her, stopping at the couch. "Then I'm excited. That means I get to spend some one-on-one time with you then? I'm in for that."

"Mr. Smith, this—"

I held up my hand. "Can you please just call me Raven? Smith is not my last name, and it's just weird for you to call me that."

"Then you should have told me your real name."

I smiled. "I told you. Tell me yours, and I'll tell you mine."

She pursed her lips. "It's Dr. Logan."

"Got it." I winked at her. "And I'm Raven."

She shook her head. "Can you please have a seat? I just have a few questions."

I watched her heels as she stepped around the chair and sat down. Crossing one leg over the other, she settled her clipboard on her lap.

I smiled, walking to the couch to join her. "Let me make this easy for you, Doc." I sat down, counting off on my fingers. "Red. A sunset. Only one. My father. And you, of course."

She stared at me for a second before asking, "And what exactly does all of that mean, Mr. Smith?"

I threw my hands to the side. "They are just my answers to the usual shrink questions." I leaned to the edge of my couch and counted off my fingers again. "What's my favorite color? Do I prefer a sunrise or a sunset? Do I have any siblings? Which parent did I seek the most love from? And who is the most gorgeous doctor I've ever met?" I leaned forward, whispering. "It's no contest with those freckles." I winked at her. "See? The usual questions." I sat back.

The lovely doctor was trying to harden her expression, but I saw the hint of a smile pull at the corners of her mouth. She broke eye contact first and looked down to her clipboard.

"Well, out of those five questions, I only was going to ask one of them. But thank you for the other information."

"You are very welcome, Doc." She pursed her lips again. I started to enjoy her frustration a little too much.

She paused for a breath and looked directly at me. "Mr. Smith, can we please just focus for a few minutes? Then you can go back to your room."

I gave her a side smile. "How about we make a deal, Doc? I'll answer all of your questions with honesty and sincerity, but only under two conditions."

"Mr. Smith, I don't have time for games."

I pushed. "That's one. You can't call me Mr. Smith anymore. It's Raven."

She stared at me, tightening her lips for a moment, before sighing. "What's the other condition?"

"See? I knew you had it in you to bend the rules."

"Mr. Sm—Raven, please—"

I held my hands up. "Okay. Sorry. I'll hold off on the commentary." I brought my hands down. "The second condition is that for every question you ask me, I get to ask you one too. But, the rule is we both have to give a completely true answer. Deal?"

She narrowed her eyes at me. "And if I don't?"

I leaned back. "Then good luck trying to decide if my answers are true or not. I'm sure my fake answers won't cause a problem for your research too much, right?"

She shook her head at me. "Why does this have to be a game? Don't you see what we are trying to do here? You came here to help us try to find a cure for so many diseases. Why can't you just answer my questions? Why do you care about what I say?"

I held her gaze. "Because you intrigue me, Doc. You are all business but wear black, double-strap high heels every day. You carry around a clipboard with paper and a pen instead of a glass tablet. You seem to be fighting to be top dog, but you don't see how the other doctors stand just slightly behind you or just to the side. They know who the alpha is, even if you don't." I saw some red tint her neck and chest. "Besides, how else am I going to find out your real name?" I winked at her, and she smiled—her real smile.

I felt my heart beat a little faster.

She nodded. "Okay, but I have two conditions of my own."

I raised an eyebrow, gesturing toward her. "By all means."

This time, she leaned forward. "First, you are not allowed to ask for my real name." I started to protest, but she raised her hand. I stopped, smiling at her. "Second, as a psychologist, everything we speak about is confidential, so I am asking for your word that any information—personal or otherwise—be kept to yourself." She met my eyes. "Do I have your word?"

I reached out with my right hand, and after a second, she took it. I ignored how soft her hand felt as I said, "You have my word."

"Thank you." She sat back in her chair. "Now, can we

proceed?"

"Please."

Doc looked at her clipboard and glanced over some notes. She looked back up at me, but before she could ask anything, a sound chimed throughout the room. She glanced down at her wrist, reading a message on her watch.

"Oh, well, they say timing is everything." She glanced back up. "It seems our session is over. Dr. Atlas needs to see me." She swiped her finger across the watch and stood. "Someone will escort you back to your room for now, and I'll see when I can reschedule."

"Sounds good, Doc."

She walked toward the door and opened it. As she stepped through the doorway, she turned back to me. "Green. A sunrise. I don't. My father. And Dr. Mikhailov." She smiled again for a brief moment before I watched her black heels walk through the door. She left me sitting alone with my own stupid grin.

Della cried out my name, her legs wrapped around my waist. My hands held hers above her head. I kissed her to soften her echoing moans against the tiled walls of the locker room.

A few minutes later, we both lay breathless beside each other, sweat dripping down our faces.

I had left the good doctor's office and came straight to find Della. My whole body was on fire by the time I left the room, the sound of those damn heels still echoing in my ears.

I grabbed Della by the hand, saying excuse me, and pulled her away from a group of people talking. She only laughed as we ran through the hallways toward the pool. I barely made it to the locker room before I pressed her up against the locker doors, my lips hungry on hers, pulling off her shirt.

Della took a deep breath beside me. "I don't know where the

hell that came from, but I hope it comes back." She laughed, rolling slightly to face me.

I grinned back at her. "I'm sorry to have interrupted your conversation."

She waved her hand. "They'll live."

Della was still taking deep breaths when I stood up, looking for the clothes we had thrown around the room in our haste.

I started to get dressed but decided on a shower first. I handed her clothes over and knelt to the floor. "I'm going to shower." I kissed her forehead. "Thank you for letting me steal you."

She smiled up at me. "Anytime."

By the time I saw Doc again, two days later, I was completely annoyed with myself. I tried everything I could to stop her clicking around in my head with her unruly red hair and freckles that danced across her face—*see? That's what I'm saying! Who cares about her freckles?*

I saw a girl. I got a girl. That's it.

It shouldn't have mattered who she was. But I didn't want her like that. Okay, let's be clear. I wanted to know what she wore under that coat more than anything I ever wanted before. That was part of the problem. If I wasn't dreaming about what color green she wore underneath, or if it was a dress, a skirt, or maybe nothing… I was lost thinking about how she tried not to smile when I gave her a hard time.

It was infuriating. I visited Della more than once since the locker room, but it wasn't helping.

So there I was, escorted to her shrink room again, and I was fuming.

What the hell is it about this doctor? What the hell makes her so damn different from every other girl I'd ever come across?

My escort stopped at her door, opened it, and ushered me in the room. I thanked him quietly and saw Doc standing at her desk, leaning over her glasstop, red strands of hair falling into her face. She looked up and met my eyes.

That was it—right there—in that look. That's what I needed. That's what I was missing.

I smiled, and all my anger and frustration melted away. "Good afternoon, Doc. It's been a time without you."

She looked back down at her specglass tablet. "Good afternoon."

"Aw, Doc. You're killing me. Are we back to being formal? We had such a nice talk the last time, didn't we?"

She didn't look up at me. "Can you please just have a seat? I'll be with you in a minute."

Her voice, the way she said please, triggered me that something was off. I walked toward her. She stood above her desk, but I realized as I got closer that she wasn't actually looking at anything.

"Doc?" She jumped. I put my hands up. "I'm sorry. I'm sorry. Are you okay?"

She cleared her throat and composed herself with a breath. "I'm fine."

I leaned slightly to the side and peered into her eyes. She wouldn't meet my gaze. "You don't look fine. I mean, you always look gorgeous-fine, but right now…" I tried catching her eyes again. "What's wrong?"

She finally looked at me. Doc just stared into my eyes for a minute, saying nothing, and I just held her eyes with mine. I saw her try to say something many times, but she fought herself. Instead, she looked back at me, eyes filled with hard emotion.

In that moment, I forgot everything around me, where I was and who we were.

I reached forward and brushed a strand of her red hair behind her ear, tracing my finger down her cheek. A tear fell from her eye then, and I wiped it away with the pad of my thumb. My fingers brushed the side of her neck. She slowly closed her eyes and sighed.

When she opened them, I saw the emotions in her eyes change. Her mind came back to her. She pulled back from me slowly, clearing her throat.

"Can you have a seat, and I'll be with you in a minute?"

I gave her a smile. "Sure, Doc, whatever you need."

I sat on the couch with my back to her, giving her a moment to recover from whatever she was feeling. When she finally walked over with her clipboard, she was back to her normal self, composed and confident. But her face seemed softer, less of a wall between us.

"Okay, Raven, let's get started." All business. *She's something else.*

I smiled. "Yes, ma'am. What can I do you for?"

"How about we start with your family history?" I nodded. "Do you have any diseases in your family? Either on your mother or father's side."

Shaking my head, I thought about my father's side. "There are none on my mother's side, but I didn't know my father after the age of seven. So I don't really remember too much about him."

She scribbled across on her pad of paper. "Okay, what about—"

"My turn."

She looked up at me. "I'm sorry?"

I held her gaze. "The deal was for every question you ask me, I get to ask you one. So that makes it my turn."

Her expression changed as different emotions crossed her face before she spoke. "How about we adjust this slightly, okay? I have so many more files to go through. How about you give me all the information I need to mark your file as reviewed, and then at the end, you can ask me your questions?"

"Like our own little personal Q&A session?"

Doc smiled. "Yes."

I considered for a moment and nodded. "Deal. Ask away."

We spent the next forty-five minutes reviewing my family histories, medical issues, fantasies—although that last one was just me adding in details to drive her a little crazy. It worked. It was a short ride through my physical, mental, and emotional life. The weirdest part was that I didn't mind answering any of the questions for her. It was a rare occasion for me to share anything about myself, and yet here I was, sharing away. This sweet doctor had some kind of voodoo over me.

"Okay, Raven. That seems to be all of my questions." She glanced up at the glass clock. "That means you have about fifteen minutes to ask me your questions."

I sat up straighter in my chair, clasping my hands together. "That's plenty. I really only have five questions."

She raised her eyebrows at me. "That's all?" She almost laughed, shaking her head. "All of this, and you only want to ask me five things?"

"Would you rather me ask you more?"

She raised her left hand in the air. "No, no. Please, proceed."

"Question one—why the color green? What makes it your favorite?"

"Technically, that's two questions, but I'll answer as they are within the same category."

"Why, thank you, Doc. It's very kind of you."

"Green is my favorite color because it makes me think of the forest and the earth. Everything that gives life to this little rock of ours is green—the grass, the leaves, the trees, the plants. Everything that is giving life and creating this circle of existence for us is green. Loving green somehow makes me feel like I am thanking the world for everything it provides us." She looked away for a second. "Sorry. I'm sure that sounds odd, like a color as a form of gratitude. It makes no sense."

"Oh, it does. When I was little, my dad started teaching me

Spanish. I learned my colors first, and the first one I ever said was red, which is *rojo*. But I couldn't pronounce the *jota* yet, so it came out *romo*. I still remember to this day how much he laughed. He picked me up and threw me in the air." I looked away for a moment. "It's one of the only good memories I have with my dad. That's when red became my favorite color."

She nodded. "It's interesting how colors can mean more than just how our eyes see them."

I glanced at her curly, red hair and smiled. "Well, you are not making it easy to change my color to anything else."

She rolled her eyes. "Next question."

"Why do you write with a paper and pen? I haven't seen anyone write with those since I was a kid. Everything is all electronic, so why does a brilliant, gorgeous—" I winked at her, "—doctor such as yourself bother with such old ways?"

Doc looked down at the bamboo pen she seemed to always have in her hand, words burned into the side, before answering. "I feel more organized this way. When I was young, and still now, math was always my favorite subject. I loved solving the long math problems that traveled down the page. When they started transitioning us from paper to tablets, I often found it to be too..." her eyes fluttered up, remembering, "...enclosing. I felt that I was confined to the glass tablet's screen, and I didn't like it. I would often have a notebook nearby to solve the problem and then recopy it over. My teachers never liked that much."

I grinned. "And I'm sure you didn't care."

She laughed. "Not in the slightest. They knew I was the smartest kid in the class, so they didn't give me a hard time about it, not too often anyway."

"Interesting. Now I know you're a math genius too. Can you get any sexier?" She shook her head, smiling, but said nothing. "Next question, but remember you have to answer all my questions."

She squinted her eyes at me. "Yes, I remember."

"Okay, good. Then, tell me, is your father the reason you're a doctor?"

Her gaze sharpened. "Why would you think that?"

"First of all, I'm the one asking the questions. You are just supposed to answer." But I saw the emotion in her eyes. "And second of all, as a freebie, I'll answer this one question. You said the answer to which parent you sought out the most love from was your father. Considering what you have to go through to get not one but two doctorates, I figured he'd be the reason."

She shook her head at me again. "And I'm supposed to be the shrink? I'm sort of impressed, actually." Doc paused to gather her thoughts. "It's true, for more than one reason. What we are trying to do here is essentially cure cancer and any other genetic disease. My father had—" Her voice trailed off, and I waited for her to continue. "My father was a great man, but I lost him to cancer. In the end, it didn't matter how great he was because cancer doesn't care. That's why I'm here, doing what I do. No one should lose their father to a disease at seventeen—a disease that we should be able to cure." Her voice hardened at the end, and my heart ached for her loss.

"I'm sorry, Doc. I didn't know."

She shook her head once. "You couldn't have. It's okay. It just pushes me to keep going every day, no matter what happens. I have to remember why we're here."

I didn't know how to reply, so I only smiled, adjusting my necklace without thought. She smiled back and tucked a loose strand behind her ear.

I was lost again. "Do you have any idea how beautiful you are?"

My eyes burned into hers, but she didn't look away. She held my gaze until a sound beeped from behind her. She looked up at the clockglass.

"Well, it looks like your fifteen minutes are up, Raven." A knock at the door came. "And your escort back to your room is waiting."

"That is totally cheating. But I'll let you have it. Next time—"

"There won't be a next time. I reviewed your file, so we have no other meetings scheduled."

I pulled my eyebrows together. "When do I get to see you again?"

She paused, staring at me, and stood up, walking to her desk. "I don't know. I'm sure we'll cross paths again soon."

I felt a weight hit my chest. "What if I want to see you again?"

"Raven—" A knock came at the door again. She cleared her throat. "You need to go."

I nodded slowly, walking backward toward the door, hoping she'd say something else. But she didn't. "Bye, Doc." I turned to the door.

"Wait… Raven, can I ask you one other question?"

I grinned as I turned back to her. "Anything for you, Doc."

She walked around the desk and stood with her arms folded. "What's your real name?"

I tilted my head to the side and laughed. "Aw, Doc, but I'm not allowed to ask yours, remember? So—"

"It's Logan. Logan Emerson Fay."

My heart jumped. It took all I had not to cross the room and pull her into my arms.

I took a steadying breath instead, only lost in her eyes for a second. She gave me her beautiful, full smile, and I steeled my legs at the next knock behind me.

I winked at her. "I'll see you soon, Logan Emerson Fay."

Her smile widened, and I turned and walked out the door, my heart pounding in my ears.

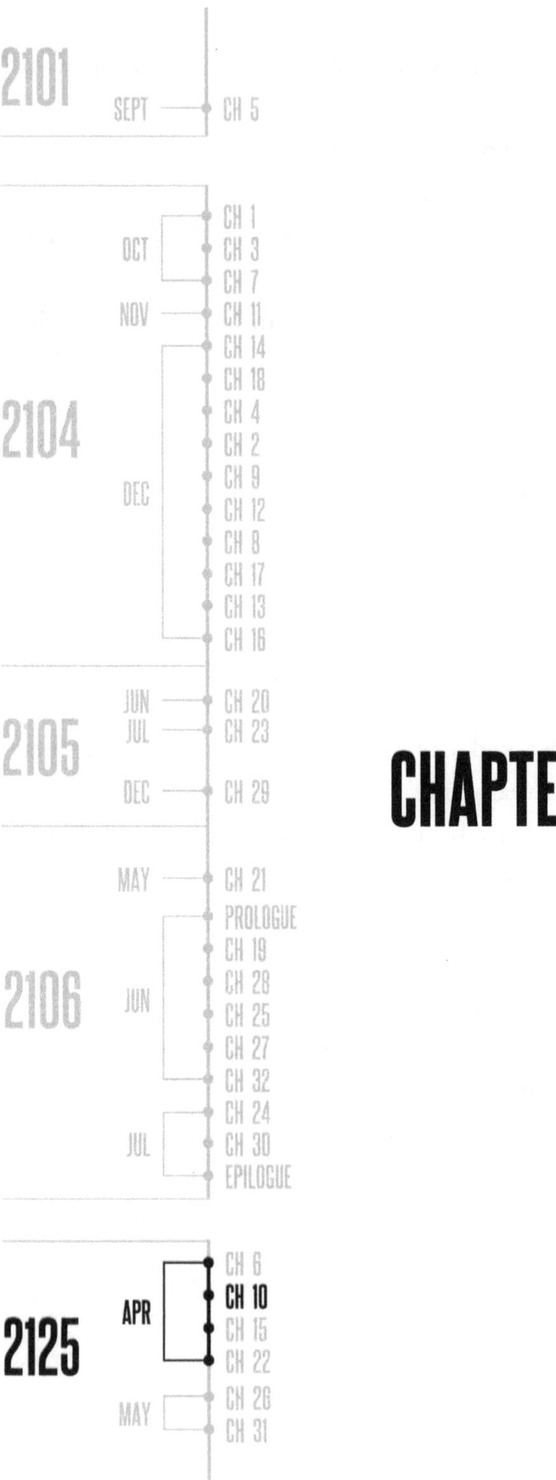

CHAPTER 10

APRIL 2125
Marina

My proximity alarm goes off throughout the room, making me open my eyes. I realize what the whooping sound means, and I jolt up in bed. I've only ever heard the alarm being tested. I never actually needed it for anything. My heart is in my throat as I pull the covers back and grab the sweatpants strewn across my nightstand.

I hop on one foot as I try to put them on and run at the same time toward the door. Instead of falling, I catch myself on the doorframe. My long hair billows around me as I run down the hallway to the stairs, leading to my observatory. I scramble as the noise gets louder.

At the top of the railing is a loft space. What once was built for relaxing now serves as my command center. A glasstop in the middle and multiple screen projections swirl around on one large, curved screen—my mom's design.

"Niko! Stop the damn noise, and show me an image of where the proximity fence was tripped!" I yell above the sound. I sigh my gratitude when the alarm stops.

"Yes, Marina. Good morning, Marina."

I wave a hand. "Yes, good morning to you too. That's a hell of a way to wake up."

I watch the main image change to the open field on the side of the house. It's closest to the garage where I keep my van. Holding my breath, I stare at the screen. Nothing moves.

"Marina."

I jump, shaking my head at my own edginess. "Yes, Niko?"

"The disturbance seems to have disappeared. I detect no movement."

I shake my head again. "But nothing just randomly trips that system. Something has to move. Wind doesn't affect it. How can—" The perimeter alarm sounds again. "Niko! Shut off the damn alarm!" The sound stops. "Where is the breach now?"

"Movement was detected near the greenhouse."

"Show me." The screen fades out from the garage and back in facing the side of the greenhouse. "Expand."

The screen resizes from its usual fifty-five-inch space to seventy-five. I lean in, willing the movement again but also praying that it's nothing. My mind races through a thousand scenarios while I try to remember the code to the weapons locker.

"Shit. How did I forget it?" I shake my head again, not taking my eyes off the screen. "Yeah, Marina, because we usually have intruders." I roll my eyes. "Niko, remind me to practice my codes daily."

"Yes, Marina. When would you like to be reminded?"

I sigh. I need to remember to program Niko with some sarcasm parameters. "Never mind, Niko." My eyes widen, trying to see the entire screen at once, waiting for any movement. "I don't understand how someone even got inside the perimeter. We have sensors set up over a mile out. We should have heard alarms going off way before this."

The anxiety in my chest tightens as I think about how someone could have disabled my sensors without me knowing. I really need to get my PHASR pistol. I'll feel safer with it on my hip, but I don't want to take my eyes off the screen. I huff as my eyes burn into the screen, wishing I could blow the specks of light out of the way.

You're not helping, Addies.

"There!" A small movement in the corner of the screen flashes quickly. "Niko, can you zoom and rerun the last ten seconds?"

"Yes, Marina."

The screen freezes, rewinds, and zooms in on the corner by the entrance to the greenhouse. I cock my head to the side.

"What?" I move close to the screen. "Niko, play it again." The image replays. I shake my head. "How's that possible?" I continue shaking my head. "That's a cat tail." I think for a moment. "But it can't be a cat. Cats died out in the first decade. If it was a real cat…" I trail off, excitement blooming in my chest. I've never seen a cat before, only in pictures. Mom insisted that I learn about everything, as if the world was the same. I wonder if it would have been easier to learn about cats if I could experience them, instead of learning about them from a glasstablet.

"Niko, reset the alarm system, but track any other movement in case the—uh—cat moves somewhere else. I'm going down to the garden."

"Yes, Marina."

I practically race down the stairs back to my room. The first thing I see when the lights come on is my disheveled bed.

"No, we don't have time. Get dressed."

I take off my dirty clothes and throw them on my bed as I grab clean clothes from my dresser. I throw on a grey t-shirt, a worn pair of jeans, and socks and twist my hair into a bun on the top of my head. Moving to leave the room, the bed catches my eye again.

"Ugh, fine."

I rush over to the opposite side of the bed I sleep on and fix it first, tossing forgotten sleeping clothes into the laundry basket, the sweats hanging over the side. I run around the bed and fix my side. Hitting the puffy comforter to smooth out the air, I toss my small decorative pillows from the floor onto the bed, placing them haphazardly beside each other.

"Good enough. Let's go, Marina."

Rushing down the hallway, I pass dozens of photos of my mom and me over the years. I take the cold hard white stairs down, instead of up this time, focusing on each step so I don't trip. After I reach the landing, I ignore the kitchen to my left, but my stomach reminds me we woke with a start. It already wants to eat. I walk through the living room to the all-glass wall that vaults up two stories, not seeing the bright rays of sunlight shining on the items on my shelves opposite the windows.

To the left of the glass wall, there is a solid metal door. I place my hand, palm open, on the glass panel beside it. "Niko, unlock the front door."

"Yes, Marina." His voice rings out in the space from hidden speakers.

The door opens, and I step outside. The sun hits me directly in the face. My home faces east, and the bright, golden light bathes my entire living room every morning. I usually enjoy my breakfast at the table outside the front window, but today, I am chasing a cat apparently—a cat that shouldn't exist. All of the domesticated animals slowly died or were killed off by wild animals. I have no idea how a regular house cat could have survived, let alone the generations after it.

"But who cares right now? Let's catch a cat!"

I start to run around the side of the house toward my greenhouse, rounding the indoor pool that also faces the same direction as the front of the house.

I'm so excited, I feel kind of dumb to be honest. I wonder what its purr really sounds like in person. Is it actually soft to the touch? Does it really *meow*?

As I approach the greenhouse, I slow down. I survey the area, looking for any sign of the cat. I creep around the side wall and peer around a corner, when I hear a crash inside of the supposedly impenetrable greenhouse. I race to the front door, placing my hand on the glass panel. The door opens as mist flutters around my face. I can hardly see through the chaos. I forgot it is time to water the plants as the system functions automatically. But from where I stand, I hear one of my smaller tomato plant trellises tip over.

"Shit." I step inside, and the door closes behind me with a swoosh. The greenhouse is the size of an old-world football field. This is not going to be easy or fast. "And if you knock over any more of my plants, cat, you and I are going to have a problem." I sigh. "You've got me using my energy way too early in the morning."

I steady my feet to ground me. Calling into my light, I close my eyes, and a bright green square of light shines in my mind. I open my eyes as I raise my hand, small green tendrils reaching out from my hand, searching for the furry intruder. I feel the dampness of the ground, the earth seeping into itself, and the movement of life inside the dirt, however small and undetectable. My green energy follows the earth about halfway down the length of the greenhouse before I sense the dark, solid void of the cat. It's under one of the tables, trying to hide its body behind a wooden table leg. It must know I'm here.

Pulling deep into my energy, I raise my hand as vines shoot up from the ground a few feet back, blocking the path of the cat, should it decide to run the other way. The movement scares it, and I feel the grey energy fly toward me. I let go of my energy—letting it rest—and open my eyes, squatting down to my ankles. I look under the many raised beds of fruits and vegetables, and my heart jumps when I see a real cat for the first time. The small specks of light also find the animal and hover a little closer than usual.

"Hey. It's okay," I whisper across the room. The cat stops mid-run and freezes, facing me. "Are you hungry? Is that why you're in here? Not that I even know how you got in here to begin with, but let's do one thing at a time." I look around me, grab a small plastic plant saucer from my pile by the door, and slowly move toward the sink to my left. Filling it, I turn toward the cat who hasn't taken its eyes off me.

"Do you want some water? Huh?" I put the saucer on the ground and back away toward the door. The cat looks at the saucer and at me a few times before taking a step toward the water and then another. I back up with each step it takes to give it some space.

Its fur is mostly white and copper around the back and its sides. There are black patches throughout, but I can't tell if they are spots or patches of dirt. It's the face that focuses most of my attention. It has two triangle ears, one black and one copper. A black crown of fur spreads from one ear to the other, separated by piercing green eyes, like human-colored eyes. I didn't know cats could have eyes colored like that.

Down the line between its eyes, there is a perfect line. One side creates a patch of black that surrounds the right eye, and the other side of the line is white fur mixed with copper. It's like seeing two faces. The patterns of its fur are so interesting. Its nose is black with small white whiskers, but its eyes are sharp and staring right at me as it dips its nose near the water, smelling it for a moment before licking happily.

I smile. "Hi. I should probably introduce myself. I'm Marina. I'm not sure how you got here, but welcome." I look around to see if there's anything I can give the cat to eat, but it's all vegetables. I'm not even sure what cats eat.

"Um, I would love to feed you, but I doubt you're going to just walk with me back to the house. So, I'll go get something. You stay here, and let's hope you don't go out the way you came. Good?" The cat, now finished with its water, sits back and stares at me.

"I'll take that as a yes." I hold my hand up. "Just stay there."

I back up toward the door, and it opens automatically. I step through, letting it shut before I take my eyes off the little Picasso. As soon as the door closes, I bolt for the house. If I lose the cat again, I'll spend even more time of my day looking for it, rather than everything else I need to do.

I shake my head, trying to ignore the anxiety building from being off schedule. "Never mind waking up to an insanely loud noise, I am spending my morning chasing a cat so far." I think about its little ears. "Okay, it's an adorable cat, but this is not helping with today's plan."

I get back to the door and walk through as it opens. "Hey, Niko. What do cats eat?"

There is a small pause before he answers, *"Cats can eat a variety of fruits and vegetables, but they are carnivores, which means meat is a good source of nutrition for cats."*

I walk over to the kitchen, maneuvering around the island in the middle of the room. "So they eat fish?"

"Yes, Marina."

"Great, me too. I'll just share some of mine. What kind of fruits?"

"Strawberries, bananas, apples—"

"Okay, got it. That's enough. I'll make a plate of fish and fruit. It can decide what it wants." I grab a pan from under the island and put it in the sink, waving my hand over the faucet to turn it on and fill it with about an inch of water. "Niko, turn on the left stove, top burner, on high. Oh, can you keep an eye on the cameras so the cat doesn't find its way out?"

"Yes, Marina."

The fire comes to life as I place the pan down. While it heats, I chop up bananas and strawberries and mash them into a small bowl. And then I wait, watching the time tick by, taking deep breaths, trying to ignore the thick bubble in my stomach.

"I know. We have a lot to do. It'll get done. Let's just take care of the cat. One thing at a time."

But it isn't working. I can't stop listing everything that needs to be done today. A solar panel on the backside of the fence needs to be rewired. My trove of vegetables needs to get canned. I need to study for my test on World War II next week. I have a pool waiting for me to do my usual sixty laps before I check the filter for the buzzing noise I keep hearing when I'm underwater. There's the damn rock I've been trying to break with my energy that I can't quite seem to accomplish.

Oh, I need to go fishing this week, as my fish supply is suddenly low. I look over at the steaming pan.

Thanks to the cat, I need to run a complete diagnostic on the entire alarm grid system and find the perimeter hole because it got in somehow, past three layers of sensors. I don't know how that's possible, but it's got me a little nervous. I've never had a visitor. Nothing has ever crossed the perimeter since Mom died. It was always just us. But she wanted to keep me safe. We don't know who survived and what their energy could do.

And she was always afraid the Doctor would find me. That's why we had so many precautions. If he was capable of killing 99.9 percent of the world's population with a smile on his face—her words—then who knows what he would do with those left behind?

I push the thoughts, fear, and anxiety down and take a deep breath. "Focus on your life, as it is, today. You will get it all done. Just breathe." I sigh.

"Marina."

I try not to flinch, annoyed that I am so jumpy this morning, and flip the fish. "Yes, Niko?"

"I discovered a broken panel on the left side of the greenhouse."

"Nicely done. Thank you, Niko. At least we know now. And I'll add that to my list of to dos. It seems to be growing since I woke up anyway. What's one more?" As soon as the fish finishes cooking, I put it on the plate, grab the bowl of fruit mash, and walk out to the door, yelling over my shoulder: "Niko, turn the burner off." I balance both plates in my hand as I use my other to open the greenhouse door. On my short walk, I decide to leave the food and extra water and get to my day. There's too much to do. Rather than sit and watch a cat eat, if it eats at all, I need to start crossing items off my list.

The mist stopped by the time I return, and as I place the plate down beside the already empty water saucer, I see little ears pop out from behind a bucket to my left. "Oh, there you are. Uh—I brought fish and fruit." I point at the dishes as I speak. "And let me get you more water." I grab the saucer and refill it, placing it back down next to the food and backing up to the door.

The cat bobs its head up and down, smelling the air. I stand as still as I can, smiling as the cat walks slowly toward the bowls.

Come on...

The cat's little black nose twitches as it smells the fruit and moves on to the fish. With one quick glance up at me to make sure I don't move, the cat begins to eat. I try to contain my excitement and only cheer internally.

The annoying anxiety pokes at me while I watch the cat eat, but I can't take my eyes off of it. I still can't believe there is another living and breathing creature here. I have been alone for two long years. I was sixteen when my mom got too sick to move, and eventually, I lost her. I was alone at sixteen. I was alone in the entire world. I shake my head, holding back tears as I watch my only connection to the world eat my fish, forgetting my original decision to leave the food and go.

When the cat finishes, it returns to the water, drinking its fill, before sitting down, tail across its feet.

I smile. "Happy now?"

The cat looks at me lazily, licking its front paws.

"I'll take that as a yes. Okay, little cat—um—I can't call you cat. That's just weird. How about—" I look at its face, and a smirk slides across my face. "Pablo. You look like a Picasso, so I'll go with that. And if you are a girl cat, which I can't tell from here, you'll be Pabla." I laugh at myself as the cat pauses its licking and stares at me.

I open my mouth to continue, but it stands and walks toward

me. Slowly, eyes darting around, the cat walks all the way to me and starts rubbing its back against my legs as it weaves in and out between them. It is the cutest thing I have ever seen.

I lower my hands. The cat smells my hands before tilting its head and rubbing its face across my knuckles.

A flash comes into my mind with a burst of energy in the shape of a sun. It hits hard and fast. I see myself standing in the street of New Eastland, my van behind me, trunk open. I see a cat, with a half-black face, jump from the window of a broken shop nearby and into the back of the van.

A second passes, and the energy is gone. I steady myself on the door frame beside me as I lower myself to the floor, overwhelmed from the wave of energy.

"Whoa. What the hell was that? That was new."

The cat stares at me as it turns away, twitching its tail.

I put my hand on my head as the feeling passes, leaving a tingling behind.

Shaking my head, I get back up to my feet, taking one more deep breath.

I glance over at the cat as it walks away. "Well, at least I know you're a Pablo now." I laugh again. "Welcome to my humble abode, Pablo."

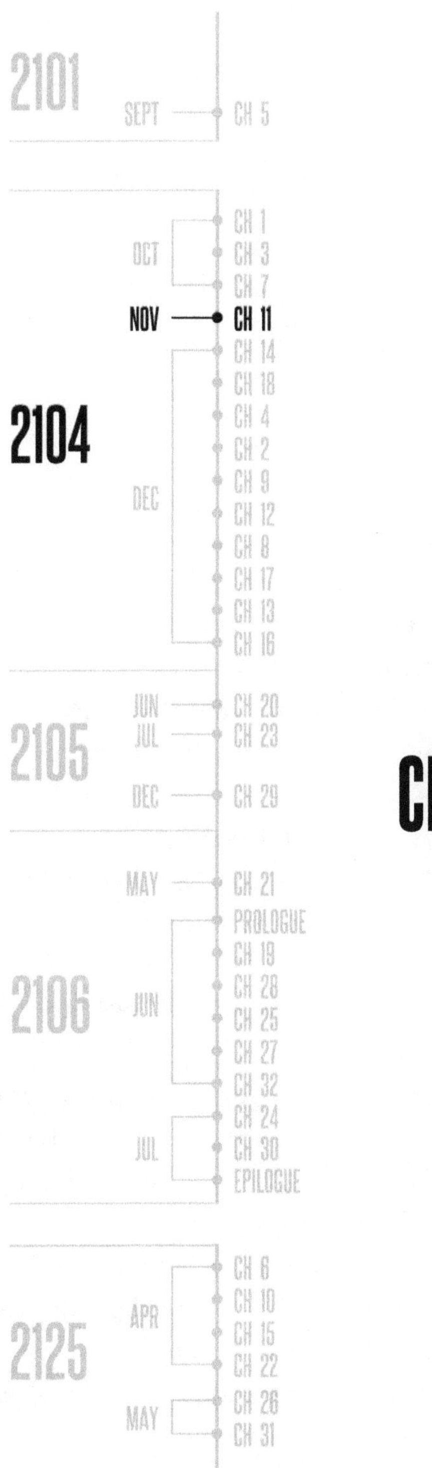

CHAPTER 11

NOVEMBER 2104
Angelia

"And do you know what he says to me?"

I sipped my coffee. "Oh no, what?"

"'No one told me it would short the system.'"

I burst into laughter. "What? Was he serious?"

"He was dead serious. I literally just stared at him. I didn't know what to say."

"Oh, man. I think I would have lost it."

Jaeden shook his head, putting another forkful of crumb cake in his mouth. He swallowed, pointing the fork at me. "What happened next was worse."

I rolled my eyes, feeling my ponytail sway to the side. "Oh no, what?"

"My director—the director for the entire division on this side of the world—comes up to me about an hour later and asks me why Route 456 is shut down. I explain to him what happened. And do you know what Mr. Director says to me?"

I set my coffee down, leaning in. "What?"

"'How would Lane know that would short the system?'"

My eyes widen, "What? That's insane."

"You're telling me." He took another sip of coffee. "Needless to say, I just finished up my work for the day, fixed Route 456—on my own—and went home."

"I can't even imagine. I would have walked out and told them all to figure it out themselves. How could they not know? I mean, there's a reason Regulation Haplan even exists."

He nodded his head, smiling. "Agreed. Can I just say how much I love that you know Regulation Haplan?"

I smiled, looking down at my cake, trying not to blush as the music changed from one song to the next.

Tonight was our fourth date in two weeks. He messaged me earlier in the day, asking if I wanted to go out after work and enjoy something small—just coffee and dessert. We'd been sitting across from each other at The Palace for about two hours already.

Save for its name, there was nothing grand about it. It didn't have high ceilings and chandeliers, but it had a live acoustic band, incredible food, and a perfect intimate setting for two young people.

Although we'd been out before, tonight, I took more time to get ready. I put on my black high-heeled boots, black leggings, and a red blouse with matching red hoops, and I pulled up my hair in the usual high ponytail. Tendrils fell around my face.

I was rewarded with a stare—closer to a gawk—when he saw me. He took a moment to find his voice. "You look beautiful. Red looks great on you."

I practically floated into his black Volkshover, smiling and thanking him before climbing into the passenger seat.

We shared stories back and forth, enjoying the music and the delicious food. The lighting was perfect to glance at him occasionally or stare at his gorgeous face. I was mesmerized by his silver eyes in the dimmed light, and when he smiled, my heart raced.

Being out with Jaeden always left me feeling like I was flying and coming down to earth at the same time. He was someone I just met, trying to remind myself he was a stranger to me. *But were we strangers now? Was he just someone?* I didn't know anymore.

All I knew was the feeling in my heart when he messaged me, how I floated as I prepared for each of our dates, and how disappointed I felt when he had to leave.

On the other side, Jaeden seemed to enjoy our time together as much as I did. He smiled and laughed—my two favorite things about him—and I caught him staring at me more than once.

"So, tell me, what's the craziest story you ever heard of why you had to fix one of the machines that came in for repair?"

I ate a bite of cake. "Hmmmm." I chewed and thought of the many strange stories over the years. It took me a second longer with his eyes on me. It was almost frustrating how distracted I was by his eyes. Finally, I picked one, through my pounding heart. "Okay, I got one."

He settled closer to hear, cup nestled in his hand.

"So this cute little old lady comes in with a garden bot. It's old and cream-colored around the edges. You can tell she uses it every day and is totally heartbroken it's malfunctioning. She's so cute and so sweet, telling me the story. She starts telling me that her garden bot doesn't like her anymore. I'm confused, so I ask her what she means. She says to me, 'Every time I get close to it, it starts humming at me. I walk away, and it stops. But I get close, and it hums.' I'm thinking I have no idea what she is talking about, but okay, it's fine. I'll check it in and see what's going on. I take the garden bot to the back. It's in a box, wrapped in a sheet. It's so endearing that she's taking care of it like a pet. Anyway, I get it to the back of the room and grab it to take it out, and so help me if the damn thing doesn't start humming at me as I get closer. I back up. It stops. I move closer, and it does it again. So now I'm thinking something's up with the sensors, but garden bots don't have that kind of sensor structure. I grab my gloves and tools, and I work on the side panel, ignoring the humming, figuring it's just some kind of malfunction. You won't believe what I found inside when I got the panel off."

"What? Broken wires?"

I shake my head. "A garter snake."

"What?" He shook his head.

"Yeah, a little black one with the yellow stripes on the sides, just curled up like it owned the place, hissing at me."

"What did you do?"

I shrugged. "I picked it up and put it in another box. On my way home, I dropped it off in the park."

"Didn't it freak you out?"

I pressed my lips together, shaking my head. "No. Snakes don't bother me. But I will say the absolute terror on Noreen's face as I walked from one side of the store to the other was the most magical part of my day."

He laughed. "Wow. You can't make those things up, can you?"

I shook my head. "Nope. Not this time."

We held each other's gaze as the music slowed with more of a melody and less of a beat. I took my last sip of coffee and wished the fluttering in my heart would stop so I could focus.

He glanced at his comm. "Oh, that would explain that."

I looked at him, confused. "Explain what?"

He gazed around the room behind me. "Why we are the only ones left."

My eyes widened as I turned to peer around the room. We were indeed the last ones. A waiter swept, while another wiped down tables, and here we were, talking away.

"I guess that means they are closing."

He flashed me his comm. "They closed twenty minutes ago, actually."

"Oh man, okay. We should go." I stood up and grabbed my jacket from the back of my chair. "That was sweet of them to let us just sit and talk."

"Yeah. I tipped them extra to let us." I snapped my head up to him. He chuckled. "No, I didn't, actually. But I would have, especially when it's the best part of my night."

I looked down and made myself busy, buttoning up my jacket. When I was done, I glanced back up at him. He was smiling at me.

He broke into an over-exaggerated British accent. "Are you ready to go, my dear?" He bowed low.

I smiled. "Why, yes, good sir. I am. Please lead the way to the carriage."

He laughed. "This way, madam."

I curtsied and walked ahead of him.

I saw the smiles on the faces of the hostesses in the front, thanking them for staying late.

"You two were having such a wonderful time. Besides, we were just cleaning up anyway."

"We appreciate it," Jaeden said before we walked out into the slightly brisk air.

We walked to the parking garage, breathing in the fresh night breeze. I didn't know what to say anyway. I just enjoyed walking beside him. When the parking garage brought the hover out for us, he held the door open for me before getting in himself.

"Do you have any preference for music on the way home?" he asked as the engines engaged.

I shook my head. "Whatever is good." I grinned as he played his usual Neoteric Beats. "You know, I was never a fan before, but they have definitely grown on me."

He drummed on the steering wheel. "Oh, good. Then my work here is complete."

The hook came in as the engine lit up, ready to go, and he started singing loudly as the thrusters kicked in.

I laughed as he rocked his head back and forth as he sang. When the hook came back on, I reached forward, turned up the volume, and started singing with him at the top of my lungs. His smile stretched ear to ear as he gave me his full smile, and we sang along for the next fifteen minutes to the band's top hits. When we pulled up to my building, I was breathless from laughing so hard. He turned down the music before the new song came on, laughing right along with me. "Well, that's one way to travel. You give an excellent concert."

I smiled. "You too."

The silence filled the hover for a moment as I looked out the window toward the building and finally back to him. He smiled at me and held my gaze. I was lost in his eyes as my heart started racing even faster.

"Well, I'll message you later. Maybe we can plan our next adventure."

I nodded, trying not to be disappointed. "Sounds fun. Thanks for the late-night treat."

"Of course. Have a good night."

"Night."

I watched him drive away before entering my building and taking the elevator to my apartment. I closed the door behind me and leaned against the door, half smiling and half frustrated.

He didn't kiss me, again.

I hung my coat on the hook along with my IDfob. As I moved from the living room, down the hallway, I thought about his little comments—my heart trying to jump out of my chest every time—when he complimented me on my tech mind or when he laughed and paused, staring into my eyes for just a second too long.

But it felt like we were just whirling through a loop. We weren't moving forward.

I slumped on my bed, pulling my boots off and tossing them closer to my closet. My dinner clothes were off and PJs on within the next minute, and I wrapped my hair into a bun. I walked to my small kitchen and sat at my even smaller table, looking at the cup with pens.

I took a deep breath and huffed it out, grabbing the green

pen before pulling the notepad toward me, a yellow page on top tonight.

Dear Mom,

I had my fourth date with Jaeden tonight. I wish you were here to talk to me through all this. I don't know what I'm doing. I don't know how he's feeling.

I stopped a second, considering, before I continued.

Maybe that's the point. Maybe he isn't feeling anything. Maybe he just sees us as friends, and I'm finding all of these little signs when they aren't anything.

My stomach twisted with the thought, but I kept writing.

Yes, to answer your next question, Mom, that would disappoint me. He's such an amazing guy. I wish you could meet him. He's so hilarious. He's gorgeous. Oh, and brilliant. Did I mention that? He literally just popped into my life and stirred up everything.

I could hear my mom's voice, in my mind, as if she asked, *"And is that not enough?"* I chewed on the pen tip and tapped my front tooth, thinking about the question.

If that is all that I could have, then it would have to be enough. Would I want to lose this new friendship because I started to feel more than just that? And the answer was a big no. I'd rather have him as a friend than as nothing.

The realization hit me in my chest, and the anxiety that had flowed through me all night slowly started to subside. I smiled, shaking my head.

And somehow, from wherever you are, you still manage to help me calm my twirling head and emotions. If friends is what he wants, then I am okay with that. Thanks, Mom, for always being here for me.

Did I mention I miss you?

Love Always and Everly, Your Lia

I grabbed my lighter and the paper and walked outside. I felt the chill of the winter air on my arms as I lit the paper on fire, breathing slowly and watching the letter turn to dust.

My heart was calm, and my head wasn't spinning. I had a new focus—just enjoy. Life was too short for anything else anyway.

Rylan

I watched as Angelia walked back inside from her balcony. It was a calm night with no rain as my cover, so I stood behind a truck bed to the left of her apartment. She smiled today when she burned her letter. She didn't do that often. I wondered what she wrote tonight.

Had she written about me? My heart jumped at the thought, but I pushed it away. The past two weeks had been really great. She was really great, greater than great. I enjoyed every second I spent with her. Everything lit up when I saw her, and I thought of nothing else the moment she was gone. My nightly routine brought me here, and the routine of it tucked my guilt away.

Some nights, I stood here and imagined what the inside of her apartment looked like. Did she have as much tech in her home as I thought? What kind of furniture did she own? What were her favorite leftovers?

I shook my head. I couldn't quell this insatiable need to

know more about her. When I delved too deep like this, usually after trying to stay away, I'd message her again to join me somewhere. We went to her favorite coffee house. We visited the VR movie theater across town to watch the newest Shaun Pelton movie. I took her to breakfast before one of her shifts so she could taste some of the best crepes in the city—at least that's what the reviews raved. Tonight, we enjoyed some incredible food at The Palace.

I laughed at her jokes, smiled at her joy, and yet cringed every time I heard her say Jaeden. I sighed and turned toward my new Volkshover parked around the corner.

Every time she said it, a pang of guilt raced through me. I lied to her. I was trying to be something—someone—I wasn't. I wasn't some young guy attending school for SoftTech engineering, although this was the very reason I worked with the Stooges.

I didn't live downtown, at least not yet. I was still working on that. So far, I managed to avoid any questions or conversations about family, but it also stopped me from asking about hers. My head throbbed with curiosity. I needed to know about the notes she burned every night.

No. What you need is to stop lying.

I waved my IDfob in front of my hover car and climbed into the driver's side. My van was parked on a side street near the same place I came to my first night over a month ago. I shook my head. A month had passed, and I was stuck in a deeper hole than when I saw her standing in the rain, my heart in my throat, lost and found at the same time.

I wanted her in my life more than I hated that I was lying to her. That was the issue. The worst part was I saw in her eyes that she wanted more from me. She leaned closer to me when we stood near each other. She let her hands linger near mine at the dinner table. She paused just for a second before getting out of the car, her eyes burning into mine.

Every one of those moments made my heart leap with joy,

while I could only smile and move on in the conversation. I was terrified to give more of myself. What happened when she found out who the real me was? What would I be then? Just a liar, a hacker, a nobody to her.

So I kept up the lie. I was Jaeden Lowe. That's who I needed to be for her.

But for how long? How long can I keep this up?

I didn't know. My hole got deeper every time I saw her smile.

Then maybe you needed to tell her that you can only be friends? That's all you want from her.

I sighed. That's another lie. But maybe it's a lie that protected her—and me—from this unknown territory. Maybe it kept us away from the places I couldn't go or had to lie about.

I fired up the engine, the soft humming from this older—yet very sleek—Volkshover model much easier to drive than my bulky, very old van. Once the thrusters engaged, I pulled out into nonexistent traffic, heading back toward my hotel.

Considering the options, the best one was to tell her we could only be friends. I'd been dancing around the idea, but my heart clenched every time I thought about putting that permanent door between us.

And the alternative?

I knew it had to be done, and done soon, before I forgot why I shouldn't, couldn't love her. Forgot the list of reasons why it wouldn't work. If I crossed that line, I wouldn't make it back without losing myself to her.

For the rest of the drive, flying over the city, I stared at the lights below me, replaying the particulars of our next conversation in my mind. Nothing felt right, but it didn't matter. It had to be done before she officially decided she wanted more from Jaeden.

I parked my hover in my usual spot and sat, contemplating whether to message her now or in the morning. I decided I couldn't wait. I pulled out my comm, clicking into messages. I typed and retyped my text, but ultimately I settled on:

"Hey, do you want to join me for some & in the morning?"

Twenty seconds later, her response pinged back with just three words. "I'd love to."

I smiled even as my anxiety rose.

"I'll pick you up at 10." Three seconds passed.

"See you then."

I shook my head, internally rolling my eyes, before getting out of my hover and walking toward my room. I was not looking forward to this, but it was the best thing for her.

For her, or for you?

Angelia

I cursed the braid I made from half of my hair as I tried to wrap it around my high ponytail. Sometimes I questioned my decision to keep my hair this long. I grabbed scissors to cut it myself a few times in the recent past. I even made appointments at salons thinking that if I set a time, I could free myself from this battle.

But then, I thought of my mom and her hair flowing down her back. She had kept my hair long since I was a toddler, never cutting more than she had to. She always told me how much she loved it, how happy it made her, how it made me look like a princess. How could I cut it?

Cursing one more time, I finally twisted the braid where I wanted. Carefully, I pulled bobby pins from my mouth and pinned the braid in place. Five bobby pins and close to ten hairpins later, I finally was happy.

I was already dressed by 9 a.m. I never usually even cracked open an eye until closer to eleven. Not only had I woken up on my own without my alarm—set for 9:30—but I bounced out of bed like it was Sci-book release day.

I took a quick shower and dressed. Today's ensemble included a black, long-sleeved turtleneck—with finger holes—tucked into my high-rise, dark navy cargo jeans, topped with a wide black belt. I even took out my Moonstruck high-tops from their box for the first time and chose them over my boots—I hoped they weren't too upset. By the time I won the epic hair battle, I was ready for breakfast. My stomach agreed. It was confused why we were up so early, considering it was the weekend, and I had a late shift today.

My heart knew the answer. Even with my newfound resolve to just be friends, it couldn't stop me from being excited to see him.

I tried to read, flip through my comm, check up on news, even put on one of the many trending shows, but I couldn't focus on anything other than the way his hair fell in his eyes and the slight dimple when he side smiled.

Well, this "just friends" thing was going well already.

I dropped my head back in exasperation. This was harder than I thought.

Finally it hit 10:00, and my comm pinged at 10:01.

"Hey, there's some hardware tech here to bring you to breakfast. Do you know this guy? 🤓"

"🤔Not sure, but if he's offering breakfast, I don't care. I'm in and staaaaaarving."

"😁"

I grabbed my coat, IDfob, bag—which I moved from one part of the room to the other multiple times earlier that morning trying to find the perfect place for them to sit so I could just grab them when I left—and shut down the lights with a quick command to Nikola.

When I reached the ground level, I realized I hadn't heard a single word from the ads. I was too busy sending ridiculous emoji faces back and forth to Jaeden.

Yup, you're not distracted by him at all. Great job.

His hover was parked outside, and as usual, he leaned against his car door, waiting for me, with my door already open.

"Good morning," he said with a smile and sparkling silver

eyes.

I smiled back. "Are you the strange hardware tech here to pick me up for breakfast?"

He shook his head. "Nope. I sent him along. I decided I'd take you."

I dramatically wiped my forehead as I walked toward the open door. "Oh good, because those hardware techs—" I threw up my hands as I climbed in the car. "I can't."

Laughing, he sat in his seat and shut both doors with a button click, shaking his head. "Well, good thing you are just stuck with me, then, huh?"

My voice wavered. "Yeah, good thing." I tried to slow my pounding heart. I reached for the screen and started searching for music to play.

"Whoa, whoa, there. Who said you had permission to touch my playlists?"

I gave a short laugh as I flipped through song after song. When I found a grouping of songs, I hit play and turned the music up, looked out the windows, and focused my mind on meaningless distractions.

I felt him glance over at me a couple of times but found myself very interested in the outside world.

We rode the short distance like this, New Age rock filling our ears the whole way, not speaking, until we came down from above the city, landing at a little place called Sunshine Café. Apparently, it had some of the best eggs in the area. And, of course he would know that. He seemed to bring me to all the more popular and trending places, and so far, each one lived up to the hype. Let's see how the Sunshine Café did.

Not that I cared. I just needed something to hold my focus, besides him. We pulled into the garage, and he turned off the hover. The silence that rang out after the thrusters shut off was unbearable. I was so grateful when he finally broke it. "Ready to eat?"

I nodded. "Yup."

Glancing around the lot, I saw a flash of a new CleanBot model for sale on the large screen across the street. It brought to mind a bunch of different sarcastic comments, but I kept them to myself. I couldn't filter through what I wanted to say and what I should say, so I just didn't say anything.

We walked into the café—he held open the door—and we picked our seats along the window, sitting across from each other.

Before silence fell between us, the waitress came to us, arms jingling from a wrist full of bracelets. "Hi, there. I'm Jillian. I'll be your server this beautiful morning. Do you want some coffee or something to get started?"

I responded a little too quickly. "I'd love a coffee, please—sweet and light."

She smiled. "Of course. And you, sir?"

I felt his eyes on me but preoccupied myself by staring at the menu. "I'll have a black coffee, please."

"You got it. I'll give you guys a few minutes." She walked away, little clinks following her.

I stared without focus on the bagel section when he spoke. "Are you okay?"

I answered back without a pause. "Yeah. I'm good. What are you having?"

Jaeden looked at me for a moment, thinking, before he answered. "Well, I heard the eggs here are phenomenal."

Trying to hide my smile, I said, "Then I will check out that section of the menu." As I flipped the page to the eggs, my menu was taken out of my hands. I jerked my head up to see him staring back at me.

"What's up? You're weird today. Something's off."

His eyes, the softest silver, held my gaze, waiting for me to answer. I couldn't hold back. It just wasn't in me to be that way. "Okay, look. I'm just—uh—not sure what we are doing." He looked around the room confused. I shook my head. "No, not literally. I mean you," I pointed to him, "and me." I pointed back at myself. "What are we doing? Are we just two friends enjoying endless hangouts or—"

"Yes." He cut me off. "We are friends, enjoying each other's company because if any software and hardware tech can find a way to coexist in harmony, it's a friendship that needs to be—um—fostered."

I sighed. "I'm being serious."

He raised his eyebrows. "So am I. It's not often two people can enjoy each other's company this much and not make it complicated. So, let's not make it complicated." He shrugged.

My stomach knotted. It was official. He wanted to just be friends. I took a deep breath—internally—before I answered and plastered a smile of false relief on my face.

"Really? That's great. I was worried there was something else happening, and that wasn't exactly the way I was leaning."

He went still for a moment before he continued. "Great. Then we're on the same page."

I nodded, though everything inside me clenched tight. "Yup, same page."

Silence dropped between us, but it was short-lived as Jillian returned to our table with two coffees in hand. "Here you go," she said as she placed them down one by one. Pulling out her glasstablet, she asked, "Okay, what do you two lovebirds want for breakfast?"

Rylan

I watched as Angelia disappeared into her apartment building. A slow and steady ache spread in my chest as she left.

Friends. That's what we were now. Just friends. I didn't know why, if this was what I wanted, I still felt so heavy and thick, like I was moving through water.

You didn't want to hurt her. And now you can't. The friend-zone is safe, which means she is safe. And so are you.

Then why did it feel like my heart was crushed when she agreed that we should be just friends?

Did you expect her to fight you for it? Did you think she would throw her hands in the air, screaming, 'No!'

I shook my head. I didn't know what I had expected, but I was pretty sure it wasn't her agreeing so easily. I guessed I read the signs wrong. She hadn't wanted more. That was a relief.

Wasn't it?

I engaged my thrusters, moving away from her building toward the closest skylane entrance down the street.

After our "just friends" conversation, she seemed to finally loosen up and relax. We laughed the rest of the meal as usual, and our sarcastic fights resumed. So, I thought the answer was yes.

I reached the long entrance line and considered playing my music, but I decided against it. I couldn't take anything else in my head right now.

Once it was my turn and I drove above the buildings, I tried to keep my mind off the new anxiety in my chest by looking at the bright, blinking adboards. I watched as the screens, currently floating to the side of the unseen skylanes, changed from ad to ad. Bright colors flashed. It wasn't as distracting in the morning. At night, the bright pinks, greens, and blues bounced off the hovers that zipped by.

As I approached my exit, an adboard displayed a series of robots—each a different size and shape. Some looked like humans, and some looked like boxes. Big white letters scrolled across at the end:

ROBOCON COMING 5-7 DECEMBER 2104 IN MONTREAL GET YOUR TICKETS NOW!

I smiled. *Friends can go to a conference together, right?* I tapped the message button on my steering wheel. It bleeped. "Message

Angelia. 'Hey, bestie. Want to go on a road trip?'"

I shook my head at my own ridiculousness and took the turn to exit the skylane. A few minutes later, I parked and entered my hotel room, when my comm alerted me.

"😂Oh, man, let's not use that word, though, k?"

I smiled, dropping my bag on one of my two beds in the room. I sent back an emoji. My comm sounded again.

"Where are we going?"

Lying down on the bed, I held the comm in my hand, considering. This could be either really good or really bad. *But we've come this far, right?*

I text back, "Want to go to RoboCon?"

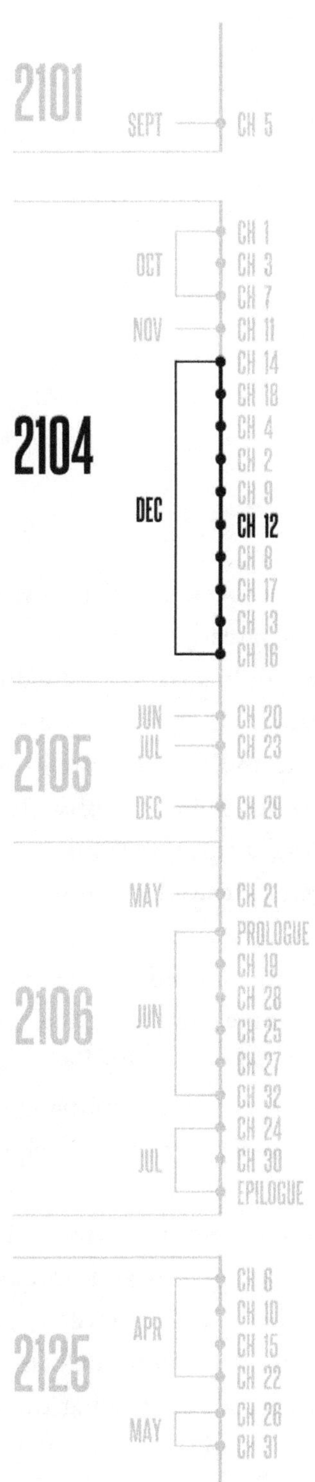

CHAPTER 12

DECEMBER 2104
Dr. Logan

The clockglass read 6:02 a.m. I had been up, sitting in my room, for an hour and three minutes already. I reviewed the newest predictions for upcoming tests, confirmed the schedule for the upcoming tests for Project E, read another chapter in my Genetics and Genome book, and meditated and worked out in my favorite VR environments. I still had another hour and fifty-eight minutes until I had to join Dr. Atlas for our morning meeting. He traveled to Montreal for a few days, so I needed to update him on more items than usual.

I sat back in my chair and glanced at the files scattered around my table. When Dr. Atlas asked me what I wanted for my office/room, I put a printer on the list. He cocked a single eyebrow at me—and it had taken a special order from a company in China—but I was grateful for being able to touch my files. It helped keep the chaos in order.

I needed to touch my files to see my patients. I needed to see the results of our newest tests with graphs and notes all at once. Techscreens felt cluttered—data piled in opaque layers—but printed, on paper, in tangible files, I could interpret all of the data. The puzzle pieces fit together easier when I could see them all at the same time.

My eyes fell on one of the top files. Mr. Smith was scrawled across the top.

My heart fluttered.

We finished our last session yesterday, and I marked his file as reviewed. He was officially confirmed able to join Project E. Guilt flashed through me, as it did every time, but this time a little heavier.

I approved and denied who entered into each of our programs. The ones with family and connections were part of our normal NOMO project. We tested and mapped the genetic sequences of each patient and used what we learned to gain a better understanding of DNA and its structure, hoping to find the way to change the DNA.

Then there was Project E. Project Evolution. It was Dr. Atlas's project he had created with Dr. Floren.

Those few individuals in Project E also had their DNA mapped, but we looked for a specific sequence of DNA—a sequence that, to date, only Dr. Atlas had within his own cells. I took a deep breath, remembering when Dr. Atlas revealed himself to me, only a few short months after he hired me.

He often called me into his office at random. An idea came to him, or he needed me to implement a process change. But, that day, he had seemed unhinged—it's the only way to say it.

His eyes looked wild and his hair and clothes unkempt. It was not normal for him to look like that. His desk was the same, devoid of any personality, but I noted a small blade sitting beside his screen. If I had been worried when I walked in the door, the sight of the blade threw me into an uncertain spiral.

Once he saw me come through the door, though, he sat behind his desk, quickly regained his composure, and steadied back to his normal self in almost an instant. "What do you know about this genetic sequence?" He jumped straight to business as if he couldn't be bothered by the small nuances of society. His fingers swiped across his desk screen, and a short DNA code projected into the space between us. He sat back to let me analyze.

I leaned forward, studying the double helix, checking the chemical bonds. Flooding through folders of information in my mind, I searched for a match. But I found nothing.

Shaking my head after a moment, I spoke. "I don't recognize it specifically. It seems to be attached to some type of healing protein, but I have never seen it before."

I saw him smile through the projected blue light shining down on his face. "You're on the right track." He stood up, hands behind his back, and walked around the desk to stand behind me. I resisted the urge to look up at him. "What if I told you this was a self-healing gene that, when active, heals almost instantaneously?"

I pressed my lips together. "I would tell you that it was not possible, but the implications would be enormous."

There was silence before I heard him cross back from behind me around to his desk once more, swiping the image away before picking up the blade. I stilled, not breathing. "Dr. Logan, please don't scream."

He sliced the top of his left forearm.

I managed to resist all urges to run and scream. Instead, I held on to my belief in the man in front of me, faith I held for so long in him and his work. And so I watched as the blood dripped down his arm. I watched the red glow form inside his arm. It swirled just out of the wound, little red specks floating in the air.

Placing the bloody blade down onto his desk, he reached into his pocket, pulling out a cloth, and wiped the blood away. Only the blood. There was no torn skin, no ripped flesh. His arm was exactly the way it was before he cut himself. With the excess blood wiped away, nothing was different, and yet everything was.

Everyone who focused on genetics and many other pockets of the scientific community knew about what happened to Dr. Atlas and Dr. Floren. The first time they conducted their test on a human subject, the NOMO machine malfunctioned, sending a lethal amount of energy and radiation out into the room. The patient died, and so did Dr. Floren. Dr. Atlas was the only survivor. He was seemingly unharmed, and many found that to be a mystery, one to which I just found the answer.

When he showed me what he had become, what changed in him that day, excitement washed away my fear. This knowledge was life-altering.

Every investor had pulled out. It took Dr. Atlas years to regain the respect and faith of the community. He resumed the NOMO project, just under different guidelines and different tests.

But that day, with only blood on that cloth, he looked at me, straight through me, and asked, "Will you help me find a way to change the world?"

A shiver ran down my arms as I looked at the files in front of me. I had watched ninety-nine people die. I laid out the schedule for their execution. I looked them each in their eyes and learned about them—their lives, thoughts, and feelings—and because of a genetic sequence they carried, I accepted them into a program that only thirty-one people knew about.

I felt like we got closer every time, and soon, we'd have the final answers to the questions. Could we create super-healing humans? Could we force evolution to speed up, or was Dr. Atlas the fluke? Was he the exception to a rule we'd never be able to duplicate?

I sighed, my eyes catching Raven's file again. He not only passed the parameters of familial attachments, but he also had a genetic sequence that matched closest to Dr. Atlas's. I put my hands over my face. *Raven.*

I was lost in emotions every time I thought of him. He was persistent in trying to break through my shield since the moment I met him. Of all days, he caught me yesterday with no defenses on the day my father died. He was always such an arrogant—yet playful—patient, but that morning, he caught me off guard with his tenderness and how he seemed to genuinely care. When he touched my face, I was swept away in that brief moment of comfort. It had been so long to feel anything soft and sweet that all I wanted was that moment to never end.

When he walked out of my office, with his gorgeous, triumphant smile, I had been so conflicted. I don't even know how it happened, how he reached so far into my heart in such a short time. I really struggled with placing him into the project rotation.

By all usual scheduling—assuming, of course, that we didn't find someone in the meantime who could withstand the radiation—he was in line to undergo the tests by the end of next week. The best I could do was move him to the end of the month, and no one would question it. But adding him to the schedule almost had me in tears.

I stood up then, angry with myself. How had I let this happen? How could I let my emotions mix with my purpose here? What was I thinking?

People came here, willing and able, and we used their lives to learn more so we could get closer and closer to saving the world, to helping the world evolve so no one else had to die from a disease like cancer. And here I was feeling like a stupid, lovesick schoolgirl.

Exasperated with myself, I decided to focus on getting dressed for my daily morning appointment with Dr. Atlas. One thing at a time. I started counting down from 100 as I grabbed my clothes for the day.

Two hours and thirty-four minutes later, I stood outside of Dr. Atlas's office door with a scone in my hand, barely breathing. My mind reeled with so much at once; I couldn't bring myself to take a step in any direction.

Dr. Atlas moved up my timeline on Raven. He wanted him for today's test. My breath caught.

Today's test was in a few hours. I barely made it through

adding him to the end of the month, and now I needed to set him up for today?

And Dr. Atlas breaking the glass?

As I watched his palm heal, I was reminded why we were here, what we were trying to accomplish. There was going to be loss so we could change the world. Wasn't that the goal?

An image of Raven's lifeless body, green smoke swirling up from his mouth, came to mind before I shook my head to clear it. I needed to see Raven—right now.

I walked back to my office as fast as my heels could carry me, dropping the scone on my desk when I entered. With my hands shaking as I picked up my comm, I entered the few lines of text to have Raven brought to me. Putting the comm in the pocket of my jacket, I stood at my desk. When I felt the anxiety start to rise as I waited, I paced. I tried sitting a few times, but nothing worked. I could hardly breathe.

Everything I worked for had led me to where I stood right now, and I was about to betray it all to save him.

I recalled Dr. Atlas's face, his expressions desperate, asking me to help him save the world, and I stopped pacing. *What am I doing?*

Before I could answer my own question, there was a knock at the door before it opened. Raven walked in. He wore a black t-shirt over black jeans with a black belt and boots. His hair was wild but kempt. The shadow of scruff on his face made me catch my breath as he smiled at me.

"Good morning, Logan." He winked at me.

My resolve disappeared with my name on his lips. I couldn't do it. I couldn't let him die. "Raven, I need you to do something for me."

His smile grew. "Oh, really? That sounds like a beautiful reason to be woken up so early. What time is it anyway? Maybe we should have some breakfast before—"

"Raven, stop." I moved toward him but stopped myself. I couldn't move. If I didn't keep still, I would unravel as I fought to push away the image of green smoke escaping his lips.

But Raven wasn't making this easy. He saw the expression on my face and closed the distance between us in five steps.

"What is it?" He searched my eyes, his face soft, smile gone. "What do you need me to do?"

I crossed my arms in front of me, steeling myself from the whirlwind in my chest. I spoke softly, "Today, members of my team will come to escort you to our Project E testing facility." His eyes locked on mine. "And I need you—" I looked around, anywhere but his eyes, burning into mine, "I need you to pretend you are sick or do whatever you can to not go with them when they come for you. I don't want you to take the test."

His smile returned. "Is that all, Doc? A test? What's—"

I stepped closer to him, needing him to understand the urgency. "Can you just do it for me? Please."

Raven's eyebrows came together. "Why? What's going to happen?"

I dropped my head. "Raven, please, for once, can't you just say yes without any questions?" I looked back in his eyes, holding his gaze. "Can you please just do this for me?" I felt tears clog in the back of my throat, and he heard it.

His smile changed, not the arrogant, "walking through life like he owned it" smile that always splashed across his face. He smiled from his heart, and I couldn't breathe staring back at him. "I'd do anything for you, Logan Emerson Fay."

His voice melted through my defenses and something in me gave way. I lost myself—in his eyes, in his smile. I closed the space between us, wrapping my arms around him and pressing my lips to his.

His hands were behind my head and my back instantly, pressing me deeper into him. He smelled like a storm, deep and wild, and he tasted even sweeter. His hands moved from outside my coat through the folds of the fabric, around my waist, and traveled up my back, pulling me closer. His fingers touched my bare skin. His tongue played with mine, and I stood wrapped in his arms until we were both breathless.

I tried pulling away, but he held me tighter, not wanting to let me go just yet. His mouth devoured mine. When I tried again, he reluctantly let me free.

We both breathed deeply with our foreheads touching for a minute. I attempted to speak first, but I couldn't find a way to say what I wanted. He broke the silence on his own.

"You have no idea how long I've wanted to kiss those lips of yours." I blushed, pulling back to look into his eyes before looking away, guilt starting to set in. He placed his finger on my chin, turning my face back to his. "Don't do that. Don't let this moment be one to forget. I won't forget it."

I smiled, and he returned it. "Okay. I know we need to talk, but right now, I need you to go back to your room. Please do what I said. Don't, under any circumstances, go with them. Is that understood?"

He winked at me. "Yes, ma'am. As long as you promise this won't be the last time I feel those lips of yours." His hungry eyes looked at my mouth, and a shock went through me. He leaned closer, lips beside mine, whispering, "Promise me." His fingertips traced my lower lip.

I closed my eyes, feeling the heat swell in my chest. I could say nothing else but the two words he wanted to hear. "I promise."

With a soft, gentle kiss on the corner of my lips, he pulled back. "I'll see you soon, Doc." And in true Raven fashion, he was out the door, leaving me breathless where I stood.

———•———

I looked at my comm again. It was 12:46 p.m. I hadn't received any notification that I needed to replace Raven. I didn't understand. They would have gone to collect him around 12:00 p.m. and brought him to the infirmary for us to draw more blood before bringing him here. But, so far, nothing.

The anxiety pounded in my stomach. I had to know what was happening.

I stood in the middle of the glass room we called Basecamp, connected to the testing room, where three chairs sat empty. Four other technicians were in the room with me, checking systems and conducting final checks, and all I could think about was where Raven was right now.

I touched the screen in front of me on the dashboard, calling out to the escorts for the three Testers.

"Dr. Pinet, are we on schedule for the Tester arrival?"

A deep voice responded. "Yes. Sorry for the delay. It took us time to track down Mr. Smith, but we found him. He was in the pool locker room with another Tester, instead of in his room. We will arrive in two minutes."

My heart dropped. *Raven is coming.* He walked to his death, and I couldn't stop it. My voice stuck in my chest, so I clicked off the comm and stared down at my clipboard. A moment later, Dr. Atlas entered the room.

"Good afternoon, Dr. Logan." He looked through the glass. "Where are the Testers?"

Despite the throbbing in my head, I managed to mumble, "ETA is two minutes."

He raised an eyebrow at my answer but continued on, checking in with the technicians.

A minute passed before the door to the testing space opened. Dr. Pinet was first in line, followed by four others, Raven among them. Squeezing my clipboard, I could only stare at him.

I was about to watch him die. *Oh my god, what have I done?*

The three testers were strapped in as I heard Dr. Atlas say my name. "Yes, Doctor?"

"Are we ready?"

I cleared my throat, hoping my voice didn't sound as shaky as I felt. "Stations A through C, confirm." Barely hearing the responses, I almost jumped when I caught Dr. Atlas's eyes on me again. He nodded at me before I continued, "Stations D through G, confirm."

My eyes never left Raven's face. From this distance, I doubted he could see me. But if he was about to take his last breath, I wasn't going to miss one second of the time he had left.

Once the other stations called back to us, Dr. Atlas spoke, "Proceed, Dr. Logan."

I took a deep breath to calm my nerves, to finish my job, the job I'd done thirty-three other times without flinching. This dream was now ripping my heart out with every passing second.

"All stations, we are confirmed. Set the sequence."

Beeps echoed through the speakers as we each put on our safety glasses. I moved closer to the window, making sure Raven could see me. He caught my eye as the final beep chimed.

He winked at me before a blinding white light enveloped the room.

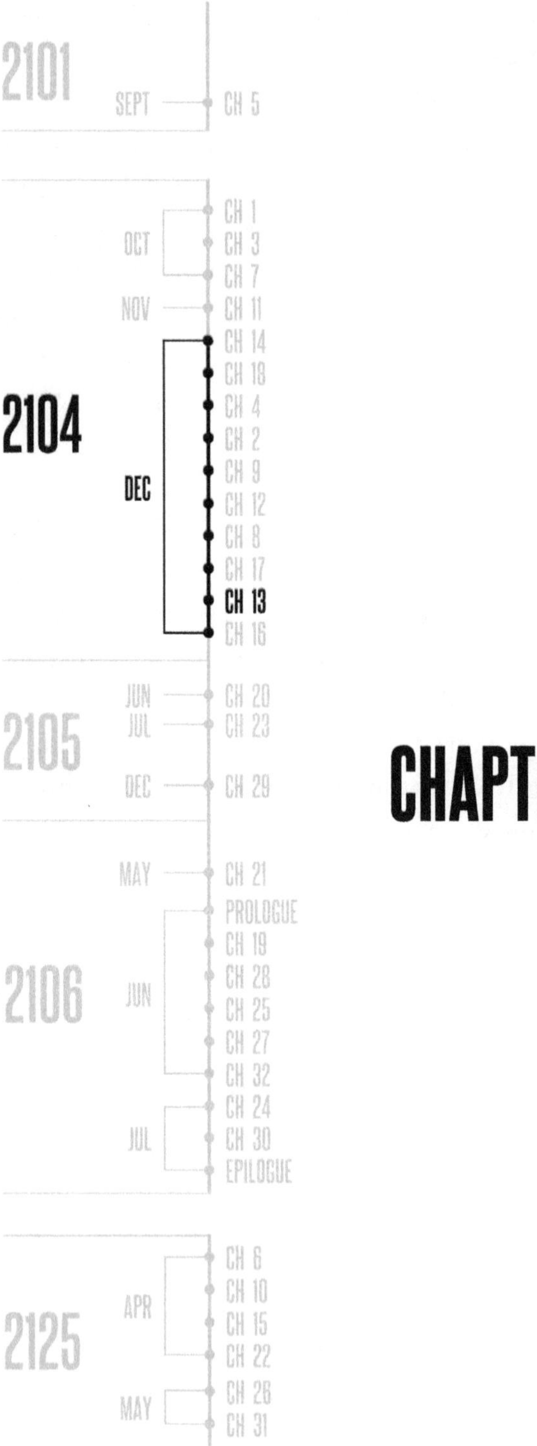

CHAPTER 13

DECEMBER 2104
Raven

My heart pounded in my chest as I ran as fast as I could. I had never been a track star, but I was always fast on my feet. Years of running from the many officers of the world helped me long before the art of the getaway. I shook my head. I knew that place had been too good to be true from the moment they rolled in at that seminar.

I glanced over to my right to see Sloan beside me, running hard to keep pace. Both of us with a backpack on our backs probably wasn't helping. It was just the two of us in a dark forest, with only the moon to light our way, running for our lives with what sounded like a dozen men coming after us with guns. It was such a great way to end a Sunday.

At least it's a clear night.

Pushing through thick forest trees, we came to a large boulder that blocked the way. Gesturing to Sloan, we moved quickly to our left to go around it. On the other side, we pressed up against the rock, both breathing hard, taking just a second to rest.

In between gasps, he asked, "How much farther? I don't know how much longer I can run like this."

I tilted my head back against the rock, blinking my eyes. "She said there was a boathouse. We can take a boat across the lake.

That's where we're going."

Sloan's eyebrows creased. "She? Who is she?"

I heard a yell in the distance behind us. "No time. Let's go." And we were off again.

The ground started to angle down as we came around the bend of a group of trees, and I briefly saw the black glass of the water. The moonlight glittered across the surface.

I smiled. *Thank you, Logan.*

A pain hit my heart as I thought of her—red hair, warm skin against mine, my name on her lips, and her moan against my hand.

I heard a rumble of thunder in the distance as I shook my head. I needed to focus. I could think about her all I wanted when we were safe.

About five minutes later, we came to a gravel road that forked off in different directions a few feet to our left and right.

Logan's voice came to my mind. *Pass the gravel road. Keep going straight. It's only another 200 yards to the house at the dock.*

"This way." I pointed into the darkness. In the small sliver of light that shone on his face, Sloan didn't look convinced, but he didn't say anything as we crossed the rocks.

As we bobbed and weaved through trees, through an almost black forest, toward a destination that I hoped was there, I couldn't help but think about how two weeks could change the course of someone's life.

You are the first, Raven—the first to survive our tests. Your friend, Sloan, is the second. Both of you are the only ones to hold the radiation, and we need to know why. He needs to know why. You aren't safe here, which is why you need to go.

I didn't fully understand the terror in her eyes, but I left. I listened to her.

She saved me. My heart sank. She saved me—but no one else before me. Logan had killed a lot of people. And me—she was going to let me…

A darkness crept into my body. It started deep in my stomach and rose to my chest. I felt an energy grow like a ball, centered over my heart. The pressure built and pushed, brightening within me. The darkness grew until a bright white circle flashed in my head, forcing me to blink my eyes.

Lightning cracked behind us. I jumped as Sloan cursed in surprise. Confusion coursed through me, but in that brief moment of light, I saw the dock house.

Freedom was right there. I took a deep breath, pushing away my thoughts of Logan, the other doctors, and all of it.

Let's just get to the damn boat first.

We reached the tree line as it opened up to the lake. There were two docks in front of us. One to the left led to the dock house, with a pile of wood and other things in front. One on the right led to a dock—and a boat. I prayed it still worked.

We stood there for a moment under the light from the moon. That's when we heard the engines—big engines and lots of them.

"Shit! They're here!" Sloan's eyes were wild and darted around.

I felt the darkness build in my chest again, and I used what energy I had left to breathe through it. I needed to focus, but the harder I held it, the more it suffocated me. I couldn't think as the pressure built. Finally without thinking, I yelled into the night sky—scaring Sloan—releasing it like a cloud into the darkness. Small reflective spots floated in the light. The sky rumbled, louder than the trucks coming for us, and the sky opened up, pouring down on us, soaking us through almost instantaneously.

The pressure was gone. Sloan stared at me. "What the fu—"

I waved my hands at him. "I don't know. They did something to us. I don't know, but I can't think about that right now. Right now, trucks are coming, filled with guys with guns. I need to think."

Looking around at the two options, I realized it would take both of us to work. Maybe we'd have a chance.

"I need you to go start the boat. Can you do that? Hey,

Sloan!" He stared past me now, through the trees, waiting with a look of terror on his face as the rain subsided. I knocked him in the shoulder. "Sloan! Can you start the boat and then pull it to the backside of the dock house?"

He shook his head, clearing his mind to refocus. "Yes, sorry. Yes. I can do that—I think. But what the hell are you going to do?"

I smiled, shrugging. "I'll distract them. Just wait for my signal to try and start the boat, or they'll hear you."

"What's the signal?"

"Something loud." I looked toward the sound of the trucks. They'd be here any second. "Listen, if they get too close, take the boat and go."

His eyebrows creased together. "What? No way, man. I'm not leaving you."

"Yes, you are. If I can't get to you, you have to go. Don't wait for me. One of us needs to get out of here. Okay?" I caught his eyes. "Sloan?"

He shook his head, but he finally replied, "Fine. But don't make me have to fucking leave you behind. Okay?" He ran off toward the boat, backpack bouncing, and left me standing there, shaking my own head.

Why am I suddenly the hero? A flash of red hair passed through my mind. *Because she thought you deserved it.*

"Well, let's hope so." I looked toward the dock house. "And let's hope you have something I can use."

Bolting for the dock that connected the shore to the front door of the boat house, I heard the trucks behind me, coming out from the tree line.

Shit.

I had no time. Bracing myself, I lowered my shoulder and prayed the door wasn't solid oak. But it was the opposite. It was old and weak, and the door crumbled. I flew through it, slamming into something hard. I quickly regained my bearings, ignoring the pain in my side. I looked around, taking stock of the room as I dropped my backpack somewhere in the darkness. I couldn't see anything, even with the moonlight shining through the small window. There were large shapes but nothing I could make out.

Raising my wrist, I swiped up on my watch face, selecting the flashlight option. "Ah, there we go."

There were dozens of crates. The lid was askew on the one closest to me. Angling my wrist higher, I peered inside, hearing the growling of engines outside. Moving back a layer of plastic packing peas, I saw dozens of bottles. They were filled with vodka.

A smile spread across my face. I always wanted to throw a Molotov cocktail.

As I shone my watch light around the room to find something I could add as the wick, I heard a voice come over a loud speaker outside.

"Raven Smith and Sloan Blic, we need you both to come outside and come with us."

Like hell we are.

Searching the room with the small flashlight on my watch was frustrating, but at least it worked. I found some scrap fabric and started ripping it into strips, shoving the pieces into my pocket, as I moved around the room looking for a fuse of some kind. The stove didn't work, although it was electric. I looked for anything flammable. I grabbed the knobs of the drawers, throwing them open. I heard the loud voice repeat itself, a little louder this time, while I searched. I found a small box and, for a second, just stared.

Did I really just find a box of matches?

I tried not to laugh as I opened them to check if they were still good. I found one inside. I took it out and looked at it. "I feel like I'm in an old action film from a hundred years ago. This is crazy." I threw my hands up. "Where's the bad guy to come make a speech?"

I heard another voice, more poised and calm, on the loudspeaker. "Mr. Smith, this is Dr. Atlas. I want to say personally that no harm will come to you or your companion, Mr. Blic."

At his name, my chest tightened. He was waiting for me—Mr. Black himself. At least they hadn't seen Sloan yet and still thought he was in here with me. The voice continued to drone on about how we were going to help so many people and how long they'd waited to find just one of us and now had two, blah blah.

I ignored the rest, walking back to the vodka bottles. I broke off the tops of ten bottles and added strips inside of each one, leaving a couple to the side to keep the flame burning—if this even worked. Then I looked at the one match now in my hand. I took a deep breath, said a prayer, and struck the match on the box.

Holy shit, it lit!

I grabbed the first bottle and lit the makeshift wick, pausing only long enough to light another one. The fire traveled up the dry fabric quicker than I thought, and I walked faster to the now broken front door. "—need you to come out willingly. We aren't going to force you, but we also can't let you leave. Let's be reasonable adults."

I blindly threw the first cocktail out the door, aiming for the pile of rubbish next to the dock. I silently cheered when it hit the target, scraps of whatever was able to light on fire. Flames rose higher. I lit another one from a burning strip, throwing it on target again. Men yelled, and orders were given. As I threw my third bottle, I heard the motor of the boat being pulled. It was too loud. They were going to hear it.

Judging by the new yelling, they already had.

I glanced to the window on my left. I saw a group of four men rushing toward the dock, where the boat waited, Sloan on top, pulling the cord again and again.

I couldn't hit them from here. A panic filled my chest. They were going to capture Sloan in less than thirty seconds if I didn't make a better plan. The scenarios played through my mind as my lungs constricted again.

Holding onto the feeling, I let it build in my center, dark

and light at the same time, watching as the men ran down the dock, yelling at Sloan.

The deeper the feeling went, the harder and harder it was to hold. I heard rumbles from the sky and watched as the light from the moon became dimmer. Clouds drifted together. Not knowing what would happen, I waited until the men were only feet from Sloan. I saw his eyes widen with fear as he jumped away from the men, high in the air. I let go of the energy, letting it fly out and upward. My arms flew up beside me.

A bright light flashed again and again in front of the running men, and with a roar, the sky opened. Rain fell hard around us.

I didn't hear a sound from any of the men, but I saw their figures lying on the dock. I searched for Sloan and saw him—thankfully and seemingly unhurt—still pulling on the cord on the boat.

I heard the engine roar to life just before a fist hit me from the side. A man grabbed me, choking me for a second as my necklace wrapped too tightly around my neck, and threw me backward. I heard the rain outside and Sloan's voice flying over the sounds, calling my name. As I shook my head, starting to stand, I felt another hit knock me sideways, smashing into some kind of glass. The crash was dulled by the rain showering down on the tin roof. I grabbed the side of one of the crates to keep from falling and kicked out with my foot, hitting my attacker in the chest. He doubled over for only a second before flying at me again. I sidestepped out of the way and dodged behind a crate as another man with a long beard flew in from behind me, fists flying at the man who hit me.

Sloan hit the man twice before grabbing him around the waist, tackling him to the ground.

"Sloan!"

But before I could move, two more men rushed in the front door, grabbing Sloan from two sides. In his twisting and thrashing, he managed to turn toward me and screamed only one word.

"GO!"

Everything told me to stay, but the look in his eyes made me move. I rushed toward the rear of the dock house to the back door, grabbing my bag as I ran. "Shit!" My foot slipped off the broken ledge of the stairs. There was a sudden drop from the back door to the boat about eight feet down. *How the hell did Sloan get up here?*

I checked around for some hold but saw nothing. I didn't know what else to do but jump.

Let's just pray the boat's not as old as the door.

I leaped into the boat, pausing for just a second to make sure I didn't fracture the wood, and then turned the rudder, cranking it to High. I aimed for the other side of the lake as fast as the little old boat could take me. My heart was still pounding as the rain subsided around me.

I woke up with a pounding headache. My head hurt like a pressure valve in the red. Under my left eye, it felt like a bowling ball had hit me. Placing both hands on my head and rubbing, I sat up slowly. I let the feeling subside before I opened my eyes and looked around. Seeing the hay around me, the night before came back to me in a wave. Now that I remembered, I wanted to go back to bed. After crossing the lake last night, I locked the engine and angled the boat back the opposite direction. With any luck, I could at least throw them off for a bit until I figured out my next steps. I had seen multiple houses dotting the shore, but I didn't want to stop as I pushed through the hills carrying my bag along with Sloan's. After another two hours, I could barely walk anymore. My head hurt worse than it did now, and I was more than exhausted.

The closest home to me at that time was a farm. I could see the house in the distance, and the different barns scattered in a few places. I walked—stumbled—into the closest one and crawled into the pile of hay before falling asleep without a second thought.

I had no idea what they would do to Sloan. Doc said there were two of us now that were—uh—changed, but I didn't see Sloan do anything other than be his normal self. Maybe the doc was wrong about him.

Doc. Logan. After all of this, part of me still wanted to be back in her office, staring at her black heels and watching her lecture me.

Stop. We have other things to focus on right now.

Checking my watch, my eyes widened. It was just before two in the afternoon. I looked at it a couple more times to make sure it was the right time. I'd slept almost twelve hours. Trying to get a grip on my new reality—ignoring the whole "being able to call lightning thing" for the moment—I thought about my next move. Whatever the plan, I needed to get lost in a big city and fast. Small homes and towns shared and talked too much. I wasn't exactly an inconspicuous character. I needed to move. My watch location panel said I was somewhere called Durhamville, over thirty miles to Syracuse. I couldn't walk that far. Plus, the next farm or home, according to my handy watch, said it was more than ten miles away. I also couldn't walk that far.

I climbed out of the hay and decided to find myself a ride while I got my bearings. I moved slow, my head still pounding, but I made it to the door and peeked around. The house was small and almost unseen from where I stood. It was mostly shaded in giant green trees. Giant cylindrical structures stood directly behind it. Tall pipes splayed down like sun beams in multiple directions, connecting to a hidden structure behind the house.

The rest of the land was flat and even greener. I peered around my barn and saw a few more to the left and right of me. This seemed to be storage of some kind, being so far from the house.

I wished that I'd find some kind of old hover or something behind one of these doors. After checking each one, I was disappointed. Contemplating my next move, I watched a dark blue truck hover drive toward the house. A small white sedan-type hover pulled in behind it. Both came around the bend from the north of the house and stopped silently in front of it.

A plan started to form in my mind, albeit not an easy one. The only way to cross the field, unseen, to those hovers was to crawl beneath the waves of grain stalks or wait until dark. Neither sounded appealing. Besides, I was thirsty and crazy hungry. I didn't want to wait a few more hours.

What if I cross in a rain and lightning storm?

I didn't know which was crazier—the fact that I actually conjured a storm just the night before or that I now counted that as an option.

I shook my head, dismissing the idea. Just because I did it once yesterday didn't mean I could do it again. The other rumblings I didn't know for sure were me. Although let's be clear, as crazy as I felt at this moment, maybe none of them were me. Maybe lightning just happened to come down right where I needed it at the exact moment I needed it, and it had nothing to do with me.

See? Crazy! You're getting crazier.

I bounced back and forth with myself for the next ten minutes about whether or not a sane person would try to use sudden—uh, supernatural?—powers so they could steal a hover. My final decision was why the hell not?

"Okay." I stood, feet apart, arms slightly away from my side, and I looked up at the sky. "Let's make some rain!" I threw my hands up in the air like I had the night before. Nothing happened.

"Of course nothing happened because you are insane." I shook my head and sat on the ground, thinking of another plan that didn't involve me standing like a lunatic in the middle of a field trying to use magic.

Listing pros and cons in my head of the two plans, crawling was out. I had to wait until nightfall.

"Fine. Then I'll go back to sleep." My stomach rumbled. "Yes, I know. But I can't help you with that unless maybe Sloan has something in his bag that I don't." I walked back into the small building that currently housed my bed, grateful that it wasn't a hundred years ago when these fields were covered in snow, instead of the cooler, milder temperatures today.

A quick inspection of Sloan's bag didn't produce any food—only clothes and a pack of cigarettes, which I wanted to save for a rainy day. *A rainy day.* I laughed at myself, feeling unbalanced as I stretched back out on my hay pile. I didn't think I could sleep any more. And then darkness swept over me.

The moon was the only available light again as I climbed into the truck hover that sat in front of the house. I'd stolen half a dozen hovers over my lifetime, and apparently, they hadn't upgraded their security systems since my teen years. I heard crickets as I closed the door.

Hovers were relatively quiet, but I held my breath as I moved around, flipping switches to engage the engine. As the final signal lit to green, I glanced in the rearview mirror to back up.

My heart stopped. A young kid stood five feet away from the bumper, bathed in the light.

Shit.

I had to back up, but he was right in my path. I guessed that was his intention. I sighed, hit standby, and opened the door, slowly.

He yelled, "Get out of my dad's truck!" The kid was no more than twelve, holding a baseball bat in one hand and a flashlight in the other.

Here we go.

I climbed out with my hands up. "Hey, there. What's your name?" My casual tone threw him off, and he looked around, confused.

"Uh—I—"

"I'm Raven, like the bird." I tilted my head to the right, showing off my bird tattoo on my neck. "I'm sure you get plenty of ravens around here, right?" The boy caught himself about to answer. His face steeled, and he gripped the bat harder.

"Get away from my dad's truck."

"Look," I said, my voice even, a smile on my face. "I don't want to keep your dad's truck. I just need to borrow it."

"No! You want to steal it, and I won't let you!"

I put my hand up higher. "I promise I don't. I just need to get to Syracuse. Have you been there before?" His eyes darted back and forth, unsure. "I'm just trying to get there, but I need a ride."

He said nothing, considering my words.

I glance at my wrist. "How about this? How about I give you my watch as collateral? I'll take your dad's truck—I'll take really good care of it—and you hold on to my watch, which I hope you'll take really good care of in return. Then, when your parents wake up in the morning, they can track their truck to wherever I leave it. They have a tracker on it, right?"

He nodded.

"See? Then all will be well. They get their truck back, I get a ride, and you can keep the watch."

The boy squinted his eyes. "Are you bribing me?"

I let out a short laugh and shrugged. "That depends. Is it working?"

He tried to hide a smile but couldn't help it. Glancing at my wrist, toward the house, and then back to me, he asked, "You promise you won't hurt the truck?"

I placed my right hand on my chest. "I promise on my mother. I will leave it at a station exactly as it is now, without a scratch. Do we have a deal?" I removed my watch and placed it gently on the backside of the white sedan hover.

Now he really smiled, looking at the watch from where he stood. “Okay.”

My smile grew. “Great. Thanks, um—?”

“Drake.”

I nodded my head at his home. “Thank you, Drake. I appreciate it. Take care.” I pointed at the watch. “It too.”

I climbed in the car before the kid could change his mind, clicking to engage it again, and waiting the five seconds before the light turned green. The car lifted, and I saw Drake move to the side before I backed up.

I saluted him as I passed, and he smiled before rushing over to grab the smart watch. He dropped the bat to inspect it further.

I grinned. “Enjoy, kid.” I clicked the navigational option on the wheel. “Directions to Syracuse.”

2101
SEPT
CH 5
CH 1
OCT
CH 3
CH 7
NOV
CH 11
CH 14
CH 18
2104
CH 4
CH 2
DEC
CH 9
CH 12
CH 8
CH 17
CH 13
CH 16
JUN
CH 20
JUL
CH 23
2105
DEC
CH 29
MAY
CH 21
PROLOGUE
CH 19
CH 28
2106
JUN
CH 25
CH 27
CH 32
CH 24
JUL
CH 30
EPILOGUE
CH 6
CH 10
APR
CH 15
2125
CH 22
CH 26
MAY
CH 31

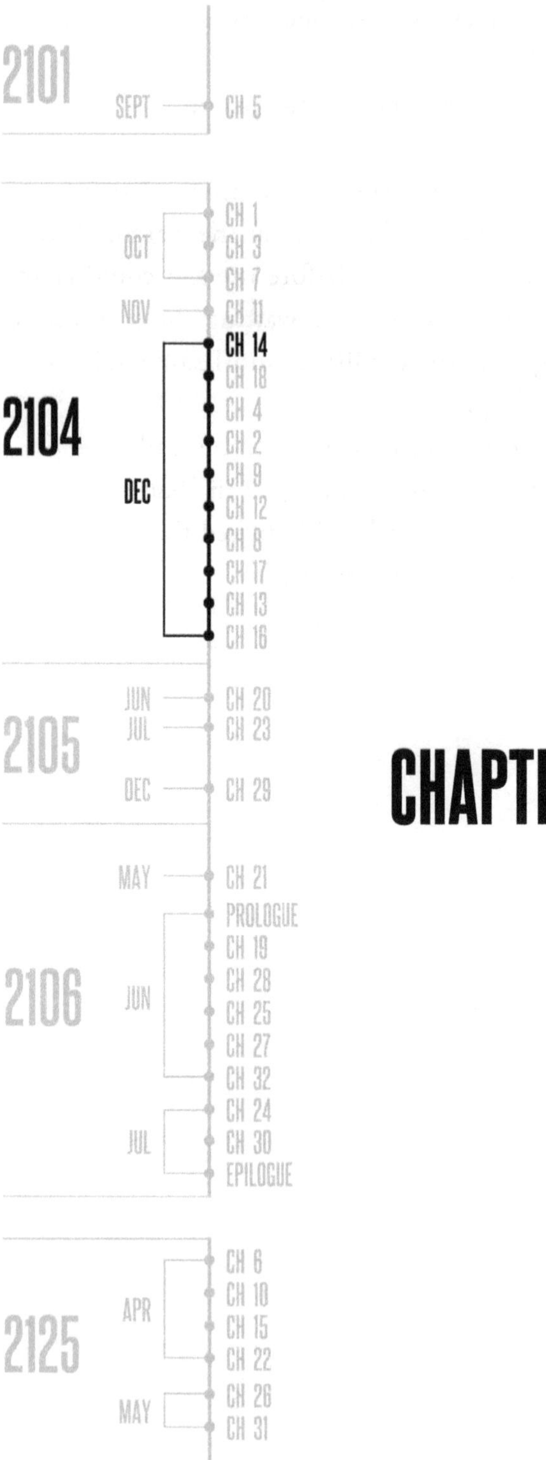

CHAPTER 14

DECEMBER 2104
Angelia

I squealed, making Jaeden jump. I laughed, staring at the names on my now-fixed specglass tablet. "Oh, sorry. I just re-read the keynote speaker list. I can't believe I'm going to be in the same room as Ronish Graves and Thatcher Hemlin. I mean, they are robot GODS!" Jaeden just watched me from across the small train table, shaking his head.

"You really are a hardware geek, aren't you?"

I pursed my lips and wiggled my head back and forth. "Um, yeah, hello, have we met?"

He laughed this time, eyes staying on mine, before looking back down to the holographic menu in front of him. "Are you going to pick something? Miss Grumpy will be back any second, and I think it's a bad idea if we don't know what we want."

"Yeah, yeah, fine." I placed my tablet beside me and swiped through the holo menu built into the table, searching through their lunch options. We'd already done this for breakfast, and our waitress was not the happiest of persons.

But it was okay. I enjoyed my travel companion more than I worried about her and her attitude. It had been a couple of weeks since we talked about being just friends, and honestly, I was happy about it. Everything was more comfortable without the expectation.

Yeah, you are just quietly falling for him now, instead of out loud. That's much easier. I found myself staring at him when he wasn't looking and hoping he'd message me to hang out. Yes, I even reached out a couple times on my own, inviting him. But I kept reminding myself that he made himself quite clear. He didn't want a relationship. We were just friends, enjoying each other's company. That was good enough for me.

Never mind how my heart raced when I caught his eyes on me, how I felt when we'd meet after not seeing each other for a few days, or the butterflies whenever he called me a silly pet name in his ridiculous British accent. Sweetheart. Darling. Love. I think "sweet" was my favorite. My heart flipped every time. I didn't care that he said it with a goofy voice. It still made my heart sing.

I had counted down the days until we officially traveled to RoboCon. We decided to take the train, enjoy the ride and the scenery, and really make a vacation out of it.

The look on Noreen's face when I finally asked for vacation for the first time since I worked with her was priceless. I took a whole week off because why the hell not? It's paid anyway.

So here we were, taking a train for ten hours to Montreal the day before the conference. We wanted to arrive early enough to get a full night's rest, all so we could wake up at six in the morning, start the festivities off right with breakfast, and find a place in line for the official opening at nine sharp.

"I still can't believe that you found rooms AT the conference center." I scrolled past the omelets to the breakfast wraps. "I mean, this was so last minute, and there just happened to be two cancellations? I wonder what we did to be so lucky."

He didn't meet my eyes as he read the menu. "Yeah, it was great, right?"

We sat in our own private train room. I would have been just fine sitting in the common area, but it was amazing that this room became available for the same price as the general admission. I thought it was a glitch in the system, but we booked it and moved along. Someone was clearly making a perfect plan for us, and I loved every second.

Our room had a small table and two chairs built out from the wall under the main window that looked out into the countryside. A few feet away was a set of couches with a table between them. At the touch of a button, the table dropped into the floor, and the couches folded down into a single bed. I blushed even thinking about it, but as couches, they were comfortable.

"So who is on your list? Who do you really want to see?"

He glanced up at me, raising an eyebrow. "You want to come with me to see software techs talk?"

I raised a hand dramatically to my chest. "Oh, well, when you say it like that, maybe not."

Jaeden laughed. "All right, all right. How about a truce for this trip? We are both lovers of technology and will enjoy it all together."

Smiling, I repeated. "Together."

The energy buzzed between us before he asked again. "Is that a yes?"

I broke eye contact and sighed. "Yup, truce." I held out my hand, and he took it. As our skin touched, I realized that we didn't touch often. The memory of each time we touched hands flooded through my mind. This was the fourth. I blinked to clear my thoughts.

Such odd things you realize sometimes, Angelia.

"So, who are you excited to see?" I repeated.

"Hands down, Dr. Atlas from the Atlas Institute. He doesn't do a lot of appearances, so I was floored when I saw his name on the list."

"Oh yeah? I've never heard his name. What's his deal?" I relished watching the excitement flash across his face.

"Dr. Atlas and his giant team of scientists are basically trying to find a cure for all of the diseases of the world, in a nutshell."

"Wow, okay. That seems like a really big undertaking. Are they close?"

He shrugged. "I don't know. It's been a while since I've heard of any new developments, but I do know they have been working on this esoskeleton technology. It works with nanobots. They are trying to not just cure the body, but repair it too."

I sat in awe. "He sounds like he's trying to change the world."

"Isn't that what all scientists try to do?"

Before I could answer, a chime at the cabin door alerted us that Miss Grumpy was back to take our order.

"Come in!" we both called out at the same time.

She opened the door and stood in the doorway. "What are you having?"

I glanced at Jaeden under my eyelashes. He hid a smile as I spoke. "I'll have the pesto chicken panini, please."

"Do you want fries or fruit?"

"Fries, please."

She looked at Jaeden, waiting for him to speak.

"Oh, sorry, uh, I'll have the cheeseburger sliders with no onions, and I'll take fries with them. Thanks."

"Got it." She walked away, closing our door behind her.

I looked back at Jaeden. "Why have a job you hate? Go work somewhere else, if you aren't happy. I don't understand."

He squinted an eye in my direction. "I'm sorry. That's a little crazy, coming from you."

"What do you mean? I love my job."

He laughed, shaking his head. "No, you don't. You are always late. You skip it whenever you feel like, and if I may say, you aren't paid nearly as much as you should be."

My brow furrowed in confusion. "How do you know how much I get paid?"

He glanced out the window before looking back at me. "I don't. I just assumed since you seem like you don't enjoy your job."

I drank from the lemonade in front of me. "Well, I do love my job. I just hate that all my efforts go into someone else's pockets."

"Why don't you open your own robo-repair shop?"

I laughed, and a piece of ice slid back into the side of my cup. "That takes capital that I don't have. But I love the idea." I took another sip before putting the cup back down.

"What if you did? Have the capital, I mean. Would you open one?"

His silver eyes focused on me, and I felt my heart speed up under his gaze.

I looked away so my mind could focus on an answer.

"Uh, yeah, I think I would. If I had the money to open one, I think so."

He leaned back in his chair. "What would you call it?"

I thought for a second, looking out through the window. I already knew the name of my store if I opened one. But I let him think I wasn't sure. I eventually answered. "I'd call it M&M Technologies."

"M&M?"

I continued to gaze out the window, watching the blur of the landscape outside. "One M for each of my parents—M for Mathieu and M for Mara." He didn't reply right away. The emotion was evident in my voice. "My dad died when I was a teenager. It was sudden." I shook my head. "My mother and father were inseparable, so no one was surprised when she got sick about six months later. She was gone shortly after that, so, I think if I was able to open a shop, I'd want to name it after them both."

"I'm sorry."

I attempted a smile. "Don't be. It was a long time ago. I'm good now. I miss them every day, but I'm okay." I glanced up at him under my lashes. "Can I tell you something crazy?"

His eyes softened. "Of course."

"I watched this Chinese documentary a long while back, shortly after my parents died. It was just something in school." I waved my hand as I talked. "Have you ever heard of Chinese spirit money?"

He shook his head and leaned in slightly to hear more.

"Well, in their culture, they take what they call spirit money—which is really just a kind of paper that they print special images on—and they burn it as an offering to their ancestors. They think the money will give their now-dead family members the ability to have everything they want in the afterlife." I paused, looking out the window for a moment, steadying my emotions. "Anyway," I cleared my throat, "I thought it was such a wonderful idea that I bought a special notepad and decided, instead of just burning some random paper, I would write letters to my parents and burn them, hoping maybe somehow they could read them or something." I shrugged. "So I do, every night. Mostly I write to my mom, but sometimes to my dad. It makes me feel better somehow, like I'm still able to share my life with them." I finally looked up into Jaeden's eyes. "Is that crazy?"

As he stared back at me, not speaking, blood rushed to my face. Maybe I shouldn't have told him that. But he surprised me.

He placed his hand over mine. "I think it's the most amazing thing I've ever heard."

We sat like that for a few minutes. With his hand over mine, my emotions roamed around the room. He confused me sometimes, but right now, I just soaked it in. I simply enjoyed his gaze on mine and the feel of his skin—for the fifth time. I intended to savor it until I couldn't anymore.

Oh dear, Angelia. You have it bad. This isn't going to end well, you know?

I didn't care. At least in this moment, everything was perfect.

Another chime signaled at the door, interrupting the blossoming silence.

Jaeden pulled his hand back and broke eye contact. "Come in."

And we're back.

I internally sighed, watching his profile as he spoke to the man who brought our lunch.

Yup, this is going to be a disaster.

Rylan

If it was even possible, she was more beautiful when she slept. We were watching some random movie on the projector when I looked down after saying something to her. She fell asleep. I don't blame her. We started our journey early this morning around five, and she had packed before that until about two.

"I've always been a procrastinator," she explained.

I got up to grab a blanket from the overhead compartment and draped it over her. She stirred for just a second before falling back to sleep. We had another three hours until we arrived in Montreal, so I planned to let her sleep for a while longer.

This was getting harder and harder. I knew this trip would be a good idea or a bad one. I enjoyed every second of her—every laugh, every smile, every moment I could look in her eyes. But, it almost hurt to not touch her when she was this close.

It took all of my restraint not to get up from the table and wrap my arms around her when she told me the story about her parents. I finally knew what she burned at night. I couldn't help but respond internally, watching her eyes as she told me. Me. Of everyone she knew, she trusted me with that information.

No, she trusts Jaeden.

I pushed away my thoughts. I'd be Jaeden forever if that's what she wanted, anything to be near her. She took a deep breath and adjusted herself in her sleep as I stared.

Shaking my head, I walked back to the chairs by the window. Plopping down, I dropped my head in my hands.

You're doing the right thing. Just don't do anything other than what friends do. Besides, she wants to be friends. Remember?

I knew it, but it was killing me.

I looked toward her sleeping body and saw the top of her head. I imagined what it would be like to just walk over to her, pull her close, and kiss the lips I'd watched since the moment I met her smile in that pizza place.

Back before I lost myself. *Or found myself.*

I didn't know which, but I knew she was the end of me. One day, I would have to walk away. Judging by this ache in my chest, it might be soon.

Maybe after this trip.

The reality hit me like a brick. Was this my goodbye trip? Was this the last time we'd be together?

If you love her, you know the answer already.

My heart pounded in my ears. I did know the answer. If I was around her much longer, I might do something dumb. Then it would get awkward between us. Or worse, she'd change her mind and would want to be more than friends. I almost laughed. Being more than friends sounded like everything I wanted, and yet—I looked back over at her as she shifted positions—it still came back to Jaeden. He's what she wanted, not me, not Rylan.

But Rylan made all the plans. He bought the Volkshover. He booked the train. He upgraded two people's reservations, so they could have rooms at the conference center. HE did that, not Jaeden. But Jaeden was who she saw, talked to, spent time with. Every time she laughed, it was with Jaeden.

I closed my eyes. *Just stay the course. Breathe. You can—*

Her cry made me jump. I was by her side in three steps. "Are you o—" She was still sleeping, but her face tensed, no longer calm and easy. It was furrowed and frustrated. She cried out again, kicking her feet out. Her arms came up suddenly, and I grabbed them without thinking, sitting on my knees and wrapping my arms around her gently. "Shh, Angelia. It's okay. It's alright. I'm here."

She stopped thrashing and settled, turning onto her side. Her face pressed against my chest. "Jaeden," she whispered into my shirt.

I couldn't breathe. I couldn't move. I held her for what felt like forever until she didn't move for a long time. I finally let go and moved back onto the couch, my legs protesting.

Her face was calm again, and I hoped she slept peacefully for the duration. As I watched her breathe in and out, I knew that this would be our last trip. I had to leave her to enjoy her life. I wouldn't stand in her way anymore. My chest clenched like a fist as I sat back to watch her sleep.

Angelia

I laughed as I bleeped us into my room.

"Why did he think I would be impressed by that line?" I shook my head as I put my bag on the chair next to the door. Jaeden walked in behind me, shrugging his shoulders.

"I don't know. But maybe 'Is this a new 150 screwdriver, or am I just happy to see you?' would have worked better?"

I laughed again as I took off my jacket and threw it on the bed. "Maybe 'Is it hot in here, or is it just you?' would have worked."

He raised an eyebrow. "Oh yeah? Then maybe he should have gone with 'I couldn't help noticing that you look a lot like my next girlfriend.'"

"Oooh, now THAT would catch my attention." I sat on the bed and started to take off my boots as Jaeden sat on the chair across the room, smiling at me.

"Okay, what about 'Would you grab my arm, so I can tell my friends I've been touched by an angel?'"

I looked over at him and saw his eyes burning into mine. My heart fluttered. I cleared my throat and forced my eyes back to my boots. "Hmm, I think I prefer 'I must be in a museum because you truly are a work of art.' It's less otherworldly and more real." I glanced at him. His eyes hadn't faltered.

His voice softened. "How about 'No wonder the sky is gray. All the color is in your eyes.'"

I stared at my second boot, trying to remember how to unzip it. My hands began to tremble.

He spoke even more softly. "Or 'I would never play hide and seek with you because someone like you is impossible to find.'"

I somehow removed my boot, but I couldn't bring myself to look at him. My heart was beating so hard I was sure he heard it. My stomach churned with anxiety. "'Do you want to go outside and get some fresh air with me? You keep taking my breath away.'" I finally found the courage to look up. He faced me, and his eyes brimmed with emotion. "'If beauty were time, you would be forever.'"

"Jaeden…" I whispered. I couldn't find the right words. He stood slowly, so slowly, and closed the distance between us. My heart leaped with every footstep.

"'Why would I want to look at the stars when I can look in your eyes?'" He crouched down in front of me. "'Wouldn't it be the perfect crime if I stole your heart, and you stole mine?'"

I caught my breath. He smiled his side smile that made me weak.

"'My heart forgets to beat the moment I see you.'"

My whole body wanted to whisper back and scream at the same time.

He looked down and reached for my hand, brushing his fingertips along my clasped hands. Fire and ice trailed where he touched. He looked back up into my eyes and through me. I could barely breathe.

Emotion flooded his eyes like a spark. His hand left mine, brushing his thumb down my cheek and across my lips. He lifted himself up closer, so close. I could almost feel his lips as he whispered, so softly, "Angelia…"

Just as his lips pressed against mine, with his hands behind my head pulling me in closer, the room shook violently, and I started to fall.

I bolted upright. Disoriented, I scanned the room. *What just happened?*

My dream flooded back to me before I realized where I was. The train. I was on the train. I took a deep breath and rubbed my hands down my face. I searched for Jaeden, but he wasn't here. *What time is it?*

I glanced over at the clockglass by the window. It was half an hour before we were due to reach Montreal. *What the hell?* I slept for almost three hours. I looked around again. *Where is Jaeden?*

As if on cue, the door to our room opened, and he walked in holding a bowl in his hand. "Hey, sleeping beauty."

"Hi," was all I could manage back.

"Need something sweet?"

I crinkled my eyebrows at him. "What?"

He smiled, lowering the bowl. It was filled with grapes, apples, melons, and strawberries. "I always need something sweet and cold after my long naps in the middle of the day. I thought you might too."

I rubbed my face to warm my cheeks. "I'm so sorry that I fell asleep on you. I'm a terrible travel companion."

"Are you kidding? It was very peaceful for once. I didn't have to hear you talk about hardware for like three hours."

I laughed. "Hey, now, we have a truce for the next three days. Remember?"

He tilted his head back. "Ah, yes, that's right. I'm sorry."

I adjusted in my seat, taking the bowl from him. "You better be." I started eating one fruit at a time. I was on my fifth piece and realized how much better I felt. "Holy crap, you're right—cold and sweet." I put another grape in my mouth. "Who knew?"

He laughed, taking the seat across from me. "Good. I'm glad

that I helped."

"No, but like really, I'm sorry. I didn't realize I was so tired. We should have watched the scenery together or something."

He waved his hand at me. "Nah. It was boring. It was just, 'Oh, look, a cow. Oh, look, another cow. Oh, look'…I think you get it."

I smiled before taking another grape, enjoying the cold juice as it squeezed in my mouth. "These are amazing. Thank you."

"You're very welcome. I planned to wake you up when I got back."

I gestured at the train. "Yeah, the lovely jolt of the train woke me up from my dreams."

"Oh, yeah? Anything good?"

My face flushed as I suddenly found interest in my bowl. "I don't remember."

He leaned forward, seeing the bowl almost empty. "Geez. Can you share?"

I gasped. "I'm sorry! I thought you brought them for me—I mean, I didn't—"

Jaeden laughed. "No, stop. I'm joking. They're all yours. Are you okay?"

I felt like a ball of emotions. That dream didn't help. I didn't even get a chance to recover before he was standing in front of me with his gorgeous silver eyes, full lips, and—

Stop. You need to stop. "I'm good, just groggy from my nap." I changed the topic. "The hover will meet us at the train station, right?" We'd talked about this already, but I picked the first thing that came to mind.

"Yup. It should already be there. Are you excited to nerd out for three days?"

I practically squealed, remembering the point in our trip. "Yes!"

He chuckled, smiling at me, as I tried to remember to breathe.

Two hours later, we stood in front of the counter at the conference center. I pushed down my growing irritation.

"We had two rooms booked, not one," Jaeden reiterated to the woman at the front desk, who couldn't stop smiling back at him.

She looked from her projection screen back to him. "I see that, and I'm so sorry. Somehow, the second room was cancelled about an hour ago. Someone else has already reserved it. They are actually already in it. I don't—I don't know what to say."

I hadn't said anything yet. I only stood next to him, shifting from foot to foot. I knew what would happen if I spoke. No F-bombs would be useful here.

He sighed. "Okay. So what are our options?"

"Um." She looked back at her screen. "We can put you both in the one other room you have booked, but it's only a single bed. I don't see anything else available at all."

He shook his head. "This is crazy. Give me a second. I need to make a call." He walked away without another word, glasstop bag in hand.

I was left standing there, waiting for him to return. I had nothing to say, although the woman apologized to me a few times. I simply nodded when she spoke. A few minutes later, he walked back.

"Okay. Sorry." The second word was directed at me. "What were you saying our other options were?"

"I'm sorry. There aren't any, unfortunately. Everything is completely booked for the next three days."

He leaned closer to the counter, his side smile flashing. "We've been on a train for over nine hours. We need real beds and real food. Can you please check again?"

She looked sympathetic as she said, "Okay," and turned back to her screen, scrolling through the rooms.

Her eyebrows crinkled together, scrolling up and down and

then back again. "Um, I don't know how that happened, but we do have one other room available. It's one of our suites, but it has two rooms. I—uh—would be happy to upgrade you at no charge, seeing how it was our fault for giving your other room away."

My jaw dropped. Three times now, some crazy level of serendipity shone good fortune on our trip. *Maybe it's Jaeden. Maybe he's lucky.*

He smiled at the woman. "That would be perfect." I have to be honest. It irked me the way she smiled back.

"Also," she said as she typed on the light keys, "this room automatically comes with a food package for breakfast, lunch, and dinner, which will automatically add to your reservation for you both for the next three days. Would that work for you two?"

Jaeden looked over at me, and I nodded. He replied, "Yes. That would be great. Thank you for accommodating us." As the woman typed, I couldn't help but smile, catching Jaeden's eye again. He shrugged, like he couldn't believe it either.

A minute later, she finished entering the information and handed us back our IDfobs, now coded with access to our room.

Our room.

As she apologized again, we said thank you and scurried away before someone changed their minds. We laughed in disbelief as we walked to the special elevators across the lobby, To Suites Only.

I bowed dramatically, gesturing toward the elevators. "This way, sir, to your suite."

He bowed back in kind. "Why, thank you, madam. Shall we?" His ridiculous British accent sharpened every word. He held out his arm, and I linked mine through his elbow, ignoring the flutter in my stomach, as we approached the shiny doors and pressed the button to go up.

The door opened, and he bowed again. "After you, sweet."

My heart rate spiked. I stammered in my own terrible, jumbled European accent, "Thank you, kind sir." I walked in and looked around. There was no screen, no ads, no BUY THIS NOW. Soft piano music played through tiny speakers in the ceiling panels. I grinned. "I could definitely get used to this."

He smiled at me as the door closed. Our room was on the eleventh floor, and the elevator traveled up without so much as a tremble.

As the doors opened, we came face to face with an older couple, dressed in white matching suits. The woman sported big glittering diamonds on her earrings. They stared at us both like we were trespassers as we exited the doors. It made me uncomfortable, and then angry that it made me feel like an imposter.

As we walked down the hallway toward the 1100-1105 section, floor-to-ceiling screens showed a scrolling view of a park. The quality of the images was impressive.

"Don't let them do that."

I snapped my head toward him. "Don't let them do what?"

His face softened. "Don't let them make you feel like you don't belong here."

"Yeah…" I watched the screens change to a bubbling fountain, complete with water. I immediately felt at peace.

Jaeden's voice interrupted my gaze with his accent. "Ahh, 1102. Here we are." He looked over at me. "Are you ready, darling?"

I rolled my eyes and laughed. "Yes, already. Can we go in?"

He swiped his IDfob over the lock, and the double doors opened before disappearing into the wall on either side. He stepped to the side and gestured for me to go first. I felt like a princess walking into her ballroom.

The ceilings were twice the height of the hallway. Everything was elegant in white with dark wooden accents on the tables, couches, beds, and molding. The main room was composed of two distinct spaces. The left had a set of white couches arranged in a U shape and an electric fireplace built into the wall. On the right, there were two bedrooms with transparent glass walls separating them. I could just make out the outlines. The doors to each room were also see-through and looked as though they floated in midair. I walked over to the opening of the doors and reached over, waving my hand over the small sensor between them. The glass walls and doors immediately frosted to an opaque white color.

"That is quite possibly the coolest thing I've ever seen."

Jaeden's voice came from beside me. "You've never seen transparent glass?"

I shook my head, admiring the wall. "I only ever read about it." His gaze and soft smile were lost on me as I looked past the rooms to the other side of the suite.

There was a dining room on the left with another set of couches to the right. A wide all-glass wall separated them with an overwhelming view of downtown Montreal.

"Wow." I breathed the word as I slowly made my way through the rooms to the window gazing out into the moving city. The sun was already setting, and the bright oranges and reds contrasted beautifully with the blue and gray buildings outside, all covered in shining lights from the hundreds of windows. I looked up higher, seeing the skylanes. Light reflected off of the hover cars as if they were stars, glittering across the sky.

I felt Jaeden beside me. His arm brushed against mine. "This is amazing," I heard him say. I smiled, knowing exactly what I wanted to tell my mom that night. I started to say as much when a chime sounded at the door.

Jaeden answered, "Come in."

A small, older man wearing a dark red uniform entered our room. "Good evening, Mr. Lowe." He nodded at me. "Ma'am. I was told to bring these to you as a further apology for our mistake."

Jaeden crossed the room to retrieve the two long, clear rectangular strips from the man. His face lit up. "Thank you so much. We'll definitely use these."

"Very good, sir. Have a great evening."

"You, too."

The man walked out of the room. As soon as the door closed, Jaeden turned toward me. An even bigger smile spread across his face.

"Didn't you say something about wanting to go to the Close-Out Dinner on Sunday night?"

My eyes widened. "Are you serious?" I walked over, taking the tickets from him and reading for myself. "Oh man! Can this trip get any better right now?" Then my face dropped. "Oh, no, what am I going to wear?"

He smiled. "I guess we'll just have to go shopping."

I looked up at him, gazing into his beautiful eyes, taking a long, deep breath. I didn't think I could fit all of today onto my small sheet of paper to my mom tonight.

What an amazing problem to have.

CHAPTER 15

APRIL 2125
Marina

Standing with my feet apart, grounded, I ignore the specks of light dancing around me. The last three times, I fell. I am tired of adding bruises to my body. I steady myself, closing my eyes. I feel the surge of energy come from within me. It's been a few days since I let my energy fly, and it feels anxious to try again.

I feel the wind billow around me as the dark center of my mind changes to a soft yellow. I pull the energy deeper into me as I start to feel a whirlwind whip at my face, clothes, and hair.

Focus. Breathe and focus.

I hold myself calm, feet rooted, and I open my eyes, narrowing in on the pot across from me on the set table. Pablo sits five feet away on a chair, tail over his paws, watching me with wide eyes.

After a quick breath in, I launch my right hand in front of me. The wind cycling around me pulls into yellow tendrils, with small yellow specks circling, shooting with force, aimed at the pot.

But I miss, terribly. Pablo looks unimpressed. Thankfully, I only lose balance this time as I drop my hand, disappointed.

"Damn. Why is it so hard to make air do what I want, Pablo? I mean, water? Got it. Earth? All good. Fire? Easy. But air? Why is air so defiant?"

I shake my head as my newest companion of a week stares back at me without a response.

"Yeah. I agree."

I walk to the chair Pablo sits on and slump down as soon as he moves for me. I feel my energy still buzzing around, wanting to do more, but my mind is distracted.

I look around at the grass field about 300 yards from my home. Another hundred yards behind me is a high cliff drop, steep enough to induce more climbing than walking if I went down. It makes for an incredible view of the valley. Tall mountains compete on either side, as the left is higher than the right. Flecks of trees, like spots, cover the top of the peak and disperse as they come down. Through the middle, a winding river snakes out as far as I can see. It glitters at night, when the sun hits the water at the right angle, but right now, it is a bright blue surrounded in browns and greens.

When my mom brought us here, she always told me it was the perfect place for us. The mountains offered protection, and we were close enough to the water to farm for ourselves. I was still in awe at the fact that my mom built our irrigation system on her own, with her own two hands, with me running around. Before that, it was all manual.

Although what is manual to me? I haven't lived in the world of online ordering and house delivery. I'll never know what it was like to have a pizza night and watch movies. I'll never take a hover down to the beach and watch the sunset with friends. I'll never walk into a store that has everything I could ever need, from food to shoes.

I shake my head at the overwhelming complexities of living without modern technology and conveniences. I have no idea what that loss really felt like for my mom. And then add in her doing it all by herself, with me meandering around. I mean, I wasn't helpful until I could use a screwdriver on my own at the age of about four.

I just can't imagine.

"Mom, you were such a powerhouse." *And what are you*

exactly? What are you doing with this life she gave you?

My gaze travels over the valley as I wonder at an answer to my own question.

The sun is high above my head, making it about 1 p.m. Just today, I already ate breakfast, enjoyed lunch, swam my usual laps, checked on a parameter sensor, and studied the Cold War. After, I decided I wanted to exercise some energy, so here I am.

My days are the same over and again. It seems silly to think of a time when people painted their nails and added color to their hair, or they worked for months to pay for a few days on a giant ship that was really just a moving city. It baffles me how people used credit and spent money they didn't have on things they thought they needed or wanted, like homes bigger than a city block or private jets to travel anywhere in the world. Oceans, mountains, valleys, ruins, and far-off cities were all accessible if you had enough money.

I sigh. But who am I to understand? To judge? At least they all had something to aim for, live for, want. What exactly am I doing? I learn facts about a world that doesn't exist anymore and never will again. I grow food to sustain myself. I maintain technology for protection. Every day, there are different objects to fix. Every day, there are different problems to solve. But it's the same—I will always be here, alone.

I glance over at Pablo, who is thoroughly cleaning himself now. "Almost alone." I grin as the fluffy cat tries to reach his back. "The life of a cat takes a lot of work, huh? I can tell." I huff out a breath. "Pablo, why am I feeling so restless lately? You think I'd feel better having you around, but I just feel so useless. You know?"

He lifts his hind leg in response and starts cleaning the inside of his thigh. "Yup. Thanks for the motivation."

I stand up and stretch, my arms pushing some Maddies out of the way. I feel the tension push against my muscles, with my energy close behind.

For a moment, I stare at my home in front of me. From

here, it looks like a giant concrete box with windows. The thick and solid gate about twenty yards away from the walls creates a solid barrier between the house and this open field. On most days, the two doors on either side are open. Every once in a while, I either want to test that they still work or just want to feel safer and close them. "Speaking of which, I haven't tested full lockdown in a long time. I should do that." I glance over at Pablo. "All right, can we go now? Are you clean enough?" He doesn't even acknowledge me. I roll my eyes and walk back toward my house, wondering what to tackle with the other eight hours of my day before bed.

I wake up with a jolt. Sweat drips down my back. I inhale slowly as my eyes look around the room.

What just happened? What woke me up?

My eyes squint and check shadows in corners.

Nothing.

I shake my head, trying to clear away the confusion. Breathing in and out through my nose, calming my nerves, I become more aware of what's around me. My heart rate slows down.

A flash hits me of my mom, crying. Emotions like waves crash against my heart. It's been a long time since I stood where my mom stood, feeling what she felt. I feel anxious and worry this chance will fall away as I try to catch the frayed ends of my dream, already floating away. I close my eyes, calming my nerves.

She was crying. Someone was hurt—no, not hurt—gone. She lost someone.

I deepen my breath, pulling into my mind. The light spins—no colors, just light, spinning faster and faster. When the pressure builds to an impossible height, I let it go, and my energy clicks in my mind. Everything shifts upside down. I feel weightless and heavy, full of energy and completely bare.

I stand in the middle of a courtyard. My disorientation takes a moment to pass, but I know I have no time. I only have seconds to see her. I turn to my left and right, searching. I look up.

There she is, standing high above me, on a building, looking down on me, at me, through me. My heart skips. I always forget how much I look like her. Our faces are the same shape. Our hair falls down our back. We both have small frames. My mom was so beautiful.

But in this moment, she is in agony. I see her tears, her shock, but the pain is the hardest to hold. I've never seen her like this. I never want to see it again. In this stolen moment, one that shouldn't be mine, I hold it gently and soak in what I can for as long as I can.

Her eyes burn through me, seeing something beyond me. I turn and find a dark, burned circle. I am standing in the middle of—

My body starts to rise. I'm not ready to go yet. I want to stay with her a little longer. I pull my energy, willing it to hold me there. I feel the pressure start to build, but it's too late. The light slows down, finally stops spinning, and I sit in my bed again, shaking.

I close my eyes, and my hands rest in my lap, as tears run down my face. I replay the dream over and over. I don't want to move. I may lose it all. I don't want to open my eyes, because I'll lose it faster.

The images start to fade into the lost moments of time. When I feel as though I can let go, I lean over to my side table and grab a journal from the drawer, touching my small tin box as I reach over. I found this old leather-bound journal around the time I lost my mom.

I had been so lost in grief at sixteen that I chanced running to the city on my own. I felt reckless and didn't care if I was found. I drove fast, too fast, to the high buildings and crumbling past. I threw bricks, rocks, and metal scraps at windows, doors, walls, and hovers. I wanted to break everything. So lost and alone, I stumbled into an old bookstore—her old bookstore. I sat there and cried for more time than I can remember, but when I finally stood up to return home, the sun started to set. A silver charm at the end of a ribbon bookmark glinted in the sunlight. The journal, attached, sat on the floor.

That day was the first time everything flipped upside down, and I saw her. I still don't know if it helped or made it worse, but it had been a long time since I saw my mother, since I felt her. I don't regret these moments.

I open the journal and turn to the last empty page. I write down whatever I can remember of these fleeting moments so I can hold on to them as long as possible. This is the nineteenth time in two years I've enjoyed random moments with her, seeing into her life. At least, that's what I think I see. It's not like I could ask.

I pick a pen from my nightstand and write. I write about how it felt, how it hurt, how it healed. When I finish, I close the pages, kiss the top of the journal, and set it back in the drawer.

Pablo sits on the floor, wide eyes staring at me. My stomach jolts, and I catch in a breath. "Holy shit, Pablo! Really?"

"*Meow.*"

"Oh, yeah?" I laugh as he dips his head up and down, looking for a place to land before he even jumps. "Got it. I'm moving over." I shift to the side and lean back. Before I tap on the bed, he's already leaping onto the new, open space. He pads over to me and rubs his face along mine, meowing and purring. "I love you too." I pet his head for a moment before he pulls away from me, walking around to find a spot to lie down. After about a dozen passes—cats are weird—he plops down.

I fall asleep to the sound of Pablo's purrs, thinking only about my mom and how I miss her, so much. I ignore the dark side of my dream, the fear in her eyes, and the feeling that the person she lost was my father.

My proximity alarm sounds as I open my eyes.

I grumble. "Not again. Pablo, can you please just stay in the damn house? How do you get out anyway?" I sit up on my elbows and start at the wide furry eyes staring back at me. "Um, okay. Sorry. Then what—"

"Good morning, Marina. Someone is approaching." My stomach drops. *Someone.*

"Um, Niko, what do you mean by someone? There are no someones. There's never been a someone." I freeze, ignoring the panic rising in my stomach.

"Someone, as in a person, is walking up toward the house."

My body finally reacts. I jump up, throw on yesterday's clothes and run down the hallway. My messy bun flops around on my head as I race up the stairs to my observatory.

The entire screen holds one image. Someone, some man, is walking toward my house with a black bag on his back. He walks nonchalantly, like he has nowhere to be, like he isn't walking into someone's home, unannounced, causing a disruption.

"Niko, close the emergency doors."

"Yes, Marina."

The loud screech of metal on metal sounds as the doors move slowly inward, closing the gap of space for the intruder to enter. I watch as he stops walking, staring at the large metal-and-stone doors, until they wind completely shut. "Niko, zoom in."

The camera shifts closer to his face, his rather stunning face, as specks float around his head. Although I've never seen another person in my entire life—in real life, not counting my mom—this is what they call beautiful. I know that immediately.

The beautiful face is actually talking. "Niko, turn on the speakers."

"—rry. I don't mean to cause any stress. Is someone in there?" He waits, and I hold my breath. "Hello?"

I think about what to do, traveling through a thousand

scenarios, most of which end badly. I take a deep breath. "Niko, open the communication line."

"Yes, Marina."

After a moment, I find my voice and speak. "You are trespassing."

His head flies up toward the sound. "Oh, good, there is someone here. I was starting to think it was just automated."

"No. I'm here, and you are trespassing."

"Yes, I got that. I'm sorry for trespassing. I'm just passing through, if that's all right."

I answer back a little too quickly. "No. It's not all right. You can't just walk through someone's property and think it's all right."

He puts his hands up. "I'm sorry. I didn't mean to cause a problem. Besides, it's not like your territory is marked with anything besides these very impressive gates." He pauses and looks around. "They're really massive. I'd be interested in learning how they connect to the security. Does the software connect to your AI? Can you shut these from any—"

I cut him off, feeling overwhelmed, feeling awkward, feeling so much. "What do you want?"

He looks up again. "Not one for small talk, huh?" He shifts on his feet. "As I said before, I'm just passing through. I just saw your home and was hoping for a place to rest that didn't include the ground." He laughs a little.

What a lovely sound—another person's laugh.

"I can understand your apprehension. I'm just some unknown, random person, but for what it's worth, I don't mean you any harm. I just want to rest before I continue on. I don't have much." He gestures to his backpack. "I won't take up too much space."

I stare at the stranger and have no idea what I should do. Part of me is so elated at the chance to talk to someone else that I want to invite him in. He can tell me about everything, just EVERYTHING. The other part of me is completely terrified. There's a reason my mom and I set up these defenses. She always wanted us—me—to be safe. After the world fell, she didn't know if those responsible would seek out others like her, like me, other Spectrals. Now, here I am, possibly speaking to one of them. But I have no idea.

I look at his face as he looks around, waiting for an answer. His features are soft, calm, and still so beautiful. It is hard to look at him for too long.

He speaks, making me jump. "It's all right. I'll go around and find another place. I'm sorry for causing a problem." He starts to move.

"Wait! I—" I don't know what's going to happen. I don't know if this is the right thing to do. I only know I don't want the first person I've ever met to walk away. He waits. "How long would you want to rest?"

He smiles. I ignore my stomach as it knots. "Would two days be too much? I promise, two days, and I'm gone. I just want to sleep somewhere else other than the dirt for once. I have nothing to trade or anything, but I'd be happy to help with whatever you need. I'm good with technology, so if you need..."

As he talks, I consider the situation. Of the five bedrooms in the house, there is one downstairs. With my door locked...it could work. I could use help fixing one of my solar panels. And I could get answers about the outside world. "Okay."

"Really?" His smile spreads across his face. "You are an incredible person. Thank you. I promise to—"

"I'll be down in a minute. I'll meet you in the yard," I say before I lose my nerve. I tap on the screen in front of me, silencing sound both ways. My hands shake slightly. "Niko, open the gate."

"Marina, there is still someone standing outside."

I huff. "Yes, Niko, I know. Let's hope this is not the worst idea in the history of ideas."

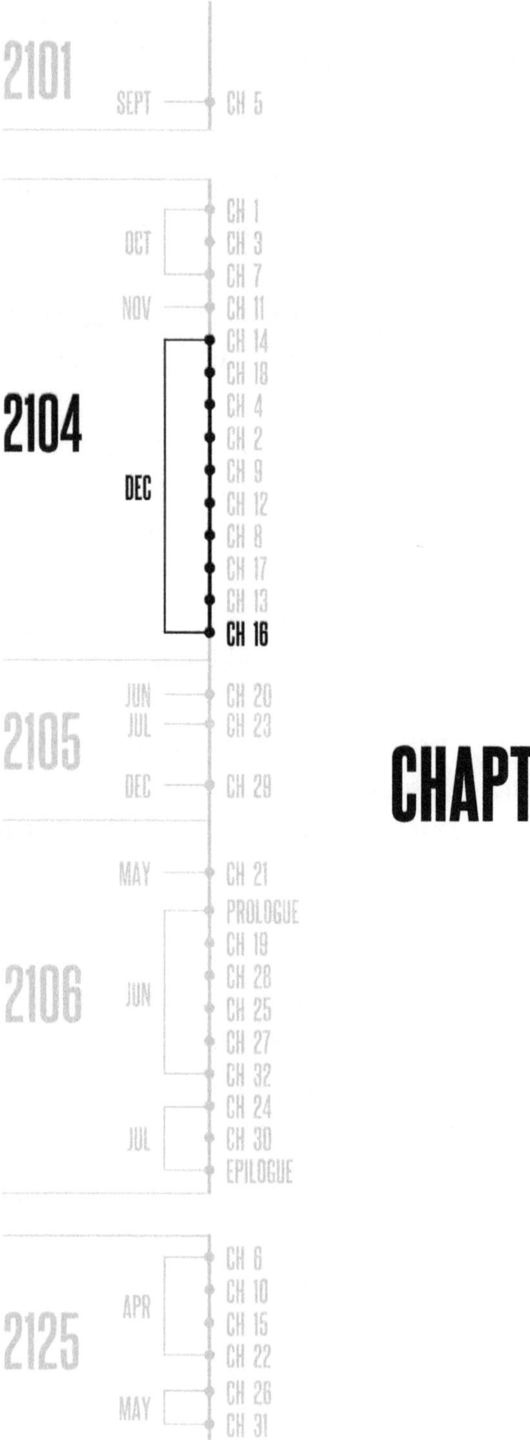

CHAPTER 16

DECEMBER 2104
Dr. Atlas

I walked from the elevator down the hallway toward the briefing room. My brain sorted through the events of the evening on repeat, and every time I reached the part where the small boat sailed away from us, I thought my rage would tear my body in two.

Then I remembered the lightning.

I was in awe of the perfectly placed storm. I felt the power come off him in waves, even from the passenger side of the truck cab. Before we arrived, I felt it like the final shockwaves of an earthquake, small and light.

The sky opened up, the lightning charged in from the sky, and a tidal wave blew against me when it hit. I barely was able to stand against its rush of energy. At first, I thought it came from Mr. Blic—Sloan—with the attack directed in front of him, but the energy burst originated from the house. It was Raven.

For a time, I watched with confusion as the scene unfolded before me. I couldn't understand what I saw—or felt. My team and I worked so hard to wake a gene that I thought only held the power to heal—the gene within me—but it seems we were wrong. I was wrong. The gene I woke was so much more.

As I considered the implications of the same gene not giving someone the same power, the same energy, I witnessed Sloan.

I was so focused on the energy I felt from Raven inside the house that I hadn't noticed the stream coming from my right. As the boat traveled behind the house, I felt the second wave, not as strong as Raven's but there, nonetheless. I yelled orders to send in more men to the house as I heard a crash, but my eyes locked on Sloan in the boat. The energy flowing from him was different, shorter, like the difference between a red and blue wavelength. The power from Raven felt like longer waves, stretched out like a red wave, while the energy from Sloan was choppier, like a blue wave.

I was lost in fascination when I felt the energy burst from Sloan. I saw him rise straight up from the boat and into the house, with trails of light flowing behind him.

There were no stairs or rope. He simply rose up, as if floating through the air, disappearing behind the house.

I was in wonder. *What can this mean?* So much changed in that moment. A higher calling crashed down into my lap, and the world was giving me everything I needed to change it.

But a minute later, the boat left the shore, with Raven aboard. I cursed under my breath. Reality came crashing back down. We lost Raven. I lost Raven.

After returning to the facility, I went straight to Dr. Logan and demanded her files on both Raven and Sloan. Arrogant, reckless, cunning, and intelligent were only some of the words she used to describe Raven, the man who now walked freely with a new power that no one understood.

All I had needed was one. But I made two.

Only that thought kept me together as I neared the end of the hallway. Two double doors led to a conference room, where five people sat waiting for me to join them. But they weren't going to be happy when I did.

I paused just before the double doors and took a deep breath. The damn vision of the boat came back to me, and I took two hard steps forward. The doors opened automatically.

I saw Dr. Logan jolt, her eyes wide and frightened. The Chief of Security—Mikhail—and Head of Tactical Operations—Harper—looked uneasy, sitting at attention, waiting for me to speak. The Director of Genetic Evaluation and Research—Dr. Maggio—tried to appear nonchalant, reviewing information on a specglass tablet in front of him. The facility's Chief Physician—Dr. Tomlan—was the only one who didn't looked moved by any emotion. As a matter of fact, he appeared bored. He was the first to speak.

"Can we skip the theatrics, please? I have piles of data to sift through, and frankly, I don't have time for this."

My eyes narrowed in on him. "I'm sorry? You have something more important to do? If you think one of the biggest discoveries of our careers walking away from us into the middle of a rather large area of land is of no consequence, by all means, get the hell out of my conference room, go back to your piles of data, and let the professionals discuss how the hell this even happened in the first place." I was yelling by the end, not caring how the anger pulled out of me.

Dr. Tomlan's face twisted into a grimace, but he said nothing.

I looked around the room face by face. "Good. Now, let me hear how we let this happen."

Mikhail spoke first, his accent thick over his perfect English. "We are still unsure how he managed to exit the restricted access area. There was no unusual activity on the scanners, and we reviewed all video footage. We have yet to find the exit they used to escape."

I practically snarled. "I suppose they vanished into thin air through the security guards that for SOME reason left their posts!"

"They received a message from you—"

"They received no such thing! Your men are completely incompetent! Why would I send a message to STOP protecting the most important assets that existed in our entire facility?" My breath came in heavy gulps, and my face burned. I forced myself to calm down, but my chest tightened. "And the footage from INSIDE the room? What of that? It shows nothing?"

Mikhail pressed his lips together. "That footage was…blank."

I stared back at him. "I'm sorry? It was what?"

Mikhail took a deep breath before continuing, "That footage will not replay from the moment he was put into the room to when my men returned to find him gone. The footage is blank. It didn't record anything."

I placed my hands on the back of the chair and squeezed. "Who was the last person to see Raven?"

He turned his head, thankful to divert my attention. "Dr. Logan."

I whipped my head over to the other side of the long table. "Tell me."

She was biting her lip for a second before steeling herself. "You told me an hour later we were to meet. I needed to confirm their state of mind was sound before I had them transported. I arrived and found no guards, which I thought was odd." She glanced at Mikhail, who scowled. "But I assumed they were in the room with the subjects, an assumption that was irrational on my part." She looked down at her hands for a moment. "It was my fault for being lost in everything going on." She cleared her throat. "Upon entering the room, I realized that it was not the case, but it was too late to turn and walk out. Raven was upset, understandably so, and I spent a few minutes reassuring him that he would get answers. I believe the only reason he was able to calm down was due to our rapport from our sessions. He believed me. I left the room about ten minutes later. I did not want to go into Sloan's room and chance the same scenario and possibly it not going as well. That's when I returned to the main hall to find the security officers."

"You could have been killed," I said, my voice laced with an edge. "We had no notion of his frame of mind. He could have attacked you. You should have waited, Dr. Logan." My voice was harsh, more so than I'd ever been with her before. She only nodded, and I felt a pang of guilt.

I turned my sights to Harper. "What's the status of your team's search for Raven?"

"We found the boat abandoned along the north east side of the bank. We reviewed satellite footage as well, but that area is so rural, no satellites were focused on that location. We've been manually searching the nearby homes and deployed tracking dogs along the countryside. Nothing as of yet."

I closed my eyes and rubbed the bridge of my nose, inhaling deeply, trying to hold myself back.

"Dr. Maggio. Tell me you have something from DNA comparisons. Anything between the two samples?"

The short man looked up from his glasstablet and only shook his head. "I'm still working on it."

I leaned forward on the desk as my blood started to rise, feeling the bubbling anger twist in my stomach. "Dr. Tomlan, what's your analysis of the patient Sloan?"

With a defiant face, he responded, "There seem to be no special qualities. He hasn't done anything different than any other human. We conducted high stress tests and changed the variables. But he doesn't react—no levitation, no anything. I don't know what I'm supposed to be looking for."

My anger flared, and my emotions spilled over. "You're supposed to be doing your jobs! All of you! Not one of you are! Do any of you understand the implications of what just happened? What we just lost because of YOUR incompetence? I don't understand how none of you seem to care. THIS is what we've been working for. THIS moment. This entire facility is built around what we finally accomplished, and all I hear is I don't know," I gestured at Mikhail, "I don't know," then to Harper, "I don't know," and over to Dr. Maggio, "and the very exciting 'I don't know.'" I flourished my hand at Dr. Tomlan.

I burned my gaze into Dr. Logan, who, although wide-eyed, sat listening and focused. I appreciated her for that.

"Dr. Logan, walk with me." I turned to stalk out of the room but paused. "I want to hear more than 'I don't know' the next time we meet or, once this fiasco is settled, you're all terminated. My reputation in this space is worth more than yours. Are we clear?" I didn't wait for a response as I walked away.

Dr. Logan's heels clicked to catch up with me.

"Why am I surrounded by such complete ineptitude? They are the highest minds, most decorated soldiers, and this is where we are," I fumed without looking at her. "Dr. Logan, how long have you been here?"

"Three years, two months, and thirty-two days."

"And in those many days, you have never failed me. You're the only person who ever understood me and what I am trying to accomplish here."

"Thank you, sir."

As we reached the elevators, I shifted to look at her. "Don't fail me now. Make sure they," I waved my hand toward the end of the hallway, "fix their damn mistakes and get me answers." I grabbed her shoulders, looking into her worried eyes. "You are my eyes and ears, and I need to know you are still with me. I am angry—so angry—but we succeeded. THAT is all that matters. So are you still with me?"

She nodded her head, eyes bright, "Yes. Yes, of course. Always."

"Great. I want the full map of Sloan's and Raven's DNA brought to my office in an hour. I want to look it over with you. Maybe you and I can find what they cannot." With that, I stepped into the waiting elevator to go to my room. The anger rolled off me in waves. *No levitation. No anything.* His jab was directed at me, letting me know that I was also wrong. I was not. I saw Sloan with my own eyes. It's not my fault that his inability to see what's there was getting in the way.

Seething, I walked to the kitchen. Perhaps some tea would calm me down so I could focus when Dr. Logan arrived. My mind still raced through the past twelve hours—success, failure, failure, failure.

I slammed the cupboard door. Failure was not something I dealt with easily. I'd been failing for so long, failing *her* for so long. I needed to finally prove to her that I deserved to be here, proof that the universe didn't make a mistake when they let me live. She couldn't walk these halls, but I could. She deserved to know that I deserved that right.

That killed me the most. The moment of our triumph, the moment of our success, walked right out the front door.

It was agonizing. The pain of failure was overwhelming. I was lost, my eyes seeing red. My breaths came in short, quick gasps. I couldn't breathe. The weight of it all hit me harder. I was crashing.

I reached for a knife from the counter and, without a second thought, placed my arm over the sink. I sliced a deep gash across the middle of my forearm. I hardly felt the pain, wrapped too tightly around the pressure in my chest. The blood spilled out and down, flowing quickly. The energy in my chest was building pressure, pushing in every direction. I held it back, willing the power in me to let me bleed. I used waves of energy to hold it back as the blood pooled in the sink.

After half a minute, I started to feel weak, heavy. The emotions subsided as my body dropped. I let go of my energy. Like a broken dam rushing in, it flooded through me and out. A red glow came from within my arm for just a moment as I watched the wound heal. My heartbeat returned to normal. My breathing slowed, and the agony in my chest calmed.

I rinsed the remaining blood down the sink and washed and dried the knife before putting it back in the knife block. With slow movements, I made my tea and sat at my usual chair after three minutes and forty-two seconds passed. As I took my first sip, the hot liquid warmed me from the inside. I took a deep breath and called out to Mendel.

"Send a message to Dr. Logan. 'Hold off on our meeting, and let the team work. We'll meet in the morning as usual. Thank you, and get some rest.'"

"Sent."

"Thank you, Mendel."

"You are welcome, Dr. Atlas."

Less than a minute later, her response came through.

"Understood. Try to get some rest too. See you in the morning."

All I wanted to do was sleep. Exhaustion overwhelmed me. As I drank the last of my tea, I stood and stretched. Maybe, for once, a few hours would settle me.

I reached the hallway when an alert chimed. *"Dr. Atlas. You have a call from Dr. Tomlan."*

"Answer."

Dr. Tomlan's voice echoed through the walls. "Dr. Atlas?"

"Yes, what is it?"

His voice sounded small, which was odd for him. "It's Sloan. He's—uh—floating."

My eyes widened. "Say that again? He's—"

"Damnit it, Garren, the man is levitating! I need you here now!"

I rushed from my room, down the hallway, and through elevators. Everything was a blur. I knew what I'd seen and was now frantic to see it again. When I finally reached the sealed doors, I was so lost in my thoughts that it took me a few tries to gain access at the eye scanner. I moved too much for it to register. I finally received the approved beep, and the door opened.

This wing contained multiple rooms connecting to a long

corridor down the middle. The room widened the farther down I traveled. I aimed for the last door on the right.

The door led into a smaller observation room, like Basecamp beside the Tester location, with a full glass wall connected to another inner room. No one was in this room, which was not protocol. I understood why when I looked through the glass to the scene unfolding in front of me.

I saw Dr. Tomlan in front of four other doctors, speaking up at an angle, toward the ceiling. From my angle, I couldn't see it. I walked forward until it came into view—the floating man in the corner.

The man looked completely terrified, eyes wide, gripping whatever he could in the corner of the room.

I looked at the floor and saw a stand flipped onto its side. Metal instruments were strewn about, including a syringe that was broken in half. Vials of blood were also broken around the room, making the small space look like a crime scene.

What happened?

I walked to the door on the left of the all-glass wall, using my palm for access. I took a breath to compose myself. All faces shifted toward me when I walked in.

"Thank GOD, Dr. Atlas. Maybe you can—"

I interrupted Dr. Tomlan. "Clear the room, please."

"What? But we—"

I held his gaze. "Clear the room, please."

Pursing his lips, he said nothing else and stalked out the door behind me, pushing past. The other three doctors followed him. Once the door shut, I turned to the control panel. With a few commands, I disabled the audio and cameras, turned the clear glass to a frosted wall, and locked the door with my own passcode.

I had no doubt that Dr. Tomlan was stringing expletives at me, but this moment wasn't his. It was mine. Turning back toward Sloan, I looked up.

"Good evening, Sloan. Is it okay if I call you that?"

"Call me whatever the hell you want, but leave me the fuck alone."

"Understood." I gazed around the room. "What happened in here? Why are you up there?"

"I don't know, man! Okay? I had my blood drawn and body poked, and then they came in with this giant needle that the guy wanted to inject into my arm. I had no idea what it was! The next thing I knew, I was up here."

Interesting. Triggered by fear. "I see."

"Well, I'm glad you do because I don't fucking get it. I'd like to get down."

I dismissed his ignorant language and grabbed a nearby chair, sitting down and looking up. "It seems you and I have something in common, Sloan."

The floating man snorted. "You and me? What could we possibly have in common?"

Don't turn back now. "I have a power too." That caught his attention. I continued. "As a matter of fact, our goal here was to find more like me. I was the first, you see. Raven, your friend, was the second, and you became our third. That makes us the only three people in the world who can do something… extraordinary."

He wasn't completely convinced, so it was time to show him.

I stood and walked over to the opposite wall of the observation room to the long counter with multiple drawers. Grabbing a sterile glass tube, I broke it on one side. I also retrieved a cloth from the side cabinet and returned to the chair.

"Are you watching, Sloan?"

He nodded. I cut across my arm, as I had many times before, showing Dr. Logan or for my own personal release of energy. The blood fell to the floor, and Sloan watched in mystified silence.

I felt my energy rush to my arm, a red glow, and then it was done. Using the towel, I wiped away the blood and looked back up at Sloan. "You are now only the third person who knows this about me."

"Why?"

"Why tell you? Because as I said, we are the same. I don't understand why I have this power any more than you do, but I am trying to figure it out. My colleagues," I gestured toward the door, "are here to help me figure you out. Then, in turn, I'll be able to figure me out."

"But why should I trust you? You chased me and Rave—"

"Because Raven was scared and didn't understand what we are trying to do. Before I could speak to him, to show him what I've shown you, he ran. He ran away from something he doesn't understand, and I want to understand. Don't you? Don't you want to know why you have this power? Why can your body hold the energy it does when we haven't found anyone else who could?" He considered my words, and I let him, giving him a moment to process.

"I don't want to be in a damn cage anymore."

"Done. I'll find better accommodations for you. But you have to promise to let us run the tests and help us figure this out. Can you do that for me?"

As in answer, he started to float down toward me, his emotions calming.

How very interesting, indeed. I watched him descend to stand in front of me.

He shifted his eyes around once he landed. "So what do I call you?"

I smiled. "I'm Dr. Atlas. Together, I know we are going to do great things."

2101
SEPT
CH 5
CH 1
OCT
CH 3
CH 7
NOV
CH 11
CH 14
CH 18
2104
CH 4
CH 2
DEC
CH 9
CH 12
CH 8
CH 17
CH 13
CH 16
JUN
CH 20
2105
JUL
CH 23
DEC
CH 29
MAY
CH 21
PROLOGUE
CH 19
2106
JUN
CH 28
CH 25
CH 27
CH 32
CH 24
JUL
CH 30
EPILOGUE
CH 6
CH 10
APR
2125
CH 15
CH 22
CH 26
MAY
CH 31

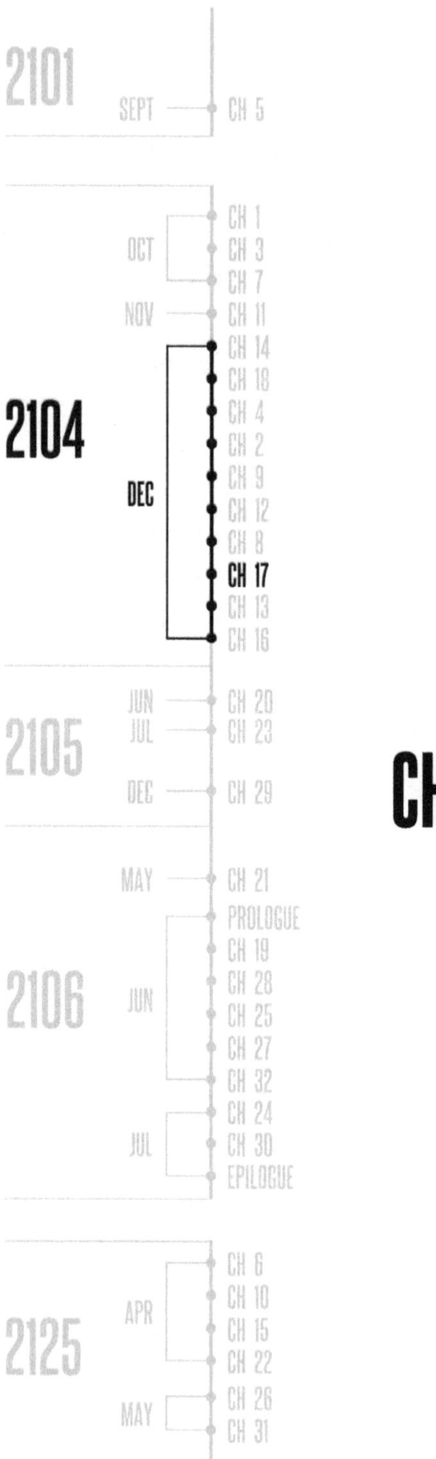

CHAPTER 17

DECEMBER 2104
Dr. Logan

He was in pain, so much pain, and it was my fault.

Raven, I'm so sorry.

Tears formed in my eyes as I watched him pull against his restraints, teeth grinding. The other Testers did the same, but I couldn't take my eyes off of him. I wouldn't leave him.

The first Tester with a white t-shirt went still first. I didn't have to look at him to see the green smoke coming from his eyes, nose, and mouth.

My heart wrenched. My stomach twisted. *Raven will be next.*

But he wasn't.

What—what am I seeing?

His body stopped trembling. He opened his eyes and looked toward the glass at me. AT ME.

There was no smoke, no green swirl. He looked at me, smiling. He was… alive. I stared back at him, blinking back my tears, and saw something even more shocking—so was the man with the long beard.

They were both alive and looking at the window as we looked back at them. I saw their mouths start to move, but I heard nothing.

I glanced over at Dr. Atlas for just a second. He was in as

much shock as I was. His face twisted with different emotions. After a moment, I heard him say, under his breath, "Haileen, I did it. Oh, my God, I did it."

He looked over and caught my eye, before I looked back at Raven, still caught in disbelief.

"I want every test, every single test imaginable, run on these two. I need to know why they are still alive." I shook my head slightly, trying to focus on his words. "Dr. Logan, did you hear me?"

I turned away from Raven and looked at Dr. Atlas, a question in my face and a darker expression on his. I'd never seen it before.

He repeated himself, his voice tense. "I need to know why they are still alive."

I nodded. "Yes, sir. I'll get—"

"Now, Dr. Logan!" I jumped at the explosion of his voice. "There is no time for talking! Just do it now!" The look in his eyes, his hard, wild eyes, scared me. They filled with unbridled emotion as he held my gaze for a moment longer, before turning to the two living men in the room.

Dr. Atlas lowered his voice, and I strained to hear him as he spoke, "We are going to figure this out, gentlemen. Even if we have to take you both apart piece by piece."

I felt a shiver run down my spine at his last words, my stomach knotting with his unspoken promise. With my heart clenched, I glanced at Raven before walking out the observatory door... *What have I done?*

My mind raced as I walked—floated—down the hallway. I didn't register the fact that I moved, the sound of my heels on the floor, or the few people who walked by me. I didn't realize I passed through doors, used scanners, and made it to the hallway to my room.

All I could see was Raven's face—the pain, the agony, and then him opening his eyes.

I felt relief, joy, guilt. I heard Dr. Atlas's voice, the strain of it, the dark emotion in every word, come through my thoughts.

Everything flooded at me all at once. I ran the rest of the way down the hallway, toward my room, pressing my palm to the scanner and rushing through the door. I felt anxiety rise up through my stomach as it constricted harder and tighter. My head started to spin as it became more difficult to breathe. I practically threw myself through the bathroom door, leaning over before my stomach heaved.

Everything screamed, spun out of control. Everything was lost. *What am I doing? What am I going to do?* So much changed in so short a time. We found what we needed. Finally.

I dropped to my knees, laying my head on my arm against the porcelain rim. I wanted the world to stop spinning, but I also wanted to stay exactly where I was, suspended between what I wanted, what I needed, and what I should do. I needed to go back to the team and start a process to run our tests. I wanted to run to Raven, throw my arms around him, and make sure he was okay. I should… I hadn't entirely decided yet. I knew I should—

A chime rang out. *"Good afternoon, Logan. Message received from Dr. Atlas."*

I stood, ignoring the stress in my head, and rinsed out my mouth before speaking. "Mika, read the message."

"Dr. Logan, I want to meet with the two men in one hour. Please see to it that it's done."

I took a steady breath. "Mika, respond. 'Will do. One hour.'"

Standing with my hands on the sink, I stared in the mirror. I looked at my face, my eyes, myself. *What have you done to get here? Didn't you have good intentions?*

Tears filled my eyes. I thought of Raven. I thought of Dr. Atlas. I saw his eyes. I heard his words.

Even if we have to take you both apart piece by piece.

I thought I'd be sick again, but after a couple of deep breaths, my eyes locked on my reflection. It didn't have to be this way. I could fix this. *Are you really going to do this?* I knew the answer before I finished the sentence.

First, I needed a key card.

Twenty minutes later, I leaned over to gain access to the Project Evolution area. Raven and Sloan were being held in separate rooms three hallways away from here. I glanced at the clockglass above the eye scanner. I had thirty minutes to get them out before Dr. Atlas came to see them.

On a regular day, walking through these halls meant encountering one or two people, but today, there were over a dozen when I stepped through the threshold. I caught my breath. I could feel the change in energy, a buzz of excitement and anticipation thick in the air. This breakthrough charged the hallways. Some weren't even going anywhere. They just waited around, waiting for news of information.

I managed to pass through the masses with only a few comments and questions and found myself rounding the final corner. The four guards stationed outside of both rooms received their new orders from Dr. Atlas—the orders I sent using Dr. Atlas's passcode from Dr. Limna's office, where I grabbed her key card—and walked the opposite direction.

Reaching the door to Raven's room, I paused with my hand above the scanner. *There's no turning back if you walk into this room.* I put my hand down and let the keypad seal my fate. I heard Raven before I saw him.

"Logan!" He rushed to me, and without any words, I threw my arms around him, pulling him close. Tears spilled from my eyes then. I could hear myself saying I was sorry, so sorry. He stroked my hair, telling me it was okay, he was okay, everything was okay.

I finally found the strength to pull back and look into his eyes, his face. He cupped my face in his two hands, wiping away my tears with his thumbs, before leaning forward and placing his lips, soft and warm, on mine. It was a sweet kiss. A welcoming blanket of emotion spread through me. I wanted to stay here, just here, with him, pressed against him.

But reality hit hard, and I pulled away. "Raven, you need to go."

He smiled and reached for me. "No. I need more of you."

I pulled back again. "You don't understand what's happening, and there's no time. Please, I need to get you out of here. They're coming for you."

The sharpness in my voice made him stop. Now he was listening. I had to lay it all out, or he wasn't going to move.

I took a deep breath and tried to steady my voice as I spoke. "Dr. Atlas isn't only using gene therapies to cure diseases. We've been—" I shook my head, feeling overwhelmed at the words spilling from my own mouth. "We've been testing ionization radiation therapy on Testers, like you, trying to change their DNA from the inside, trying to give them the ability to heal themselves."

Raven didn't look convinced. "Doc, we do that already. Band-Aids help with that, too." He smirked with sarcasm in his voice. "I don't—"

I don't know how else to say it. "We changed you, Raven, from the inside. You're the first since..." I knew how crazy this was going to sound. "You're the first since Dr. Atlas. He has a supernatural ability to heal instantly." His eyebrows pulled together, and I continued. "I watched him take a scalpel and slice himself across his forearm, and within seconds, the wound was gone. Since then, we've been trying to duplicate the results." Guilt flashed through me, but I pushed away the thoughts of the many lives lost.

"You are the first, Raven—the first to survive our tests. Your friend, Sloan, is the second. Both of you are the only ones to hold the radiation, and we need to know why. HE needs to know why. You aren't safe here, which is why you need to go."

I didn't know how to be the doctor that woke up this morning, searching through data and Tester files, uncaring of the names that passed in and out. All I saw was the end goal. All I saw were numbers, probabilities, and statistics. I looked into Raven's eyes, my own brimming with pain, guilt, and tears.

He was so much more than a number. "I'm so sorry."

I could see him thinking, processing through the little bits I gave him. Finally, he spoke. "I'm the first to live, which means... They all died?"

I nodded, the pain in my chest tightening.

"How many before me?"

"Before today," I took a shaky breath, "ninety-nine."

Disgust washed over his face, and he shook his head in disbelief. His reaction crushed me. I looked down, unable to say anything else, not even sure what I could say.

"What's going to happen to me?" I heard him ask.

I stared at the fabric weave in his shirt. "We don't know. That's why he needs you and Sloan. He needs to know what makes you two different from the oth—others."

His finger slid under my chin, and he lifted my face to his. "Look, I don't know the why, but I see you, your passion for what you do and how you believe in what you are doing. And I don't care about the rest. I care about this."

Raven leaned forward, placing his lips on mine. Warmth spread through me, and he made me feel less like the monster I was every day. I enjoyed his comfort wrapped around me for a moment longer before I pulled back.

"Please, Raven. You need to go, and I need to tell you how. I don't know what he's going to do, but I know I can't let it happen."

His eyes held mine. "How can I go? How can I just leave you here? I may not see you again."

I looked away, his words sinking in my heart. "I know. You probably won't. But you'll be alive. That's what matters." I placed my hands over his.

He looked conflicted, but I saw the resolution bloom. He knew he needed to go. He knew I was right. I could see it in his eyes. "How long do we have?"

I glanced up at the clockglass. "Maybe ten minutes."

A smile spread across his face as he pulled me closer. "That's plenty of time." His mouth was on mine before I could protest. His hands found their way under my coat, pulling at my black dress, pulling it up. He pushed me backward until I was against the wall, his body hard against mine.

I wanted to tell him to stop, that we didn't have time. But, all I could feel was his heat as he pressed my chin up with one hand, trailing his lips down my neck to my collarbone. I forgot reality for just a moment, letting it all go, melting into him. "Raven..."

His mouth was back on mine, and my arms wrapped around his neck, pulling him closer. Breathing heavily, his hot lips traveling across my jaw, he whispered, "I won't leave until I can feel you from the inside first."

I came undone.

I pulled at his shirt, up and over his head. I caught my breath at his body, exactly how I imagined it—strong, lean and absolutely beautiful. I trailed my fingertips across the bird tattoo on his neck. He closed his eyes as I moved down his chest, to the soft skin below his stomach.

His eyes flew open, changed, filled with a hunger. He grabbed me by the shoulders and flipped me toward the wall, pulling my coat down by the shoulders. I felt his breath against my neck as he pulled down my red lace straps, his lips finding my skin. He moved my dress up, moving any fabric between us. I felt his hot skin pressed up against mine when his voice came back to my ear.

"Tell me to stop, Logan. Just tell me, and I will."

I couldn't breathe. A wave of heat engulfed me, the sensation of his skin, his fingertips trailing down my hips, touching me softly between my legs. "I can't."

"Tell me why." His breath against my neck sent a shiver down my skin while his fingers teased me from the inside. I moved against him.

"Because I want you to. Please, Raven, I want you to."

He put his hand over my mouth as his thrust himself deep into me. He captured my cry between his fingers, and I bit down, moaning quietly against his skin. His face was buried in my hair, against my neck, and he whispered soft things that made me burn.

I didn't know how long we were one person, lost in how we felt, with so many words but nothing to say. We were nothing but raw need and emotion. The sensations rose higher and higher. It felt like a sweet fire, lifting me up.

When I couldn't hold it anymore, I exploded into everything around me, calling out his name, his release following mine.

Our bodies slowed and stilled. His body pressed into mine, his breathing heavy against me. He pulled my hair to the side and placed his lips on the soft part of my neck.

"Logan, how am I going to leave you now?"

Taking a couple deep breaths before turning slowly in his arms, we became two people again instead of one. "Because I'm asking you to. You said you'd do anything for me. Was it true?"

His eyes swam with emotion. "It was."

I wrapped my arms around him, kissing him softly, gently, and—for just a moment—with a spike of passion. I pulled back, and my eyes locked onto his. "Then you are going to listen to what you need to do, and then you are leaving because you have to go, right now."

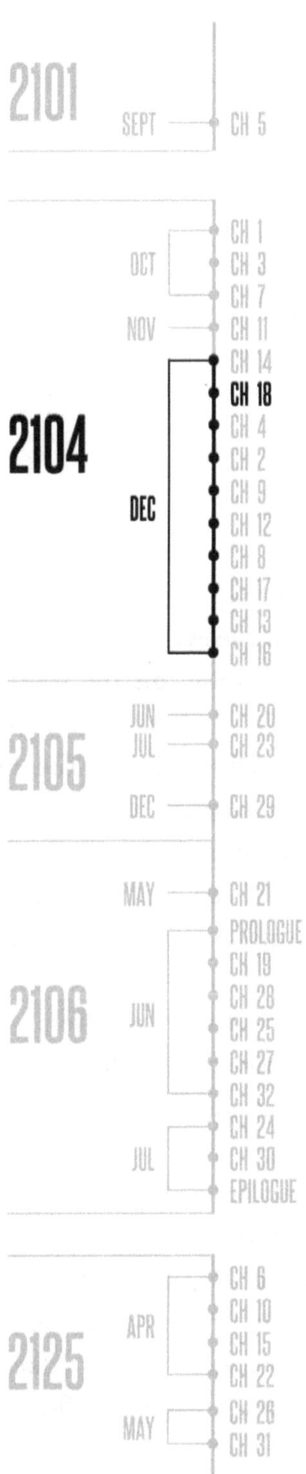

CHAPTER 18

DECEMBER 2104
Angelia

The air hummed with chatting nerds all around me, seated and waiting for the final symposium of the event. Lights from the white stage danced around the room, reflecting off the walls and across people's faces. Two large glowing pillars on either side of the bright stage projected the words "The Atlas Institute: The Esoskeleton" into the air. Almost every chair was already filled with people. The walkways filled with even more searching for a seat or walking back out to find standing room. It was the last night of RoboCon, and I could almost feel the collective sadness of the event ending.

What. A. Freaking. Ride.

I had my mind blown more than once from the different technology displayed around the convention. There was so much to see. I knew we missed a lot of it, but we tried to see what interested us the most—which was everything.

Never being into the software side of the world, it was interesting to hear the advances and the updates to many of the robots I worked on every day. Jaeden was like a kid in a candy store, eyes wide, drinking in every word. It was cute to see him so excited.

At one point, one of the software techies talked about the CleanBots' software update and how a software malfunction resulted in the sudden explosion of water from the tank in the recent weeks. I thought about Mrs. Heels, suddenly soaked and furious, before she had brought hers in for repair. I actually laughed out loud, making Jaeden turn and look at me.

"I'll tell you about it later," I whispered.

He smiled and returned his attention to the presentation. My eyes lingered on his profile for just a second before I listened with him.

RoboCon was the most incredible experience I ever had, and yet I knew it wouldn't have been the case if I went alone—or with anyone else.

Jaeden made everything just so seamless, so calm, so hilarious. Everything without stress or tension. We simply enjoyed each other's company with no awkward moments, even while technically sharing the same room. We spent our days laughing and gaping at the many companies, vendors, and even a few diehard fans dressed as robots—weirdest thing I'd ever seen—and then at night, talked for hours over dinner, enjoying the food of a random restaurant within the convention center, and returned to our room to talk more. It was like we never ran out of topics to discuss.

I tried not to think about this weekend ending, like it would never or could never be duplicated again, so I did my best to savor every minute.

A voice over a loud speaker brought me out of my thoughts. "Ladies and gentlemen, the presentation of the Atlas Institute will begin in five minutes' time. Please take your seats."

I heard someone say from behind me, dripping in sarcasm, "If there were any seats left."

I looked over my shoulder, searching the many people walking down the aisles for Jaeden, not seeing him yet. He'd gone to grab us something to munch on and a drink while I protected his seat beside me. We crammed in so much on our last day that we skipped lunch. My job was to shoo away poachers.

We planned to eat tonight, but dinner wasn't for a few more hours. And we had to go shopping. Tonight was the Close-Out Dinner, which meant an outfit other than cargo pants and a long-sleeved shirt. I actually had to wear a dress. I was not sure how it was supposed to happen in such a short timeframe, but once this was over, we were heading over to Luciole Lux down the street. I never shopped there in my life. It wasn't my style, nor my price tag, but tonight was a big night. For once, I wanted to play the part of a pretty girl on the arm of a gorgeous man.

I actually wanted to wear a dress. *What has Jaeden done to me?*

I heard his voice say, "Excuse me." I looked up as a couple of people stood up, letting him travel down the aisle. He held water bottles in one hand, two small bags in the other, and what looked like a convention promo bag hanging from his wrist.

And he was wearing a new shirt. I could only make out a white rectangle before the graphic on the t-shirt came into focus as he moved down the aisle. It said "Atlas Institute" across the front.

I looked up at him, shaking my head. "It looks like you drank the Kool-Aid too, huh?"

He pointed proudly at the shirt. "Come on, you love it." I rolled my eyes.

"Well, don't be jealous," he said, holding up the wrist with the promo bag. "You have one too."

I laughed. "I guess we both drank the Kool-Aid today. Thanks for reeling me in." He laughed with me as I moved our jackets—my sign the seat was taken, yet people still asked—and he plopped down beside me, handing me a water, a bag of pretzels, and the promo bag. I said my thank yous and was rewarded with his smile before he surveyed the room. "Holy crap! This room right now is insane."

I looked around as even more groups flooded in, and the aisles filled with standing people. "That's not a safety violation or anything."

He followed my gaze. "Yeah, no, that looks really safe. If

there's a fire, we'll just fly out the back."

I laughed. "Great emergency plan."

"Thanks. I pitched it to the convention center guys, and they were all in." I shook my head as I opened the pretzel bag, putting four in my mouth at once.

Jaeden made a dramatic face. "Are you all right? Do you want a straw to drink them with or something?"

I smacked his arm while I chewed through the crunchy snack, unable to reply. He only shook his head, opened his own bag, and angled toward the stage below us.

"I wonder what they are going to announce today. I know they've been working on the esoskeleton for a few years. I've seen most of the replays of Dr. Atlas's presentations. He's a little flashy and dramatic, but he's a genius. So he gets away with it." He popped a couple pretzels in his mouth.

I swallowed my second handful, about to ask him to elaborate, when the lights dimmed. The buzzing of voices became whispers and then anticipated silence. I gazed around the room, feeling the immediate calm of everyone. It felt like the entire world paused. It made me even more excited to see what Dr. Atlas had to say.

The room darkened, and the speaker sounded with a new announcement in an animated and excited voice. "Ladies and gentlemen, please help us in welcoming a scientist whose work in genetic engineering is changing the way the world sees diseases, a scientist whose goal is to change the world from the inside out. Let's welcome Dr. Atlas!"

The unseen crowd screamed, cheered, and roared. Hands clapped, echoing around me.

When the lights flashed back on, a man in all black and striking silver hair stood in the middle of the stage, smiling, with his hands at his sides, palms up. If it was even possible, the crowd got louder. Even Jaeden hollered along with them. *Who is this guy?*

The doctor spoke, his voice filled with energy. "Thank you!

Thank you, everyone! How is everyone doing today?" He moved around the stage, gazing around the room as the crowd cheered. There was definitely something about him. He appeared methodical and yet graceful as he moved. He stood tall and walked with purpose.

I was intrigued.

"I'm thrilled to hear that!" I heard him say. I brought my attention back to his words. "I myself am thrilled to be here and am excited to share with you the newest, the latest and greatest. Now who is ready?"

I waited until the cheers calmed down, watching the doctor smile with patience. "Okay, but first, I have a story to tell." The crowd quieted, anticipating.

The projection above Dr. Atlas changed. A collage video started playing of a young kid, no older than me, riding a hover bike, laughing with friends, and jumping off a wall to a hoop in a Flyball game.

Dr. Atlas pointed up with both hands. "This is Griffin. He has always been at the top of his class. Star Flyball athlete for twelve years. Full scholarship to Notre Dame. Loving family. A long life ahead of him."

Images of Griffin's life flashed between his sentences. "And as life does, it struck with tragedy."

The white lights of the stage darkened, as if on cue, and the image changed to a hover wreck, metal in pieces everywhere. The lights of medics flashed in different scenes.

"Griffin was in an accident. The accident should have killed him, and everyone inside, but..."

His voice faded into the background as I leaned over to Jaeden, trying to talk so only he heard. "You were right about him being flashy and dramatic." Jaeden raised his eyebrows and nodding before focusing back to the stage.

While Dr. Atlas spoke about the horrific accident, adding in details of pain and suffering, I gazed around the room. I seemed to be the only one not lost in the doctor's words. Every face, every pair of eyes, were trained to the front of the room, captivated. Jaeden's included.

I looked back to the stage. His eyes, the emotions behind them, didn't quite connect from his words to his face. His eyes were dark, hidden, and protected. But his face showed warmth and excitement, even as he told a story of destruction.

"...but it got worse for young Griffin. His entire future career was dependent on his role as star quarterback at Notre Dame. If he didn't play, he didn't get a scholarship. At the pivotal moment of his life, he lost something that day that a year ago would have been impossible to replace." He paused for dramatic effect. The crowd hushed, waiting. "He lost his entire left hand."

Gasps popped out across the room as the image changed to Griffin lying in a hospital bed, nothing but a white bandage wrapped over his arm that ended at the wrist. After a few images passed, Dr. Atlas moved across the stage, more animated.

"Griffin's hand was severed at the wrist from the impact, crushed beyond repair. At best, a perfect cut can be repaired within six hours, but by the time he and his passengers were removed from the wreckage and brought to the hospital, hours had already elapsed." He stopped walking, standing with confidence, on the left side of the stage. "And that, my friends, is where the Atlas Institute's Esoskeleton nanoarchitectonics stepped in to save this young man's body, his future, and his life." He turned toward the back of the room. "Griffin? Can you please come say hello to everyone?"

Even with the dramatics, I couldn't help but lean in as the young, blonde Griffin walked out from the back of the stage, with his arms behind his back. I don't think anyone took a breath.

Smiling around the room, Dr. Atlas leaned over to the young man, now standing beside him. "Go ahead, son. Show them."

Griffin waved to the crowd with his perfectly normal, uninjured left hand. More gasps spread through the rows. I even glanced at Jaeden, both of us awestruck.

"How does it feel, Griffin?"

Griffin smiled, if awkwardly. "It feels normal, like nothing ever happened."

Dr. Atlas gazed back at the crowd. "Let's give Griffin a round of applause for his bravery and fortitude." The crowd erupted as the shy Griffin smiled back, waving his intact hand. "Thank you, Griffin."

The kid nodded, waved again, and exited the stage to a loud roar of applause. I jumped at Jaeden's voice beside me, "Tell me I was wrong. He's good, right?"

I nodded, eyes wide, as the doctor continued. "Griffin was our first human esoskeleton patient. We have been testing our nanotechnology on the reattachment of limbs of smaller creatures, but this was a turning point, a point where we could finally use the esoskeleton for a purpose to change the course of his history. This was our opportunity to make history what we wanted, instead of leaving it to the fate of time." His eyes darkened as he spoke, his eyes wild and fevered, lost in an emotion. "For we are the ones who design history. We are the ones who make it what we want. Nothing should stand in our way of victory." For just a moment, he seemed absorbed by his words, as if he forgot where he stood, speaking to someone else, instead of a crowd of young fans.

But the moment passed, and his face lit up once more with his wide, bold smile. "Anyone want to know how the technology works?" Screams and shouts came from every direction. His smile spread. "I thought you might. Let's get to it, then. Shall we?"

Cheers echoed off the wall as the images changed above him.

For the next hour, Dr. Atlas walked us through the entire history of nanotechnology and where his company made breakthroughs like no one had before them. I was intrigued at the technology behind the nanobots and even more fascinated in his discussion about the possible effectiveness of picobots for repairing damage at the cellular level. His fevered look never returned, but the image of his momentarily wild eyes hadn't left my mind while he spoke.

It was an hour to remember, for sure.

"And that is our goal. To continue to serve our great community, pushing for ways to repair what we once couldn't. So far, we have restored seven different severed limbs, all of which healed completely from the inside. With a 100 percent success rate at this point, we are seven leaps closer to building a network of nanobots available to everyone." His arms raised in the air on the last word as the audience stood on their feet, cheering louder than ever before.

I watched as Dr. Atlas waved his goodbyes to the crowd, saying thank you even though they couldn't hear his words. I shook my head in disbelief as I looked over at Jaeden, who looked as enthralled as everyone else.

He pointed toward the stage, yelling at me over the chaos. "That man is going to change the world. I just know it."

As the doctor in black walked off the stage, his back now to the auditorium, I knew that Jaeden was right. But I still wasn't sure if it would be for the good of us all.

Rylan

I didn't know why I was so nervous. It felt like first-date jitters. I didn't understand it. We'd hung out dozens of times before today, been to dinner more than once, spent every second together for days now, and yet, right now, standing in front of the bathroom mirror, staring at my reflection, I was nervous.

Maybe because it's our last night together.

I reached for my black jacket, lying across the small table in my bathroom, pulled it on, and adjusted my collar and sleeves. I glanced at my reflection, my new black suit with a white collared shirt. I slid a white handkerchief into my breast pocket, and the overhead light reflecting off the shoes caught my eye.

I had no idea who this guy was looking back at me in the mirror. He was a guy with a future, a guy with a plan. This guy needed a gorgeous woman on his arm. These past three days had been a sweet torture. I spent every waking moment with Angelia. I constantly reminded myself that this was in fact the last time, that I was leaving after this, that I'd never hear her laugh again. I had to crush the emotion as far down as I could force it. It was too much.

Today was by far my favorite day out of the whole weekend. Going to Luciole Lux tonight gave me a chance to see Angelia in a rare state of disarray. She was always so confident and proud. She just didn't care and did what she wanted. Either way, she was always sure of her actions. But here she was, trying on dresses in uncharted territory. Being out of her element brought out the smallest of whiny and flustered tendencies, so small she probably didn't even notice them, but I did. Her voice trembled slightly at her own frustration as she tried on dress after dress. She let out a quick exasperated breath as she stared at yet another dress. And I thought I couldn't love her more.

My heart swelled every time she grabbed another handful, looking defeated and disappearing into the changing room. It took all I had not to pull her into my arms and kiss her pouting, defeated lips. Instead, I took deep breaths as waves of overwhelming emotion came over me, and for once, I let them come. I knew I'd never feel this joy again. I wanted to hold on to every wave as it crashed into my heart.

In the end, she finally picked a dark-blue gown, which I only knew from a piece of fabric that fell from the garment bag. It matched her ocean eyes, and I was anxious to see her in it.

Now we were getting ready, in our respective rooms of course. I was excited and still dreaded stepping out of this bathroom, starting my last night out with her. I pulled at my sleeves, slicked my hands over my hair for the tenth time, and took a deep breath.

Just make it a night to remember.

I stood taller. I turned, walking out through the bathroom, across my bedroom, and through the door to the living room.

Angelia wasn't out here yet, but remnants of her were strewn about—our shoes by the door, her two different pairs of black boots, a sweatshirt on one couch, and a sweater crumpled up on the other.

On the table sat a book, a real printed book. I didn't even know they existed anymore. I delighted in listening and watching her beam with joy as she told me about Sci-book release day. She lit up even more talking about her books than she had when she talked about the machines she worked on. I learned so much about this quirky, passionate, beautiful girl in seventy-two hours. I knew there was so much more to learn, so much more I wanted to learn.

I shook my head, walking out toward the balcony. I needed some air to help calm my nerves.

Stepping out the door, a breeze brushed past my cheeks. The city seemed darker tonight. Buildings blurred into each other, and against the sky, only shapes dancing across the horizon with hundreds of moving lights in the sky. It was still beautiful, even in its stillness and dark shade—

A small sound behind me paused my thoughts. I turned around slowly, and my breath caught in my throat.

Standing with her heeled toes pointed inward, her hands clasped by their fingers in front of her, Angelia stood in a sea of blue that made her eyes light up like white fire. So help me, I couldn't do anything but stare at her, feeling my heart pound in my chest.

Her long hair—that was always up, always pulled back—cascaded in waves over her shoulders. The thin straps of her dress showed skin I'd never seen before, including a patch of freckles on her left shoulder. My lips itched to touch them. The dress crisscrossed over her chest, stomach, and hips to a slit on the right, showing part of her legs and leaving the rest to mystery.

The meek, unsure, sweet, and innocent expression on her face made her look only more radiant. "How do I look?" she asked, twisting her lips into an unsure smile.

My heart answered before my mind could stop it. "Like the most beautiful woman I've ever seen."

She blushed. And my heart stopped. She looked up from under her lashes. "You look incredibly beautiful too."

We stood there, at a crossing. I knew she felt it. I could see it on her face.

All at once, my control snapped. I forgot who I was, who I was supposed to be. I crossed the space between us and grabbed her hands, pulling her to me. Her eyes locked on mine, wondering—so much wonder in her eyes. I couldn't hold it anymore. Her eyes broke me. "You are the most beautiful woman I've ever seen. I have wanted to tell you that every day since I first saw you. Your light, your energy, beams through everything you do. I felt it when we met and every time I see you. Whenever I leave you, I feel like I've lost something, like I'm not whole until I see you again." Her hands tightened around mine as I brushed my thumbs along her knuckles.

I gazed into her eyes, feeling the world inside of them as she looked back at me.

"I tried to stay away. I tried so hard, but you don't make it easy on me. The more I'm with you, the more I need to be with you." I could barely breathe. My mind told me to stop, but I couldn't. I'd already started, and I couldn't take it back.

"I know we both said we wanted to be friends. I know that I'm stepping over a boundary that we both made, but I don't think I can—I don't think I can do this anymore without telling you."

Her eyes, those blue eyes, pulled me in deeper. I fell into them, in their emotion. But she said nothing, only staring back at me.

My heartbeat echoed through me, and my stomach clenched, waiting. "Say something, please. I'm lost right now. Tell me if it's just me. Just tell me, and—"

"I think I'm in love with you." She smiled slowly and let

out a breath, like she'd been holding it for days. "I think I've always loved you, since the day you walked into my store, your eyes seeing through me. I think I've been chasing that day ever since. And this weekend, oh man, this weekend only showed me my heart was right. You are..." She trailed off, thinking, as I stood frozen, eyes locked on hers. "You are everything. You became everything so quickly. I don't know how to make you anything else. I wanted so badly to tell you for so long. I just—"

I kissed her, my lips finding a soft ecstasy on hers. Fireworks exploded in my chest. She reached up and wrapped her arms around my neck. Pulling her in tighter against me, I let everything go. With every second that passed, another rope untied from my heart.

My mind screamed the lies I used to tell myself—this wouldn't work. I would hurt her. I was going to lose her. I needed to stop. I could still stop.

I felt her tongue touch mine and heard the soft whisper from her lips. I knew then that I couldn't stop. Never again would I try to stop loving her.

I leaned over and swept her into my arms, carrying her over to the white couches. My lips returned to hers as I walked, lost in the beat of my heart.

Angelia

He tasted sweet, like honey, sugar, and spice all mixed together. He was delicious. And I finally felt found in his arms.

He set me down on the couch, gently, leaving me for a moment to remove his coat and throw it to the side before lying on top of me, pulling me against him. It wasn't enough. I wanted to feel his skin.

"Take this off," I whispered, tugging on his sleeves.

He leaned back, his side smile making my heart flutter. Standing up again, he started to undo every button, deliberately taking his time. His eyes never left mine. I sucked in a breath as he pulled his shirt over his shoulders. He stood there, his perfect skin finally bare for me to see. Under his heart, along his ribcage, three words were tattooed in black ink. *It's the journey.*

I sat up, my head level with his stomach, and traced the script with my fingertips. I heard him inhale as I leaned forward and followed the same trail with my lips. He dropped to his knees, gently pushing my legs open with both hands, and shifted his body between mine. His hands trailed behind my neck and back, luring me into a slow, deep kiss, like he was savoring the taste of me, not wanting to stop. My body started to burn, thinking, wondering, guessing how he'd feel completely bare against me.

I felt both of his hands on my shoulders. His fingertips brushed the straps of my dress, but he hesitated, unsure. I reached up and pulled both straps down. My dainty dress fell to my waist. Still kissing him, I took his hands and ran them down my collarbone, down my chest, over my breasts. I heard him groan softly through our lips. My body responded, aching now, needing his skin. I needed to feel him.

He pushed me back on the couch. His lips left mine, leaving me breathless, as he traced down my neck, across my shoulders—pausing on my patch of freckles—and down my chest. His tongue lingered on one breast, and then the other, before trailing farther down my stomach. With his hands holding my dress by the straps, he pulled the folds of chiffon down over my hips, caressing my skin as he went. Pausing to kiss under my belly button—warming me from the inside—he continued kissing down to my knees before taking off the last pieces of fabric covering my body. My heels followed shortly after.

I lay there, naked, as he devoured me with his eyes. "And I thought you couldn't be more beautiful."

I smiled up at him. "Come here. I need to feel your skin against mine." He started to lean toward me, but I stopped him. "No, I want all of you."

His smile gripped my heart as I watched him unbuckle his belt. A few moments later, his skin was as bare as mine as he lay down beside me. I closed my eyes as his fingers trailed up and down my body. I'd looked at his eyes so many times. But right now...right now, they saw straight into me. The tips of his fingers skimmed along my chin, tilting it up, so he could kiss across my neck, leaving fire behind.

My stomach knotted as I waited patiently for his lips to come back to mine. Lost in everything I held back from him for so long, I drew his body against mine, tasting him, needing him. I felt his hand move across my chest and down my stomach, finding where I needed him the most. I moaned softly as his fingers touched me gently before he pushed into me as my need grew. I felt his body respond beside me.

His lips were at my ear, pressing deeper into me. I bit my lip as I heard him speak. "Tell me what you want. Whatever you want, just tell me."

I could barely answer. Just one word was all I had to say. "You."

My heart and body fell, fading into his words, his hands. He shifted his body on top of me, lips finding mine, fingers laced together, a sweet passion taking over us both.

Then slowly, so torturously slow, he pressed himself into me, filling me gently, driving me to the edge. I tried to pull him against me, but he pushed me down with his hands, holding me, taking his time until he completed me. "Angelia," he whispered, catching my eyes, and holding me still with his gaze. "I love you. I have loved you since I met you. I want you to know that before I show you that it's true."

The emotions welled up from my heart. I couldn't say a word as he moved against me. His eyes, his silver, perfect eyes locked on mine.

We moved together. Seconds—minutes—forever—passed,

slow and filled with everything he ever wanted to say to me. He said it with his eyes, his lips, his body.

I couldn't get enough. I angled my hips to move with his as he moved deeper. Our arms wrapped around each other, our bodies intertwined. My heart swelled, and my body flew with his, in the sky, through the world, and right here, exactly where we were.

"Tell me again," I heard myself say through the pleasure building within me. "Tell me again that you love me."

His voice, soft and sensuous, complied. "I love you, Angelia." He moved faster, sensing my need, feeling it grow. "I love you like I never knew I could love before."

At his last words, I felt a white-hot light shoot through me as I pulled him closer. Hot and cold fire raced through me. I cried out as the world burst into pieces of raw need, pleasure, emotion, and love. Before I could fall back to earth, he hit the edge of the horizon and fell with me. Holding me tighter, our bodies rocked against each other slowly, breathing in the world around us, knowing it was not the same world we woke up to hours before.

He laid his head on my chest, both of us breathing heavy, hands folded together. I gazed down, seeing his hair and a small outline of his face.

"Hey," I said softly.

He tilted his head up so he could see my eyes.

"Hey." He smiled, and, as always, my stomach flipped.

"I guess we're not making the party, huh?"

He laughed through his deep breaths. "No. I suppose not."

I thought for a second. "Then can we do this for the rest of the night?" He lifted his head, leaning toward me. My body still felt the deep cascading waves as he moved. He kissed me gently. I smiled. "Or, what if we do this for the rest of forever?" My eyes found his, emotions flowing through us both. "I love you."

He took a deep breath, smiling. "I loved you first."

"But—" I started to protest, and he laughed, kissing me

again, making me forget about anything else but how his lips and his body—and his heart—felt tangled with mine.

PART TWO

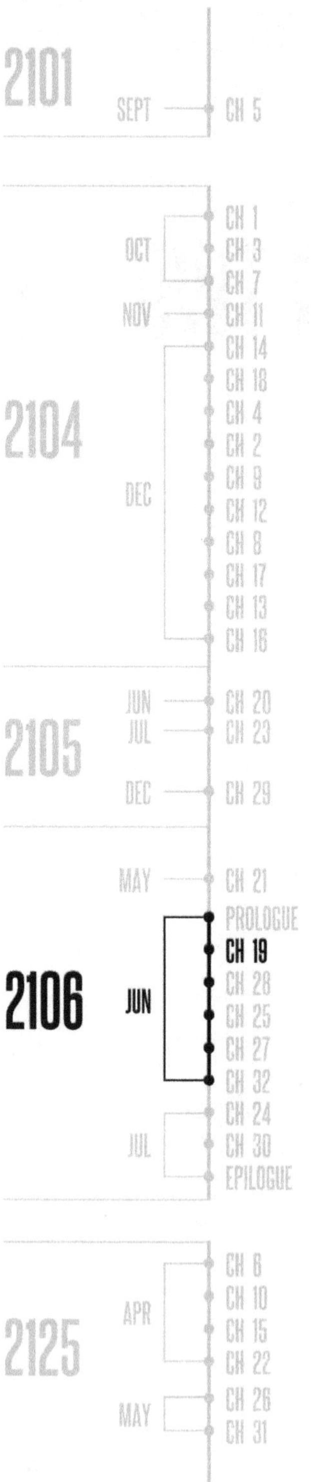

CHAPTER 19

JUNE 2106
Angelia

I lifted my black hood over my head. It wasn't cold, and I wasn't sick. I was terrified, and nothing made me feel safe anymore.

The projectionTV screen in front of me was the only light in the room, bouncing shadows off the walls. I closed the shades and curtains over a week ago. I didn't want to exist to anyone. I didn't want anyone to see me on accident.

I didn't want anyone to see what I could do now.

I pulled the strings of my sweatshirt tighter around my face while staring at the screen. The sound was on mute. It was too much to hear everyone talking. Somehow, I thought the words were less stressful, less real, less everything if I couldn't hear them. The problem was I couldn't stay away from what was happening on the news.

The news had one broadcast, always talking about the same story—the day the world went bright and people changed in New Eastland. People like me.

I glanced over at the glasstech controller on the table about four feet in front of me. I slowly raised my right hand in the air. Color swirled in my mind, grey turning to black, and I pulled at the energy. The controller flew into my hand.

The day the world went bright, and I changed.

I shook my head, feeling crazy, still having a hard time believing what I could do, and threw the controller down beside me like it was a dirty rag. I pulled my fingers back into my sweatshirt, tugging on my strings again. Only my eyes were visible now.

The projected image showed a man speaking to a reporter, the background filled with dozens of protestors. The lower third of the screen had two words scrolling across the image: SPECTRALS DISAPPEARING.

That's what we are now. Spectrals. That's what I'd been for two weeks. My eyes widened. *Two weeks? That's all?* I couldn't believe it.

Two weeks ago, my body lit on fire, and I felt the worst pain that I'd ever experienced, a pain I couldn't describe even if I tried.

But I'm not the only one who felt it, so I didn't have to.

I watched as the projection changed to rotating images of different protestors with their signs. It's a new century, and protesting was still the same. But this time, I agreed with the protestors.

The world changed when random people throughout New Eastland exhibited powers after Spectral Day—*clever name, let me tell you.* But then, many of them started disappearing, and it became an even bigger problem.

That's why I was hiding in my apartment. No one knew where they were, where they were going, or even HOW. There was no trace. They were just gone. I was terrified it would happen to me sooner than later. I shook my head trying to ignore the fear creeping into my mind and the weight in my chest.

I even missed my first Sci-book day in over a decade being locked away. In the grand scheme of everything happening, it wasn't the end of the world, but in my little world, it had killed me all day not to go. I grumbled, still filled with regret.

The only positive out of the entire two weeks was the perfectly cleaned and sparkling apartment I now inhabited. Boredom, in between waves of terror and staring at my silent projector, led me to clean.

And clean. And clean some more.

Laundry didn't litter my floor. My bed was made. I even organized my workshop this past weekend. Wires, bolts, and data boards all nestled in their place. I was actually running out of things to organize, and I could only make my toilet shine so much.

I took a deep breath and blew it out, feeling the heat from my breath inside my sweatshirt, the sweatshirt that I stole from Jaeden. Sorry, Rylan. It was Rylan. Whatever his name was, I still had moments when I wished he was here. Moments that I became so lost in missing him I thought I should throw away this black sweatshirt with the words "Neoteric Beats" across it. I remembered moments filled with his laughter and his smile. Moments—

Okay, let's not do this. We made it all the way to the evening. It was five already. I didn't want to spend the night crying. Again.

Let's focus on something else. What is on the menu for dinner?

I should just take the time and order groceries, instead of ordering every meal, but I didn't have it in me. It seemed so...normal to order groceries. I wasn't feeling—normal. I mean, me cleaning was OUT of the norm for me, so it worked. Living in darkness at all times was out of the norm. I couldn't even bring myself to read. I kept trying, but it didn't feel right, acting like nothing happened, like the world didn't just upend itself in the city.

I sighed. Sadly, missing Jaeden—Rylan—was also normal. So I didn't feel like doing it anymore.

And there it was—a wave of emotion. It crashed down on me, hard. I thought of his smile, his laugh, his hands holding mine, and his eyes when we made love. I thought of how he told me he loved me, would always love me.

I closed my eyes. *Please. Not now. I can't. I'm too tired. Too scared. Too lost to do this right now.*

Taking deep breaths, I somehow calmed my heart rate, and the knot in my stomach let go. I decided to focus and find what

I wanted to order. I looked over at my comm sitting on my tiny kitchen table, contemplating if I was really hungry enough to have to get up and get it.

Or I could just reach for it, and it'd fly across the room.

The thought scared and thrilled me at the same time. Maybe I could…I shook my head.

No, no. I'm not doing this.

I stood up more quickly than I needed to, pulled my sweatshirt mask away from my face, and crossed the room to the kitchen. Normally, I'd need light, but having turned into a nocturnal animal, seeing in the dark wasn't as hard as it should be.

Another reason why I was crazy.

I huffed for the thousandth time that day and opened the cabinet to grab a mug. Maybe another cup of coffee could hold me over while I waited for whatever I decided to order.

I pretended to ignore the mugs to the right of the door. The white one that always sat in front displayed the saying, "There's no place like 137.44.62.1." It had been a stupid software gift that I found while scrolling through random techie gifts one day. I added my apartment IP address to it and bought it without really thinking.

But the look on his face when he opened the box, like I'd given him something he never had before and couldn't have been more grateful, still lingered in my mind. He never left after that night. We added his car—the car still parked there today—to the tenant roster for the parking garage, and my apartment became ours.

It's still a stupid gift.

I reached past it to grab my yellow flower mug. The flowers themselves were carved delicately into the mug, making small impressions everywhere. The mug always lifted me up, reminding me of the beauty of life, but today—and thirteen days before—it brought me no joy. There was no sunlight to dance across the bright color, just shadows and the unknown.

I closed the cabinet door and turned to the coffee machine

built into the wall on my small counter, one perk of this small apartment. All I had to do was keep my machine stocked with grounds. The water connected through the piping in the walls. Plus, it connected to my AI. It was like this coffee made itself.

It's the small things.

Placing my grey-should-have-been-yellow mug under the brewer, I spoke, "Nikola, make me a cappuccino, please."

"Yes, Angelia."

I made a face. My voice sounded so strange to me, probably because I hadn't heard a voice in days now. No news. No family. No friends. There was no one who needed to check on me anyway.

I silently berated myself for being so damn dramatic this evening and grabbed my comm. The HubSpot was my go-to and listed all of my recent orders. All of my credits were going to the HubSpot, judging by the number of restaurants and cafés as I scrolled. I wonder if—oooh—The Sunshine Bistro had a two-for-one carne asada burrito special. That could be dinner today and tomorrow.

I clicked and swiped through the prompts, placing my order. A popup alert told me my food would arrive in twenty to forty minutes.

I can think of a few things we can do for twenty to forty minutes while we wait. The memory hit me like they usually did, reminding me what I lost and what changed. His voice matched the mischievous smile as he pulled me into his arms. The food ended up sitting outside for another hour before we got to it.

I shook my head. I needed to do something else besides think. I needed to clean something.

Two hours later, my kitchen smelled like lavender Lysol, which was to say it just smelled like chemicals. They all smelled the same—harsh and strong—but I was sure my kitchen was saying thank you. I cleared out all of my cabinets and the pantry and wiped down everything before putting it all back. I finally stopped to enjoy my now-cold burrito.

As I did after most of my long cleaning stretches, I decided to take a shower. I always felt like the chemicals seeped through me with all the dirt, and I needed to scrub it all away. Besides, a nice, warm shower before I posted myself in front of the projector screen again sounded like a great idea, except when I got lost in memories of Rylan.

I usually could make it halfway through my shower before my mind lost its exhausting battle. I tried not to think about him. I couldn't help but think about him. If I was lucky, I made it through without all of the emotions spilling over into tears. Considering my earlier episode, I doubted it, so I opted for a short shower, just to warm up and rinse. I was in and out in less than six minutes.

Ten minutes later, I was dry and dressed in my favorite red sweatpants that tapered tighter to the ankle, with the word LOVE in white down my calf. I put on my cropped white tank top with no bra—*because why?*—and threw on Rylan's stolen sweatshirt. It didn't smell like him anymore since I'd been wearing it so much. I couldn't remember the last time I wore a different sweatshirt. I did wash it, though, due to some random, accidental food happenings. It didn't stop me from occasionally thinking his scent was nearby.

With my hair braided to one side, I grabbed a refilled water bottle from the fridge and made my way back to the couch, reaching for my comm on the kitchen table as I went.

I jumped as it pinged, with my hand hovering over it. It wasn't just any ping. It was a specific ping—Rylan's ping—one that I hadn't heard in over six months. He had made it just for him so I would know when he messaged me.

My hand froze above the comm, and my heart froze in my chest.

I'd waited for months to hear from him. I begged the universe one day and then told it to forget my request the next. But mostly, I waited. And now I couldn't get my hand to move to see what he finally decided to say to me.

"Good afternoon, Angelia. You have a message from Jaeden. Would you like me to read it to you?"

My heart skipped. I never changed his name in my comm. I didn't know which was harder, hearing the only name I knew him by or knowing it should be something else.

I knew if I didn't answer, Nikola would read it anyway, but I couldn't decide what I wanted.

"Angelia, now reading your newest message. 'I know I am the last person you want to hear from right now, but I need you to listen to me. They know what you can do, and they are coming for you. They are coming right now.' Would you like me to send a reply?"

I stood in shock and confusion. I grabbed my comm and opened the message to read it again. As I reached the end, a new message popped in.

"I know you're reading this. Please, I need you to pack a bag, only the essentials. But you need to do it now. Message me back when you're done."

I stared at the words, trying to process what was going on. *Who are "they?" How does he know they are coming? And how does he know I am reading his messages?* I looked around the room. All the windows were still shut. How could he—A chill went up my spine. *Is there a camera in the house? Is he watching me?*

My heart pounded. After everything I found out… maybe it was true…

I shook my head. I needed to focus. I considered putting my comm down and ignoring him, but I kept reading the same part over and over again.

They know what you can do, and they are coming for you. My fears realized in one sentence.

Whatever this was, I didn't think I could ignore it. Another message came in.

"We are running out of time."

My heart pounded, wanting, wishing, but my mind told me

my next decision would lead to regret and, soon after, more pain.

"Angelia, please, I will explain everything."

I finally moved. Running down the hallway into my room, I rushed to my closet and grabbed my black-and-grey duffel bag. With everything in its place, packing a bag in thirty seconds was much easier. I snatched as many long-sleeved shirts, tank tops, and cargo pants as I could, one handful at a time before moving to my drawers and scooping out bras, underwear, socks, t-shirts, and sweatpants. I pulled out my favorite black boots and threw my high tops into the bag. I stopped quickly in the bathroom for five items for washing, brushing, and conditioning and darted back down the hallway to my kitchen table. Grabbing my cup of pens, paper pile, and lighter, I set them gently on top of everything else before adding in my specglass tablet, chargers, and five of my favorite books.

I was stepping into my boots as I received a new message.

"If you're done, I need you to do one more thing. I need you to move the couch and table out of the way to the other side of the room."

I read the message twice, confused, before a knock at the door drew my attention. My heart skipped.

"Angelia Solis?"

I looked down at my phone as it buzzed again.

"I know they're there. They won't stay outside the door for long. Did you move the couch and table yet?"

Another pound at the door. "Angelia, we know you are in there. Please open the door. We need to speak with you."

"I know how crazy this sounds. Please, if you only trust me one more time in your life, let it be today."

I pushed back tears. Too much, this was all too much. But I didn't have time. I needed to move the couch. I pushed my comm into my pocket, dropped my bag, and rushed forward.

I took a breath—ignoring another harder, more frantic knock—and pushed the couch off the rug to the other side of the room before doing the same with the table.

I pulled out my comm and typed back: *"Done."*

"Okay, stand by the kitchen and be ready. Don't be scared."

I didn't understand anything. The pounding became steady, and the angry tone of the man calling my name got louder. I tried to breathe.

Don't be scared? Right now, I'm terrif—

A bright, blinding light, with multiple strands of yellow light, swirled around in a circle. Small specks of light danced around. The circle of light grew wider until it was suddenly gone. Instead, there in the middle of my rug, in my living room, where I'd seen him hundreds of times was Jaeden—Rylan. He stared at me with those same beautiful eyes.

Even after everything, it still took all of me not to run and throw my arms around him. He crossed the room and took the bag from me.

"Come on. Let's go." He grabbed my hand and pulled me back toward the living room, but I held fast, feet planted. The yelling got louder outside the door, and I was frozen where I stood. I couldn't move.

And then he stood in front of me. His face was the only thing I could see. His eyes locked on mine, big and beautiful, and for a moment, I saw my Jaeden. I saw the man I'd loved for almost a year and mourned for the last six months.

"Angelia. Please."

I let go. I nodded and let him lead me back to the rug. He slung my bag over his shoulder. He stood me in front of him and wrapped his arms around me, his lips near my ear.

"This is going to feel weird."

I glanced over at the news still projecting in the air. The lower text banner now displayed new words. HOW DID THIS HAPPEN. Before I could take in a full breath, faintly aware that my door burst open from the outside, shards of wood scattering in every direction, my body felt as though it shrank and expanded all at once.

I was light, and I was darkness. I was wide. I was thin. My skin stretched and felt like water rushing over me. I spun, tumbled, and flew. I closed my eyes tight and reached my arms over his arms, across my chest, and held on until— The world came back to me. My body stopped moving. All was calm.

I opened my eyes. We stood in a park. I looked up at the skyline in front of me—New Eastland. I felt his arms around me, and for just a moment, just one more, I felt him close to me before letting go of him and pulling away.

"We need to go. Come on." He started walking toward a black hover van parked a few yards away, engaged and floating inches above the ground.

I didn't move.

He turned around, looking at me. He let out a breath. "Look, I get it. There is so much happening right now. I want to answer all of your questions. I do, but I need to get you out of here first. Can we do that? Then you can ask me anything. Let me just get you safe."

Dozens of thoughts and emotions—pain, anger, confusion, shock, awe—ran through my head. I just teleported from one part of the city to another. The love of my life was a Spectral like me. We just ran away from who the hell knew. Everything felt upside down.

Of the many things I wanted to say, I couldn't voice any of them. It was all too fresh and overwhelming. I chose to simply nod and walked toward him, climbing into the passenger's side. As he set the sequence to take off, I glanced behind me into the van's interior. One side of the back was a desk with multiple monitors, keyboards, and wires, and the other had been built into a makeshift bed. The very back of the van looked like piles of clothes and random belongings.

I turned back to the front and caught his eyes on me. Pain flashed in his eyes before he turned back to the front window, acknowledging the sequence on his dashboard, and finally setting off toward a main street.

I didn't know who this man was beside me or how he had pretended to be someone he wasn't for so long. But I knew he was here now. I knew I should feel anger. I should have been furious with him. I should feel the pain of hating him. I should have been lost in the days I wished he never existed.

But I didn't feel anything but an odd hum coming from inside of me and from beside me. I dismissed it as a side effect from warping through space.

I closed my eyes for a moment, numb to everything.

I would process all of this later. Let my emotions flow later. I'd be angry later. Right now, I opened my eyes, stared out my window, and watched my home, my city, fly by for what very well could be the last time.

After two weeks of feeling terrified, wrapped in my own haunted thoughts, I found a strange kind of peace beside him.

CHAPTER 20

JUNE 2105
Dr. Atlas

Green smoke spiraled into the air. I punched the table in front of me, making everyone in the room jump, including Dr. Logan.

I didn't apologize. I simply stood there, staring at the three dead Testers before me.

This was the twentieth attempt to duplicate Raven and Sloan's results. We spent the last six months combing through every aspect of Sloan's DNA. We found the gene—the one that matched mine, the one that changed a human into something more—and yet we couldn't seem to replicate the results.

Although the two men stood right where these bodies were now, although we saw—I saw—with my own eyes, felt through my own energy what they could do, although we tested Sloan and over the months helped him control his ability, although all of this happened, it's like it didn't exist if we couldn't DUPLICATE it.

I closed my eyes and took a deep breath. *If only I had Raven.*

His DNA compared against Sloan's and mine would yield three points of data. With three points of proof, we could figure out this elusive puzzle. The usual anger began to bubble and rise as I thought about him escaping, but I pushed the flood of emotion back down. The past was the past. I needed to move above it.

Dr. Logan cleared her throat beside me. "Excuse me, Dr. Atlas." I almost cringed at the sound of her meek, soft voice. Raven's escape seemed to affect her, defeat her, change her into something weaker, something—less.

It annoyed me. There was so much to discover, and she seemed to have lost her passion. I didn't have time to bring it back for her. I clenched my fists and finally turned toward her.

"What, Dr. Logan?" The words came out harsher than she expected, and I saw her eyes cloud as she stared back at me.

"I—I was just going to say that the data is coming in, a-and—"

"What data? The data that tells me we failed again? Thank you for your proficient ability to state the obvious." I scanned the room. All eyes rested on me. "How many more geneticists does it take to find ONE matching gene pair?"

"Dr. Atlas, I—" Her face scrunched up with—I didn't know—regret, remorse, maybe pity. For herself or for me, I couldn't tell. Either way, it brought my anger boiling to the surface.

I waved her off. "I don't want to hear any more. I'll be in my room. Notify me when you find another way for us to fail."

I stormed out, unable to look at her expression any longer. I knew I should be compassionate. She felt guilty, like it was somehow her fault the subjects escaped. I knew that. I could see it in her eyes every time it came up in conversation. She needed to get past it. There were hours of researching and continued, never-ending mapping to do. I had to figure this out, and she needed to help me. So far, her observations into the complete DNA maps from Sloan and Raven before they changed brought us insight into other aspects of their DNA that could cause a difference. She made eight discoveries of matching pairs in the sequences between Sloan, myself, and Raven. Without having Raven's DNA after he changed, we played more of a guessing game without an answer key. Every time she found a combination that could be the trigger, though, we found Testers and attempted the same range of ionization radiation as Sloan and Raven.

None of them worked. None of them survived. None of it made a difference. My eyes trained on the wall in front of me as I tried to regulate my breathing.

I didn't see the doctors, scientists, and assistants who walked past me, people who had worked with me for years. They were all just a blur as I clambered down the hallways, turning automatically toward my destination, stopping only briefly to scan my eyes before continuing back to my room.

My room was dark when I walked in, and I didn't bother turning on any lights. I just wanted to sit. I didn't even want to think. I felt as though all I did was think, and none of it helped.

I saw the glow from my techscreen in the corner of the room, and five minutes later, I combed through strands of DNA, thinking with a cup of tea in my hand. A double helix reflected as a 3D projection in the air as I spun and twisted it, comparing it to another beside it. My DNA and Sloan's were almost identical. Almost—

A chime sounded. *"Dr. Atlas, you have a call from Dr. Tomlan."*

"Answer."

Dr. Tomlan's voice came through in the middle of a sentence. "—you please relax?"

I heard a voice in the background, yelling, "I want Dr. Atlas here now!"

"Okay, okay!" I heard Dr. Tomlan reply.

"Mendel, disconnect the call, and message Dr. Tomlan. 'I'm on my way.'"

"Yes, Dr. Atlas."

Sloan. I pinched the bridge of my nose. This man was slightly infuriating on his own. Not being very bright didn't help matters. I felt like I was babysitting a child—a child with an unexplainable superhuman ability. At least Raven had some fire, some confidence. He wouldn't have needed to be coaxed and coddled every day. But

Sloan…

I shook my head, took one more sip of my tea before closing down my techscreen and placing my cup by the sink.

I crossed the compound before exiting out a door. We reconstructed the back living quarters into his space. We knocked down walls and created a two-story space where he could practice his levitation. He demanded an all-tech living room and a large bathroom with a hot tub. I was happy to oblige it all, as long as he kept letting us run tests. Most days he did, except for days like today, apparently, where he went off and became uncooperative.

I placed my face in front of the scanner, and the doors opened. The hallway was carpeted, as were all of the other rooms. We originally added hardwood floors, but one bad dream caused him to float. He fell—quite hard, I may add—onto the floor, almost breaking his elbow. We since added the thickest, most plush carpet manufactured to every room.

I passed through the living room, the kitchen—although he didn't need one with our new chef Henri and his team—and the back double doors that opened to the two-story section of Sloan's home.

He sat in the upper left corner, much like I found him the first time we met, but this time, his arms were crossed over his chest. His expression was not one of fear but of twisted anger.

Dr. Tomlan sat in a nearby chair, glasses on his face, reading on his specglass tablet. Out of the corner of his eye, he saw me enter, hands behind my back.

"Oh, good. The calvary has arrived." He swept past me, whispering as he went. "Good luck." With that, he walked out the door.

I looked up at Sloan. I adopted a friendly face and held my annoyance at bay. "Good afternoon, Sloan. What seems to be the issue?" *Today?*

He started in as soon as I finished my sentence. The few phrases I actually caught in his rambling anger included "tired of being here," "you said it was temporary," and "when can I leave?"

Just the usual issues it seems.

"Why do you want to leave? You have everything you need right here—food, shelter, all the technology you can buy. What else do you want?"

"I want girls, man. I want to fuck someone. I've been in here for almost six months, and there ARE. NO. GIRLS."

Oh, dear God. Is this what my life had become?

I kept my face on an even keel, not chancing to offend him with my revolted reaction. "Ah, I can see the trouble. Do you want me to have someone brought in? Perhaps regularly?"

I saw his eyes light up as he lowered himself from the ceiling down to where I stood. "You—you can do that?" He practically drooled at the thoughts in his own head.

I smiled then. "I can do anything."

He ran his hand through his hair, smiling back at me. "I—that—yes. I want you to do that."

"Consider it done. I will send in one of my assistants to get your—uh—type, and we'll see who we can find." I looked around the room and tried not to grimace at the sight of clothes, dishes, and random other things strewn about. "And I'll see about getting a caretaker in here to straighten up for you. How does that sound?"

He beamed. "How does that sound? It sounds amazing! I mean, this isn't as easy as you made it seem. You know? I just sit around. Let people run tests. That's it. No, this is hard, really hard. Levitate here. Levitate there. Can you make this thing levitate? No, no I can't! And I'm tired, man. I'm so tired. I just—" He ran his hand through his hair again. "I just don't even feel like I'm human anymore. You know?"

A shock went through me, and I stilled. "What did you say?"

He looked at me, confused. "I said I just don't even feel human anymore. Why? What's up?"

My eyes widened as I stared back at him. "You're a genius."

He looked almost frightened at the wide-eyed, crazed expression on my face. "Um, okay, thanks?"

I turned and rushed toward the door. "I'll get someone here to talk to you about—uh—the girls. I have to go. Sorry. Um, let Dr. Tomlan do whatever he needs in the meantime. Deal?"

I didn't look over my shoulder as I raced out the door, hearing him respond behind me.

Dr. Tomlan sat on a kitchen stool as I ran by him, not saying anything. "Dr. Atlas? Hey—Garren? What's—"

I didn't hear his words either as I went through the door to the hallway. I pulled out my comm as I crossed the distance to the other buildings, barely breathing. My message to Dr. Logan went through as I crossed back into my building. Instead of turning left toward my room, I went right to the large conference room. The techscreen was larger and could show us more detail.

I reached the room and started the display as Dr. Logan walked in, eyes wide and concerned.

"Dr. Atlas? What is it? Is everything okay?"

My eyes blazed, and I felt like I was floating. "You've been looking in the wrong place, my dearest Dr. Logan. The wrong place." I pulled up the command to show the double helixes I was reviewing earlier in my room. A few seconds later, the three before-radiation DNA sequences now projected side by side—first mine, then Sloan's, and Raven's.

She stared at me, eyes focused, unclouded for once. Her curiosity was piqued.

I pointed to the DNA strands. "Here we are, normal humans going about our lives. There's nothing new, nothing special, about us. It's boring DNA that you and I could map in our sleep, yes?"

"Yes." The light from the projection danced off the walls and reflected in her eyes as she listened.

I swiped across the techscreen. The DNA strands disappeared, and another two loaded—mine and Sloan's after we were exposed.

"Cells may contain the same sequence of DNA, but not every gene within every cell is active. Millions of combinations occur simultaneously across the body."

"Yes, I know. That's Genetics 101."

I looked over at her, happy to see her fire return, even if just for a moment. "You've been searching through them all to find the one that allowed this superpower—this unnatural gene—to activate or mutate. I know now we've been looking in the wrong place."

She looked anxious, waiting, holding her breath.

I typed in a command, holding my hand above the key to enter it. "The DNA sequence that makes us human, that marks us as human, the few genes in our body that ONLY humans have—"

"The Triad. Yes, go on."

I smiled. "What if what makes us human is what changed? What if the Triad itself changed?"

Her eyes went wide. "But that would mean you wouldn't be—"

"Human anymore."

I entered the command on the keyboard and held my breath. The double helixes twisted in front of us, and the computer brought the Triad sequence into view. I heard her gasp.

There in front of us, highlighted with perfect precision, was what used to be the Triad sequence. Humans were the only species with this combination of genes—the 1 percent of what made us different from our primate cousins.

Instead, a new, bold sequence was marked as an error. The word unknown blinked across the top of the screen. I put my hands on the desk to steady myself as I looked at Dr. Logan, tears streaming down her face.

I stood in disbelief, staring at the blinking word. Minutes passed until I finally found my voice. "That, Dr. Logan, is what evolution looks like. We ARE evolution."

She covered her mouth with her hand, wiped at her tears,

and cleared her throat. “Congratulations, Dr. Atlas. You finally did it. You found the evolution gene.”

“No. Dr. Logan, we did it.” I shook my head, still in a fog. “Do you remember what I said to you at your interview so many years ago?”

She smiled. “How can I forget? You said ‘Let me show you how you’re going to help me change the world.’”

I nodded. “That I did.” I gestured to the sequence. “And today, we did that together. Today, we changed the world.”

Emotion flooded through me, and tears welled behind my eyes. I closed them, remembering everything it had taken to get here. “I did it, Haileen. I promised you I would. I did it. I kept my promise.”

My tears fell as I imagined her smiling down on me, proud of what I’d done.

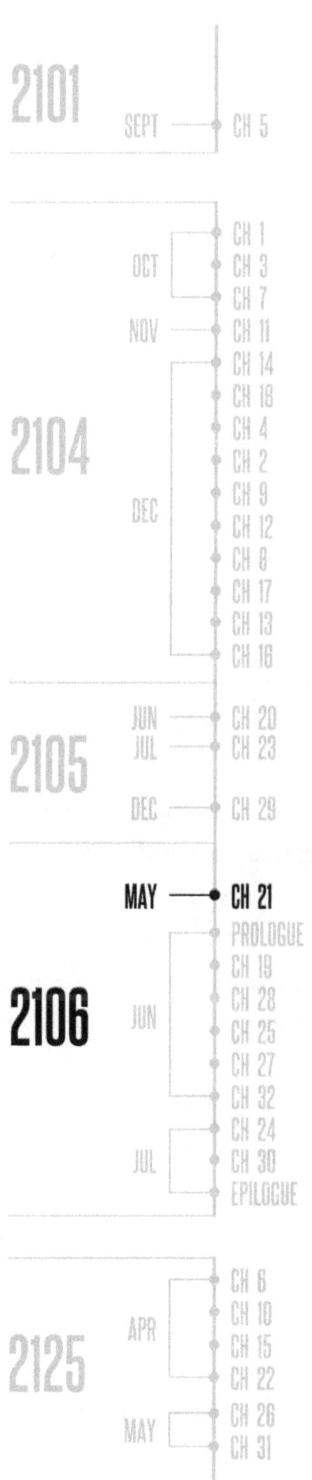

CHAPTER 21

MAY 2106
Raven

I felt her shudder against me, both of us wrapped up together, with her legs over mine in the middle of her bed.

At this point, I guessed it was our bed, but I didn't really feel that way. It was hers, and I didn't want it. To be honest, I didn't even really want her either.

She rocked her hips against me, letting her head fall back, smiling. More out of habit, I leaned forward and kissed her neck, and I heard her sigh. She started to laugh.

"My goodness, if you aren't a gift from Heaven just for me, Raven." Her voice had a little country in it, which was actually one of the things I still liked about Moira. In the beginning, there was plenty to like about her.

She was, for one, drop-dead gorgeous—blonde hair down her shoulders, bright blue eyes, and a body that, for months, I couldn't keep my hands off of for longer than a night or two. I found myself waking her up in the middle of the night, my mouth finding her sweet lips between her thighs before she was completely awake. She helped me forget the compound, the tests, and the redhead. I could almost forget my redhead.

If ever I got lost in thoughts or emotions, I just grabbed

Moira and did what we seemed to do rather well together. Her cries off the wall kept me grounded and focused on her, on where I was, that I was hidden.

I didn't want to think about the future, where I wanted to go, or what I needed to do. I just wanted a place to stay, a woman to fuck, and food to eat. But there were times that all I could see was red hair and sharp eyes.

"Raven? Did you hear me?"

I snapped back to the girl sitting in my lap and smiled. "Sorry. I was lost in your skin, honey. What was that?"

She giggled, another cute sound of hers that simply faded into the mundane over time. "I said I need to take a shower and get to work."

"Oh, okay. I guess I'll have to let you go, then." She smiled as I kissed her, holding her just an extra second, before letting her pull away from me. She walked naked toward the shower, and I noticed, for the first time, the sun rays streaming in through the windows in front of her.

It wasn't that I didn't care for this girl. I did. Moira saved me when I needed her. I found her at a local bar in Syracuse shortly after I dropped off the truck at a station nearby. She was visiting for a work trip. The next morning, she planned to drive home.

We talked all night, drank all night, and then walked to her place and fucked all night. I told her I just happened to be heading that way for a trip to visit family in New Eastland. She was more than happy to give me a ride. She invited me to stay the first night with her when we reached South Albany—an even bigger city, even more people, a better place to get lost—and I just never left.

That was over a year ago.

Moira worked every day at some city job located deeper in the city, so she left early in the morning and came home late. She also worked a second job on the weekends, which meant she was gone Friday and Saturday nights too. I stayed at her house all day and kept it clean, cooked dinner before she got home, and made sure she was satisfied every day, one way or another. I'm sure no one had ever given her body the attention I did.

She got all of me, and I got to hide away, forgetting a little more every day about how, once upon a time, I could control storms. It was a perfect arrangement. I lay backwards on the bed, closing my eyes to fall back to sleep. With nothing to do for a few hours. I might as well get more beauty sleep. It's what I did all day anyway. All day. Every day.

A little while later, I woke up slightly to a soft kiss on my lips. I heard her whisper, "I love you, Raven. I'll see you later." A ball of anxiety twisted in my stomach as I pretended to be asleep, like I hadn't heard her.

I'd never said those words back to any woman before, but I'd heard them enough times to know how dangerous they were for everyone involved. The closest I ever came—to knowing that feeling—was with the doctor in the double-strap black heels.

I shook my head. I wasn't starting my day with these thoughts. I rolled over the opposite direction and pushed the sheet off of me, letting the cool air from the morning touch my hot skin. I heard the front door close before I settled in and fell back into blackness.

I placed the two plates of baked stuffed shells on the table when I heard Moira come in the door. She wore black slacks with a white, flowy, button-up top. Her hair was ironed straight, but it still framed around her face. She looked like power and smiled like sweetness, and yet these moments didn't offer me anything—no rush, no emotion. It was actually frustrating. I had a great thing here. Instead of just enjoying it, I had to put on a show.

"Hey, babe. How was work?" I asked her, turning back to the kitchen to grab the salads.

I heard her heels drop by the door as I came back into the dining room. I looked at her. Her face twisted with emotion.

Oh, no, she had a bad day.

I set the salads down. "What happened? Rough day?"

She burst into tears, and I rushed to her side. The sounds of her overwhelmed cries hit me like a brick. I pulled her into my arms. I couldn't handle it when she cried, when any woman cried. Not much affected me. I could get through anything. I had been through more than I wanted to remember, but this—these tears filled with pain and distress—was my Achilles heel. I hated feeling useless, like I couldn't fix it. It made me feel as if I couldn't fix anything, ever.

All I could do was what I did best—distract her.

I pulled her into my arms and started with her lips, kissing them softly to calm her, to stop her tears. I played gently with her tongue. She responded, kissing me back, forgetting her tears. I unbuttoned her blouse and let it fall to the floor. I left her lips and kissed down her neck, pulling her to me, making her sigh as I kissed lower. I unclipped the top of her pants and slid my hand down, finding where I need to touch her to make her forget, to make her calm again.

I moved deeper into her, kissing her, moving until I felt her build as high as she could before crying out, arms around me, lips on mine.

After a minute, she let me go, and I pulled back, kissing her forehead. "Feel better?"

She smiled at me. It was a beautiful smile. Her smile said so much, but it meant nothing to me. At least she wasn't crying anymore.

"I'm always better when you're around." I knew she meant it, which pained me. I kissed her softly before turning back to the kitchen to grab the rest of our dinner.

I heard her pull out her chair at the head of the table and sit down. "What'd you do today while I was out?" she called out from the dining room. This question came every night as if she expected me to give a unique answer. I returned with a side of asparagus and rolls and placed them beside the shells. "I read, watched TV, and cleaned up a bit." I sat down beside her. "I cooked dinner and then just waited for you to come home." I reached over and grabbed her hand. She gave me a light smile before grabbing her fork and looking over the food in front of her.

"This looks great. Thanks for dinner."

"Of course."

We ate in silence for the next few minutes, which was odd. She usually told stories or shared gossip, but she seemed distracted. Somehow, I got the feeling that my distraction wasn't strong enough to keep whatever it was in her mind from jumping around. I kept silent, not wanting to be a trigger.

I turned my own attention away from her and looked around the room. The house was an old cottage. Parts of it were converted into an apartment. The bathrooms and kitchen were upgraded to be more modern, while the rest remained as it had been. There was still a half wall near the entrance and small windows throughout. It was one of the few closed-concept homes I'd been in. It was tight and cozy. Moira added her own touches throughout.

I glanced over at her. *Here is a beautiful girl with a gorgeous body and great home. What is my problem?*

I took another bite of a shell when she finally spoke. "Raven, what are we doing?" Before I could say anything, she continued. "I mean, this is great." She gestured at the food. "You are great." She gestured at me. "What we do together is amazing." I couldn't help but smile when she said that part. "But I can't keep working, and you just sitting home all day. Our lives can't be like this forever. I mean, this apartment can't hold a family. We need more space."

And there it is. Shit.

We had this conversation at least three other times before, but judging by the serious expression on her face, this wouldn't go away with some finesse. It was only going to go away with a lie.

"Then I'll get a job. I'm sure there's something in town I can—" She pushed back her chair before I could finish my sentence and jumped into my lap, kissing me.

"I told them you would. They said you were just using me, my home, and my money. It made me so angry, but I told them we had something more than that, more than they could see." She kissed me again.

I played along. I smiled and laughed as we tumbled to the floor, all the while thinking and calculating how the hell I would get out of here. How long could I push this off? How long until I had to find a new home?

I barely felt her take off my shirt as I tried to get lost in my thoughts of the future. Flashes of red hair came to my mind. I didn't respond as I moved in her, hearing her say she loved me, remembering how soft Logan felt in my arms.

I felt even less as we lay breathless beside each other before Moira moved to get ready for her second job that night. All I could see were double-strap black heels.

Less than an hour later, I kissed Moira goodbye for the second time that day. Her eyes were so full of light and hope. It took more than usual to push the guilt down.

I watched the headlights of her black sports hover pull out of her driveway and disappear around the bend of her street. I quickly changed into the clothes I mentally picked out—my grey shirt, worn black jeans, black boots, topped with my leather jacket—and walked out the door. Moira's other IDfob nestled in my hand.

I just need to get out of the house. She wouldn't be home until about 4 a.m., if it was her usual shift. I had a few hours to get lost in bottles of alcohol and music. Moira's apartment was at the tip of downtown South Albany. Farther down, closer to the river, there was more life, more bars, more excitement. But that's not what I wanted tonight. I wanted a clear glass that didn't run empty.

I took a left at the end of the curve toward The Wild River Pub, already feeling lighter as I drove closer. There were no lines outside the door, no security, just a door and an entrance. I felt mentally fried and wanted to numb for a few hours. Tomorrow, I'd figure out what I should do next. Maybe moving along was in the cards now. No one had come to find me since I escaped. Maybe I was safe. Maybe I could go where I wanted. Maybe I was just being paranoid.

Maybe they were waiting for me to slip up so they could bring me back to the compound. See? This was why I was drinking tonight.

As I opened the door, music hit me from every angle, a popping beat with some R&B undertones. The dance floor was filled, but the room wasn't overcrowded. Random strangers sat around at the various tables drinking with another someone or watching the crazies dance.

As per the name, everything was river decor. Oars in an X crossed the top of the bar. Random fishing knickknacks hung from the ceiling. An anchor was visible in every corner. Flat metal signs were arranged in collages on most of the wall space in between small shelves of random items.

For me, it was the color. It was blue, white, and grey. There might have been a lot to look at, but the colors blended from one to the next in a calming way. I was sure it was an accident because everything seemed to be scattered around. Somehow, it worked.

The bar made a U shape, and I chose an empty seat on the bartender's right side. The register was closer, so I could always get his attention. He caught sight of me and came over. "How's it going, Raven?"

I pointed to a bottle behind him, liquid as clear as water. "River House Whiskey, please, Galen."

He raised an eyebrow, "That good, huh?" He reached back to grab it.

"Yes, that good."

Galen grabbed two shot glasses and a wider whiskey glass. He poured into all three.

I knocked back the two shot glasses and saluted him with the wider one. "Thank you."

"Sure." He placed the bottle down in front of me. "Try not to drink it too fast." I downed what was left in the glass and nodded at him, pouring more.

He shook his head and walked away to a couple who approached the bar on the other side. The brunette leaned against the man and whispered in his ear, making him laugh as he tried to focus on the bartender to give him their order. The girl was not making it easy for him.

I looked away, now sipping from my glass. My body was lit up and warm. I already felt a calm spreading through me. Maybe I wouldn't need a full bottle tonight. Sipping my way through another two glasses, I stared out at the dance floor. Songs started to blend together, and the lights and colors started to blur.

That was what I wanted. That was what I needed.

I signaled over to Galen I'd be right back and—with focus—got down from my stool, heading toward the head. When I came back a few minutes later, the music seemed louder, and the bar was more packed. A new group of a younger crowd had come in while I was gone. I could gawk happily at quite a lovely array of young women. I moved face to face, body to body.

I heard a laugh that stole my attention away from the rest. My heart jumped when my eyes landed on her. Standing between two others was a shorter girl with red hair around her face and green eyes that sparkled through the darkness of the room. My whole body came alive. She could be her younger sister—same high cheekbones, same upturned nose, same lips... My stomach twisted as emotions flooding through me.

I remembered her lips on mine, her warm skin, when I heard the crack of lightning. I ignored it. It wasn't happening. I just kept staring at her as she spoke, laughed, placed her hand on her friend's arm. I felt jealousy rise in me.

Crack.

This time, I wasn't the only one who heard it. Others looked around, whispering to someone next to them.

Then came the rain. A torrential downpour clacked down on the roof of the bar so hard it drowned out some of the music.

The redhead looked up then, and she caught me, eyes trained on her. I expected her to look away, to give me a snarky expression, but she just smiled at me, blushing. I smiled back.

I held up one finger before leaning over the bar and grabbing a second glass from the many laid out in a row. She watched me, nibbling on the side of her lip. With two glasses in hand, and the bottle in the other, I gestured with my eyes and headed toward a booth toward the back of the bar, holding up both filled hands.

She glanced down briefly before looking back at her friends, who now talked to another side of the group, not seeing her. She turned back to me, flicking her head to the booth, and nodded.

As we both walked at an angle to intersect at the booth, I heard the rain slow. The crashing changed from waves to soft drops, and by the time I reached the booth, the rain stopped.

I watched as she came around a table to stand in front of me. I hadn't noticed her short white dress that showed all the curves of her body before, but now that I did, more than one thought ran through my mind.

I set the bottle and glasses on the table, offering my hand. "Raven."

She blushed under my gaze and put her soft hand in mine. "Ivy."

At that moment, all I wanted to hear was my name on her lips, with her white dress crumpled somewhere on the floor.

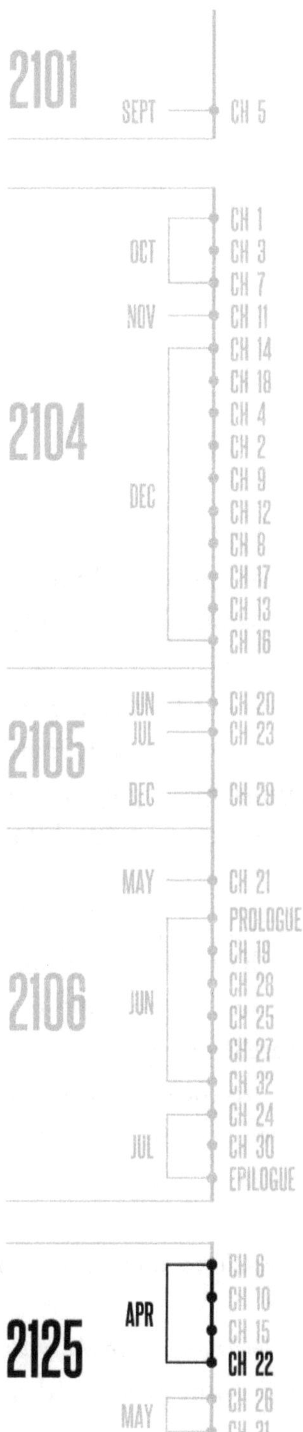

CHAPTER 22

APRIL 2125
Marina

My weapons locker bleeps—my code now firmly planted into my mind—and I grab my PHASR pistol, placing it into the holster already strapped to my leg.

I am not taking any chances, beautiful face or not.

Closing the locker, I catch my reflection in the mirror. I changed into a pair of white leggings and a grey tank top. I didn't want extra or loose fabric to make me feel constricted. I look into my own eyes and take a deep breath.

"Am I crazy? Is this completely crazy?" My wide, green eyes stare back. Glancing up, I realize my hair is still in a funky, messy bun on my head, and I quickly pull out the elastic. I flip over, pulling it into the sleekest ponytail I can before flipping back up and wrapping my hair into a bun on the top of my head. The smaller pieces of bangs fall around my face, but I have no time to fix that. I just need to look—

"Look like what?"

I don't know. I just don't want to meet my first-ever other human being looking like a disaster.

Oh, sure. His beautiful face has nothing to do with it.

I roll my eyes. No. It has nothing to do with it. A shot of

excitement trickles through me. He is another person, like me, with energy that builds inside of them. I wonder if he ever feels overwhelmed by it. I wonder if he ever feels it moving within him or begging to come out. There are so many things that I want to ask him. But right now—

"I need to get downstairs." I realize he is still waiting for me to join him. I refuse to look at my bed as I walk by, knowing the comforter is on the floor with my sheets. "I'll deal with it later." I ignore the nagging in my mind.

Walking down the stairs, I feel the heavy metal of the pistol bounce against my leg, making me feel on some level safer and also reminding me of the situation I'm about to walk into. The sound of my bare feet echoes down the stairs. "Shit, I forgot shoes." Shaking my head at myself, I spot my boots across the room by the front door and push back the annoying inner monologue that prompts me not to put on boots without socks.

"Don't right now. I have enough to worry about." My voice bounces off the walls like I'm talking inside of a glass bubble. I hear everything—the water flowing through the pipes, the coffee dripping into the pot. That means it's now seven in the morning. The silence seems louder than usual.

"Yup, I'm definitely crazy."

From where I stand, I see the outline of my guest's body through the window. His head and torso get bigger—closer—and I'm trying not to freak out. Not caring about my white pants on the floor, I sit down and tug on my boots. "Oh, Mom, why can't you be here? I don't know if I should do this." My eyes fly up to nothing. "Niko."

"Yes, Marina."

"Run a risk assessment of the current situation."

"Yes, Marina. What are the parameters?"

I huff, tying the first boot. "The parameters? I'm about to let another person, someone I don't know, into my home. This person could be dangerous and could be here to hurt me. I may not know it until it's too late."

"Then I would say the risk is high, Marina."

I shake my head. "And if I said a gorgeous stranger was here to sweep me off my feet and carry me away to live happily ever after, then what would you say?"

"I do not understand the parameters."

I groan as I finish tying my second boot and jump to my feet, glancing back out the window. He stands in the middle of the courtyard area, looking around at the house. His posture appears calm, with one hand on his backpack strap and the other stuffed in his pocket.

Why does that annoy me so much?

"Maybe because you're an emotional wreck, torn in a thousand different ways, and he looks like he's waiting to go for a walk. Ugh. Okay, I'm doing this." I take deep breaths as I place my palm on the keypad. The door opens, and I walk through the threshold, take a few tentative steps toward him. Streaks of sunlight filter through the high trees behind him. For just a moment, the world seems at peace with this stranger who stands in the middle of it, like he belongs here.

The Addies, Maddies, and Saddies float around the stranger in my yard as if they sense his presence. They dart back and forth around him, catching the light. I see him glance around at them with a curious look on his face. *Are these little specks of light not everywhere?*

I walk toward him, and as I get closer, I can feel—I don't know—HIM. I can feel him, his energy, his light, like a pulsing hum in my mind. *That's so interesting.*

The last time I felt this level of energy was with my mom. With her power and her ability, our energy always reached out toward each other. It was normal. We didn't pay any attention to it. But now with another person standing in front of me, after so long of not feeling that from someone else, I realize how much I miss that feeling. It's like a warm, comforting blanket. It feels different, though.

Why does it feel different? So many questions. So many things to learn.

He catches sight of me and turns to face me. His calm and cool composure changes. He stares at me, eyes wide, as some emotion twists across his face for just a second. It passes quickly, and he smiles as if nothing happened.

"Good morning," he greets me with a bigger smile.

I glance down at his plain white t-shirt and dark blue jeans. His sneakers seem strange to me. They don't look worn for someone who says he's been walking. The backpack looks light on his back, so he doesn't have much inside—

I realize I am taking too long to answer when I catch him still looking at me. "Good morning. I—you're not carrying much with you."

His eyes light up with his smile. "No, just a few essentials." He gestures behind me. "It's a beautiful house. Is it just you here?"

My heart stops, and my anxiety rises. *I knew it. I knew it. This is a bad idea.*

He must see a new expression on my face. "Oh, sorry. I didn't mean—sorry. I just meant," he gestures toward my house again, "it's just a lot of house for one person." His exasperation somehow makes me feel better.

I nod, calmer now, looking back over my shoulder, admiring the way the light slants over the house.

"It used to be me and my mom," I reply as I turn back to face him. "But she died a couple of years ago, so now it's just me." I shrug, holding back the emotion that threatens to flood through me.

His eyes are blank for a moment, saying nothing, but he seems to find the words. "I'm sorry for your loss." His voice is heavy with emotion, and it's strange to me how he seems affected. I wonder who he's lost. He isn't much older than me, so we have that in common.

His expression changes again. "I'm sure your father—"

"I never knew my father. But to be fair, he didn't know about me either." The words stumble out of my mouth before I stop them. I don't know if I'm sharing too much, but, oddly, I don't seem to care. I simply revel in the chance to speak to someone else.

He nods, lost in thoughts I can't hear. "So the giant gate and the—uh—gun on your thigh?"

I startle at his words, looking down briefly. "Uh, yeah, I—well, I don't know you or your intentions, and—well—"

"Your mom always taught you to be prepared." He smiles.

I half-smile back. "Yes."

He nods again and gazes around the space. "Well, you and your mom made a beautiful home."

I stand there, staring at him, watching him. The buzz in my mind is louder than before. *It's so strange. Am I extra crazy today?*

"I'm Blade, by the way." He extends his hand.

I step forward and shake it—an image of a girl standing in the rain floods my mind. I blink my eyes, shaking my head. I catch his eyes staring at me, and the image vanishes.

I clear my throat, feeling even more unbalanced than I did before. "Marina."

"Beautiful name."

I smile. "Thanks." I peer into his eyes. They are grey, almost white. I've never seen eyes like that in all my research. They are amazing. Distracted by his unique eyes, I realize we're still shaking hands. I pull back, probably too quickly, and then regret it. I hate feeling so out of sorts. "Sorry. I'm—I'm not myself today."

He put his hands up. "I get it. Some stranger comes in and wrecks your normal day. I'm sorry by the way, again—I keep saying it, but really. I'm sure you didn't even have breakfast yet."

My stomach answers his question. I press my lips together. "As a matter of fact, I haven't. Would—" I take a deep breath. He has to come in at some point. "Would you like some breakfast?"

He grins. "I'd love some." He looks down at my PHASR. "Are you bringing it to breakfast too?"

I hold back a smile, slightly twisting to the side. "Yes. But, how about we just pretend it's not there? It'll make me feel better until I know you better. I promise not to shoot you, you know, unless you try something. Is that all right?"

Blade laughs before responding, "Perfect."

"Okay, great. Then, come on. Come meet the house." I turn toward the door, ignoring the hum in the back of my mind. Blade follows behind me as we walk up to the house. It takes focus not to spin around and watch him while we walk. I don't want to turn my back on him, but I don't know how to bring myself to walk beside him either.

I hate feeling like this.

I pause at the threshold, turning to him. He gestures forward with his hand. "Ladies first."

I smile at the old saying and walk through the door without responding. I think thank you would have been correct. I berate myself for not saying it.

The light from the outside spills through the windows, sending patterned streaks across the room floor. I walk toward the kitchen to the right as he stands in the landing, looking up and around the room.

"It's clean in here," he says with an edge of surprise in his voice.

I turn to him, confused. "Why wouldn't it be?"

He shrugs. "I don't know. I guess I figured without anyone else but yourself, why bother?"

I consider for a moment. "But why would I want to live in a mess, even if I was alone?"

His response is simply to nod. He spots the shelves on the wall across from the window and gravitates toward it as I pull out fruit and eggs from the fridge and a small frozen loaf of bread from the freezer.

I keep my eyes on him as much as I can, watching him move, as questions race through my mind.

Is everyone like him? Where does he come from? Where is he going? Why is he walking? Who says ladies first anymore?

I see him glance at the gear coupler on the shelf as he looks around at the other random items. He turns to me. "Can I ask you why you have a giant, broken piece of glass on the shelf?"

I grab two small bowls and two plates from the cabinet. "Each item you see is from all the times something went wrong when I visited the city."

Blade tilts his head. "So you have shelves of mistakes that you look at every day? Isn't that a bit negative?"

"I don't see them as negative." I pile fruit in the bowls. "I see them as positive because they gently remind me what happened. They make sure that I don't repeat the same mistakes again." I glance up. "Niko, turn on the griddle."

"Yes, Marina."

Blade jumps at the sound of Niko's voice, and I chuckle at the expression on his face. "Sorry. I didn't think to warn you."

He looks over at me as he crosses the living room and walks to the counter. "Is your AI integrated into all of your house systems?" I shoot him a look, and he throws his hands up. "I promise I won't use the information for evil. I am just curious how such a big house can be connected with an interface like that."

I smile as I break an egg over the griddle. "He's integrated into most of them. My mom worked hard to connect all of the hardware and software. She wanted the house to run seamlessly without too much need for human touch. Sadly, robots are still robots, and they need a human to fix them."

"And that's why you go into the city? You need to get parts and tools? Is it okay if I sit?" He gestures to the stool in front of him.

"Please." I put the cut bread into the toaster. "Niko, set the toaster oven to three minutes."

"Yes, Marina."

"Does he say anything else besides that?"

I laugh. "Yeah, although Niko is not one for conversation."

"No? It seems an AI with a giant house would have tons to talk about."

"Yeah, you would think so, but nope. I spend most of the time talking to myself." I cringe at my last words.

I see the empathy cross his face, but before he can say anything, a big ball of fluff jumps onto the counter right in front of his face.

I smile. "Good morning, Pablo." The cat ignores me and starts rubbing his head onto Blade's hand, without even a glance in my direction. "That's interesting." Blade pets his head and whispers silly words I can't totally understand.

"What's interesting?"

"He definitely didn't like me when he first saw me. He wouldn't come near me until I fed him. Here you are, and he's in love already."

He scratches Pablo behind his ears. "Eh, maybe he just knows I'm a cat lover." I dwell on the image before me—a beautiful stranger loving on my cat. Huh.

I leave the cat to purr as I prepare breakfast. The toast is done. The eggs are flipped. What else? "Do you want tea?"

He looks up. "You have tea?"

I shrug, smiling. "Yeah. I grow tea trees outside by the greenhouse."

His eyes grow wide. "What else do you grow?"

Pride swells in my chest. "I grow everything I eat, actually. I grow fruits on the vine, like strawberries, green vegetables—a ton of them—uh, potatoes, corn, lettuce, and onions. There are peppers and spices, like basil and oregano." I close my eyes. "My basil is delicious. I love eating it right off the branch. Although I have to say that my tomatoes are the best. The soil is perfect for them, and they are very happy. What else? Oh, I have a small wheat section near the trees for things like bread." I gesture behind me at the toaster.

I beam with a sense of accomplishment. He just looks at me. I'm so confused. What does his face mean?

When he doesn't say anything, I ask again. "Soo, is that a yes to tea?"

Blinking his eyes, he shakes his head a bit before answering. "Yes. That would be great. I am just, I guess, surprised how self-sufficient this place is. I mean, eggs." He points to the sizzling griddle. I turn around, having forgotten the eggs, and remove them from the hot surface. "That means you have chickens."

I grab the tea bags from a nearby jar, placing them beside the kettle already on the stove. "Niko, turn on the tea burner."

"Yes, Marina."

"I do. We have about twenty in the back. Mom came across a chicken farm on her way here, still pregnant with me, and one day went back to see if there were any left. There had been thankfully not just chickens but a few roosters too. We've managed to keep the line going for a long while now."

He sat back, shocked. "Amazing. Do you eat the chickens too?"

I scrunch my face and shake my head in dramatic disgust. "No way. I raised these babies. I can't eat them. That's terrible."

He laughs. "All right, sorry. So what do you do for meat? Anything? Don't tell me you have a cow farm too?"

The toaster oven pings as I roll my eyes, and I plate the warm bread. I shift to the fridge, opening it with one hand and pulling out a small jar of almond butter with the other. Grabbing a knife, I open the jar and spread it over the bread. "Nope, but there's a pond nearby, so I get fish once a week for protein and such. Almonds," I raise the bread in my hand, "are also grown in the back for almond milk and butter."

He says nothing, seemingly mystified by my life. I bring all of the food over to the barstools for us to eat.

Blade looks over the food plates. "This is amazing. It's like the world didn't stop in these walls. It's impressive the amount that you were able to adapt to this new type of living environment. And although you're alone, you seem to have found a little piece of paradise. You're flourishing."

"I don't know if being alone could ever be considered paradise," I look around anywhere but his eyes. "But you and I both grew up in this world, our parents in the old one. We will never really know what was truly lost. No matter how normal all of this feels, everything just hurts around me." I let the words spill out, unable to stop. "I can still feel that a lot is missing. I can feel that the world is not whole. It's not the way that it should be." I look into his eyes. "Do you ever feel like that?"

He diverts his gaze. Emotion flashes across his face, which is answer enough for me.

I shrug my shoulders and smile. "You're the first person that I've ever met besides my mom, and so far, I think we're doing pretty okay."

His jaw drops, and his eyes widen, his white eyes. "The only person you've ever met?"

That awkward feeling returns to me then. "Yes? I mean, maybe where you're from, there are more people. For me, I only grew up with my mom until I lost her, and now you're here." I wait to see if he wants to reply, but he seems lost in his own head. I keep talking, trying to fill the air with words, instead of so much emotion. "What's it like where you're from? Is it far from here?"

So many questions flood through me then. Curiosity overtakes everything. Of all the questions, I want to ask him what he can do, what his energy can do, but it's a personal thing. *Isn't it?* I know I don't want to just reveal mine all of a sudden. Besides, I don't think I could just meet someone, and they would suddenly tell me their superpower. That seems intrusive.

But I am so curious, so I bite down on my lip to keep from asking that particular question. My questions seem to unsettle him even more as he tries to find a way to answer.

As if on cue, the tea kettle whistles. I place two homemade tea bags into mugs from the cabinet. Pouring over the steaming hot water, I try to rein in everything that I am feeling. Suddenly, I feel self-conscious.

Am I giving away too much of myself, too much of my home, too much of my mom? Is that why he can't answer? It's too much?

But I find it so easy to talk to Blade. I'm not sure if it's because he's the first person that I've ever met, or if it is him personally. How would I know the difference? All I know is it feels nice to talk to someone other than myself, even if only about the mundane things of the world.

I turn back with the mugs and place them down in front of us and decide to just keep talking. "We don't have sugar, but I have almond milk. Would that work?"

He finally smiles. "Yes, thank you. That would be great."

I grab the almond milk from the refrigerator and pour it into our mugs. "Go ahead. Try it. Tell me what you think." I watch him with excitement. "I've never had anyone try my tea before. My mom passed before the trees were ready to harvest." I look away for a second. "I think she would've loved the flavor. It is very rich and earthy, at least to me. Anyway, that's enough of my tea nonsense. Try it."

I watch as Blade picks up the oversized mug. A solid silver band rests on his ring finger on his right hand. I didn't notice it before. It's a beautiful color, much like his eyes.

He drinks, and his eyes shine. "Okay, that's really good. Compliments to the owner of this tea." He tips his cup at me as I pick up my own.

"Really? That makes me happy. I'm so glad. All right, I'll stop talking. Let's eat."

We eat mostly in silence, saying a word or two here and there, focusing mostly on the food and—for me—the conversation we just had. When we are both done, I set the plates in the sink.

"It was delicious. Thank you." He puts his hands in the air. "All of this is just amazing. And I'm still shocked at how everything seems so seamless." He gestures toward the dishes now in the sink. "You didn't need to do this, so I very much appreciate it. Really."

I shrug again. "Of course. I mean, you're my first guest, um, ever. And since I'm the one walking around with a pistol on my leg, I figured I could at least feed you."

He laughs. "Well, maybe our next meal won't need a firearm."

I purse my lips. "Eh, that's still up for debate." He smiles. *I am beginning to really like that smile.* "Um, well, I have to go check on a few things. Why don't I show you your room, and then maybe we can meet back up in a bit? I can give you a little tour of my gardens outside? You can see the food?"

He beams at me. "I would absolutely love that."

"Great. Okay, well, come this way. I'll show you."

I start walking toward the back room, finally feeling more at ease that I made the right decision.

First a cat. Now a human. What will stray into my home next?

Blade

I lie down on the bed, feeling the air leave the sheets.

What am I doing? How did I think this was going to be easy? I'd just walk in and see her and everything would be fine?

I shake my head, covering my face with my hands.

Everything about her confuses me—her eyes, her face, her hair, the way she walks, the way she laughs.

Oh, but the pain. I wasn't expecting the pain. It is like a shard of glass through my heart, piercing, constant, and overwhelming.

And the jealousy. It feels like poison, running through me

like ice. I can hardly contain it. It makes me angry, which makes it even harder to focus. All at once, I don't know if I can do this.

I sit up then, swinging my legs over the side of the bed. This is too much. She isn't what I thought she'd be at all, but I should have known. I mean, she's her daughter.

I should have known.

I hit my hands on my knees before standing, pacing the small room. *It's not like you have a choice, right? I mean, you're here now. Not that you had a choice about it to begin with, but...* I stop walking and take a deep breath. I hear Leeya's voice in my mind.

"You are the only one that can make her believe. You need to make her believe." I still don't understand why it has to be me. But Leeya went through so much to find me, sacrificed so much to tell me. Letting out another breath, I know I can't give up now, no matter the pain.

Billions. Remember the billions we need to save.

I nod to myself and do my best to ignore my shattered heart, thinking of the one I couldn't save.

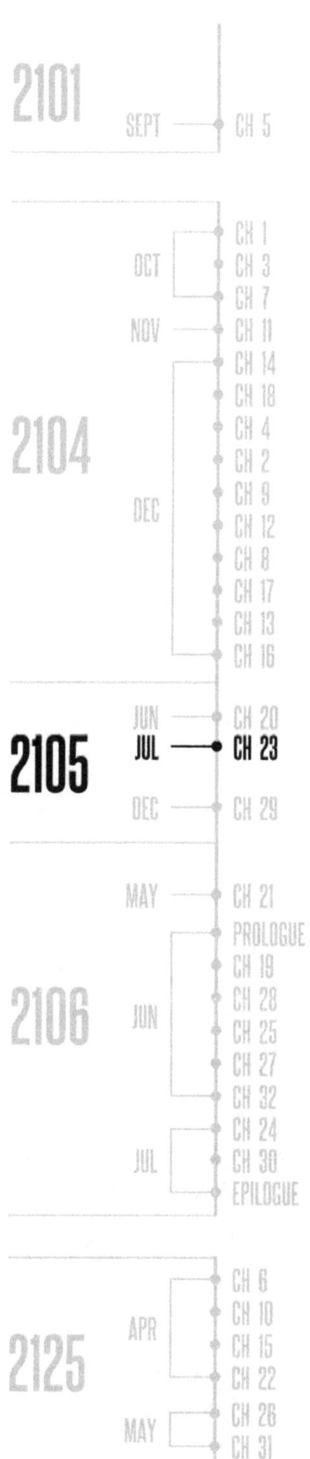

CHAPTER 23

JULY 2105
Angelia

The sun woke me up. Bright rays of light streamed in from outside and found their way through my sheer curtains.

I stretched my arms above my head, enjoying the feeling as blood rushed around my body. I turned my head to the side to see my favorite view every morning.

Jaeden.

He was still sound asleep, his hair falling in his face, eyes soft, lips closed, lying on his stomach with his arms shoved under the pillow. He had no shirt on—or anything else, as usual during the summer—but the sheets stopped at his waist. His broad shoulders and incredibly soft skin just begged to be kissed. *Who am I to argue?*

I sat up on my elbows and leaned over, pressing my lips softly and gently to the middle of his back. I heard him sigh.

Trailing one kiss after the other between his shoulder blades, I listened to his breathing, knowing I'd woken him just enough for him to know I was there. I sat back, watching the light drift across his skin the way my lips had, and my heart smiled with me.

He is so beautiful. And he is mine.

He'd been mine for just over six months now, and it was an incredible six months. Nothing stood between us, no barrier to stop our emotions, and there were no rules we were trying to follow. It was all so effortless. We held hands when we walked out onto the street. He kissed me when we went to bed before saying goodnight. I threw my legs over his when we watched a movie before he pulled a soft blanket over me. It was all as it should be, as it always should have been.

Going to RoboCon had been one of those decisions that changed the course of our lives and brought us together. I was happy, like so stupidly happy that it was hard to hold in my heart on some days.

Like now, my heart swelled, looking down on him. I leaned over to start my journey back up his back. But as my lips touched his skin, the damn clockglass went off, completely shattering my thoughts.

"Ugh," I groaned, leaning the opposite direction to turn off the soft music floating from the clockglass. It wasn't the music. It was the morning. No, it wasn't just morning. It was seven o'clock in the morning. I never went in early, but Noreen and I had to do inventory for the next two days. I didn't want to, not even a little bit. Counting every single nut and bolt for the next twelve hours today and tomorrow did not make any part of me happy. But two extra days off next week would.

If I survive it.

I lay down, flat on my back, refusing to get up, when Jaeden shifted beside me. "You know you need to go shower, right?" he said with a half asleep voice.

I huffed. "Yeah. I'm going."

He smiled, with his eyes still closed. "Yup. Totally sounds like it."

I squeezed my lips together. "I don't want to. Can't she pay someone else to come in to do this?"

He cracked an eye open. "You want someone else touching *your* parts from *your* bins and putting them back where *they* want to put them?"

My eyes widened. "That sounds awful."

He laughed. "I know. So get in the shower and prevent such an awful occurrence from… occurring."

I shook my head, smiling. "You're half asleep. Go back to bed."

He reached over then, grabbing me around the waist, pulling me closer to him, laying his head on my bare chest.

"Or you could just stay here." He lifted his head, kissing my stomach. "The nuts and bolts may be messed up and in totally different bins, but it's totally okay if you don't get up."

"Uggh. These are the reasons I hate you. You know that?"

His kisses softened. "Oh really? I don't think that's true. I think you love me."

I shook my head. "Nope. Right now, I hate you."

His lips trailed lower. "Are you sure?"

My eyes closed, losing my train of thought, not answering.

"I'm sorry. I don't believe I heard an answer." His fingers tugged at my shorts, pulling them down. I never had a chance to answer before his lips found one of my favorite places for him to kiss.

Half an hour later, I was showered, dressed, and making coffee. I cleaned his favorite white mug with our IP address on it—he wouldn't drink out of anything else since I gave it to him a few weeks ago—and I already had bagels in the toaster. I planned on driving myself to work, but he said he would, which just meant more time with him. Plus, when this crazy long day ended, I'd be able to see him as soon as I left the walls of my prison.

The toaster sounded, and I reached for the fridge. "Butter or cream cheese?" I called down the hallway.

"Butter" was the answer this morning, and I decided to join him as I grabbed the container from the shelf. I layered more butter than I should, wanting it to melt into all of the crevices of the bagel—best way to eat it. Grabbing the coffee, I added milk and sugar to mine and brought my mug and his black coffee to our newest addition to the kitchen area.

Jaeden had been sleeping over basically every night since our trip to Montreal, and it became quickly apparent that we needed a bigger table for two people to eat comfortably. Before I could find one, he came home one day with a big box, followed by two more big boxes. He had to take two trips from the hallway. The table was an elegant white circle sitting on an hourglass base. Oh, and the chairs were rich wood. The legs were brown like coffee, and the backs the same color with three horizontal lines carved into the wood. But I loved the seats of the chairs the most. They were a yellow corduroy and SO pretty. I was surprised he managed to pick out something that suited me so well. I smiled every time I walked to our kitchen table. This morning was no different.

I placed the bagels and coffee mugs down. "Are you coming, or am I eating without you?"

I looked up to see him walking down the hallway, dressed in a white t-shirt and black jeans, barefoot and gorgeous. *Will I ever get tired of looking at him?* He crossed the room and swept me into his arms, kissing me. *Nope. Not a chance.* He put me back down and sat in his chair, closest to the window.

"Thanks, beautiful."

I smiled, blushing. "Of course. I mean, if you're going to drive me, you might as well eat something. Which by the way, you don't need to. Really. I can go."

He crunched down on the bagel, swallowing before answering, as I took a bite of my own. "First of all, it's faster with my hover license. Second, you do realize that I'm sitting around here ALL day for the next twelve hours without you? What the hell am I going to do with myself? So please, let me get any extra time I can."

I shook my head, picking up my mug. "You'll get bored of me soon. Just you wait." The smell of coffee reached my nose before my lips. I closed my eyes as I felt the coffee warm me, tasting the first sip of the day, relishing in its warmth and flavor. When I opened my eyes, his silver eyes glowed with emotion.

"I don't think so," he said before taking another bite.

I tried not to smile as I sipped from my mug. I bit into my bagel, and the butter dripped down my fingers, exactly how I loved it. "What do you want to do when I get home?" I asked.

He raised an eyebrow at me.

I laughed. "No, I mean to relax."

He set his bagel down. "Oh, that's very relaxing. Didn't I relax you this morning just fine?"

I blushed, looking away toward the living room. I could see Jaeden's computer area by the living room table. Two glasstops were set up on a double mobile standing desk. Jaeden often worked for hours on his computer, so he needed to be able to move around as he worked. The screens were connected to our new projectionTV that he brought with him from his place.

There wasn't much else that he brought, besides clothes and such, just his glasstops, the projectionTV, and a few small things. When I asked him about his furniture, telling him it was fine that he could bring whatever he wanted, he simply said he liked my stuff better. *Fine by me.* It's not like he wasn't everywhere in my—our—apartment now. His own new books were strewn about. After finding the print-on-demand option for books, he ordered many of his own, and they sat all around the room on every surface. Seeing his books everywhere brought me more joy than my own books.

I looked around and saw clothes of ours tossed everywhere from the night before. We hadn't made it to our room, after that look in his eyes. I'd pick those up later. "Want to finish the movie you interrupted last night?"

"I interrupted? I'm sorry. Is it my fault that you accidentally," he put dramatic quotes around the word with his fingers, "took off your tank top when you took off your sweatshirt? I mean…what was I supposed to do? Keep watching the movie?"

I tilted my head. "Um, yes, actually. I was excited to watch *The Darkness.* I've been waiting."

"Well, next time, don't distract me with your bare skin."

"I—" I threw a piece of bagel at him. He knocked it out of the way and lunged at me. I twisted out of my chair in time for him to tackle me to the floor. We laughed as we rolled and wrestled, trying to win the battle and end up on top of the other. I never let him win without a fight that usually left me breathless, but as usual, he eventually took the advantage and had my hands pinned above my head, his lips inches from mine.

His eyes burned fire into mine as we breathed heavily. "I love you," he said.

I smiled, warmth blooming in my chest. "I love you."

Rylan

I almost pulled her back into my car and took her home after she said goodbye to me at work. She kissed me once, shut the door, and then came back in for another kiss. I finally let her go and watched her walk into TechHalo, waving as she walked through the door.

Now I sat in the car, window down, arm resting on the ledge, wondering what to do with myself.

I didn't want her to work. I wanted her to just stay home with me all day, but I had no way of explaining where all my credits came from. At this point, she thought I wrote software for a tech company, which was why I could work from home. I took days off when she did and treated it more like a part-time job, which was—interestingly—the kind of job that I always wanted in the first place.

Until I saw her jumping through puddles, her soul on her sleeve.

Now our days were spent wrapped up in each other or me waiting for her to come home from work.

I told her one day how much I was paid. I chose a number three times more than her salary so she couldn't argue when I said I wanted to pay the rent on the apartment. She only agreed if she took care of all the other expenses. She wasn't used to being taken care of.

I had enough credits for us to buy a house and live off the rest for years to come. I even considered creating the identity of a rich uncle somewhere that left me an inheritance and taking her away to wherever she wanted to go. I considered trying to find a way that we won some kind of contest, and I'd whisk her to multiple countries around the world and watch her eyes light up with excitement at every place we would visit.

Instead, we were limited to these ever-closing walls of the city. I didn't know if it made me lucky or cursed that she was all I needed. It scared me to think of a time she might never be with me. It confused me to think of a time she wasn't. We met a year and two months ago, and I felt like I spent another life with her.

There was my life before I came to New Eastland, with the Three Stooges. Then, the life before we went to Montreal—lost behind a barrier of friendship. The new life that we created IN Montreal was free and full of excitement. And the one we had now intertwined everything.

I took a deep breath and hit the engage sequence on my hover.

She seemed happy with me—the new me—and I decided to be Jaeden for the rest of my life. If it meant her in my life, I would never go back to being Rylan—a hacker and a thief. I wasn't those anymore. I was Jaeden, and I would protect that secret forever.

I pulled out of the lot and headed toward the skylanes, stealing one last look through the glass walls of TechHalo in case I could catch a glimpse of her for just a moment. When I saw nothing, I continued on my way toward the entrance to the skylanes at the back of the strip mall, pausing at the four-way stop before the exit.

The warm July air swept through my car for a moment. The breeze brought a familiar smell, one I hadn't breathed in for months. My heart started racing as I looked around.

A black hover with tinted windows parked behind the strip mall buildings. From where I sat, I saw the small orange glow get brighter as the person inside breathed in. Very few people smoked real cigarettes anymore, but there was always one person who swore he'd never give it up.

Cristian. The Moe to my Three Stooges. And he was sitting across from me in the parking lot.

My first instinct was to turn around and get Angelia. But my hands stayed glued to the steering wheel. *What am I saying? He's the only person who smokes cigarettes?* My eyes fixed on the black hover as it engaged its engines and pulled away.

I sat at the four-way stop until the black hover disappeared from sight behind me. I took a deep breath and shook my head. I was overthinking. *Just relax. You tracked them last week, and they were on the other side of the country. It's fine.*

I took another deep breath, trying to clear my head, as I pulled past the sign and got in line for the skylane entrance. It took another ten minutes to slow down my heartbeat and convince myself that I was overreacting to a simple coincidence.

I used to scoff when someone said smell was tied to memory stronger than other senses. Never again.

Once the fog in my head cleared, I turned up the music, feeling normal again by the time the chorus looped around twice. I had more important things to think about.

Angelia.

I needed to find something I could do for her, some way to bring her the joy she deserved. Her birthday was coming—our first to celebrate together. None of my ideas were big enough, and yet they required a lot of credits. I didn't want to push it.

What's that old saying? I just want to give her the world on a silver platter.

Cliché. And true.

I needed to figure out a way to give her an experience that

didn't take us too far from our own four walls. An idea sparked. Maybe it didn't need to be within the four corners of our walls at all. Maybe she needed a new set of walls. It would take longer than I had until her birthday. *Maybe for our anniversary in a few months?*

I smiled, thinking of her possible reaction. She'd always wanted a little piece of her own world, so that's what I'd give her.

Angelia

At 8:34 p.m., I trudged out to the waiting Volkshover, shoulders slumped and exhausted. I couldn't wait to climb into the passenger seat, see his face, and be done with the day.

I opened the door, and before I could even get in, he handed me a croissant with a chocolate center from The Dark Roast.

"Ohh, my favorite! I love you. Thank you." I took a bite, sat down, and leaned over to kiss him, still chewing.

He smiled and kissed me. "That good, huh?"

I took another bite. "Everything is way sorer than I expected. I won't even tell you how many times I went up and down that damn ladder or how many cups of coffee I drank."

"Sorry, love. What do you want to grab for dinner on the way? Anything you want."

That offer sparked a smile as I chewed my third bite. "I want a burger and fries with a soda AND a milkshake."

He laughed as he reversed the hover. "American Café, then?"

I groaned, my mouth already watering at the thought of their semi-sweet burgers and spicy fries. "Yes, yes, double yes."

"You got it, beautiful."

The trip from TechHalo to home with a stop to American Café in between took about thirty-five minutes. On the way, I pulled the burger out, took one big bite, and wrapped it back up, following it with a handful of fries. I also fed some to Jaeden as he drove before closing the bag to keep the food warm.

Once we reached the parking structure, I unraveled myself

from the front seat as my back protested every move. *How am I going to do this again tomorrow?*

Without speaking, I dragged myself to the elevator, leaning on Jaeden as we went. I thought of sleeping for another few years, at least, as I waved my IDfob at our door's keypad—Jaeden held our food and drinks—and walked through the door.

I dragged myself straight to the living room and slumped on the couch, leaning over to lie on my side. I pulled my feet up and closed my eyes.

"No. Don't do that. You need to eat." I heard him set dinner on the table and walk over to the couch. "Hey, you should eat before you sleep." He swept a few strands of hair from my face that had escaped my braid throughout my workday and kissed my forehead.

He removed my boots and socks, and I floated in his arms. My head rested on his chest, and he carried me down the hallway, my toes brushing my books a couple times as we passed. He laid me on my side of the bed. My eyes never opened. I was too tired to even think about the effort.

He kissed my cheek, brushing a soft kiss across my lips. "I love you. Goodnight, beautiful." I didn't hear him close the door as I fell into a deep sleep, dreaming of nothing, lost in exhaustion and yet still filled with joy in my heart.

Cristian

I flicked my cigarette through the open window and stared at the guy walking into the apartment building with food and drinks in his hands. This same guy apparently left us to chase a piece of ass and play house.

I was pissed. *No, I am fucking furious.*

I shook my head and pulled out another cigarette. I couldn't breathe in fast enough once it was lit, taking a deep drag. I ignored the patient faces of the three men sitting beside and behind me. I needed to find a way to calm the hell down. They were waiting to hear what I had to say, and they knew better than to rush me. When the second cigarette hit the ground, I finally spoke. "Good work, Trey. You found him."

Seann took that as permission to speak. "It's definitely him, Cris?"

I nodded. "Yup. It seems he found a new life, one that doesn't include the word loyalty. And I think, unless anyone disagrees, that we should show him what it means to be loyal and what happens when you aren't."

Brente said nothing, but I could see him grinding his teeth in the rearview mirror, choking back words. He finally managed just one. "When?"

I looked over at Trey sitting beside me. "Well, we got, what, two more jobs lined up right now?"

He answered, "Yes, in Jersey and DC. They should only take a few weeks. We could come back—"

I held my hand up, stopping him. "There's no question we're coming back. The question is how badly he'll beg us to stop when we do." I looked in the mirror and watched a smile spread across Brente's face. "We found Rylan, boys. Too bad he won't like the reunion we have planned for him."

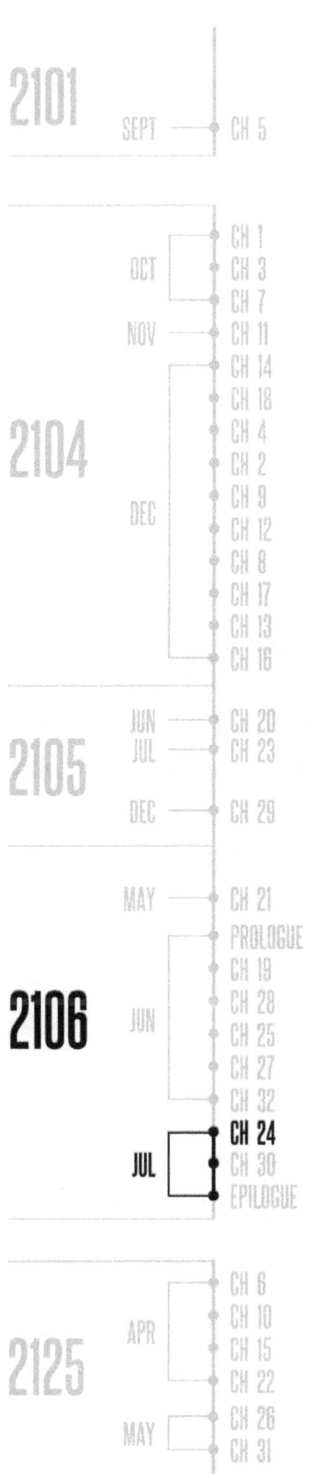

CHAPTER 24

JULY 2106
Dr. Logan

I missed the quiet. I missed the peace. I missed the calm.Now all I seemed to do was drift through chaos—loud, messy chaos.

I graduated summa cum laude, earlier than anyone else in my class—classes two years earlier or after. I had two PhDs. I conducted thousands of hours of research and development, hundreds of tests, compiling years of viable experience.

And for a month, I'd been nothing but a glorified babysitter.

Normally, I jumped out of bed every day, ready to serve my passion, a purpose, a focus. Now, I snoozed for at least an hour before even getting out of bed to dress for the day.

My alarm rang out for the second time. *Speak of the devil.* "Mika, shut off the alarm, please."

I pulled back the covers. I immediately felt cold, even though the room was its usual, comfortable seventy-three degrees. In the shower, I enjoyed the few sweet minutes of warmth before my first meeting of the day.

Planning and logistics really just felt more like complaining about all the things that weren't going right. I guess I'd see how today would go.

I chose a pair of black slacks, a long-sleeved black shirt, and flat loafers with a silver chain across the top. I hadn't worn my heels since Raven left, one year and 209 days ago.

Every day, I hoped he was okay. And every day, I missed him.

My "ten minutes 'til" reminder went off. I left my room, grabbed my comm and clipboard from the living room table, and walked toward the door. I stepped over the papers scattered around the floor, ignored the dishes in the sink, and looked past the pile of laundry by the front door. I just wanted to get through my meetings and get back in bed.

I took a deep breath, raised my head a little higher, and opened the door… to chaos.

There were just so many people.

Doctors. Technicians. Construction workers. Spectrals.

All of them mixed together in this whirlwind of a facility. Each one of us were just trying to survive, trying to get through each day.

As I walked down the hallways, my eyes scanned over the dozens of crates in stacks along the walls. Bags of clothes that needed to be washed sat outside of the many doors I passed. This part of the facility used to house members of the staff, those honored with an opportunity to work with Dr. Atlas and his team. Now, it housed dozens of Spectrals in as small a space as we could fit them, which meant doctors and scientists found roommates. Everyone had to find someone, except me and Dr. Atlas. For that, I would be eternally grateful.

Voices trailed around the room, bouncing off the walls. Many talked to other scientists in white lab coats, some complained loudly, and others looked scared. The Spectrals happily walking around, displaying their powers. One man phased a ball from one hand to the other. Another wrote in the air with her finger, leaving a trail of light.

Every power I'd seen so far was as beautiful as it was terrifying. We started this—to find a way to give humans extraordinary healing abilities so we could save the people of the world from harrowing diseases, cure us all from the inside out. Now our experiments resulted in people who could levitate, throw ice, project emotion, or even phase themselves through other objects. The list kept going.

The world changed, all right.

I rounded a few more corners. The noise and number of people calmed as I walked farther away from the sleeping quarters. I scanned my palm and walked into a large room, thankful that I went unseen by the many who needed my attention.

I was the first one to the conference room, which was normal. I looked around the room, praying the coffee station was ready to go, and found the small miracle sat on the left side of the room. Some luxuries were hit or miss with such an influx of more people and only so much staff to take care of it all. Food, cleaning, laundry, and everything else that happened in the background fell behind every day. I waited for the day someone forgot the coffee.

I poured a black cup and drank, inviting the warmth to sit with me. I sat at the head of the table and waited. It was the same room we had discussed how we "lost" Raven and Sloan, after I helped them escape and lied to Dr. Atlas for the first and only time in our lives together. I took another sip and pushed the guilt down. I didn't regret my decision and never would. Raven was alive, and that's all that mattered.

As I drank more coffee, calming my nerves, one doctor, scientist, and team lead after another entered the room and filled the chairs. Normally, ten of us attended this daily meeting. I glanced at the clockglass. Exactly at ten, I was surprised when Dr. Atlas walked through the door.

I awkwardly stood up as quick as I could. "Dr. Atlas, I didn't expect you to be here."

His face was soft but serious. "Am I not invited to my own meetings?"

"No, I didn't mean—of course you are. It's just—"

"Don't be flustered. I'm not here to change anything. I just thought for once I'd sit in the meeting and hear the updates so you didn't have to repeat it all later this evening."

I nodded. "Sounds good. Would you like to sit here?" I gestured toward my chair.

He waved me off. "Not at all. I'll stand in the back and listen in, but thank you." He walked toward the opposite end of the room and settled himself against a table, nodding to a few as he passed.

I checked the time and saw most of the faces, so I began. "Good morning, everyone. Let's get through this quickly because we have a lot to do. Sawye, let's start with you. I know we received the final shipments of supplies, so we're all anxious to hear when your team will finish extending our facilities including the new Spectral wing."

A short, stocky man with darker skin coughed and waved at everyone. "The—uh—extended facilities are going to take, at minimum, three months to complete."

Groans rang out around the table. Sawye straightened his back. "Our men are working around the clock. I have a full-time crew morning and night."

Dr. Tomlan cut in. "Yes, we know. We can hear them."

Sawye shot him a look. "My point is we are going as fast as we can, and to be clear, I don't recommend doing this in three months. It really needs triple that amount of time. It's rather—"

I held up my hand. "Let's not go back into past concerns. We have too much to cover. So three months? Then how soon can we utilize the new space? When's the open date?"

He crossed his arms over his chest. "December 1."

I nodded. "Okay. Great. Thank you, Sawye, and thank your team. I know you are all doing the best you can as fast as you can. I can speak for Dr. Atlas as well when I say we appreciate it." Sawye smiled and nodded his gratitude for my words. I turned to another doctor sitting to my left. Her short salt-and-pepper hair framed her face in curls like mine. "Dr. Fraklin, how's the move going? Is Michigan ready? Any good news on that front?"

"I don't know about good news but news just the same. It's going to take another two weeks before we can be fully out of here." She threw her hands up. "And before you go throwing groans at me, it's not on us. We are ready to go. The Michigan facility is dragging their feet. We could drive away tomorrow."

I glanced back at Dr. Atlas. He nodded at me. "Then go. I already spoke to Dr. Atlas about it. If fifty-three people show up, they'll get their act together pretty quick. It's my understanding they are mostly done at this point anyway. The facilities to continue the research and development of our other projects are set to go. The rooms for all of you are set up. I think they are just concerned about the shift of resources, but Dr. Atlas spoke to their Facilities Director. They are on notice. We just don't have time to wait around with more Spectrals arriving every day." I looked at Dr. Fraklin. "Let's connect later to discuss final logistics. Okay?" She nodded as we both turned our attention to the small blonde near the door. "Janelle, what are the numbers now?"

"Good morning, everyone. We now have exactly two hundred and forty-four Spectrals, including Sloan and the Trio. On average, about seven Spectrals come in every day, but it's increasing. In another two weeks, we project we'll see more than double here."

Many shook their heads. Dr. Tomlan's face turned red. I headed him off. "Dr. Tomlan, how are the Spectrals?"

"Besides too many in number?" He paused to take a breath. "They are all healthy. None of them seem to have any type of disease or history of disease. Dr. Maggio and I," he acknowledged the doctor beside him checking a specglass tablet, "are mapping each profile as fast as we can, but you can imagine the flood is proving to be difficult."

"Has the age range changed?"

He shook his head. "Everyone is between the age of twenty

and forty. Dr. Maggio is—Dr. Maggio, you tell them."

The tablet clacked down on the table as his brown eyes looked up at me. "As we map, I am paying particular attention to the age markers, as well as the growth markers. At quick analysis, there seems to be a correlation between when the gene becomes active and when it can no longer be."

"Like a shelf life?" I asked, intrigued.

He raised his eyebrows, pondering my question. "Yes, actually, nicely said. It's exactly like that. But we need definitive answers, not more guessing as we go."

"Please keep us updated." He nodded and returned to his tablet. "Since we're already on the topic, Harper, how is Spectral Operations?"

"Guns are easier," he said flatly.

"Would you like to elaborate?"

He put his hands up. "No one knows what we are doing with these Spectrals. I've seen one walk through a wall through a portal he made. I've seen ice crystals thrown across the room. We are trying to inventory them as accurately as possible, but some of these people can't control what they do. Some don't even know what they can do. I'm no doctor, and trying to group these different... abilities... together is damn near impossible." Over the past two weeks, I watched Harper change from his calm, albeit rigid self to this new unfettered person. I feared I wasn't the only one unraveling around here.

"How about an additional team? Your team can focus on the abilities while a new group works on the database and cross-references."

He nodded. "I'll take it."

"Great. Done. I'll work on that today." I looked over at Mikhail, our Chief of Security. "Do you have any concerns we need to be aware of?"

He shook his head. "Everything is in place," he said with his accent. "We know every coming and going. We know where everyone is. Thanks to these new bracelets, we are all tagged." He raised his hand to show the thin translucent band on his wrist, a band we all wore now.

As more Spectrals flooded in, Dr. Atlas wanted to be able to track everyone within the facility, specifically noting who was who. The Raven episode spurred him to take extra precautions.

"Yeah, like dogs," said Dr. Tomlan, rolling his eyes.

"You're free to leave the facility whenever you like," Mikhail quipped back.

Dr. Tomlan swiveled in his chair. "Am I? The last I heard, we weren't allowed to leave, so don't tell me what I can and can't do!"

Before Mikhail could reply, Dr. Atlas spoke from the back of the room. "That's enough, Dr. Tomlan. This has been difficult for all of us, but once the processes are all in place, we will be able to move forward and help these Spectrals with their new abilities. Let's all remember these people are the future. If you and Dr. Maggio are correct, and they have no diseases, then future generations won't either. Please understand the implications of this before you complain about a bracelet." Dr. Tomlan lowered his eyes, turned his chair toward me, and remained silent.

Dr. Atlas motioned toward me. "Please continue."

I nodded. "Okay. That leaves you, Glenn. We received word last night that your second crew will arrive tomorrow. You're getting another fifteen people to help with the housing and logistics of the facility. I know the basic tasks are backing up, so they will be here soon."

"That's incredible news! This was becoming more than unbearable—" He stopped there, not wanting to stir up the room again. "I look forward to meeting my new team. Oh, but can I ask one thing? When are we going to get everyone occupying the locked wing into the system? It's tedious to have two of my guys stand there to let people in from one side and out from the other."

I looked back at Mikhail. "Is there an update on that?"

"I'll send a team to go room by room, scan everyone, and set them up."

"Thank you." I look back at Glenn. "In the meantime, why don't you have them pass through the supply door with our generic keycards at the back of the facility?"

Glenn's brow furrowed in confusion. "The supply door?"

I nodded. "Yes, at the back of the facility. It's the one door you can pass through without the retinal scan. Have them move through there for now. It takes a little longer to walk around, but it should alleviate a bit of the front-end traffic."

He nodded. "That's great. I'll get started with that now. Thanks, Dr. Logan."

"No problem." I looked around the room. "Is there anything else?" I saw nods around the room, but no one spoke. "Great. Let's get to whatever the day brings us, and I'll see you all tomorrow morning."

There were scrapes and bumps as everyone stood, walking out one at a time. As Dr. Fraklin walked by, she put her hand on my arm and whispered, "You're doing fine." I rested my hand over hers briefly, smiling, before she walked out.

Dr. Atlas came to the front of the room as soon as it cleared. "Well, that was… enlightening." He stared off into the distance before he refocused his eyes on me. "Where are you off to now?"

Grabbing my clipboard off the table, I moved toward the door with him. "I am going to visit the Trio and Harper. I want to check in briefly with them, see how the Trio is doing, and get more details on what kind of team Harper needs."

He nodded. "Then I'll speak with you later." Dr. Atlas turned the opposite way. I watched him disappear into the chaos of the hallway before making my way to the testing part of the facility.

A few minutes later, I stood in one of the testing rooms we set up for Spectrals, watching the Trio practice their new abilities.

Lin was a small girl, half Japanese, and fierce. Aside from the fire she held in the palm of her hands, she was sharp and quick-witted. Beside her was Xander, a tall blonde with deep-set eyes. His hand rested on Lin's shoulder, absorbing her ability and creating his own fire in his left hand. The last of the Trio was Eton. He stood in front of a table with multiple random objects on it—a book, a glass cup, and a piece of wood.

As he extended his hand, Eton closed his eyes. I watched as the tips of his fingers turned translucent. Then his fingers, his hand, all the way to his wrist also changed. Slowly, he waved his semitransparent hand through the glass cup. It phased through, and I watched in awe. I turned to Harper. "They've come a long way."

He nodded. "They have. They have the most control of their abilities because they've had them the longest, aside from Sloan, who has about six months on them. He can turn his on and off like a water faucet. These guys are basically there too."

I watched as Lin changed her fire into a bright white-and-blue flame, and the one in Xander's hand shifted to match.

"Incredible."

When Dr. Atlas made his discovery last year, we checked the genomes of the remaining thirty-nine Testers. Only three others—they became known as the Trio—held the right sequence, in the right order, with the right set of markers. I remembered the shock that rushed through me as Dr. Atlas and I looked through the glass, and three more humans with supernatural abilities sat on the other side. No one said a word. The hush in the room filled with so much emotion. We finally found a way to test for this gene—that we now called the Spectral gene thanks to the media—and were able to confirm if a Tester had it on the spot, which made it easier to weed out the Testers we brought back to the facility. The problem was the gene only existed in twenty-to forty-year-olds. Even then, it was less than a 5 percent possibility they had the gene. Five people in every 100 had it, and it was challenging enough to get even fifty people to attend our seminars.

...until the day, a month ago, when we released a gamma bomb over New Eastland and thousands of people changed.

"You know what scares me?" Harper's voice beside me brought me out of my thoughts.

I glanced at him. Dressed in a military-type uniform, with broad shoulders and cut muscles, I wondered how anything could scare this man. "What's that?"

His face lit up with red light as Lin threw a fireball at the glass where we stood, laughing when Harper flinched. He sighed and looked over at me.

"What happens when they figure out they are stronger than us, that they don't have to be in a cage? They can go and do and be whatever they want, wherever they want. What happens when we can't stop them?"

Xander walked over to Eton, placing one hand on his friend's shoulder, and watched as his own hand turned transparent. Lin began throwing fire in the air and catching it, like a hot game of catch.

I had no answer to give Harper. A small fear crept into my mind, watching the three of them laugh together, seeing the future of evolution and the dangers that came with it.

I was exhausted by the time I returned to my room. I dropped my clipboard on the table, passed the piles on the floor, and kicked off my shoes before plopping down on the couch. I had just leaned over to lie down when I heard a message *ping*. I groaned.

"Mika, read my new message."

"Yes, Logan. Message from Dr. Atlas. 'Dr. Logan, please meet me in Basecamp. I need to speak with you in regard to something important.' End of message."

I covered my face with both of my hands, talking through my fingers. "Mika, reply, 'Okay. I am on my way. Meet you in five minutes.'"

"Yes, Logan. Sent."

I stood from the couch and grabbed my shoes from either side of the living room. *Let's go see what he needs…I hope it's good news.*

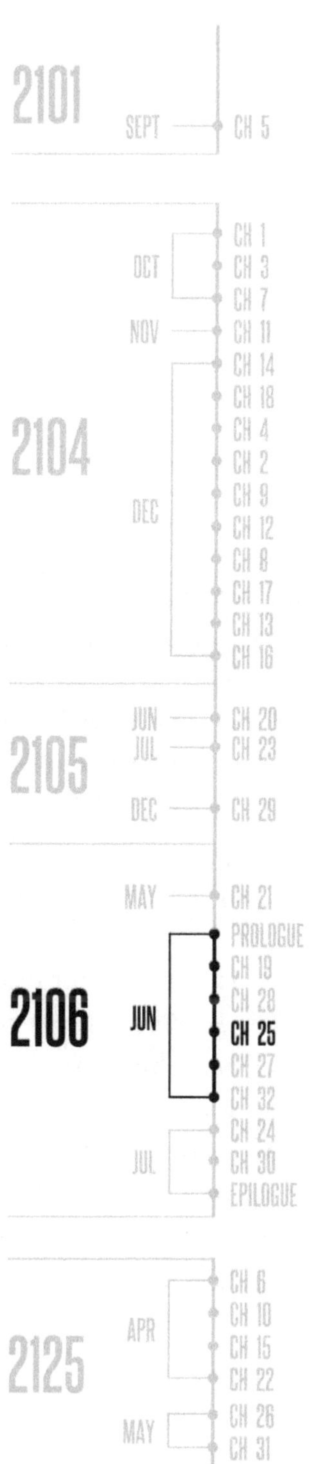

CHAPTER 25

JUNE 2106
Angelia

I woke up to a sore neck. *Why am I so uncomfortable in my bed? And why is there music in my room? I never sleep with music. And what is that hum in the back of my head?*

Everything flooded back to me. The news broadcast about missing Spectrals. The pounding voice that came for me. And—

My eyes flew open.

I teleported with—

I sat up too quickly, paying for it with a pinch in my side. "Whoa, hey. You're okay."

My eyes found Rylan's, happy to see them for just a moment before I remembered everything else. It was a strange sensation to hate and love someone at the same time, but here I was, rocking those feelings simultaneously. *What a way to wake up.*

I looked out the car window at the hover lights under the many cars traveling the same way we were. We weren't in a skylane anymore, which meant we were out of New Eastland. All the original foundational roads were used outside of big cities. Maybe one day, skylanes would span across the country, but for now, we used the same infrastructure for hundreds of years.

Where are we?

"We're still in New York. It took almost three hours to get out of the city. It seems we aren't the only ones trying to leave."

Thoughts spun in my head, and I didn't know which to follow. My emotions spiked. I reached forward and shut the music off, dropping us both into a deafening silence. "Why are you here? Where are we going? And who the hell broke down my damn door? What's going on, Jae—"

He stiffened, and I stopped. We both stilled in the silence that flooded the hover. *You need to get it together. Stop it.*

I took a deep breath and settled my nerves best I could. "What's going on?"

"First, tell me what do you know about all of this?"

Anger shot through me. "What do I know? Seriously? I know that one day I was standing in my shop," I ignored the emotions that pulsed through me, "and felt the worst pain I ever experienced in my life. I came home, and I could—" My mouth snapped shut.

I couldn't say the words out loud, like somehow it made it real if I did. Besides, I didn't know if he knew exactly what I could do. Suddenly, I didn't want to share it, like it was some kind of disease.

"I could… do something I couldn't do before. I haven't left my house since. For two weeks, I've been sitting in my apartment, watching the news. I watched as Spectrals, people like me—" I looked over at him. "People like us apparently are disappearing." I threw my hands in the air, feeling the emotions boil over as I spoke faster and louder. "That's what I know. I know that I know nothing. And then you show up. This has been the most eventful hour of the past two weeks. So, please, Rylan, why don't YOU tell me what's going on so maybe, for once, I can feel calmer than I have in a long while." I crossed my arms over my chest and leaned against the passenger door, staring at him.

He glanced at me from the corner of his eye before he answered. "Okay, well, where do you want to start?"

"How about we start with who the hell broke down my door?"

He nodded. "We can start there." He let out a long breath before continuing. "Do you remember when we went to Montreal—"

"How could I forget?"

"—and we saw Dr. Atlas from the Atlas Institute?"

"Yes. What does he have to do with this?"

"Everything."

That quieted me. I decided to just listen and say nothing.

He saw my shift and resumed. "After Spectral Day, and the pain—you were right about that—the worst I've ever felt too, physically anyway…" He looked down briefly.

I ignored the pain in his voice. It wasn't my job anymore to care how he felt. I refocused on his words.

"I was clenching through the pain when I suddenly found myself on the other side of the city. I don't know how to explain it. I felt like I was drowning and—"

"Flying?"

"Yeah, flying—both at the same time. That's how it felt for you too?"

I nodded. "It was like being lost in a flying bubble, wet and dry at the same time. It was the strangest feeling." I caught his eyes when I looked up, and my heart lurched. "Anyway, continue."

"Yeah—well, before I got back—uh—home, I had hundreds of notifications from companies I follow."

There was an undertone of what sounded like guilt when he said home, but I pressed my lips together.

Not. My. Job.

"Every news station was broadcasting about people with special abilities—Spectrals—and that's when I found out I wasn't the only one. I didn't sleep for the next few days. I scoured every source I could until I started to see a pattern of information. All of it surrounded the Atlas Institute. I read crazy things. The Institute conducting experiments on people, some people going into their complex and never leaving again, and so much more. So, I did what I always do—"

"—you followed the trail."

He gave me a half smile, nodding. If it wasn't for the shattered pieces of my heart nagging me, I would have smiled back at his boyish excitement.

"I tracked the trail backwards." He shook his head in disbelief. "It's amazing what information people leave behind without realizing it."

"So, you found that they were responsible for this, then? How?"

"That's the thing. At first, I found information about what they called 'seminars.' These events are common for companies like the Atlas Institute when they look for volunteers for their tests and such, so that wasn't weird to find out. But, when I was researching the capacity of the Atlas Institute and reviewing the results and names listed as volunteers, the numbers didn't add up. So I dug deeper and found a new trail—or dozens of trails. I started looking for people who just disappeared, dropped off the grid, or no longer had an imprint. Then, I went back to the Atlas Institute and found all these new shipments of food, clothing, and other construction materials being commissioned."

I narrowed my eyes. "How do you know all of this?"

He looked out the window beside him, avoiding my eyes.

"You hacked their system, right?" I felt my anger rise again. "Or whatever the hell you call it."

"Yes."

I shook my head, trying to keep it under control. "Okay. Keep going."

"Since I was already in their system, I decided to tap into their communications and track what was going on. That's when I learned how often people were coming, where they were disappearing from, and how they were found. Some seemed to go willingly to the Atlas Institute, while others, well, weren't being asked as easily."

"That's who came for me? People from the Atlas Institute?" My eyes opened wide, remembering the banging and shouts behind the door. "But how did they find me? How are they finding any of us? I don't understand."

"I'm still not 100 percent sure of that either. I only have bits and pieces, something about energy waves. The only thing I can figure out is that they have some way of detecting the energy coming from Spectrals."

The thought terrified me. "They can detect us? I—I don't..." I didn't know how to express the thoughts racing through my mind. When Rylan appeared in my living room, I somehow started to feel better about the world, safer. Now I felt scared again.

"I don't know. I plan on figuring it out, but right now, I just know they can." He paused, deciding what to share next. I waited, emotions swirling. "I didn't know if you were one of the Spectrals. I didn't know if you were okay or what had happened to you or if—"

"Well, you wouldn't really know, would you? You chose to cut off that communication on your own, if you remember."

He ignored my jab, taking a deep breath, and continued. "When I started to realize the Institute was taking people, I wrote new code and set my program to specifically pick up your address if it ever came up."

I didn't want to believe he cared, so I shoved the emotion down, listening.

"A few days later, your address triggered. I traced the information, and somehow, they had your name. The only information I could see was a date and time—which was about four hours ago."

So the Institute can't only sense the energy but find who it came from?

Anxiety rose in my chest, and I leaned my head back, closing my eyes. I wanted to go back to sleep. It was much calmer and easier when I was sleeping.

"I came as fast as I could to get you out of there."
"How chivalrous of you."

The words flew out of my mouth before I could stop them, much harsher than I intended. But I didn't take them back, not after the six months I went through without him. He didn't deserve my sweetness. He took it for granted for a year and then left it behind without a second thought, so I didn't care how I sounded to him.

"Look, Angelia—"

With my eyes still closed, I held up a hand. "Don't. Please. I need—I need a minute. Just tell me where we are going so I know. Then I need some time to let all this, I don't know, sit. Okay?"

He sighed. "The Atlas Institute is north of New Eastland around the Syracuse area, so I am taking us west through Pennsylvania. Hopefully, they can't reach us or detect us that far away. We're actually going to stop in about a half an hour at an inn to sleep, if that's okay. We can regroup before we keep driving. Is that—"

"It's fine." *Just leave me alone for a minute.*

That's what I really wanted to say. As angry as I was, it still hurt to throw my anger at him. All of this was too much. I didn't know how much more my emotions, my heart, could take. I just wanted to sleep.

Just let me sleep.

About thirty minutes later, I felt the hover slow down as it turned off the main road. I hadn't opened my eyes or said a word since I told him it was fine. I couldn't figure out what I wanted to say. I just tried to process the new information with what happened before.

It was so hard trying to sort through it all, sitting near the person who used to help me sort through life. I finally opened my eyes as the hover parked.

The small inn off the highway was about ten stories high

and shaped like an L. I could see a pool to the right, with strings of lights around the seating area. I imagined people sitting under a fake umbrella without a care in the world, drinking a fruity cocktail, laughing together. I glanced over at Rylan, who toggled off the hover and shut down the thrusters. The silence filled the car as we just stared at each other for a moment. He opened his mouth to say something, but I turned and stepped out of the van.

I am not doing this right now.

I stretched, taking my time as he grabbed our bags from the side door. I walked around, grabbed mine from him, and threw it over my shoulder, leaving him behind me.

"Angelia, wait—"

A shock went through me. I barely stopped a growl coming out of my throat. "Can you call me something else, please?"

He stopped in his tracks, looking confused. "What else can I call you? I've always—"

"I know. That's my point. You were always the only one who ever called me that, and I want you to stop. Just call me Lia, like everyone else in the world." I didn't wait for an answer and continued my trek to the front office. I didn't want to feel angry, but I couldn't seem to resist it. Everything about him reminded me of what I had and what I lost.

As I walked up to the counter, a man with glasses looked up at me. I hadn't seen someone wear glasses since I was a kid, not since they approved the OpticOculus serum to be used in infants, repairing any defects before they even could see. I liked the retro style of his wide frames.

I opened my mouth when Rylan spoke first. "Hi, good evening. We need a room with two beds."

Mr. Glasses smiled as he looked from me to Rylan. "Sure. Let me see what we have available."

I didn't care to listen to the jumble of conversation surrounding a room, expense, and all the nonsense of the mundane.

I felt heavier and more tired by the second. I just wanted a bed with a pillow and blanket.

I slumped down into a nearby chair and stared without focus at the projectionTV in front of me. The sound was off—apparently I wasn't the only one—and showing the same newsreel as when I left my apartment.

All of my things. My… everything…is in that apartment.

I mourned the life I had built on my own for so long, shared with Rylan for a blink of it, and now probably had lost forever. I became numb again. And it felt good. I was done, so done.

Please, I am so done.

Rylan approached me then. "We're set."

I jumped up, with my waning energy, and walked toward the elevators. He hit the button to our floor. I barely registered the ads promoting household products above my head. My gaze remained unfocused on the shiny interior walls.

The doors opened what felt like hours later, and I walked out, standing to the side so I could follow him. Five doors down, he waved his IDfob over the door and let us in. He walked in first, and the lights triggered. There was a bathroom on the right, a small closet in front of it on the left, two beds stacked side by side, and a window with the shades drawn, although outside was probably pitch black anyway.

I walked past him to the bed nearest the window, dropping my bag on the floor. I barely kicked my boots off before I flopped down, fully clothed, on the bed, not saying a word, closing my eyes.

He sat on his bed. "Lia?"

I didn't answer, wouldn't answer… couldn't.

"I know how angry you are, and I don't know what to say besides I'm sorry. I didn't want to hurt you. I wanted to protect you—to just let you be happy."

My eyes welled with tears. "I was happy."

I thought he'd say something else, but nothing came. He

clicked the lamp off beside our beds, and the tension slowly seeped from my body, letting the numbness take me away to a calmer place.

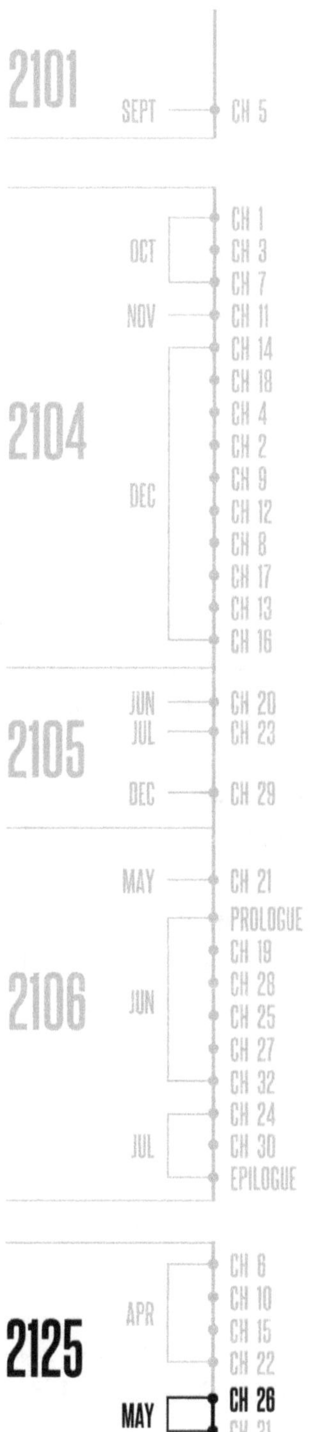

CHAPTER 26

MAY 2125
Marina

While holding the small screws in my mouth, I set the drill down on the grass. A bad habit I learned from my mom, but it works—I never lose a screw. The hot sun reflects off the metal panel. I hear the click against the wall as I slide the metal door to the left.

"Geez, finally. Why was that so difficult?" My words sound more like a muffled mess than a sentence.

I lay the panel flat on the grass and drop the six tiny screws into my hand, wiping the metallic taste from my lips before putting them into my small pocket. I peer inside the opening.

"Let's see what the problem is today." I check section by section from the top to the bottom, moving wires, looking at connections, and feeling the seals. Nothing seems to be wrong, except the power in the house flickers, like there's a short.

"Where the hell are you?"

"Here."

I jump at the sound of Blade's voice and slice my hand on the sharp panel edge.

"Oh, sorry. Shit. Are you okay?"

A small line of blood forms, but it isn't bad enough to need immediate attention. I wave him off. "I'm fine. It's my fault for forgetting there's another human here."

He smiles. "Still not used to me, huh? It's been a month."

"I know. Aren't you leaving yet? Haven't you overstayed your welcome?" I laugh at his dramatic face, feigning shock and offense.

"Didn't someone ask me to stay to help realign her solar panels?"

I roll my eyes. "Maybe."

"And who asked me to help lay the foundation for her expanded irrigation system?"

I press my lips together. "Also, maybe."

He widens his eyes at me. "After all of this truly meaningful work, you don't remember I'm here?"

I scrunch up the side of my face. "Yeah, but maybe I'm rethinking this arrangement."

He clutches his chest. "I'm hurt. I thought we were friends."

I wiggle my head at him. "Eh, debatable." We smile at each other, and I look at the panel.

Blade has been here for exactly thirty days today. On the second day, he prepared to leave and be on his way, but I got scared, like down-to-my-bones terrified. I was scared of what it meant if he left, scared to be alone again.

That's what it came down to, being alone. I couldn't imagine being alone again, so I thought of some small jobs here and there where I could use his help. He was more than willing. Then bigger jobs came to mind. I knew it would keep him here.

And now?

Now, I just don't want him to leave. Such a small amount of time has passed, and I'm scared not to see him—or feel him—again when I wake up. It is a strange feeling, but I feel it.

So here he is, still helping with tasks around my home. Whenever I think about him leaving, I become anxious. I have to stop and breathe. But I leave it where I found it and move on, until the next time the thought hits me and knocks me down.

It's very frustrating.

He walks over to stand beside me, looking at the tall machine I am currently sticking my hands into. "Of all the machines I've seen around here, how have I not seen this one yet?"

I shrug, peering deeper into the open space revealed behind the panel.

"Did you get this from a charging station?" he asks.

I nod. "Yup. Mom and I took two." I pull out a bottom rack to check the first layer of fuses. "There is one on the backside of the garage for the hover. You haven't seen it since we haven't gone anywhere, but it's there. I'll show you later when we get ready to leave." Each fuse seems intact as I assess the row of ten. "Mom wanted to make sure we could travel whenever we wanted, so we have a whole solar panel system just for that. The one you helped me rearrange? That's the one that feeds directly to the cell charger for the hover." I close the rack and open the next one. "And then we took this one a few years later, so we had a way to recharge the solar panel distribution system."

I glance back over at him, and he shakes his head in disbelief. "What?"

He lets out a breath of air. "You and your mom are geniuses. That's an incredible idea."

I feel my face flush at his compliment and look back at the last rack of fuses. "Thanks. My mom always knew what and how to connect everything to make it work for us. She was the genius. I'm just the student. And—" On the last fuse, I find it. "And there you are, my little friend, causing me all the trouble. Damn."

"I'm sorry. Is this a good thing or a bad thing?"

"Well, both. It's a good thing because now I know what the problem is. I'll just add it to the list of what I need from the city today."

"And the bad?"

"The bad news is I don't know if I'll be able to find this fuse in the store we're going to." I pause for a second, mentally cataloguing what I remember about M&M Technologies. "But honestly, the place had everything else I needed the last time I was there. They might just have it. If they do, I'll take every one I can find."

"You mean there's something you don't have in your workshop?" he asks with a sarcastic tone.

I laugh. "Crazy, right?"

He leans forward. "I'm really excited to go, which is actually why I came over here. I wanted to let you know that the food, drinks, and bags you wanted are ready to be loaded in the hover. Everything is sitting on the kitchen table. So if you're ready, I'm ready."

I grab the last fuse on the end and wiggle it until it releases. I pull it free, careful to not hit any of the others. I hold it up. "Now I'm ready."

Fifteen minutes later, I'm changed with my long braid fed through a white ball cap. I changed out my t-shirt for a tank top, expecting the heat to be more uncomfortable than usual in the city. It will only get hotter.

I grab my black backpack, filled with tools, and the empty bag to add the parts and supplies we find in the city, and meet Blade at the kitchen table.

He looks up at me, wearing a dark gray t-shirt and blue jeans. Hair falls into his eyes. Emotions flutter in my belly as I see him standing there, but I take a deep breath, ignoring it. "All right, I'm finally ready to go."

"Awesome." He grabs our bag of food and the case of water bottles and follows me toward the front door. "So just the hardware store? What else?"

I pause to put my palm on the screen. "We'll hit the hardware store, a new food store to check on some cans, and then one other place I want to show you." I look at him out of the corner of my eye. "But that's a secret."

He smiles. "Sounds like an adventure."

I type my security code into the panel, speaking out loud, "Niko, Lockdown Phase II. Set Phase III at fifteen minutes."

"Yes, Marina. Have a safe trip."

"Thanks, Niko."

Before the door opens, I hear a meow behind me. I turn to see Pablo sitting in the middle of the floor.

"Hi, baby boy." I kneel down, reaching my hand out. He trots over to me, rubbing his head in my hand. "Don't worry. We'll be back tonight. Okay?" He meows again before I stand back up.

The door slides open, and I see Pablo's bright eyes staring at us through the crack of the door as it closes.

Out in the early morning sun, we make our way toward the garage, walking side by side. "When's the last time you were in the city?" I ask as we walk.

He shrugs, looking across the grass area. "I don't even remember. A long time ago."

I smile. "Well, I'm excited to be your guide, then. The store we are going to go to first is huge. It has so much. I wasn't there long enough to see everything last month, so I think maybe this time we can take an inventory. Is that okay with you?"

"Sure. I'm just excited not to have to walk there."

I laugh. "Oh, I can imagine." I unlock the garage with the palm scanner, and the door slowly lifts, revealing the black hover van inside. "Here she is, the best hover ever." I walk toward the van, opening the side door and dropping my tool bag inside. I turn back to find Blade standing in place, eyes trailing over the hover. "Never seen a hover van before?"

"No, I—" He clears his throat. "I just wasn't expecting a van. I thought it was more of a sedan."

"Oh, yeah, no. Mom and I needed more room than just a small sedan to travel with supplies, trees, machines, whatever. Besides, she had this van since forever. It was hers before—um—before everything."

Blade nods, not moving, rooted where he stands. "Are you good with a van? You seem a little—"

He shook his head. "Yeah, I'm good. Let's go." He drops the bags beside mine, only inches from me. I feel the familiar hum from him standing so close to me. I smell his familiar scent. I blink and move away from him, ignoring the incessant butterflies in my stomach.

Just get in the car.

I hop in the driver's side and start to engage the engine while he climbs into the passenger's side of the van. He scans, from the front of the van to the back. I follow his eyes. "It didn't always have all this empty space. Would you believe that this van used to have a full computer setup, with multiple screens, stations, and even a place to sleep? Mom said it had been her home a few times. I would have loved to see it then, but Mom took everything out of the van before I could walk. Now, it's just open and cleared out of anything, except for what we travel with."

"I'm sure it was a very fancy van back then."

"Oh, it was." The sequence finishes and beeps. "Okay. Let's finally get moving."

"Okay, S…umm…" I look out the window. "Sign!"

"Come on! That's easy!" Blade throws his hands in the air.

"It starts with an S, so it works. Now you go, T."

Blade searches out the window, looking for— "T, trash! Boom!"

I laugh. "Oh yeah, now that wasn't easy or anything."

"No comments from you. Go. U."

"As in U are going to lose?"

He chuckles. "We'll see who lands on X."

"Um, that'd also be U." I laugh harder as he drops his head

backward and groans, realizing it's true.

He peeks over at me. "Who started this game, anyway?"

"U. I'm so winning at this!"

He rolls his eyes. "Remind me not to play games with you again."

"No! This is awesome. I never played games in the hover before. It seems so old world."

"Oh, it was. Driving across the country, playing games, was the only way to keep your mind focused on something other than tree, tree, tree—oh, rock—tree."

I giggle. "Wow. What an idea, to drive across the country just because, not for a need, not for a damn fuse—just for the fun of it." I shake my head. "It seems fun, actually."

He looks off in the distance with a faraway haze over his features. "I think we should stop at U and just let you win. I don't think we'll find anything for the rest of the letters."

"What? No zebras running around the empty roads?"

He presses his lips together. "Nope. I doubt it."

"All right, fine. I'll let it go. Besides, we're almost there."

I turn onto one of the main roads that spins its way through the top of the giant island, once called Manhattan, and make our way south. Some roads are blocked. Some are gone. Some are overgrown. It takes a lot of navigating to reach our destination, or it would if I didn't engage the thrusters and fly over it all. I feel gravity push down as we rise up.

Blade presses his forehead to the window and looks down at the empty streets winding in every direction. His eyes devour our surroundings. The sun is high, and the sky is clear, which makes an even stronger edge to the city. Vines cover the buildings, and trees and rubble surround the bases of many of the taller skyscrapers. The battle continues between green and brown as the land starts to take back its territory.

Over my trips to the city, I counted about eight satellites that crashed in New Eastland. From where we sit, I can see two. It is a magnificent sight, a mixture of beauty and decimation.

I haven't looked at the world the way he is in a very long time, as if the loss is fresh and new to him. I forget it's hard to remember the world as it was when you don't see this kind of destruction on a regular basis.

"It's a little intense, right?"

He doesn't speak for a second, taking it all in. He clears his throat. "It's very intense."

I fly the hover over the larger part of the city, moving toward the middle, where M&M Technologies is situated. I make a short U-turn, find the best approach, and start to descend.

I glance over at him. He seems frozen, looking at the ground, his face pale. His eyes dart back and forth. "Blade?" I feel the shift in his body. "Blade, are you okay?"

I feel a ripple of energy pop in and through the hover. One second, I am looking at him, feeling the shift of energy from a hum to a rush in every direction. My own energy reacts and pulses. A second later, there is a bright flash of yellow. And Blade is gone.

Nothing but small specks of yellow light float above his seat. "Blade!" I look down, searching for him on the ground below, but there's nothing. My head is heavy as my stomach knots. "What the hell just happened?!"

I try my best not to lose my head, as I still hover in midair. I take a few deep breaths and lower my van to the front entrance of M&M Technologies. I jump out of the van after the locks disengage.

"Blade!" I look around, heart beating hard inside my chest, searching for any movement. Anything. Minutes pass. I stop calling his name. Wherever he is, he doesn't hear me. I start to panic.

I sit down on a bench covered in vines from a small nearby tree. My heart is racing. My stomach is in knots. I'm thinking about being alone again. My head gets dizzy, feeling empty with his energy gone.

I force a deep breath. Then another. My stomach eventually stops churning, but then I start getting anxious thinking about sitting and waiting. "Let's just go get what we need. Let's focus on one thing at a time."

I ignore the small flips in my stomach as I grab my comm from the front seat holder, along with my tool bag from the side of the van. I review my list and pretend my head isn't pounding as I walk up to the store.

I focus on what I need and walk through the door, taking deep breaths whenever a wave of emotion—fear, confusion, worry—comes over me. *Breathe. Just find what you need.*

It takes about half an hour, but I find everything on my list—oddly, the easiest shopping trip ever—including the fuses for the solar panel distribution system. As I add the pack into my bag, I hear a door open at the front of the store.

I drop the bag of tools and rush toward the sound, seeing Blade standing in the entrance area. I run down the center aisle and, without thinking, throw my arms around him. I squeeze him, tears coming to my eyes.

I'm too emotional to register the image of the girl in the rain this time, but it's there, like an itch in the back of my mind.

He hugs me back as the image vanishes. He pulls me away, hands still on my arms. He tries to hide a grimace with a smile, which tells me a lot and yet not enough at the same time.

"I'm sorry. I didn't mean to scare you. Are you okay?"

"Am I okay? Are you serious? Are you okay? What happened? You were there, and then you weren't. I don't know what happened." I hug him again. "I was so scared something happened to you."

He takes a deep breath and pulls back to look at me in the eyes. "I'm sorry."

I wipe the tears from my eyes, feeling silly as my face flushes. "No. I'm sorry for the tears. I don't know what came over me. I was—I am—I don't know, just scared." I turn away from him, feeling too awkward by my reaction.

"Well, at least the cat's out of the bag. You know what my power is now. I'm sure you've been wondering."

"Are you kidding? I've been wondering since I met you. I didn't even know what other kinds of abilities existed. Yours is pretty amazing." Questions flood my mind. "What does it feel like?"

He shrugs. "Like being in a washing machine."

I tilt my head. "Really? That's weird and great at the same time." I shake my head. "Teleportation… I can only imagine what else there is." I jolt as I catch him staring at me. "What?"

"What, what?"

I squint my eyes. "Why are you looking at me like that?"

"Oh, I don't know. Maybe I'm waiting for the part where you tell me what you can do." He raises his eyebrows at me.

I laugh. "Yeah, uh, I can, um—how about I show you?"

Blade smiles. "Even better."

"All right." I walk past him out the door, and he follows behind me. I search the area for something to use. I see some overgrown trees to the left, vines hanging down low and around the trunks. *That'll work.*

I ground my feet, looking over at him, feeling like I'm on display. I refocus my attention on the trees, taking a deep breath, three times.

I fall down in my mind, finding my energy ready to go. I pull it up and reach out with one hand toward the vines. I feel the energy leave my body in waves. I open my eyes and see the familiar green threads travel out toward the vines.

I pull my hands up as the vines lift off the ground, almost as if fluttering in the wind. I separate them into three chunks, and, pulling my hands back and forth, I make the vines form into a giant braid. One set of vines moves over the other, one at a time.

When it's done, I let the energy pull back into my mind, and I lower my hands. Blade stands quietly beside me as I turn toward him. "That's it."

He raises his eyebrows. "You can use your power to make trees do what you want?"

"Yeah... and anything of the earth—trees, flowers. Then there's the ability to move water, air, and, um, fire. Yeah, that's it."

He just stares at me before shaking his head. "We need to work on your modesty." He breathes out his nose quickly. "Wow. Elemental powers. That's amazing."

I flush. "Yeah? You think so?"

"Definitely. Are you able to control them all the same?"

I shake my head. "No. I'm still working on them. I'm not able to move a mountain or anything, and air just doesn't like to listen to me. But I practice when I can."

"Yeah? Wow. Just wow. I think you win in the power area."

I laugh. "No. Teleporting is pretty incredible."

He puts his hands in his pockets. "Maybe."

I focus on him. "Speaking of, you're okay, right? From earlier?"

He shrugs. "I'm fine. It just happens sometimes when I'm overwhelmed. It was just... a lot... seeing the city like this. It's been a long time. You forget what it was at one point. And seeing it like this? It was just too much all of a sudden."

My lips twist to the side. "Then I'm sorry too. I'm so used to coming here. It's nothing to me. I didn't even consider how it would be for you."

"It's fine. I'm good. You're good. I teleport. You have elemental powers. And it looks like you found what you needed." He tilts his head back toward the shop.

I follow his eyes. "Yeah, I found it all."

"Fuses too?"

"Yup."

"That's great. So what else is left?"

"Are you sure? We don't have to do any more. I know we just

got here, but—"

"No, really. I'm fine. What else did you want to do before we left?"

A smile spreads across my face. "Have you ever seen a real book?"

Blade

I think Marina is trying to kill me.

It's like she knows it hurts and twists it deeper into my heart.

But I know she doesn't. She doesn't have a clue, which makes it even harder.

I smile and wow with her as she takes me to The Last Review, showing me the books, telling me how they used to be made. All the while I break, crumbling into the pages of the lost books no one will ever read again.

I need to tell her the truth. I need her to know who I am and why I'm here. But I don't know if she is ready.

Would anyone ever be ready?

I shake my head. She doesn't deserve this. She's beautiful, smart, and hilarious, just like her mother. I sigh.

I need to tell her. I need to do it soon, before I lose myself in this world and forget I still need to save the one I come from.

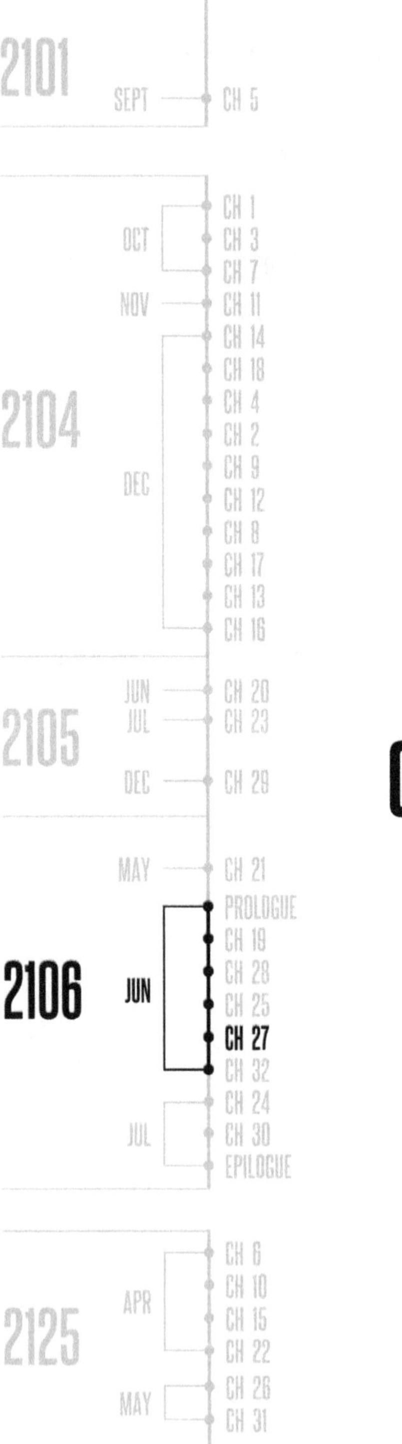

CHAPTER 27

JUNE 2106
Angelia

I woke up to an empty room the next morning. It took a few minutes of convincing to tell myself that he hadn't left me behind, that he had a good reason for leaving me alone. I tried to remind myself that it didn't matter either way, but I knew better. I was terrified without him. I needed him beside me, angry or not. It was just me and him. He was all I had.

Just like before.

He walked in a few minutes later with a platter of food—much like he had long ago in Montreal. I pushed away the memory.

"Morning. I thought we should eat before we continue on our way."

I eyed the food on the tray. I was starving. I hadn't eaten since the burrito. I saw bagels, bananas, muffins, eggs, bacon, grapes, cheese—and coffee. I reached for that first. This was definitely a day that needed to start with caffeine.

"Thank you," I said softly, grabbing one of the two plates from the tray.

His smile didn't reach his eyes. "Of course."

I ate a little bit of everything. The grapes and cheese were the best part. I never understood why grapes and cheese—of all food combinations—tasted so perfectly paired when they went together. One grape to cheese cube ratio was three times more delicious than either of the two by themselves. At least, that's what Jaeden and I always said.

I glanced over at him. He drank a cup of coffee, sat on his bed, and flipped through his comm. He didn't eat anything. Before I could stop myself, I asked, "Do you want cream cheese or butter on the other bagel?"

Rylan looked up at me, startled, not expecting to hear from me, I guessed. I instantly regretted speaking. "Sorry. I—"

He shook his head. "It's okay. I'm good. Thanks, though."

We sat in silence until I finished, when I stood to clear the mess. "I'm ready when you are."

His eyes flickered to my chest before looking back in my eyes when I remembered which sweatshirt I wore, the same one he had always worn. He had said it was his favorite and so became my property as soon as he moved in. I walked around in this sweatshirt all winter. So often, I sat on his lap in nothing but this sweatshirt while I worked to steal his attention away.

I felt my face flush. I started to move, but Rylan grabbed my hand before I could turn away, standing up beside the bed. His skin was soft. I closed my eyes, trying to hold back the flood of emotion that came with his touch.

"Angelia…"

His voice confused me. My mind was at war with itself, the same way it had been so long ago. We both thought the other wanted to be friends, but it hadn't been that at all. It had all been a lie. Our relationship had been built on so many lies. But my heart didn't care as I felt him pull me closer to him, grabbing my other hand. My eyes stayed closed, not wanting to see what I felt so strongly.

"Look at me."

I took a deep breath before opening my eyes. His gaze pierced through me, conveying so much of what he always used to say to me.

"I'm sorry. I'm sorry I made the wrong choice. I'm sorry that I left you alone. I never should have left you. I should have been here."

I felt the cracks in my heart turn into small fissures. His eyes pulled me in, as they always could. I missed being lost in his eyes. I missed him. I missed my Jaeden—

My walls flew up, crashing into my heart. I closed my eyes again and backed away from him.

"Please, don't. I can't… I've spent months trying to move on. I can't do this again. I can't." I hurried over to my bag and picked it up, walking back toward the bathroom. "I want to shower before we go. I'll meet you outside in the van in twenty minutes."

I shut the door and turned the shower on, covering my mouth as I broke down in tears.

Half an hour later, I walked down the path from the night before toward the van. His sweatshirt was rolled into a ball in the bag. Instead, I wore a long-sleeved black shirt with a pair of cargo pants and my boots. I left my hair down to air dry. It swayed around my hips as I walked.

Rylan sat inside the hover ready to go. I glanced up at the cloudy sky. Normally, the hint of rain would make me happy, but I didn't care much anymore. Rainy days were just that, days filled with rain.

He said nothing as I settled into the van, feeling the new hum between us, and placed my bag at my feet. I didn't want to put it on the side, and I wasn't about to hand it to him. Besides, its weight at my feet was somehow comforting. Stranger still, so was the hum in the back of my mind.

At least something is comforting…

He waited for me to say something, but when I didn't, he engaged the thrusters and backed up. We drove for about forty minutes in silence. His Neoteric Beats played in the background, but I barely heard them. I stared out the window, watching the haze of life pass by. It seemed everywhere was a somber day today. I saw homes pass on the horizon. Farms and animals came into view a few times and then disappeared behind the hills. I kept my eyes focused on everything that existed outside the window to occupy my mind.

"I need to stop and refuel one of the cells. Are you good with stopping for a few minutes?"

"Whatever you want to do." I watched a large red building with white stripes come into and out of view.

Rylan took the off ramp toward a recharging station. Bright lights blinked, even in the daytime. It looked like the gas stations of a few hundred years ago. Everything had changed from hybrid to all-electric and finally to hover cars. I couldn't even imagine what it must have been like to drive a car that could explode. That seemed surreal.

Although I can move things with my mind, and I was just running away from people who wanted to kidnap me and make me part of their... whatever... so yeah... Maybe there are stranger things.

Two stalls were open and available for charging. Rylan backed in next to the one on the left, shut the hover down without a word to me—which was fine—and got out of the van after he disengaged the cells from the engine. I heard the lock click as he opened the small hatch on his side of the engine block. A bright blue glow lit up his face. He pulled out the dimmer cell. They charged in rotation so the hover could still function with just one cell, if needed. It wouldn't be able to move much more than a crawl in that case, but at least the driver wouldn't be stranded.

I watched as he held it with his bare hands. I never understood how something so small could hold so much energy and yet be cool to the touch. I pondered the technology as Rylan opened the thick glass door to the charger and inserted the cell into one of the three slots. A screen projected in front of him, and he chose a few options on the screen before returning to the open van door.

"Do you want something from inside? Water or anything?"

I shook my head. "No. Thank you." I actually wanted water. It sounded really good, but I didn't want anything from him. I just wanted to get moving. I felt anxious, exposed, sitting here.

Rylan disappeared into the shop, IDfob in hand. I wondered if it was even real credit on his fob or if it was still his stolen money. I closed my eyes and took a deep breath. I didn't want to go down that route right now. I wanted to just sit. Gazing out the window, I looked at the forest trees situated around us.

The day was still grey, but it wasn't as ugly as this morning. It was actually—

I heard a growling noise from my left. An all-black sports sedan squealed into the charging station. The car turned to the right, slamming on its brakes, and took the slot next to ours. I saw a man behind the wheel.

The car door opened, and Mr. Speedy stepped out and stood there for a minute. I couldn't take my eyes off of him. He wore all black, from his leather jacket to his boots. I stared at the bird tattoo on his neck when he glanced over at me, catching me in the act.

My stomach jolted. I felt my face turn red, but I didn't look away. His green eyes locked on mine. A surge of energy swelled within me. It felt like a whirlwind gaining speed, like it was trying to reach out and away from me.

He felt it too. I saw the confusion cross his face for a split second before he smiled. I smiled back, warmth spreading through me.

Rylan climbed back in the van, snapping my attention away. He handed me a water bottle and a bag of Doritos, and then he got back out to check the power cell before I could say anything.

I looked back to the man in all black. I saw him walk into the shop like he owned the world, like nothing ever got in his way. *What must it feel like to carry confidence in your back pocket like that?*

A few minutes later, Rylan reinserted the cell, now glowing brighter than the others, into the engine and closed the hatch, letting the lock reengage. He started the hover, and as Rylan pulled the van forward and out of the stall, the man in black came out of the shop. He caught my eye as we started to turn the other direction. I watched as he stood, staring at me for just a moment, and winked as I went past.

I smiled again, feeling the buzz inside me subside the farther away we drove from Mr. Black. We merged back onto the main road, finally on our way again. I opened my bottle and took a drink, but I didn't touch the chips. I didn't feel like snacking, so I put them on top of my bag. I honestly thought I would take a nap. I was tired of looking out the window at line after line of trees. I shifted to lay my head against the door.

"We didn't finish talking yesterday. I'm sure there's a lot more you want to know."

My eyes closed. "No. Not really." But as I thought about it, I opened my eyes. "Actually, there is one thing. Where are we going? I know you said Pennsylvania, but you didn't say where or even why Pennsylvania."

He looked out the window. Apparently, I'd asked the wrong question, a question he didn't want to answer.

"Rylan? Where are we going?" The anxiety rose in my chest. I hated it. I hated feeling anxious around him.

He blew out a long breath. "I'm taking you to my house."

My stomach dropped. "I'm sorry? Your house? Don't you live in New Eastland?"

He shook his head slowly. "No. When I... left, I moved out of the city. I couldn't be nearby."

Emotions hit me like a wave. So many nights, I had found comfort looking out of my balcony, knowing he was at an apartment somewhere. It had given me peace on hard nights. And it was all a lie. He not only left me. He left everything. *Why did that hurt even more than before?*

I sat in shock. But then… "Wait. Then what were you doing

in New Eastland on Spectral day? You had to be within the city limits."

He tensed—another question he didn't want to answer. My heart clenched in anticipation. Rylan shook his head, as if fighting with himself, and it angered me. "Oh, out with it already. I think everything I've found out about you is worse than anything you have to tell me now. Why were you in the city?"

He looked over at me then, eyes overflowing with emotion. "I missed you. I couldn't focus where I was. I wasn't sleeping. I needed to—I needed to see you."

I felt sick. I needed out. I needed out of the van. "Pull over," I stammered, trying to breathe.

His face contorted with concern. "What? Now?"

"Yes. Pull over now. I want out. Dammit, now, Rylan!"

He swerved the van to the shoulder and slowed down. As soon as the safety locks disengaged, I pushed open the door, stumbling onto the grass and escaping into the brush of trees. I heard Rylan call my name from the car.

I trudged deeper into the trees, stomping over fallen leaves, skirting around low branches.

"Angelia! Wait! Where are you going?"

"Away from you," I yelled over my shoulder.

"What? Come on. Stop. Can we talk, please? Angelia?"

I heard him move faster to try to catch up with me, and I started to run. I didn't want to talk. I didn't even want to look at him. I just wanted him to go away. I ignored his calls as I ran as fast as I could through the brush. I eventually broke out of the trees and into a large open and bare field. No trees to hide in meant nothing to keep him from catching me. So I turned, feet planted, rage in my eyes.

He slowed down as he saw me and stopped about five feet away. "Angelia—"

I threw my hands up. "Stop calling me that! You're not

allowed to call me that anymore! Don't you get it? Don't you see that? You're not allowed to miss me. You're not allowed to come see me," I practically growled as I paced in a circle. "After everything, you came back to spy on me. AGAIN. I can't—I don't—How long were you watching me this time, Rylan? How long?"

He stood still, arms at his side. His shoulders slumped, already in defeat, like nothing could get worse. "I got there two days before Spectral day."

I shook my head. "And what did I do for those two days? How much of my days did you watch?"

He rubbed his forehead briefly before answering. "I saw you go to your shop. I watched you drink coffee—"

"Burn my notes?"

He nodded so gently I almost didn't notice. I tried to steady my breathing. *Lies. He is just always full of lies.* I put my hands over my face, wanting to shut out what was happening, when I heard him step toward me.

I threw my hands out. "Stop! Don't. I can't trust you or anything you say. Why did I even come with you? Maybe it would have been better to go with the guys who came for me. At least I wouldn't have this… this knife in my heart every time I look at you." I was overwhelmed by my emotions now. Nothing stopped the anger or sorrow from flooding out of me, fast and hard. "And you want to know the craziest part? I forgave you. After everything that happened, after those men told me all about you, after everything I learned, I still forgave you. I wanted YOU. I loved YOU. But you didn't want me. You didn't want us. You chose to leave."

His face and body suddenly animated, finally speaking. "Do you think I wanted to leave? You honestly think that it didn't take every ounce of strength I had to leave you sleeping in bed that morning? That it didn't hurt? That I wanted to go? Is that what you think?"

"I think you left me and didn't care what happened."

"That's the only reason I left!" His voice exploded as it rose to meet mine. "I left because I cared. I knew it wouldn't last."

I shook my head to clear my vision. The trees swayed behind him, speaking to the wind. "I didn't ask you to go. I asked you to stay." I looked back into his eyes, my voice dropping. "Don't you remember? I asked you to stay." Tears filled my eyes.

"Yes, you did. *That* day. But I knew, one day, you'd change your mind. You'd wake up and realize who was lying beside you. You would have to make the decision. I didn't want you to have to make it, so I made it. I made it so you could move on with your life and have a chance at being truly happy with someone you could love and trust, not someone like me."

I took in a shaky breath and turned away from him, tears spilling down my face. I felt the breeze across my cheeks and something… something else. I looked across the field. A buzz—I'd felt it before—came from the other side. All I could see was a giant cream-colored boulder. But I felt it, like the wind in my hair, a caress across my face.

"I'm sorry…" I heard Rylan speak from behind me. "I would take it back if I could."

I spun around then, anger flaring. "Would you? Tell me what, exactly, would you take back? Stalking me for weeks? Lying to me about who you were? Making me love you, knowing everything you said was a lie? Making yourself my everything? Do you know that, Rylan? I thought you were my forever! That we were forever!" I practically screamed the last sentence, drowning in so much pain I thought I would never resurface.

The pain burst through me in waves of energy. It exploded out of me like a surge of power. I saw strings of black light shoot out in every direction. Small white specks of light flowed beside them. They flew outward, knocking into Rylan, pushing him down to the ground. I watched as the surrounding trees swayed and bent, some snapping from the strings of energy.

The surge released, I fell to my knees. Rylan rushed to my side. "Are you okay?" He cupped my face in his hands, looking into my eyes.

I put my hands on his chest, feeling around where the wave hit him. "Are you okay? I'm sorry. I didn't know. I didn't know I could—"

He hugged me then, arms wrapped around me, holding me against him.

And I let him.

I wrapped my arms around his neck and held him back, crying into his shoulder, wishing the world was different. I wished we were back in our apartment, lying in bed, kissing each other while we talked just to interrupt, just to make the other one smile.

I felt the numbness come back then, flowing over me like a blanket. All of the energy was gone from my body. I could barely open my eyes. The tears stopped. My legs were weak. My knees buckled.

Rylan caught me, scooping me up into his arms. "Hold on, Angelia. Let me get you back to the van. Just hold on."

The world twisted and spun. It was wet and dry as I tumbled. And then I was whole again.

He opened the side door and laid me on the bed he had made on the inside, the bed he slept in while he watched me. I shook my head to quiet the memories.

"You'll be okay. Just sleep. Sleep as long as you need." His hand grazed my forehead, brushing strands of hair to the side. "You were my forever too. You've always been my forever."

My heart would have smiled if given the chance, but the darkness came for me then. I let it have me.

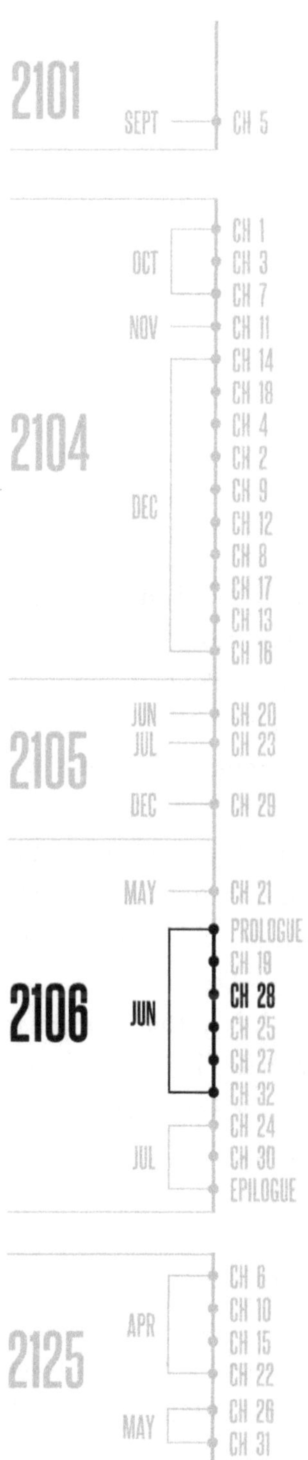

CHAPTER 28

JUNE 2106
Raven

The house was painfully silent as I closed the door quietly behind me. I knew there were bound to be more creaks in the floorboards down the middle of the kitchen, so I walked around the side through the living room. I removed my boots and put them by the other shoes, along with my jacket on its hook, and I made my way to the stairs. I looked up at the fourteen steps to the top.

The hardest part about sneaking back into this house was going up the stairs. If she was awake, it didn't matter. She'd hear me. But, if she was still sleeping, it was possible. I stood and stared, not ready to chance it yet.

I accidentally fell asleep with Ivy. That was not the plan, nor had it been in the past. I always returned home before Moira to make sure that everything stayed exactly the way that it was. But today, I fell asleep next to my newest redhead.

Stupid. Stupid. Stupid.

Up I climbed, one stair at a time. One creak, I stopped. I made it up five steps when a loud screech rang out through the stairwell, and I froze, waiting for any signal that Moira was awake. Thankfully, I heard nothing. I continued. When I reached the top, I started taking off my clothes. I was completely naked, everything all bunched in my hand, as I walked into the room. Call it a sort of insurance plan. If she caught me sliding into bed, I could easily lie and say that I was getting up to use the bathroom.

I walked into the room. I saw her stir and look toward the door, so I bolted into the bathroom, shoving my clothes in the hamper as fast as possible.

"Babe?" she called from the bedroom.

I whispered, "Sorry, hun. Did I wake you?"

"Are you just getting home?" I heard the edge to her voice as I flushed the toilet and walked out of the bathroom.

"No. I came home a couple hours ago, but you were sleeping. I figured you were exhausted, so I just got in bed."

I crawled into the bed, hoping she wouldn't notice as I pulled the blankets apart, making them messy as I got in. She didn't say anything. I held my breath, not expecting her to believe me, but then she surprised me and rolled over, wrapping her body around mine.

"I was worried when I got home and you weren't here. There are too many crazy things happening in New Eastland. It stressed me out."

I pulled her closer to me, my heart stinging with guilt for pretending to be what she wanted, for being someone I wasn't.

I held her close and stroked her hair. "It's okay. I'm okay. Don't worry. Go back to sleep."

She did, but I couldn't. I knew whatever happened in New Eastland was because of the Atlas Institute and, in turn, Logan too. That's why I was at Ivy's house.

Every time I said it was the last time, something triggered, and I had to see her. I could barely contain the storm that raged by the time I reached her house. I heard the lightning behind me as she opened the door. When she saw it was me, she smiled, dragging me into the house, and our lips touched before the door fully closed.

I knew I was chasing something that wasn't mine. I knew I was running away from something that might not even be an issue any more, but I felt stuck, with Moira, with Logan. Now, I was stuck with Ivy to get me through being stuck with them all.

I sighed quietly. Something had to change. I was losing my mind.

The next morning, I flipped pancakes as Moira came down the stairs. I got the usual hug and kiss before she sat down and turned on the projectionTV, flipping to the news channel.

I ignored the news at all costs, not wanting to get wrapped up in any emotional nonsense about Logan, so I steered clear. In the mornings, though, I couldn't escape.

"Oh, wow. There's a protest going on in New Eastland. Raven, look."

I added the two new pancakes to our stacks before turning toward the screen. "What are they protesting today?"

"It looks like too many Spectrals are disappearing, and people aren't happy about it."

That caught my attention. I sat at the breakfast bar to watch the segment. "Turn it up," I said, straining to hear the words from the reporter.

She scrolled up on the glasstech controller, and the words came into focus. "…knows why this is happening. It seems only about 5 percent of the populace of New Eastland were affected by what is being called Spectral Day. At this point, scientists are still speculating on why those 5 percent and not any others. Dr. Atlas of The Atlas Institute commented, saying they are unsure of the origin of this gene mutation but are willing to open their doors for any exploratory testing." I scoffed but kept my comments to myself. "Renowned philanthropist and billionaire Kane Tummult says the implications of this new discovery will change the course of the human race. Many may agree, but at this point, many are unsure. As you can see behind me, the protest started early again this morning, going on day two, and will continue to go well into the day as many are frustrated without any answers to their questions. Why did this happen? Who is responsible? And where are the Spectrals disappearing to? This is Chance Parker. Back to you, Alex."

The picture changed to the news room. I felt my anxiety levels rise.

Spectrals are disappearing? I guess I should have been watching the news. Shit.

How were they being found? What did the compound develop to find Spectrals?

Oh, shit, to find me.

I was right in the middle between them and New Eastland. I needed to go. I needed to go now.

So many thoughts flowed through my head, and it took a second for me to realize that Moira was talking.

"Babe? Hey, are you okay? You look, I don't know, off. Are you all right?"

I nodded, blinking a few times before smiling. "Yes. I'm sorry. It's just—uh—a lot to take in, with everything going on in New Eastland. Do you want to eat?"

She hugged me. "It's okay. It's hours away from us. Like you said last night, there's no need to be worried." I smiled at her before grabbing our plates.

I didn't taste the pancakes, the homemade syrup, or the hazelnut coffee or really hear Moira as she talked to me about her plans for the day with one of her friends. I was stuck, lost in a sea of fear. I hadn't felt like this since I left the compound, and now, they'd found a way to track people like me.

If they looked for me once, they'd do it again.

I somehow got through eating breakfast and cleaning up while she got ready. As she walked back down the stairs, looking beautiful, sadness welled up in my chest. She'd been so good to me, taken me in, and loved me—she really had. I didn't think I would, but I was going to miss her.

After she put on her boots, she walked over to hug me goodbye. I pulled her close, arms around her waist, and held her tighter before kissing her softly, deeply.

She smiled. "What was that for?"

"I don't think I ever say thank you enough for what you do for me."

"Yes, you do, every day." She kissed me, and I heard her comm chime with an alert. "I'll see you later. Nella's outside. Hold this thought until I get home. Okay?"

I winked at her. "You got it."

I watched as she walked out the door, climbed into the waiting hover, and drove off, out of my life, for the last time.

Less than fifteen minutes later, I was packed. I didn't have much to bring with me, just a duffle bag full of clothes, shoes, and other random belongings. Really, everything was Moira's, and I didn't want to take anything of hers—except for her hover, cigarettes, and credits from her account. I needed those. Before I could take any of it, though, I had to remove the tracking device.

Grabbing a screwdriver, a butcher knife, and matches, I went to the garage and slid under the car toward the rear of the bumper. Within ten minutes, I was done. Of the many things I learned on the streets over the years, right now, I was thankful the most for this one.

I walked back into the house and put my thieving tools away. I opened her specglass tablet and transferred credits from her account to mine. I'd done it before—she'd given me permission—but this time, I took enough to last me for a few weeks.

I pushed the guilt down as I put her tablet back. I stopped. I should leave her with something. A note? A goodbye? An apology? None of it seemed right, so I changed my mind and just left the tablet on the table.

Moving back to the living room, I grabbed my duffle bag and

took my jacket off the hook. I started to walk toward the garage door and took one last look around the room, at the only place I've ever lived longer than a few weeks since I was a kid.

The stillness of the house followed me outside as I got in the black sports hover and drove down the street. I drove nowhere specific, just west and away from this goddamn state.

I was almost to Pennsylvania and finally out of New York. Before I crossed the border, I needed to refuel, not only the hover but me too. The last thing I wanted to do was stop, but considering my New York plates, I didn't want to flag anything in Pennsylvania until I had to. Besides, I was not a short person, and sports hovers were not made for men my size.

Checking the navigation, I found a charging station only a few miles away. That worked for me.

I pulled in—a little fast, I thought—and parked my hover across from a large black hover van. As I got out to stretch, feeling the warmth of the summer sun on my face, my energy stirred, almost like a buzz. That was odd.

I was usually thinking of Logan when I felt these rumblings. I looked up right into the bright blue eyes of a shockingly beautiful girl sitting in the black hover beside me.

She flushed when I caught her looking at me but didn't look away.

The pulse was there, and it grew stronger as I held her eyes. It felt like power. *And it felt good.* I smiled at her. She smiled back.

And then the moment vanished as someone walked up to the driver's side of the van and stole her attention. I took a breath and walked away, trying to clear my head, turning my thoughts away from the blue-eyed beauty to what food I wanted before I charged the cells.

A few minutes later, I walked back out of the small store, having already devoured the sandwich I bought inside, now only holding the rest of my energy drink. The black van made a U-turn in front of me. I stopped and looked at the passenger side window for another glimpse of the beautiful girl with the blue eyes.

And there she was. I winked at her as the car turned, and I saw her smile again. *A beautiful smile to match.*

The cells took about ten more minutes to charge. Apparently, Moira hadn't charged the others, so I had to recharge them all. Waiting made me anxious. I just wanted to hit the road already.

I finally received green lights across the three cells, and I put them back in as fast as I could. The car was hot from sitting in the sun, so I blasted the air conditioning.

Maybe I could make it to the middle of Pennsylvania by nightfall. I hoped so. I wouldn't feel better until I was far enough away that I couldn't watch any local news from New York.

As I entered the main road, I turned left, driving toward the state line. Both sides of the road were lined with trees, just green for miles. Watching the tree line get denser, I cursed myself.

Those blue eyes were so distracting that I forgot my restroom break. Annoyed, I pulled off to the side of the road just before a wide bend that curved around a large expanse of trees. Instead of standing right out for anyone to see—I had some modesty, after all—I decided to walk a little farther into the tree line. As I adjusted my pants, I heard voices coming from inside of the dense brush in front of me. I paused to hear the muffled conversation. I didn't quite understand why anyone would be in the forest itself. One of the voices got louder. Now I was too curious not to go look.

I walked through the thick bushes and trees toward the voices on the other side. A short way from where I stood, I came to a clearing with a large boulder. Across the clearing of wild grass, I saw two people, a guy and a girl, having an argument. I saw the guy pleading with the girl, but her back was to me.

I felt the hum return like a little scratch at the back of my head. It got stronger and stronger as I heard her voice get louder and louder.

Then, suddenly, she rotated and stared directly at me with bright blue eyes. This was the same girl who, a few minutes before, distracted me and sent my energy into a slight blaze. Her gaze became unfocused, and I realized that the boulder hid me from her sight.

I continued to watch as she turned back to the man. Her arms flung out, and she screamed loud enough for me to pick up phrases. The words "we were forever" echoed through the open space between us.

And then waves of black light burst from her body, flowing out from the center where she stood, traveling out in every direction. Small white spots swirled around, like little webs of energy.

The guy slammed into the ground, and trees buckled and bent where her energy hit them.

My body wanted to respond. I could feel the energy as it burst from her, and it sparked my own to do the same. It was intoxicating.

She fell to the floor, making me step forward. But I remembered myself. I remembered our situation and watched as the guy ran to her side, picking her up.

I waited to see if she was okay when suddenly there was a flash of yellow light, and they were gone.

I stood there in the wake of the energy flowing through me while feeling a strange loss in my body. Shocked, I stared at the field, at where the young couple had just been. I didn't know how it happened, how they came to be here, but I knew they were Spectrals—Spectrals like me.

I knew I needed to follow them. I had too many questions, and maybe they had answers. I raced toward my hover, knowing I couldn't let her energy get away.

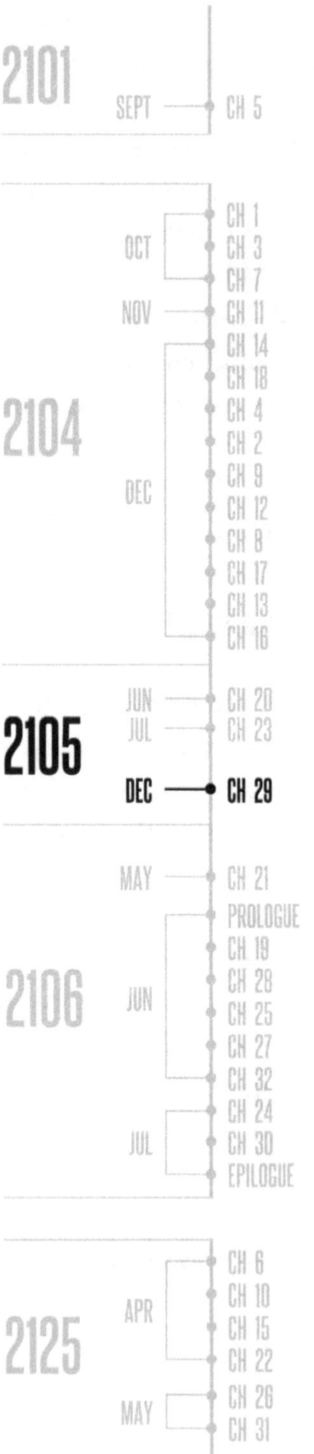

CHAPTER 29

DECEMBER 2105
Angelia

"Nope." Jaeden shook his head, smiling at me.

I huffed. "Come on. You said you'd give me a hint."

He raised his eyebrows at me. "When did I say that?" I scrunched my lips together. "Exactly. So will you get dressed now, please?"

Jaeden turned around from his spot on the couch, looking over the back. I stood as if on stage in front of him between the window and the kitchen. I was trying to convince him to tell me where he planned to take me for our first-ever anniversary.

"Well, can you give me a hint after I get dressed?"

He shook his head, grinning. "How did I not know that you hate surprises?"

I scoffed. "That's not true! I love surprises." I crossed my arms. "Just not having a hint makes it harder to deal with it."

"You know, you're cute when you pout."

Taking two steps forward, I grabbed a pillow from the couch and threw it at him.

He caught it, laughing, and threw it back at me. "Can you go get dressed now?"

I spun around, exasperated, thinking of something I could

offer him. I twisted my lips. "How about I owe you a REALLY long body massage? I'll get out some candles and some music." I smiled. "I'll do it naked."

He put one hand in the air. "First of all, you already owe me like five body massages. I'm still waiting on those. How is adding another one to my list going to help you?"

"Ughhh. You're killing me." Another idea came then. I smiled, looking at him from under my lashes. "How about I just get undressed, instead of dressed?"

His laughter was cut short.

I pulled his favorite sweatshirt, with the words "Neoteric Beats," over my head and dropped it to the floor. I had nothing on underneath, except a pair of shorts, which quickly followed.

His eyes raked over my body. I tingled in all the places his eyes touched from across the room. Jaeden stood up from the couch and didn't take his eyes off me as he came around to where I stood. I was trying to win the battle, but as he got closer, with that fire in his eyes, I forgot which battle I wanted to win.

He brushed his fingertips down my neck and over my shoulders, crossing my collarbone on both sides. A shiver ran down my body as I closed my eyes, lost to the sensations he left across my skin. He pulled me into him, nuzzling the soft curve of my neck. My hands ran through his hair as his lips explored the top part of my body. His hands explored the bottom.

Everything about his touch was soft, gentle, sweet, until it became filled with need. He couldn't get enough. He couldn't touch me enough. His lips were on mine, his body hard against me, and I fell into the sensation of him.

He let me go for just a second to grab our grey throw off the couch and lay it down where we stood. I laid down, watching him undress, with a smirk on my face.

"Do you have any idea how beautiful you are?" I said as my eyes followed the same pattern over his body that his had on mine.

He smiled at me as he pushed his pile of clothes to the side, lying down beside me. With one hand holding up his head, the other drew a line up to the hollow of my throat and down to just below my belly button. Up and down, I could only lie there, enjoying his soft tease.

"You know, this doesn't change anything. I'm still not giving you a hint."

I reached for him and kissed him with my own passion, my own need. His arms around me, pressed up against him, I whispered against his lips, "Right now, I want something else from you."

He traced down my side with his left hand, lower and lower. His fingertips brushed the inside of my thighs. "Oh yeah? What's that exactly?"

"I—"

His fingers pressed deeply into me, cutting off my words, my thoughts, everything, as I cried out. His lips came back to mine as sensations started to blend together. My heartbeat, my breath, his skin, our bodies, everything blurred as he shifted his body on top of mine. Our arms and legs intertwined. "Is this what you want?" he asked gently between breaths, pressing himself into me. I nodded, eyes closed, reveling in the softness of his skin, his smell, his weight on me, in me.

I loved how time froze when we were together like this.

No, that's not right.

There was no time. There was just our heartbeat.

Just our lips touching.

Just our bodies moving as one.

Just our love. And I could stay here with him forever every time.

Rylan

An hour later, we were finally in my hover and on our way. I glanced over at her. She looked out the window, watching the different buildings pass by, trying to figure out where I was taking her. She had not made it easy to get out the door. We were a little behind schedule, but I was not disappointed in the way our morning started.

Our fingers were intertwined between us, and I pulled her toward me to kiss the back of her hand. "Are you excited?"

A smile spread across her face. "Yes. Are you kidding? This is the biggest secret of my life right now. How much longer until we get there?"

"Less than ten minutes."

She squealed, her side braid shifting in her excitement, and looked back out the window.

Angelia was a perfect picture in her long-sleeved black top with a deep scoop neckline. Her dark blue jeans flared out, with rips across the knees and of course her oversized cargo pockets. She tapped the toes of her usual black boots and fidgeted with the buttons on her grey overcoat, sitting over her lap while we drove. I didn't want to take my eyes off her, but being in midair made that a necessity, so I stole glances as I could. I still didn't know how I got to be so lucky. Shifting my focus back to the road in front of me, I saw our exit up ahead.

She squealed again, looking over at me. "Are we going to the TechHub Outlets?"

I wanted to laugh, but I only smiled, nodding. She giggled with delight. We were about five minutes away, and the knot in my stomach worsened.

I had been working on this gift for six months. It took time and quite a bit of money to set this up. I prayed she didn't hold the last part against me.

You'll find out soon enough.

I looped around two streets and pulled into a shopping center in the middle of one of the busiest parts of the city. It was called TechHub for a reason. It was like a giant outdoor mall for technology. Every store, shop, booth, and vendor specialized in software or hardware.

Along the sides of the skylane, signs floated on drones, each flashing news of a special deal or asking us what we needed so it could direct us. I already knew where I was going.

We sat in the line to descend longer than expected, and I could feel Angelia's growing anxiety. She started picking under her nails while staring out the window. Finally it was our turn, and I followed the flow to park.

After today, we'd probably park somewhere else, but for now, I chose the front parking area, like a regular patron.

She wiggled back and forth in her seat as I disengaged the hover and let the engines shut down. As soon as the locks let go, she practically jumped out the door, her coat flying out onto the pavement as she did.

I laughed and came around the side, picking up her coat and helping her put it on. I pulled her to me by the lapels. "Why are you such a kid right now? Is it Christmas?" She laughed as I kissed her.

"Yes, maybe. It depends on what we are doing." She looked around. "Where are we going?"

I grabbed both of her hands, interlacing them in mine, and wrapped our arms around her back, holding her against me.

"Well, we are going to have a delicious lunch. It would have been breakfast, but someone distracted me and wouldn't get dressed this morning." She wrinkled her nose at me. "But first, I think I'm just as anxious as you to give you your present first. Is that okay?"

She scrunched up her shoulders. "Yes, yes!"

"Okay, then. Come on." I let go of one hand and led her with the other toward a corner of the shopping center. We wound through hovers, bikes, and people to reach the corner. She was distracted, soaking in everything with wide eyes. Robots traveled around holding signs, and small hovers floated with sample products from various stores. She was in heaven.

We finally made it to the sidewalk, and I ignored my stomach doing flips in my chest. I could hardly breathe as we passed two shops on our right. I stopped in front of one. She was too busy staring at a couple at a projection screen placing an order for a CleanBot, watching the visual change as the couple picked different options from the kiosk, to realize that we weren't moving.

She turned to me. "What's up? Why'd we stop?"

I shrugged. "We're here."

She looked at the store in front of us. The windows displayed a store with empty shelves. Confusion flashed across her face as she glanced at the sign above the window. M&M TECHNOLOGIES was sprawled across the top in black and red letters. My heart soared at her changing expression. Tears formed in her eyes and then fell as I held her hand, waiting, just waiting for her to say something. This was her moment, and I was just a passenger beside her.

After a minute, she wiped the fallen tears from her face. "How did you…" She stopped again, overcome by emotion. I pulled her to me, resting her forehead against my cheek.

I spoke softly, "I might not be able to give you the whole world, so I wanted to give you a little piece of it." She wrapped her arms around me, and we stood there, embracing each other and all that this new piece of life meant for her, for us.

She finally pulled back, smiling at me. "Can we go inside?"

I took a quick breath, releasing my anxiety. She wasn't mad. She wasn't fighting me. I pulled out her IDfob from my back pocket, holding it by the metal ring she never added anything to. "It was coded for access yesterday."

Her eyes widened, and she snatched it from my hand. She stepped toward the door and stopped, turning back to me. She stood there, just looking at me. Before I could ask, she threw her arms around me again and kissed me like it was the first time. Now breathless, she leaned her forehead against mine.

"Thank you. With all of my heart, thank you."

"With all of mine, you're welcome." I kissed her forehead. "Come on. Let's go inside."

Angelia

I soared in a sea of emotions—shock, excitement, fear. There was so much to feel at one time for so many different reasons.

I was still in shock, processing what it took Jaeden to do this, from the location, which was near impossible to begin with, to the cost. I didn't know how he did it, but I was saving that conversation for some other time.

I felt excitement because, well, this was my future—our future. I was now the owner of a shop. *My shop?* Oh, man, what a feeling. It was mine.

What if I screw it up? I shook my head. I wouldn't. I planned on putting my soul into this. The fear started to drop away as the excitement built the closer we got to the door.

I stopped at the front door panel, staring at it, my IDfob in my hand. I reached up and kissed Jaeden on the lips, softly, saying as much as I could with that one moment. He smiled, his beautiful smile, as I scanned the IDfob over the panel. The lock released.

The room smelled like paint, plastic, and metal. Most of all, it smelled brand new, like a room that'd never been touched. There was a long walkway down the middle of the room, leading from the front door to the back, that ended at a pair of double doors. I saw rows and rows of empty shelves, many with bins of different sizes on them to my left and my right.

I gasped. "Holy shit. It keeps going?"

He laughed. "Yup. I wasn't going to limit you to a small space." I wrapped my arms around his waist and squeezed. "The inventory is in the back in boxes. More is coming next week. I basically ordered everything on the manifest for TechHalo and some other things I thought you might want."

I pulled back and looked at him. "What? You couldn't

organize the bins for me? Sheesh. Who are you?"

He laughed. "I was not about to screw up where you wanted everything. I wouldn't hear the end of it."

I nodded. "True."

"And I wouldn't rob you of that joy for anything."

I kissed him. "You know me so well."

"I do."

I smiled, gazing around. "Show me more. Is there an office?"

"Yeah, this way."

I practically jumped up and down and ran to the back of the shop. For the next hour, we explored every nook and cranny of the store. I saw the office, which only had a desk, a chair, and a techscreen.

He hadn't wanted to furnish more than that so I could customize and set the room up the way I wanted it. But he painted the walls a soft yellow, which made me giggly.

We walked through the receiving room in the back. It was full of crates with a manifest of over 100 items. My eyes were as big as plates. I couldn't wait to start unpacking.

Then, beyond the double doors, we found the repair room. I stood in awe. Eight stations were set up, each with the same layout—a table with a light and a metal cabinet. Yellow pegboards hung above each table with hooks ready for supplies.

In the middle of the room was a large, yellow, rolling toolbox and two smaller ones. A large, centralized desk sat in the middle of the semi-circle of stations with gloves and other random tools. I walked through the room, running my hands across everything.

When he asked if I liked it, I burst into happy tears and hugged him again.

We traveled back down the main walkway toward the front of the store, hand in hand. He twirled me, mid-walk, pulling me in for a kiss. "Are you happy?"

"Um, are you crazy? What, if anything, of the past couple of hours would say otherwise?"

He laughed and kissed me again.

I pulled back then, standing to the side. "But you know I have to ask. How did you pay for all of this? I mean, I know you have a good savings account, and you make good money, but this is a little beyond all of that, isn't it?"

The look on his face shifted. Before he could answer my question, another voice interrupted from the front of the shop.

"Yes, Rylan, why don't you tell her where you got the money."

Four men stood at the front of my shop. I'd never seen them before, but their stern faces and cold demeanor made me feel anxious.

Jaeden's eyes widened with recognition. He knew who they were. I didn't know why, but that scared me. I looked from Jaeden to the man in front with a shaved head. He shot me a sinister smile, sending shivers down my spine.

"I'm sorry. You don't know him as Rylan. Right? Damn. Which alias does he use with you?" He glanced up at the ceiling, as if trying to figure out a math problem before looking back at me. "Oh, that's right. He's Jaeden Lowe to you. Isn't he?"

I didn't understand. Jaeden shifted himself in front of me, his arm holding me behind him, protecting me from whoever they were. His posture scared me even more. *Something was wrong. Something was very wrong.*

"What do you want?" he asked.

The bald man laughed. "What do I want? Honestly, what I wanted for a long time was what you promised us and then failed to deliver. But, thankfully, we have Trey now. He can do your job better than you ever did."

The man tilted to the side to look me in the eye. I could just see his face over Jaeden's shoulder.

"Did he ever tell you about his job before he met you? No? I suppose not. It would kill all this magic you seem to have together."

I looked up at Jaeden, but he didn't say anything. He just

stared straight ahead at the men in front of us.

"Oh, come on, Jaeden, or Rylan, or whoever you are. Let's all be friends. No one needs to get hurt." His smile didn't match his words.

"Whatever you want from me, just tell me, Cristian. Whatever you want, just leave her out of this."

Cristian glared back. "But this all has to do with her. If it wasn't for her, then you wouldn't have betrayed every single one of us. Right?"

Jaeden turned his body, completely hiding me from the men standing in front of us. I grabbed his arm from behind, unsure what to do or say.

Cristian peered around Jaeden and spoke to me again. "Don't you want to know who it is that you're building a life with? Don't you want to know his real name?" I felt angry at this man trying to cause chaos.

With a surge of courage, I yelled back. "His name is Jaeden. I don't know what you want, but there's nothing that you can say that's going to change anything."

Cristian chuckled. "Nothing I can say? Oh, I highly doubt that. Since we're calling you Jaeden for right now, let's go with that." He rubbed his hands together before crossing his arms over his chest. "So, Jaeden, how long did you stalk the beautiful Angelia before you finally spoke to her?" Jaeden stiffened beside me. "Did you know that, sweetheart? Do you know that he stalked you for weeks before he finally had the courage to come talk to you?"

"Cristian, stop it," Jaeden said, with a fear in his voice.

"No. I think it's important for her to know. If she thinks she wants to spend her life with you, shouldn't she know who it is that sleeps next to her every night?" He looked back at me again. "Didn't you find it strange that he happened to know your favorite coffee place? How about when you went to Montreal?" He eyed the other men still standing silently beside them. "Of all the ones you found,

Trey, this one's my favorite." He looked back at us. "In Montreal, didn't you find it strange how everything just kept happening so serendipitously for both of you? Did you really think that you guys were just that lucky?"

The knot in my stomach twisted. His questions mirrored my own from those days. I didn't understand how or why, but I felt he was telling the truth. "Jaeden?"

He didn't answer. He didn't turn. He just stared back at Cristian.

"Do you want to tell her what you actually do for a living, Jaeden? Do you want to tell her that you spent months with us traveling across the country stealing from the elite? Do you want to tell her how many houses you helped us break into with your programs? Go ahead and tell her how you are able to hack into any technology, any IDfob, any security system, anything. Why don't you tell her that, Jaeden? She's listening now. She might be very impressed by the fact that you can do that. If she loves you as much as she says she does, why not just tell her the truth?" His smile turned into a grimace. "Tell her that you're a thief. Look her in the eyes and tell her that everything you have is stolen. If not for that, you'd have nothing. You'd be worthless."

Tears stung the back of my eyes. I stepped away from Jaeden, letting go of his arm.

He finally turned to look at me, when he felt me pull away. "Angelia…"

I didn't know what to say. I just looked him in the eyes, wishing and hoping that Cristian was wrong, that he wasn't this person. But his eyes told me the truth.

My heart shattered, feeling like little pieces were breaking off and falling to the floor. "It's true, isn't it? What he's saying is true, right?" I whispered.

He grabbed both of my hands, his eyes on mine. "Whether it's true or not doesn't change how much I love you. I fell in love with you as somebody else—that might be true—but I have always loved you with all of me."

I wanted to believe him. There was a war in my heart, my mind. I didn't know what to think, what to feel. I opened my mouth to speak when I realized we both had lost track of the four men standing by the door.

Hands grabbed me from behind, while two other men approached Jaeden from either side. We were both yanked away from each other. I started to pull away while Jaeden tried to free himself.

Cristian walked up to me and looked me in the eye. "Don't be upset. This is who he is. This is what he's always been, what he'll always be. You should be grateful that I told you before you guys got married, before you married a stranger."

I lashed out and kicked him as hard as I could between his legs. He doubled over but quickly stood back up, yelling with rage in his eyes. I didn't see his fist, but I felt the pain across my face. I heard Jaeden scream as I hit the floor, stunned and dizzy.

I couldn't move as I watched Jaeden hit, twist, and try to get away from the men that held him. The ringing in my ears slowly started to subside.

"This is what happens when you betray your family." Pulling back his fist, Cristian hit Jaeden over and over again. Blood came down Jaeden's nose, his mouth, and I screamed for them to stop.

Cristian hit him in the chest, in the sides, wherever he could reach. Then, when he couldn't stand anymore, the two men dropped Jaeden and started using their feet.

I could only lie there in shock, in pain, as they hurt the only person I ever loved.

They finally stopped. Jaeden wasn't moving. Cristian grabbed him by the hair and pulled his face to his. "You have a week to send us the rest of your cut, with interest. Don't make me come back and find you, or you won't leave with your life." Cristian looked over at me, eyes sharp and vicious. "Happy anniversary." He laughed as he dropped Jaeden's head to the floor and walked away, leaving us both.

My head was spinning. I couldn't keep my eyes open. I fought, strained to stay awake, to stay there, with Jaeden. But it hurt. Everything hurt—my heart, my head—and I felt a numbness sweep over me then. I closed my eyes and hated myself as I fell into darkness, hearing his voice call my name.

Rylan

I opened my eyes, or tried to. They felt heavy, like lead, like I hadn't ever opened them. My head was spinning, but I willed an eye to crack open. Light flooded in, and I winced, the pain shooting to the back of my skull. I tried to move my mouth, move my tongue, but it felt like cotton. I was so confused. *What's going on? What's wrong with me?*

A machine beeped near me as the sounds of the room became clearer. I turned my head toward the sound but couldn't focus on anything. All I saw were blurs of color.

And then I heard a gasp, followed by footsteps.

"Gillian! Gillian! He's opening his eyes!" A pause. "Yes, yes, got it. Okay. Thank you." The muffled voice sounded familiar. I didn't know. I just knew I needed to open my eyes. I did my best to focus on that.

The footsteps came back closer to me. Light flooded back into my eyes. This time, I ignored the pain, pushing my eyes all the way open. The fuzzy light took a second to shape and form until I was able to focus on the person standing in front of me. Tears streamed down her cheeks, and her hands were folded inside her sweatshirt—my sweatshirt—where she stood.

My eyes moved around her face, and a rush of emotions slammed into me when I saw the red, swollen side of her cheek and larger, colorful areas of bruising. Memories flooded back to me. *Cristian.*

I tried to sit up then, my muscles screaming at me. Angelia

rushed forward to put her hands on me, but she stopped right above me, taking a step back. "It's okay. Just relax. You're okay… You're okay."

Guilt, anger, and loss washed over me. It hurt more than I could imagine for her to back away from me.

I opened my mouth, frustrated at my body. I managed to croak out just a few words. "Are you okay?"

Tears brimmed in her eyes again. "I'm fine. But you… you've been… really hurt… for a while. You were… in a coma." She spoke carefully, as if the words were glass and they hurt to say.

I lifted my head to look at her, but the muscles were too weak. I took a deep breath. "How long?"

She pressed her lips together, holding back tears. "Four days."

My eyes went wide, which sent a pain through my head. Four days. They'd beaten me into a coma for four days. Angelia was alone for four days.

I lifted my head again, ignoring my numb muscles, looking back at her cheek. "Are you okay?" I was out of breath after just a few words, which frustrated me. But it was nothing compared to the shame, the guilt I felt looking at her face, remembering her fall to the floor, me not being able to do anything.

She nodded. "I'm okay. I had a mild concussion, but—"

I hissed in my anger. My head spun, and I felt sick. I dropped my head backward, hitting the pillow with more force than I should have. I saw spots in front of my eyes.

She stepped forward again, hands clasped. "I'm okay. Really, I'm okay. Don't… don't be upset. I'm just… so glad you're okay." Tears fell down her cheeks again, and I felt my own surface. I glanced over to the chair she'd been sitting in. There was a pile of books, a trash can filled with remnants of food, a blanket, and a pillow. She'd been sleeping there.

Oh, god, did she stay here for four days?

She turned her head to see what I was looking at and lowered her eyes. "I couldn't leave you. I needed—"

A doctor walked in, cutting her off. "Hi, Mr. Lowe. I'm Dr. Meursin. How are you feeling?" It hurt to take my eyes off of her, but I turned my attention to him.

For ten minutes, I answered the usual questions the best I could. He poked and pressed on different parts of my body, listened to my heart and my breathing, and checked the bandage I didn't even know I had wrapped around my head. When he was done, he draped his stethoscope back around his neck. "Everything seems to be healing the way we want it to. Now that you're awake, it should be even faster. We don't like to use the regenerator when a patient is unconscious, so if you are still feeling better later today, you'll have your first session. It should take about three sessions—one per day—to get you fully healed and on your way home." He glanced over at Angelia. "She's been here by your side since you came through the doors. I'm sure she'll be happy to get you home too."

I tried to catch her eyes, but she kept looking down, biting her lip.

"Well, I'll leave you to rest, and we'll come in to check on you in a bit. You're very lucky those men didn't kill you, Mr. Lowe. I guess no one can be too careful. Rest. I'll see you later."
He nodded at Angelia, who attempted a smile.

"Thank you, Doctor." She still wouldn't look at me as he left, finding somewhere else to let her eyes fall. "I told them we were attacked by strangers," she explained softly. "I didn't want them asking more questions about them… about you. So, I just made it seem random."

My stomach twisted. *What have I done?* "Angelia… I'm… I don't know what to say. I'm sorry."

She pressed her lips together and shook her head. "I've been sitting here so worried about you for days. I've barely slept, watching you breathing, praying for you to open your eyes."

I felt tears come again as I saw the pain cross her face, pain I caused.

She spoke between the tears. "I've been angry. I've been confused. I've been so many things, but mostly, I've been grateful." She looked at me then, her eyes focused. "I'm grateful they didn't kill you. I'm grateful for the past year. I wouldn't change one day we had together."

"Angelia..."

She held her hands up, stepping closer to me. "No. Let me finish while I still can. I know now what it really is to love someone, which sounds stupid and cliché, but it's true. I don't care what they said. I don't care what you did. It doesn't change how much I love you. It doesn't change that, and that is all that matters." She took a deep breath. "So I want you to stay. Stay and be with me. Give them whatever they want, and then be whoever you want. Your name doesn't matter. Who you were before me doesn't matter. It's who you are now that matters, and I know you love me." She looked down for a brief moment. "And I'm grateful for that too."

Tears flowed down my face as I lay there, speechless. *She still loved me. She still wanted me.*

I reached out with one hand, my arm shaking, and she took it. Her hand was so warm, like the flood of emotion in my heart. "I don't..." Tears overwhelmed me. She waited while I took a breath and composed myself. "I don't deserve you."

She smiled then, sniffling, a soft, playful look on her face. "No, you don't."

It hurt to smile, but I did, pulling her toward me. "Come here." She climbed gently onto the bed, careful not to hurt me. She laid her head on my chest, and I rested my cheek against her hair.

I felt her breathe me in and sigh. "I was so scared I lost you."

I kissed her head. "I'm here. I'm not going anywhere."

And I had meant it—that day, the next, and even the one after that, the day I finally got to go home.

We laughed as she pushed me out of the hospital in a

wheelchair, even though I could walk just fine. The regenerator had done its job, as expected. "Policy," the nurses said. She wound me around the hallways, running and taking the corners too sharp, almost toppling me at least twice. But we made it to my Volkshover with no real problems.

I started to climb into the passenger seat as Angelia brought the wheelchair back inside. My comm went off in my pocket, a message from an unknown number.

"Look up."

Across the street, in the courtyard of the hospital, stood Cristian in the overcast light of the day, staring at me. I felt sick and angry all over again. I had to remember that Angelia was coming back soon. It was the only thing that kept me from crossing the street.

He typed more into his comm and hit send. *"Your deadline is tonight. Don't forget, for her sake."*

I looked back up at him, but he was already walking away, his back to me.

My stomach dropped, and all the anxiety and guilt flooded back. I caused all of this. I turned her life upside down, and it would always be this way. She would never be safe with me.

So I went through the motions when she came back to the car, my heart breaking with every word I said. Every word brought me closer to my last.

She deserved something better. She deserved someone better. It wasn't me.

It wasn't Rylan.

She loved Jaeden. But I wasn't him.

I smiled when I should and laughed when the time was right. I let her lead me into the house and took the glasstop from her when she handed it to me, saying, "Do what they want, so we can just be done. I'll be in bed waiting."

I felt numb as I sat down without a word and went into my

personal account. I typed through my programs, fingers speeding through as fast as I could, and transferred the remaining 4.8 million credits evenly over the three accounts I created so many lifetimes ago.

I took a breath, hit send, and watched the number turn to zero.

I shut off the glasstop. The good news was that they didn't know about my second account. That and the fact that she was okay.

Angelia is okay.

I didn't know how I was going to do this, how I was going to leave her, or survive without her.

But it's not about you now. It's about her. It's always been about her.

I walked down the hallway to our room—I paused, her room—and stopped in the doorway. She sat in her bed with only a sheet around her waist. Holding her hands up to me, I crossed the room, taking them both, lost and confused. Her eyes were so big and beautiful, inviting me, asking me.

If this was the last time we'd be together, I'd be here. I'd be present and give her all of me.

She reached for me and kissed me, softly, and then with that need I knew and had felt so many times. Pulling away just enough, she whispered, "I love you, more than you know. I missed you so much."

My heart ached as I let my body show her just how much I felt the same. We stayed in bed for hours into the night. Finally feeling her fall asleep beside me, curled up against me, I lay awake, watching her. I kissed her on the forehead before getting up slowly, careful to not wake her.

And the pain, the agony, the heartache of a thousand lives walked out the door with me.

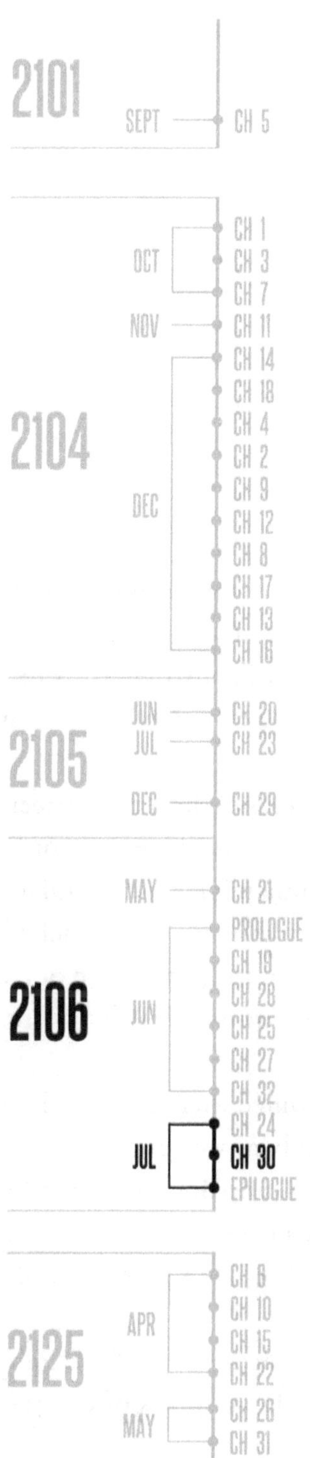

CHAPTER 30

JULY 2106
Dr. Atlas

The bottle felt cool in my hand as I poured myself a glass of Louis Jadot Bonnes-Mares. It was a favorite of mine and had been lying in my wine cabinet for some time. I finally opened it today.

Today marked four weeks since we set off the gamma bomb over New Eastland.

Four weeks since I sat behind the multi-screen command station in our temporary "war" room and gave the word.

Four weeks since the gamma missile we manufactured with a team of fifty over the course of ten months was launched.

Four weeks since 5 percent of the population of New Eastland felt the pain of evolution and grew into something more, something better.

Four weeks since we welcomed them into our home, opening our doors and expanding as quickly as we could.

I sighed, breathing in the red wine, letting it fill my senses before I closed my eyes and took a drink. The cool liquid rolled over my tongue before I swallowed it. The Louis Jadot went down smooth and lovely, as always.

I glanced at the projected map in front of me, light shining up from the techscreen, showing the large spikes of energy throughout

New Eastland. Each spike represented a Spectral—as they were now called—whose energy was strong enough to be detected without needing Greysin.

It became apparent rather quickly that the abilities of some were stronger than others. Some could bend and mold matter, while others simply used their own energy to project their power, like Sloan.

He could levitate but was still unable to levitate anything else. The power was within him, but he couldn't project it outward.

Then, there were Spectrals like Lin, one of the Trio. She created fire from within herself, not just a flame, but different types of fire. Her blue flame was the most lethal and, as of now, could burn through any material we have given her. It was just incredible. I took another drink, reveling in the taste as it went down. Every new ability we found, the more incredible the scenario became. And yet…

I hadn't found what I was looking for to begin with—the power to heal. I was still the only one with the power to heal myself. Much like Sloan, my power only worked on me. I could never heal anyone else. Never a more frustrating circumstance, but it was as evolution dictated.

When I made my discovery over a year ago, I floated through the cosmos for days before I could reel it in and refocus my energy, my direction. I needed to test as many people as possible to find more with my ability, but it proved difficult with Testers. Only about 2 percent of those who walked through our doors had the right gene to begin with. And every time we stirred and woke a new genetic sequence from within a new Spectral, they had a new power, a new ability.

It was as frustrating as it was fascinating.

I watched the spikes on the map fluctuate as powers were used. The wave didn't tell me what it was, just the level of energy. I thanked Greysin for this bit of technology.

He was one of the first Spectrals to join our new extended family last year before the summer ended. At first, we didn't know what his ability was—as it happened with some—and it wasn't until his fifth trip to the infirmary that we realized his episodes of overwhelming dissociation were directly related to the tests we ran every day at the same time on other Spectrals. Once we narrowed it down, we started to spread out the tests until he could get a handle on his power. Originally part of the architectural world, Greysin had ideas of how we could use his ability through technology. And here we were. We now had a physical tracking device on Spectrals.

Greysin also quickly became the fourth person to know about my own ability. To date, I never shared with anyone else besides Dr. Logan and Sloan about what my body could do. I didn't deem it of importance or relevance for that matter, but it didn't matter to Greysin. He felt waves whether we used our powers or not. He walked into my office one day before announcing himself and said, "We need to talk."

I looked up from my techscreen at the thirty-two-year-old Spectral demanding my attention. "Of course. First, why don't you sit down?" I waited until he did before I continued. "Thank you. Now, what do we need to discuss?"

His face contorted in anger, but I remained calm, having become used to the outbursts of new Spectrals coming to terms with their abilities. "We need to discuss the fact that you are lying to us all."

I simply took a breath, lacing my fingers together. "Lying about what, Greysin?"

"You have power, just like the rest of us."

Interestingly, I didn't even think that he would be able to detect me, considering I hadn't used my ability in many months. The learning curve for the many abilities was high.

By the end of our conversation, we came to an easy agreement of silence in exchange for better accommodations for him. Was it blackmail? It could be seen that way. But since our arrangement, he'd been like my other right hand—Logan always being my first—for everything I needed, especially finding the most powerful Spectrals.

Most Spectrals at the Institute found us through others who previously had come to us. The word and whispers moved throughout the city, but some, most, of the strongest, most connected to their power, didn't always come forward. So we sought them out. Once we explained the situation, most came freely. Most came excitedly. But there were a few who didn't want to come at all.

I don't give them the choice.

My first right hand didn't know this and would more than likely disapprove of my tactical team. I recruited other Spectrals with abilities—such as completely silencing sounds, like doors broken down, and a type of cloaking ability, to bend light—to hide someone being escorted away.

But this was the way of the world. I wasn't leaving it to them. I gave them this power, and I needed to know everything I could. The ones with the most power were the answers to questions I didn't even know I had yet.

I finished my drink as I heard an alarm ring out.

"Dr. Atlas, this is your meeting reminder. It starts in ten minutes."

"Thank you, Mendel."

My 10 a.m. glass of wine was finished, and I needed to leave for the meet- ing. I normally didn't make an appearance, but I felt, this once, it was a good day to breathe in the world I created.

Dr. Logan talked, and I couldn't help but smile at how she handled Dr. Tomlan. I'd known him for over thirty years—he's one of the few who knew Haileen—and he was positively brilliant, albeit abrasive at times. He never fazed Dr. Logan, although this particular time I felt like I needed to step in.

"That's enough, Dr. Tomlan. This has been difficult for all of us, but once the processes are all in place, we will be able to move forward and help these Spectrals with their new abilities. Let's all remember these people are the future. If you and Dr. Maggio are correct, and they have no diseases, then future generations won't either. Please understand the implications before you complain about a bracelet." Dr. Tomlan turned the back of his chair toward me in silence, and I gestured to Dr. Logan. "Please continue."

I listened as she spoke about the new crew. Most of the important elements of the conversation already passed, but I didn't want to be rude and leave the room in the middle of the meeting. I waited until she finished speaking with Glenn.

"In the meantime, why don't you have them pass through the supply door with our generic keycards at the back of the facility?"

Her words piqued my interest. An odd sensation gnawed at me, like someone scratching the back of my ear, and I didn't know why.

"The supply door?" Glenn asked.

"Yes, at the back of the facility. It's the one door that you can pass through without the retinal scan. Have them move through there for now. It takes a little longer to walk around, but it should alleviate a bit of the front-end traffic."

And that's when it struck me. *Raven.*

My heart dropped. Thoughts and emotions flooded through my mind.

It couldn't be true. I didn't want it to be true. *And somehow…*

The meeting ended. I tried to convey my normal self, but inside, I could only think about the supply door.

"Well, that was… enlightening. Where are you off to now?"

She looked tired, worn down, but still pushing through. My head started to throb.

"I am going to visit the Trio and Harper. I want to check in briefly with them, see how the Trio is doing, and get more details on what kind of team Harper needs."

I nodded. "Then I'll speak with you later."

I walked out into the hallway, conscious to acknowledge anyone who reached out to speak to me, but I wanted to return to my private room as quickly as possible. Once I reached my own hallway, I raced to my door and rushed inside. "Mendel, lights on and turn on my techscreen." I moved to the desk in the back of my room and started typing across the already lit screen. "The footage. I need the footage."

I knew I still had it on my techscreen from over a year ago when I requested it to review. I swiped across the screen as it projected in front of me. The light was bright against the background of darkness.

I typed in a command, pulling up the footage from the day that Raven escaped, tapping through different camera views and angles until I found the supply room door. I scrubbed through the footage of that day, stopping about twenty minutes after Dr. Logan said she had entered Raven's room.

There was the answer to my question. Raven and Sloan escaped through the supply room door with a key card. I watched as Raven pulled a key card from his pocket and swiped along the access pad, and Sloan moved nervously from foot to foot beside him.

I called up the security logs on my techscreen from that day. Dr. Limna's key card was used for that door at that time.

My hands froze above the keyboard with my next thought. I knew there would be no turning back.

I took a breath. And then another. I thought of everything we accomplished together. I remembered every conversation, the tears in her eyes, and the emotion in mine.

I thought of the people that we killed together for the greater good. I was terrified to look for what I knew I would find.

I stood in the shadows, waiting for her. My black coat blended into the wall beside me.

A single light in the room illuminated the three chairs where we had put dozens of Testers over the years. And I waited.

A few minutes later, I watched her enter the room and look around, confused, realizing that I wasn't there. I stepped out of the shadows and nodded for her to come through the side door. Without any hesitation, she did.

Dr. Logan looked at me with concern in her eyes. "Dr. Atlas, is everything okay?" Over the years, we endured so much. She always knew how to read me.

In five minutes, she'd never be able to read me again.

I unfolded my arms from my chest. "How long have we worked together, Dr. Logan?"

"Four years, nine months, and twenty-five days."

I couldn't help but smile. "You were always so beautifully precise with your numbers. I always admired that about you. You were always everything I ever needed for Project E." I walked around from behind the chairs to stand closer to her, pacing as I spoke. "We were going to change the world, you and I. Remember? That was the plan. Wasn't that always OUR plan?"

She looked at me, unsure what to say, so she didn't say anything at all.

"You know what was always hard for me to get past?"

Her head shake was almost imperceptible as she watched me.

"Raven. I never understood how that whole day

happened. With so many security measures in place, and so many contingencies, it never made sense. I found myself searching the footage of that day over and over again for weeks, months even, trying to find what happened. I couldn't believe the incompetence of my men, that somehow they had failed me and didn't even know how." I stopped pacing. "Do you know what always struck me as odd?"

She shook her head again, holding her breath.

"When you walked into Raven's room, there was a split second hesitation, like a…" I put a finger over my mouth, considering the words. "…reconsideration, a second thought. There was a moment where you must have thought about whether you wanted to really do it."

Fear flashed in her eyes, but she said nothing, rooted in place.

"And then, today, you let it slip. After lying to my face for over a year, you finally let it go. You don't even realize that you did. Or do you?"

I searched her wide eyes, her scared eyes.

"No, you really don't." I repeated her words from earlier today. "'In the meantime, why don't you have them pass through the supply door with our generic keycards at the back of the facility?' Do you remember now?"

Her eyes froze, locked on mine.

"The only door that doesn't need a retinal scan to exit is the supply connection door at the back of the facility. You knew this and never told anyone about it, never hinted at it, until today. When you finally let it out, the wheels turned. I checked the footage right away. Wouldn't you guess, when I checked the footage of that door, I finally solved the mystery of the vanished subjects."

I looked down for a moment as pain and anger filled my chest before glaring back at her.

"And do you know how much it destroyed me when I checked the footage of Dr. Limna's office earlier that day and found you walking in and grabbing her keycard? I had to stop the footage as I watched you type into the glasstop, which I can only assume was the message from me the guards received a little while later. You have no idea the pain I felt as I watched you betray our plan, our team, our dream." I lowered my voice. "As I watched you betray me." I shook my head, having a hard time hearing my own words. "You've been like a daughter to me. I brought you here." I threw my hands up. "I brought you into my world. I showed you my secret! And this? This is what you do. Why? Why did you throw it all away for this—for Raven?" I practically spat the last words between the betrayal surrounding my heart. My eyes were wild, and my chest heaved.

She said nothing. Her glassy eyes just stared back at me, infuriating me even more.

"Speak!" I screamed. She jumped, her eyes finding mine, and I felt gratification at her reaction.

Tears spilled down her cheeks, as she opened her quivering mouth to answer. "I fell in love with him. I had given you so many others, helped you kill so many others. I couldn't—"

My head felt like it was going to split in half. "Love? You think you loved that pig? How could you even breathe the same air as him? You are above him! Above everyone!"

"Dr. Atlas—"

"No! I don't want to hear it! You betrayed us! You betrayed everything! You betrayed me! So help me if you don't deserve to die with the rest of them!" I ran at her, grabbing her by the shoulders and twisting her down into the chair—the straps already detached and waiting for her. I closed one side, and she screamed. She struggled, calling my name, kicking at me.

I ignored her as I closed her second arm, tightening the sides until she couldn't move anything but her feet.

She cried, "Dr. Atlas, please. I'm sorry. I brought him here. I brought him here to die, and when he didn't, I didn't have it in me to go through it again. Please, forgive me. I'm here. I'm here now. Please. I've done everything you ever asked of me. Everything! I killed every person you asked me to! Every single one! Please don't do this!"

But I backed away from her, tears in my own eyes. "You were like a daughter to me," I said again. "We were going to change the world together."

I turned my back on her and her screams as I walked through the door into the observatory room. The sound dropped out as soon as the door closed behind me. I watched as she writhed, pulled, and kicked, screaming words I couldn't hear.

I wiped the tears from my eyes as I set the sequence, hearing the long series of beeps through the speakers.

She paused for just a moment, looking up, hearing the sounds, and knowing what they meant.

I leaned over and typed in the command to light the observatory room. I wanted her to see me. I wanted to be the last thing she ever saw.

The first warning bell went off. She pulled and pulled against her restraints. The second warning bell sounded. She stopped fighting, lowering her head, taking deep breaths.

The third and final rang out. She looked up at me, right in my eyes, head held high, jaw set, ready to face her final seconds.

I turned my head away as the bright light filled the room. Waves of pain flooded through me. Tears welled up from inside, and heaving breaths broke and scattered until the light stopped.

Opening my eyes, I looked at her. She screamed again, this time in pain. Her body twisted from side to side. I waited, watched, ready for her body to fall, for the green wisps to come.

The screaming flooded my mind—high, sharp, excruciating sounds at levels that made me cover my ears. But it didn't help. The sound was in my head, tearing through me.

I saw her screaming… and then she wasn't. The sound in my head stopped.

The pain subsided. I dropped my hands, staring at her.

No smoke.

No pain.

No death.

She stared back at me. Her voice echoed in my head. *Let me out. Let me out now!*

Nothing in my body could deny her. I moved like a puppet on a string as I walked away from the station, through the door to where she sat, and unlocked her without any power to stop myself.

I felt cold, empty. I felt like nothing. I was nothing.

She stood up as soon as the second restraint was released, and she shoved me as hard as she could, knocking me backward as she raced toward the door. I landed hard on the floor, feeling a crack in my arm as I hit. I came back to myself then, a whole person again—complete.

I yelled out to her. "Wait! Logan! Stop!"

She turned on me then, wild and lost in fury. "You tried to kill me!"

You tried to kill me!

The screams in my head were crippling as she rushed at me.

I threw my hands up. "And yet I saved you! Don't you see? You're like me now. You're a Spectral!" Warmth bloomed in my chest, pride rushing through me. "Together, we can still save the world. You and me."

She stopped steps from me, glaring.

You made me a monster! I hate you!

I slowly stood up, my hands still raised, blinking my eyes through the wails in my head. "Where will you go? What will you do? You are one of us. You ARE evolution. You have to see it through. What other choice do you have?" I saw her eyes shift back and forth, twisting her mind. Agony and confusion rushed over her features. Her legs buckled beneath her, and she fell to the floor.

I rushed to her, not caring what happened. I pulled her into my arms as she cried, deep waves of tears. My skin tingled as it touched hers. Warmth flooded through me, and she stopped crying. Her breath caught in her throat. A channel of energy opened. I watched the red light from my hands travel down into her body and back again. It rushed through me. It was intoxicating.

I was dizzy with the delicious feel of it, lost in the buzz, the high of the energy as it moved from her body to mine.

She gasped, like it hurt to breathe. Her eyes flew open, staring beyond me. "Raven…" she whispered. "Raven, I'm sorry…"

Anger, then fury, coursed through me. Still she called to him, called to that rat. My grip on her tightened.

She tried to pull away, feeling her energy leave her body. She pushed me, kicking, and the screaming rushed back into my head. She used every drop of strength she had left, but I blocked it out until I had it all. I wanted it all, every drop of it. It was mine.

She didn't deserve it.

I watched as her skin changed colors. Black lines stretched across her skin, flowing up to my hand. I held on, taking it all, everything, until she stopped moving.

Her eyes were glassy, her heart still, her life lost.

But the voices were not. I heard them all at once from all over the compound. Some I recognized. Some I didn't. Hundreds of voices roared through my mind. Every thought, every word, hissing through me.

I looked down at her lifeless body, and my mind cracked.

I didn't see Dr. Logan. I saw Haileen, with her pale skin and black lines, lines that traveled to my hands.

Reality spiraled.

I hadn't been the healer. Healing hadn't been my ability.

It had been *hers.*

The pain seared through me like a knife as I realized the one piece of the puzzle I'd always been missing. I could never grasp it, no matter how I hard I tried. This piece told me why I lost Haileen—my perfect, beautiful Haileen.

I doubled over, consumed by my own anguish as it all snapped into place.

The power to take. The power to heal.

One was mine. One was hers.

Oh, God. I had killed her. I killed Haileen.

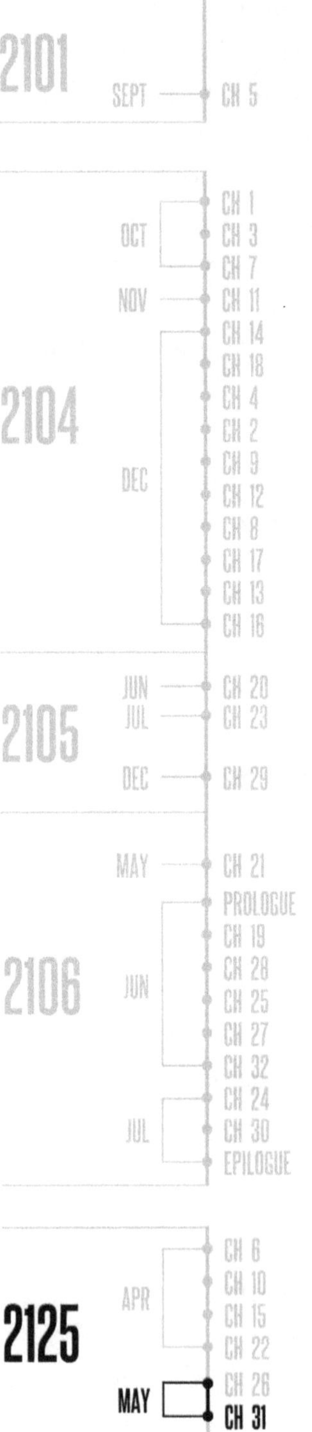

CHAPTER 31

MAY 2125
Marina

My eyes water as I chop onions, Pablo jumping onto the counter, wrapping his tail around his paws. I smile as he pokes his nose toward the smell.

"Nope. None for you, little kitty."

He meows at me and jumps down, clearly not interested in what I'm cooking.

The tomatoes are already diced into small cubes along with the green, orange, and yellow peppers. I add a teaspoon of almond butter and let it simmer before I add the onions.

The smell of sizzling vegetables always makes me smile. It reminds me of my mom when she cooked the same sauce. It was her favorite, or at least this version of her favorite, not having oil after a few years. I watched her make it so many times I learned by sight.

I only make it every year on her birthday, but I am making an exception tonight. I toss in the peppers, turning them around in the butter, wafting the smell toward me to see what else I need to add. I toss in some oregano, some salt, and pepper flakes.

I know Blade likes spicy food from the day I showed him the vegetables in my greenhouse. He'd taken a spicy pepper right off the branch and ate it, complimenting me afterward. So I make sure to cut them too and add them in.

I plan to make him a delicious dinner. Up until this point, we haven't had a gourmet dinner. We've feasted on just the usual, normal, sparse dinners. But tonight is different.

Tonight, I will ask Blade to stay, indefinitely.

Since we returned from the city about a week ago, I haven't been able to think about anything else. When he and his energy disappeared, I had felt more alone than ever before.

But I have to be honest with myself, I know for certain that this isn't just about being alone now either. I'm not just used to him. I'm not just comfortable. I want him here—him, not someone else. I want him, and his smile and his laugh, to stay.

So here I am, cooking my special sauce on a day I don't usually, mentally going over how I want to tell him. I say the words over and over in my head, making my stomach twist each time.

I told him in the morning that I was getting bored with the plain meals and would make something special for us. I played it off as though we deserved a fancy night for once. We talked about eating out under the stars, by a fire, and dressing up. He seemed excited about it, and I couldn't wait.

I just hope he's as excited about what I have to say.

I move from one side of the kitchen to the other, moving plates and utensils to where I need them. I also cut up vegetables for a salad, make fresh bread, roast two fish with potatoes and gather pasta from the last time I made it by hand.

I hear the door behind me open as I check the fish in the oven.

"Fire is lit, my lady."

I turn and smile at him. "Oh yeah? It's good?"

"Yup. I even moved the table and chairs over."

I stir the sauce. "I would have helped you."

He shrugs. "Yeah, but you're doing all the cooking. I figured I'd be useful. Besides, teleportation makes that pretty easy."

I spin to look at him. "You can do that? With things?"

"Yeah, small things. Nothing crazy. I haven't tried a car yet."

I shake my head. "Please don't. That's crazy. Besides, I like my van. Get your own van, if you want to try it out."

He presses his lips together before he throws his hands up. "All right, all right. No van for practice. Got it." He breathes in, closing his eyes. "Wow, it smells good in here."

I can't help but smile again, feeling my face flush. "Thanks. I hope you like it all."

He sits down on the stool. "I love it already. Are you kidding?"

"Good." I grab the pasta from the jar sitting beside the stove and drop in the long noodles. "Can you set the table? It's done in—Mika, set a timer for four minutes."

"Yes, Marina."

I look at Blade. "In four minutes."

He stands up. "Then, yes, I will go set the table."

Walking around the island, he reaches up for two plates while I move around him to grab the spoon on the other side of him. He reaches across to put the plates down and open the utensils as I move to the cabinet across from him for a bowl to strain the pasta.

It's like a dance. And I can't let this dance get away.

He takes the plates, utensils, and glasses out to the table as I plate dinner—including the finished pasta—into the array of serving dishes I placed on the counter earlier. I take off my apron as he walks back in.

"Okay, go."

I look at him confused. "What?"

"Go change. I'll take these out and run back in and change. Go get ready."

I beam at him. "Okay. I'll see you downstairs. I only need five minutes."

He waves me off. "Yeah, yeah. Let's see who's ready first."

I laugh as I run up the stairs and rush into my room, heading straight to my closet. I have one dress in the many things I've collected over the years. One. Clothes to dress up in wasn't something I ever wanted an abundance of, although today I wish I had more choices.

As I pull the dress up over my hips, dropping the thin straps on either side of my shoulders, I am pleasantly surprised. It fits perfectly and looks rather flattering, if I can say so. The dress is a forest green, matching my eyes, and scoops in the front. It's short but falls a couple inches past my fingertips with my hands by my side. I don't own a pair of heels, but I grab my black sandals that tie up the ankle—a gift from my mom when I was thirteen. I never wore them before today, and I love how they look on my feet.

My hair had been up in a messy bun while I cooked, but now, I want to let it down. I choose to French braid it from the front and down along the side, tying it off with a black elastic.

I check the mirror, turning from one side to the other, and am happy with the final product. I look cute. Step one is complete.

I find Blade standing at the bottom of the stairs, waiting for me, looking like a dream in a black button-down and black pants. I almost miss a step on my way down with his wide eyes on me.

He offers his arm as I hit the bottom step. "May I?"

I take his arm, smiling, ignoring the image of rain and long hair in my mind. "Why, thank you."

He leads me through the kitchen and out the back door. We walk in silence as the warm air hits my bare skin, calming my nerves from the inside. The sun starts to set, and a warm glow flows across the horizon.

Coming around the side of the house, I see the table Blade set for us. He somehow found string lights and hung them from the corner of the house, wrapping them to make almost a halo above our seats.

"I found some in the garage in a box. I thought they looked nice."

They look like glittering lights, but different from the light specks that float around. These have a purpose, like a constellation in the sky. "I think they look beautiful."

He smiles, and my stomach flips. *I don't know if I can do this.*

We both sit on either side of the table, the five serving dishes perfectly between us. "This is more than I pictured in my head." I look up at him. "Thanks, Blade."

He smiles. "Of course. Thanks for cooking. This look amazing."

I reach for his plate. "Let me serve you. I'll give you a little bit of everything."

"Thanks."

I take his plate and pile on the pasta with sauce, some fish and potatoes, a chunk of the bread with almond butter, and a scoop of tomato salad with cucumbers and onions. He sets the plate back in front of him, looking at me.

I look back. "What?"

"I'm not eating without you."

I laugh. "Oh, sorry." I add the same foods on my plate. "Okay, I have food. Eat. I'm dying to know how much you like it." I watch with eager eyes as he picks up his fork, spiraling the long, red-sauced pasta onto the fork. His silver ring glimmers from the warm lights above us.

He pauses. "Can you stop staring? I have a hard time eating on display."

I sit back. "Sorry. I'm just excited to see what you think."

"I see that. How about you eat AND I eat, and we comment together?"

I smile. "Deal." I pick up my fork and knife, cutting the pasta into smaller pieces before scooping it up toward my mouth.

He stares again with a half-smile and squinty eyes. "Why make long pasta and then cut it into pieces?"

I roll my eyes. "Can you just take a bite, and we talk about my eating habits later, please? I want to know if you like it."

He stifles a laugh at my exasperation and finally takes a bite. His eyebrows raise. He nods. My heart floats—he likes the pasta. And the fish, potatoes, salad, and bread. He melts every time he takes a new bite, and my stomach cartwheels.

He dips the bread in the pasta sauce again. "This is my favorite. I can't believe you make bread and all of this on your own. It's amazing."

I swallow the bite of fish in my mouth and smile. "Thank you. I learned from the best, actually. Mom was an incredible cook. Even with the small ingredients we had, she always made something delicious."

His eyes glass over for a second before he reaches for another piece of his bread. "I think your mother could do anything, it seems."

"I'd agree with you. We wouldn't have any of this if it wasn't for her, so I'm pretty grateful." I reach for my glass and take a drink of the homemade fruit juice.

"Tell me about her," he says. "Do you mind? I'd love to hear, if you want to share. What was she like before the world became," he points at the Maddies floating by, "this?"

"Oh, that's a question. Um, I don't actually know too much about her life before this. I know she worked with machines. She always had a passion for that. I know that after the world changed, she came here, and the rest is history. Most of what I know of her is what I know from growing up. But she was my whole world, so I learned everything from her." I take another sip of juice. "I will say I think she loved my father very much."

He starts to take a bite but pauses, looking down at his plate as he asks, "Why do you say that?"

"Because she had this little box, filled with mementos. I found it after she passed away. It has old cards, ticket stubs, random receipts, and one small, blurry picture."

He looks up at me then, eyes serious. "You have a picture of them together?"

"Yeah. It's not a very good one, though. I know it's my mom, but because it's blurry, she even looks different. But it's all I have of my parents." I stop for a moment. "Well, I mean, I always guessed it was my father. She never told me or showed me otherwise. She was always very quiet about him. Who else could it be?"

I glance at him, his lips pressed together. "Can I ask what your father's name was?"

I wonder at his line of questioning, but I answer him. "Jona. Jona Tennet."

He nods, staring off into the distance. After a minute, he asks, "Do you know the name Rylan Wris?"

I think about it. "No. I never heard that name before. Was he a history—"

He cuts me off. "Can you do me a favor?"

Surprise spikes through me. "Of course."

"Can you go get that box of your mom's?"

My eyebrows scrunch together, confused. "Why?"

"Can you just get it? I promise I'll explain everything."

I don't understand. But I stand up and make my way back to my room where I keep the box. It is a small tin box made to look like a package that traveled the world, complete with images of old stamps. The top is the prettiest part of the box with black-and-white sketched roses sitting in the center. It is always next to my journal in my drawer. I pick it up and walk back down to the table, box in hand. Blade stands, pacing, looking nervous. I hold the box out for him to see.

His eyes widen, and he looks away, emotion coming over him as I stand nearby, even more confused than before. He tries to turn back to me but can't. "I'm sorry. I need a second." He walks away, toward the house, leaving me in my dress, holding a box, not understanding anything.

After a minute, I sit down in my chair, move the plates away from me, and open the lid to the box. I haven't opened it in such a long time. I take out the cards, opening each one, reading the short notes, all signed with a J at the bottom. I look at the names of the places on the receipts one by one—coffee shops, bookstores, restaurants.

"She loved to go to The Dark Roast. It was her favorite coffee shop in the whole city."

I turn to face him. He stands with the last of the light shining on his face as the sun finally dips behind the horizon. He smiles, his real smile, deep and happy. "She usually went there on the last Thursday of the month to read her new Sci-book and would read for hours. She always wore pants with cargo pockets in them in case she found something she wanted to bring home with her for her workshop." He looks up for a second before continuing. "She always wore her hair up in a high ponytail when she worked, but she looked like a dream when it was down." He walks closer to me. "She got whiny when she was emotional and hated making decisions about clothes. It was her least favorite thing—to go shopping." He steps next to me, peering into my emotional eyes. "And this," he picks up the picture, holding it close to him, "was the last date we had before we tried to save the world. That was the same day she gave me this ring." He twists the ring with his thumb.

Chills run all over my body, and tears fill my eyes. My mind is confused. My heart is smiling. I don't know what to say.

He hands me the picture. "You can see the ring in the picture."

I take it from him, unbelieving, looking at the two people in the photo. He's right. I see the bright silver band, shining even through the hazy image.

"Wait. I don't understand. How is this you," I point to the picture, "and this is you?" I gesture to him. "Your name is—"

"Rylan Wris."

I freeze. "But, I thought…" I look around, trying to grasp a thought. "The cards—they aren't signed with an R. They are signed with a J."

He presses his lips together. "Jaeden Lowe. That's who I was to her for a long time."

"Wait, does that mean you're my—"

He shakes his head. "No. You have his name right. It's not me."

I let out a loud breath, wiping my hands down my face, trying to breathe. "Okay. Let's hold off on the whole name thing for a minute. How are you here? I mean, if you are from when my mom was—uh—this age, then how are you here? Wait." I narrow my eyes at him. "Why did you leave her? Why was she alone?" I stand up as anger flares through me. "Why did you leave her in that world alone? Who is Jona, then? I don't understand any of this."

He stares at me, not speaking for a time, considering his words. "I didn't want to leave your mother. She was the love of my life, and I spent the best years of my life with her."

I say nothing, trying to process his words.

He takes a deep breath, running his hands through his hair. "Look. I know all of this is confusing—"

"Insane is more like it."

"Agreed. It's incredibly insane. But it's true." He pauses, staring into the night. "The doctor you spoke about once? His name was Dr. Atlas. He is the reason this," he holds his hands up, "happened. Your mom and I, and… others, tried to stop him, and we… failed."

"No. No, that's not true. Mom would have told me. She was just a city girl who made it through and came here. I don't understand any of this." I put my hand to my forehead. "Can we just start with how you're here? How did you—uh—I guess, travel through time?" I shake my head. "This is insane."

He looks at me. "About as insane as billions of people dead in a breath and the only ones left having supernatural powers."

I catch his eyes. "Okay. Then tell me—what's my mom's full

name?"

He smiles. "Angelia Marina Solis. She always loved her middle name and hoped to give it to her daughter someday. Although most people called her Lia, I wouldn't do it. Her full name was too beautiful not to say."

Tears spring to my eyes and fall before I can stop them. I shake my head. "How—how is this possible?"

He bends his knees, coming down to my eye level. His eyes fill with so much emotion. "I'm here, Marina, because…" he takes a deep breath and lets it out slowly, "we are going to bring them all back. Together. You and me and, if it all goes to plan, your mother too."

More tears come. "What are you saying?"

He grabs my hands, looking through me, his eyes the color of the moon. "I'm here because you're going to help me save the world."

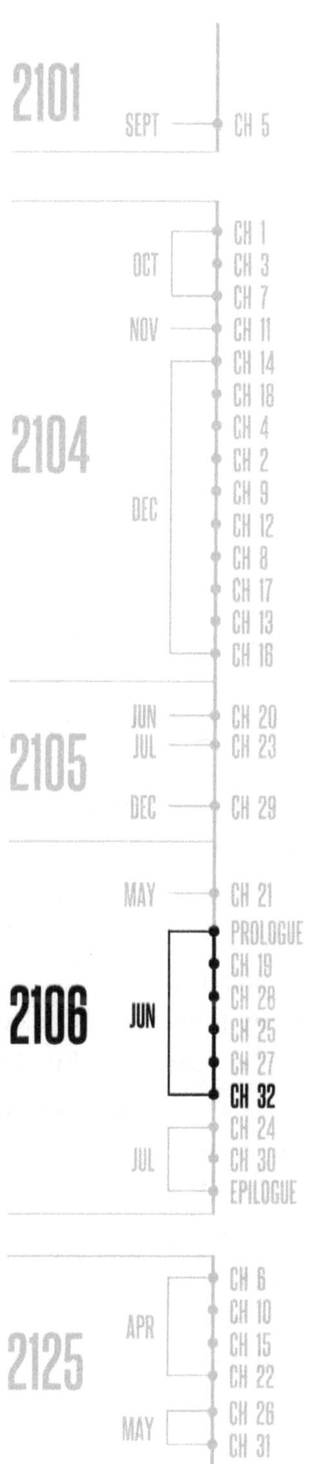

CHAPTER 32

JUNE 2106
Angelia

My eyes flew open. "Rylan!"

He appeared from around the side of the van. "I'm here. It's okay. I'm here."

He put his hand on my forehead, his fingertips running through my hair. "You're okay."

I reached my hands out without thinking, putting my hands on his chest, checking him as I had before.

"I'm fine. You only knocked the wind out of me a bit. I'm fine," he repeats, seeing the look on my face.

"I'm sorry," I whispered. "I didn't mean to."

I felt his soft fingers across my forehead. "It's okay."

We stared at each other for just a second before I pulled back from him, trying to sit up. He put his hands on my arms, making sure I was steady. Once I sat upright, he removed his hands and stepped back. I wished he hadn't. I wanted him closer. I was so confused and so lost, but somehow, I managed to find a sliver of safety when I was close to him. I just felt alone with him far away.

I looked around where we parked.

"Where are we?" I asked, feeling slightly woozy but trying to breathe through it.

"I didn't want us to sit on the main road. There were too many hovers, so I pulled us around another street off the main road. It's quieter. Is that okay?"

I nodded but said nothing. I wasn't sure even what to say.

"So, am I allowed to say that what you did was amazing?"

My eyebrows flew up. "Amazing? You think that was amazing?"

He nodded. "Yeah. It was pretty spectacular, actually. I've never seen anything like it."

"Says the guy who can teleport."

He threw his hands up. "I'm just saying it was amazing." He paused, as if debating whether to finish his thought. "What else can you do?"

I sighed. "I don't think this is the time."

He swiveled around, hands still up. "Is there a better time? I mean, you just knocked me and trees down with an incredibly strong force coming from your body. I can't think of a better time."

I nodded. "Okay, fair point." I looked around. "Where's your IDfob?" He pulled it out of his pocket, holding it out in his palm.

I waved him back. "Step back a few feet."

He turned behind him, looking toward the road, making sure it was clear before stepping back.

"Now hold it up."

Rylan held his hand up the height of his shoulder, watching me.

I held my right hand up and closed my eyes, finding my energy and sending it out. The IDfob flew from his hand to mine.

"Holy shit."

I pursed my lips, shrugging. "Yeah."

He stepped back to me. "You're telekinetic?"

"I guess so." I shook my head. "That sounds insane."

"About as insane as you telling me I can teleport."

I nodded again and bit my lip, thinking. "Can you do anything else?"

He shook his head. "No. That's it—one place to another."

I took a deep breath. "Incredible."

"That's what I'm saying."

"Can I ask you why you wanted me to move the couch in the living room?"

He shrugged. "I don't know what happens if I teleport to the same place as something else. I mean, does it move? Do I—um—phase through it?" He shook his head. "It's weird to say this out loud. I've said it in my head a million times, but to say it out loud… it makes it—"

"Real?"

He nodded. "Yeah, exactly. Real."

"I get it. Well, considering we don't know anything, I think that was a good call to move the couch. You wouldn't make a good couch. Just saying."

He looked at me, unsure how to react. I smiled. He smiled back. I missed that smile, so damn much.

But this is not the time.

I cleared my throat, breaking eye contact and looking down the street. "So, uh, where are we going?"

"Well, if you are feeling better, we can go back the way we came, get back on the main road. It's less than an hour to the Pennsylvania border and then another four hours to my—" He stopped.

I finished the sentence for him. "Your house."

"Yeah."

I took a deep breath, pushing aside the emotions that flooded through me. "Look. There's obviously a lot happening here, not just between us, but everywhere. I know I've been kind of a bitch about everything—"

"You haven't been a bitch at all."

"It's just everything is confusing and emotional. It's just a lot." He nodded as I spoke. "So, how about we just focus on getting to your—your house, and then we come up with a plan. You were right when you said to me, let's just get me safe. But it's not just me. It's us. We are both Spectrals. We need to get somewhere safe, and then we can talk about… everything." I looked around, away from his eyes that burned into mine. "I'll pause my emotions. I mean, I feel like I have a right to feel the way I do… But I want to just leave it alone right now and get to where we're going. Is that okay?" I held my hand out toward him. "Truce?"

He smiled, his beautiful, gorgeous smile, and took my hand. "Truce."

I ignored the warmth of his skin where we touched. I ignored the hum that grew in my mind, flowing through my energy, my power. I ignored the look in his eyes, knowing he was trying to ignore it too. And I ignored the fact that we held hands for just too much longer.

I pulled my hand away first. "Okay, then. Let's get back on the road."

He moved back as I stepped down from the side of the van, and we both climbed in the front seats. As he engaged the engine, I let my eyes fall across his profile—his hair falling in his face, the silver in his eyes, the fullness in his lips—lips that I missed on mine.

He turned then, caught me staring, and smiled. I looked away, blushing, to look out the window.

"Rylan, can I say one more thing before we drive off?"

"Of course."

I turned back to him. "Thank you."

He looked confused. "Thank you for what? I didn't—"

"But you did, though. You saved me from whoever that was back at my apartment. You are taking me to your home when you don't have to. You carried me after I—knocked you out with my crazy brain abilities."

He laughed. "Yeah, that was pretty crazy."

"Yeah." I took a breath. "I just want you to know that I appreciate it. That's all."

He nodded, a sadness behind his eyes. "You are most welcome."

I smiled before looking back toward the window.

"Can I just say one thing too?"

I looked back. "Sure."

"If you want to use your telekinesis again, can you aim it in a different direction? I mean, it was badass and all, but I'm a little scared of you now."

I laughed then, shaking my head. "Good. You should be scared of me. I may blow something up next time."

His eyes widen. "Can you do that?"

I shrugged. "How about we do our best not to test that out?"

"Agreed." The signal chimed that the hover was ready. "Good?"

I nodded. "Good."

As he turned the wheel to go back to the main road, I almost smiled, feeling it was true for the first time in over six months.

Rylan

We sat in a long row of traffic and moved at a crawl. There seemed to be a blockade of some kind in front of us. They checked one car at time.

"I don't like this," Angelia said between her teeth, biting on her fingertips. "I really don't like this."

"It's going to be fine. We haven't done anything. There's no reason not to let me through. I live in Pennsylvania."

She didn't seem convinced. I watched her nibble, a nervous habit I'd never seen before, and tried to forget how cute she was in these moments of stress.

"But didn't you say they had my name?"

I smiled. "Yes, but that was the Institute, not the government. Really, we're going to be fine."

I looked back to the road and hoped I was right. I watched her as she shifted in her seat, anxious.

"Here." I leaned forward. "How about this?" I turned up the Neoteric Beats playing in the background. "Come on. You love this song." I started singing, swaying in my seat.

She looked at me from the corner of her eyes, trying to hold back her smile.

"Come on. I can't do this solo by myself." I sang louder. She turned to face me and laughed. Then, she started singing the chorus with me and turned the volume up even louder.

I drummed on the steering wheel, singing loudly, until I heard a honk from behind me. We both jumped.

I checked the road. The hovers had moved, but we hadn't.

"Oops." She laughed as I moved forward. "Thanks. That helped."

I smiled. "Good. That was the point."

Two more cars were now ahead of us before the checkpoint. She folded her legs under her and pulled her sleeves down over her fingers.

And then it was our turn. I lowered the window. "Good afternoon."

The officer looked eye level at me before looking over at Angelia. "Afternoon. I need your ID. We are only letting Pennsylvania residents through."

"Sure." I grabbed my IDfob from the small compartment on the dash and handed it over.

He looked past me to Angelia. "Yours too."

I didn't miss a beat. "We live together."

He shifted his eyes to me. "I still need to scan her ID."

"Got it. Okay, one second." He leaned over to me. "Let me have your ID so they can verify." Her eyes were wide, terrified. "It's okay. They just want to verify where you live." She swallowed and handed me her IDfob from her bag.

I handed it over to the officer.

"Thanks." He turned and walked away. Before he was out of sight, I whipped around, reaching for my bag in the back seat. I couldn't reach it from where I was.

"What do you need?"

"My glasstop. Quick."

She turned her body, angled herself to grab it from the bag, and handed it to me.

I swept across the screen, and it started right away. I added in my password, entered the network, and searched through the departments, finding the DMV. I scrolled and input my programming code as fast as I could.

She watched me, looking between my screen and the officer still standing at his protection scanner.

I found her. *Angelia M. Solis, Resident, New Eastland, New York.*

My fingers flew across the screen. I typed in the new information and hit submit. I looked up as the officer walked back toward us. *Shit.*

"Can you pull off to the side, please?"

"Is there something wrong, officer?" I saw the sunlight behind him dim as the sky darkened.

He pointed to the side where another two police hovers were parked. "Please just pull to the side over there."

"Yes, sir."

I heard a rumble in the distance as I closed the window, turning the wheel. A bright light flashed, followed by a crack that resonated through the hover like a wave.

I watched as a lightning bolt struck through one of the hovers. Angelia screamed beside me.

Raven

I saw the officer walk away from their van. He had their IDs in his hand.

I shook my head.

This is not good.

I looked side to side. There was no way out without being seen—or stopped.

I was six cars behind them, not sure what to do, but I knew if they were detained, it wouldn't end well.

After I had seen them disappear, I had ran back to my hover and raced around the corner, hoping to find them on the other side of the bend. I saw the black van parked down a side street. I parked up a way to the side, waiting. When they came back to the main highway, I followed them. Interestingly, they were traveling the same direction I was.

Now we were both parked, here, stuck, and I got the feeling there was only one thing I could do. I got out of my car. I left it, right where it was, grabbing my bag from the back, and walked off to the side. I knew others could see me. If all went well, they wouldn't for long.

I steadied my feet and closed my eyes, focusing on the last time I saw Logan. I saw her smile, her lips. Feeling my energy build and spiral, the sky darkened around us. I remembered her warm skin and how she tasted as the pressure pushed and pulled inside of me, asking me to let go. The rumble of rain closed in as I thought of my hand closed over her mouth as my name escaped her lips. I heard her moans in my ears.

And then I remembered—I'd never touch her again.

My heart twisted and shattered as I shot my hands out, releasing every ounce of energy, straight toward the two police hovers in front of me. A light, a crack, and a bolt slammed into one of the hovers, splitting it in half.

I heard muffled screams from inside cars as I pulled my hands back. Rain fell from the black sky, making it hard to see. I ran toward the van, bag in hand.

I pictured Logan standing behind the glass as she watched people die, as she sent them to die—as she had sent me to die. With my hand in the sky, I pulled another bolt down, crashing it into the other hover. This time, it hit the engine. A fire exploded outward with a rush of sound and metal.

I made it to the van, racing down the passenger's side, my energy draining. A heaviness washed over me. I slammed my side against her window, hitting the glass. She jumped, a small scream escaping from her mouth.

"Let me in! Unlock the door!"

She shook her head, staring at me wide-eyed.

"I am like you. You know I am." I caught her eyes with mine. "You can feel me too. I know you can. Let me in! We don't have time—I can't bring down another bolt." I felt sluggish, my energy waning.

I saw her turn to the man in the driver seat and say something. She yelled at him, and then the door unlocked.

The window came down enough for her to speak through the opening. "Get in on the other side. Now! Go!"

I watched as more officers ran past me, trying to put out the fire spreading through every part of the hovers. I climbed in, soaking wet, and slammed the door shut.

The man in the front seat turned toward me. "Who the hell are you? What do you want?"

I laughed. "Right now, I want to get the fuck out of here. Let's go." I lay back, feeling my energy drag me down. I looked up, feeling her eyes on me. "I'm right. Aren't I? You can feel it too?"

She nodded her head.

I nodded back. "I'm Raven," I said, closing my eyes.

"I'm Angelia. This is Rylan."

"Nice to meet you both." I put my arm over my face. "Now

if you'll excuse me, I need to sleep. I'm losing..."

I was dragged down into nothing before I could finish my sentence.

Angelia

I stared at the man in the back of the van. He was soaking wet and unconscious, and yet I could still feel him—feel Raven.

The energy pulsed from him, like a warmth on my skin. I felt it before at the charge station, and I was surprised how much stronger it was with him closer to me.

I looked over at Rylan, who locked eyes with me as he drove away from the line of stopped and burning hovers.

"Who the hell is he? You know him?"

I shook my head. "No. I just met him."

"Well, he seems to think you can feel him. What does that even mean?" Jealousy didn't look good on him. At any other time, I would have laughed.

I glanced back at Raven, his breaths slow and even. "I can feel his energy, more than I can feel yours. You know what I'm talking about. Right?" I brought my eyes back to Rylan's. His face twisted, clearly upset with this man in the back of his van, but he nodded. "He's one of us. He's a Spectral."

"Great. That doesn't mean we can trust him."

"Considering he just put two lightning bolts through those hovers to get us away from the blockade, I think we can."

Rylan checked the mirror behind us as he pushed the hover faster. "How do we know he even did that?"

I looked back over my shoulder. "Because I felt him when he did it."

Rylan held my eyes for a moment before bringing his attention back to the road. He huffed out a breath. "Let's just get farther into Pennsylvania. Then, we can stop at some inn and talk. I don't know. But I don't want to take this guy with us, without knowing more about him."

"Fair enough."

I turned my body so I could see Rylan and Raven at the same time. My movement was not lost on Rylan, but he chose to stay quiet. I watched him. His eyes moved around when he was upset. He sat straighter in his seat. The man of my dreams sat across from me, everything I ever wanted, and yet a complete stranger to me in so many ways.

I looked over at Raven. His tattoo was covered, but I knew it was there. Raven was a stranger who I had never met before today, and yet I felt his energy pulse through him like a heartbeat alongside my own.

I put my hands together, laying my folded hands against my lips. *What the hell have we all gotten ourselves into?* I prayed the coming days would yield more answers, instead of more questions.

Rylan spoke softly. "Hey, are you okay?"

I nodded, letting out a breath. "I'm okay."

And I hoped through the beating of my heart, through the ripples of light and energy, through the layers of emotion, that it was true.

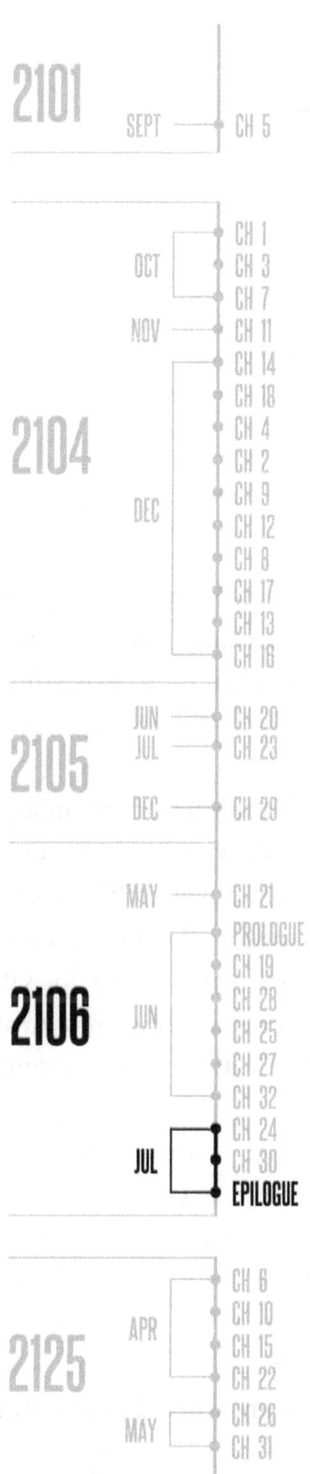

EPILOGUE

JULY 2106
Dr. Atlas

Reni Harrington was our first subject. He was a forty-year-old man who suffered from Stage Two lung cancer and was one of the most ornery men I'd ever met. He grumbled about everything. It was a wonder he had even volunteered, but I supposed even the ornery men wanted to live.

After dozens of tests and months of mapping his DNA, we finally had a plan of action. We were ready to test the newly programmed machine on his tumors down to his DNA. When the day came, we decided on a small team, which consisted of just me, Haileen, and Reni. We didn't want anyone nearby for safety reasons and for the deep responsibility and liability of our future actions. Whatever happened, it was on us. We didn't want anyone to share in the potentially negative outcome.

I brought Reni to a glass box of a room and set him into a long white chair that bent in two places, once at the tailbone and once at the knees. It was made to follow the curve of a body so someone could sit comfortably. The NOMO was above him like a tent, with a large pyramid pointing downward toward where he now sat, looking around the room. There was a machine with a screen beside him and even more monitors outside the room, where Haileen and I stood.

Everything had been set days before he arrived, and Haileen and I reviewed the plan a thousand times. We had his DNA map. We had the markers in place. We had the exact positions of the burst marked on his body. It had been successful in rodents and primates. Now, it needed to succeed for a human—for just one of the many who needed our help.

I pushed away the memory of how many rules, regulations, meetings, and committees it took to get to this point, to obtain the final approval, to test it finally on a person.

Haileen and I looked at each other and clasped hands in celebration that our moment finally arrived and at how proud of each other we were for what we accomplished. It was time. Finally, it all came to this.

But the darkness in the world was using us, filling our minds with hope when it had its own plan.

NOMO turned on and hummed. The tented pyramid began its first rotation, starting to pulse where we marked. I glanced at Haileen through my protective glasses, seeing a spark of anticipation in her eyes. She returned an encouraging smile as the second rotation began.

On its third rotation, the alarms sounded, and the scales on the screens tipped. Red flashed on every screen, and before we could react, a bright, blinding light flashed as a part of the system overcharged.

I felt rays of light ripple through my body. My whole body to my core shuddered and vibrated, pain split through me.

Then, Haileen started screaming. That's the last thing I heard before I lost consciousness.

When I woke up, my head pounded, like I had extreme dehydration. I tried to figure out where I was and what happened.

I sat up slowly. The glass barrier between the Observing Room and Reni's had shattered inward from the overload. I reached up and touched my face, and my fingers brought back the stain of blood. Little sharp pains pricked around my cheeks and forehead. I must have had glass shards across my face. The stinging worsened as I looked into the room and saw the now-lifeless Reni, with green smoke spiraling up from his eyes. My heart clenched, and I caught my breath.

I snapped my neck to the side to find Haileen, and I saw her slumped against the monitor on the side wall. The blast knocked her backward. She was unconscious and had lines of blood dripping down her cheek. I scrambled over to her on my hands and knees, ignoring the biting glass that sliced into my palm. I was inches away from Haileen when I stopped, staring at her face. The blood dripped, but there were no wounds. There were no puncture marks, gashes, or even small cuts.

I looked back at that moment and wished I would have thought more about it. I wished I would have used the brilliant mind that I was given to find an answer. But, I knew what happened next would have happened either way. It was the world's plan, after all.

I reached for Haileen and wrapped my arms around her shoulders, pulling her gently into my arms. I called her name as I tried to wake her up, to find out if she was badly injured, to try to help the love of my life. I brushed her hair from her face and rested my hand just below her neck, feeling her breath.

I felt a shock when my skin touched hers. A warm tingling started where our skin touched, the heat getting hotter the longer my hand touched her. Tiny prickles of light—the only way I could explain it—traced up my arm, over my shoulder, and centered in my chest. The warmth was inviting and sweet, and the tingling was a dizzying delight, making my head spin and my skin shiver with a soft ecstasy.

A muted gasp came from Haileen, as if she was choking and that's all she could manage. I looked down at her and froze. Her skin had turned a milky white color, and black lines stretched from my hand, over her chest, and up her neck and face.

I ripped my hand off of her. Her eyes bore into mine. There was pain and surprise. And goodbye.

I called her name. I told her no, not to leave me, but her eyelids drooped and closed, leaving me alone, forever.

My heart snapped, ripped, broke. I went numb, and every nerve exploded. I felt dizzy, spiraling. The room tilted on its side, and my whole existence was crushed. Everything was heavy, bearing down on me. My eyes couldn't see through my tears. My lungs couldn't breathe. My heart couldn't beat.

I plunged my shaking hand through my hair and ran down my face. I braced for the sting, the pain. I welcomed it, hoped for it, asked for it. I waited for something to ground me, to weigh my feet down before I floated away, without Haileen.

But I felt nothing. I felt no pain.

I no longer had any wounds, puncture marks, gashes, or small cuts. Nothing on my face marked the glass that had drawn blood.

I looked down at Haileen's lifeless face and cried.

I shook my head, thinking about how long I sat there, holding her, until someone finally came. I stared into nothing while I waited to be questioned.

After the funeral, I stood at her grave. I was sad, bitter, and mourning until I became angry, furious, and hateful. I became so outraged at the entire world that I no longer wanted to be a part of it. I tried to cut my wrists to the bone after numbing myself with whiskey straight from a bottle.

How long after that had my wounds healed? Seconds. The blood barely had time to drip down my arm and touch the sides of my chair before the wounds were gone. Again.

I took the knife and cut again and again and watched my wounds heal over and over. Every cut released the pain that I felt—the torment, the sorrow, the anger. It all dissipated one slice at a time, until all that was left was knowing what I needed to do. I knew my new path.

Haileen and I were still going to change the world. But instead of saving it, we were going to evolve it. Because now I knew.

She was dead because of me, of what I became. I was never meant to heal.

I was meant to destroy.

And this time, I was going to take the rest of humanity with me.

The Story Continues...

Book 2
Beyond Ruin: Origins

Exclusive Excerpt

38 years before Beyond Power, Book 1

PROLOGUE

MAY 2067

Blood was everywhere—on my neck, my pants, my hands. I couldn't look anywhere and not see red.

The pain in my chest felt like a spear between my lungs. I couldn't breathe. I couldn't focus. I didn't know if my heart was beating or if it was lost in waves of pain. I didn't know what to do. I didn't know if I could do anything. I didn't know if it was better to do nothing.

Trace had blood on her hands too, bright red dripping blood.

I just stared at everything around me in an unnatural stillness. Time slowed. But the noise—everyone, everything was so loud, shouting so many words. So much noise, yet nothing was happening.

Time crawled to nothing, and I wished it was true. We didn't have time. It was running out with every drop of blood. How could I fix this? How could I stop time from bringing us seconds closer to an ending that I couldn't survive? An ending I knew I wouldn't survive.

I'd lived through pain, turmoil, and loss. But this was not a loss I could stomach, accept, or move past. It wasn't real. It must be a dream.

I heard the rumble of the boat, the splash of water, and the screams of those chasing us.

We sped across the water as fast as we could, away from the flying bullets. I heard them around us, hitting the sides of the boat, the water, everything. I wondered if I'd be hit by one next. I wondered if my blood would soon stain hands, clothes, and the bottom of this boat.

I saw the red mix with water, swirling in circles. It was as beautiful as it was terrifying.

Someone needed to do something. Someone needed to stop the blood. Someone.

I flew forward and pressed my hands on the open wound that poured, spilled, and soiled everything it touched.

"Move!" I heard Trace shout beside me.

"Not on your life!" I yelled back. I pressed down with every ounce of my strength.

The blood had to stop, before my heart stopped first.

1

MAY 2066
Ellura

The smoke filled my lungs, burning me from the inside. It was hot, so hot. If I could breathe, I was sure ash would trail on my scorched breath.

My sister cried beside me, and I squeezed her hands. I watched as the bright orange flames snaked across our floor, catching the pink tassels of our rug on fire like candles on a birthday cake.

Heat from the fire trailed up my throat as it filled my head, clouding it, making it hard to think. It made me tired. Weak. I wanted to close my eyes. I wanted to sleep.

I slumped down to my knees, leaning against Tania. She wasn't crying anymore, her breath so slow I couldn't feel it. I thought maybe I'd take a nap next to her. Maybe when we woke up, we could walk to the park. Maybe Mom and Dad could take us. Maybe…

***

A scream woke me from a cold, deep sleep. The shrill, abrupt sound echoed off the abandoned subway walls, one section at a time. I lifted my head just a few inches, peering around the mounds of blankets surrounding me. None of the other three dozen sleeping people moved, noticed, or cared. I waited for another scream, but silence settled in once again. I tried to close my eyes and find calm beyond my nightmares, but my mind wouldn't let go. It held me awake with regretful, racing thoughts, so I gave up and decided to start another day.

I sat up on my makeshift bed made of layers of old blankets and sheets. I never removed a blanket. I only added one on top of the others. After stacking them for the past three years, the pile was as thick as a regular mattress, which thankfully made sleeping on the concrete floors much easier.

Pulling my greasy hair from its bun, I fluffed it with my fingers. It felt good to scratch my scalp and let it breathe. Many girls my age didn't bother to keep long hair anymore. They just buzzed it off or kept it short to their jaw. I couldn't bring myself to do it. I might not see my hair flow in waves around my shoulders anymore, locked up in a bun, but I loved my long blonde hair and wasn't about to let it go any time soon. I slicked it up, using my fingers as a brush, twisted it into a sleek bun, and wrapped the thick black elastic band twice to keep it in place.

I looked around the subway. No one had any use for these old tunnels anymore, so they became the warmest places for us to sleep. I glanced up at the walls. It was just about sunrise, judging by the darkness in the tunnels and the orange lights on the wall. If the internal lights were still on, there was no natural light outside. In the artificial glow, the entire world down here seemed even more unreal than this harsh reality—people living in huddles and piles of their meager possessions.

We are one big, disconnected family.

On most mornings, I was the first one out of the Caves because it was easier to find a place to perch before the crowd arrived. But crowds weren't all bad. More people meant more opportunities to steal. The weekly New Harlem market was the perfect spot to find what I needed—food or money. My stomach growled. This morning, I needed both.

I spent the last five years of my short eighteen years on the streets. Sleep. Eat. Survive. That's all there was, nothing more. I didn't need anything else.

Grabbing a water bottle and a rag from beside my bed, I used it to clean the sweat and dirt from my face, neck, and hands. I might have been a needy cutpurse, but looking like one didn't help me move through the crowds.

For as long as I could remember, I took whatever I wanted, whenever I wanted. In this world of constant poverty, it was never enough, so I just kept taking. Thankfully, my big sister taught me well. Of all her life lessons, this was one of the good ones.

When I finished washing myself, I stretched my body to the side, mindful of the close body next to me. Jann had been my left-side sleeper for a couple of years now, and on my right was Ricen. He arrived only about six months ago. I glanced around at the dozens more surrounding me.

Each one of us was desperate and full of despair. We fought for everything, wishing for a better life but just grateful for another day. The future was unknown with hope forgotten, and survival was the only remaining instinct we had left.

New York City fell a year ago. The government threw its hands in the air and decided to focus on bigger battles elsewhere in the country. The people were left to fend for themselves. New York City, the rest of the boroughs, and Long Island—now simply called the Island—were abandoned by any kind of authority to keep them together. The Social War destroyed all remaining infrastructure. Lucky for me, cash was king again, despite the law that converted everything to digital currency twenty years ago. Now, I could live off my trade.

I stood up and slowly wound my way out of the maze of sleepers. As I passed, a few people, other early birds like me, started to wake up. I stole a quick glance over my shoulder toward the wall directly under one of the large orange lights. I wondered for just a second if Dregg was awake before continuing my slow dance through the tunnel. I made it to the stairs when a voice sounded from behind me.

"Saturday, the best day of the week."

I turned to see Dregg smiling at me as he joined me on my climb. Ignoring the small twang of displeasure that always showed up when I interacted with someone, I continued my way up the steps.

I met Dregg the first day I came to these subways. He was two years younger than me and had been stuck in the city for much longer than me. While he was a sweet kid, I had no desire for connection or friends. I had enough to worry about and had no time in my day to add anything else.

Some mornings, he found me before I left the Caves, like today, and he walked with me to the market. He often came up with random competitions for the two of us, like who could get the most money in an hour, or challenged us to the same mark to see who could score first. I knew he only did it to spend time with me, and sometimes I was in a good enough mood to play the game. Besides, he knew I was the better thief. He just never admitted it, no matter how many times I won—which was every time.

My stomach growled again, this time loud enough for Dregg to hear, as we walked up the first flight of stairs.

"Yeah, I hear that." He looked behind us to see a few others following along. "What side of the market are you off to today?"

I shrugged. "I haven't decided." I traced the patterns in the decorative mosaic tiles on the wall with my fingers as I climbed. It was the prettiest part of the subway.

He brushed the sandy brown hair out of his eyes. "I wonder if the taco stand will be there this week. It wasn't last Saturday…"

I listened to him drone on about his plans for the day with only half a mind.

We reached the top of the last set of stairs and proceeded

uptown on Frederick Douglass Boulevard. I peered behind me and saw the edges of the Central Park tree line. The sun wasn't usually high enough this early to shine through the buildings of old New York City, but here—where there were more trees than anywhere else—I could see the faint glow of the sun rising. It's why I slept on this side of the City, why I claimed my spot in this subway entrance, and why a small scar—one of many—sat above my right eyebrow from defending my stake. It was the only beautiful part of the city left, and I wanted to see it every day.

Everywhere else was filled with trash. Huge piles of it littered every corner. I guessed that happened with no government and therefore no regular disposal services.

New York City became the focus of rebirth and transformation a few years after the Social War became a force the country could no longer ignore. Long Island was forgotten and left to dozens of factions fighting to control their piece of the outskirts. Seven out of the nine original bridges were destroyed in attempts to protect Long Island from the chaos of the City, but in the end, the Island fell too. Thousands fled West before the final wave of raids. Once a flourishing island that sat beside NYC, it was now so divided that those who craved power had found their way to the top of their towns. After even bloodier fights between those who remained, the factions split into their own dominions, each with a Duke to look over them all.

Saturdays in Harlem were one of the few occasions when the factions came together in one place. It was a place to sell, trade, and barter. Anything and everything went, with no rules—except no stealing. I ignored this one rule regularly, with nothing but survival fueling me.

Dregg and I walked the seventeen blocks deeper into Harlem, dodging the piles of trash and ignoring the few people we saw on the streets. Block after block was as silent as they were empty. An occasional, unknown sound, a hint of life between the folds of neglect, echoed off the abandoned brick buildings, but otherwise, there wasn't a peep—except for Dregg. His thoughts—and mouth—never seemed to stop.

We turned left on W 127th Street and right onto Convent Avenue before embarking on the last three blocks. I smiled. I never tired of the shift from one life to another as we walked down Convent.

The buzz of conversation and occasional laughter broke the eerie silence of our early journey. The world transformed as though the city became alive and breathed into everything on this one street. Hundreds of people, many just claiming their spots for the day, set up their booths, put out their goods, or sat around and waited for business to start.

Oh, and the smell of delicious food and pastries.

My stomach reacted immediately, and I took a deep breath, trying—to no avail—to settle it back down. The usual bland colors of cement and buildings now blended with the lively colors of people moving from one place to another. In this sea of color, sound, smell, my senses became drunk on it all.

I needed this—the hustle and bustle of life.

We passed vendor after vendor, moving deeper into the heart of the market. It took all of my strength not to look at the food in a nearby pita stand, but I felt a tug on my sleeve. Dregg stared off into the distance, eyes wide.

With a whisper, he asked, "Can you get us breakfast?"

My heart twisted. This was why I didn't make connections. I couldn't take this burden, like a weight on my chest. He didn't ask me very often to steal for him. Everything was always a competition. So for him to ask…

I searched the steadily growing crowd and looked back at him. "Meet me by the statue in fifteen minutes." He smiled and disappeared to my right.

I made my way through the vendors and other guests, making sure to stand tall, and searched for the best place to grab and go.

A small cart caught my eye. Someone handed cardboard bowls of breakfast food through a window, and a second worker placed the food on a nearby table. If I timed it right, I could grab one of those containers when they both turned their backs. I watched the pattern as both men continued to turn, pass new food from one to the other, and set it down. It was like finding the rhythm in a dance I didn't know, but once I learned it, I could dance it too.

I moved quickly, looping around behind another patron to make sure I had the right beats, because the music would end as soon as the spaces for bowls filled. I approached the cart with purpose.

Turn, pass, set, turn, pass, set—I grabbed two bowls, one in each hand, spun in the opposite direction, and crossed behind the cart. I glanced over my shoulder. The worker put down the new bowls in his hands and went right back to his dance, without breaking his rhythm.

I met Dregg at the statue, and his eyes lit up when he saw me. "Thank you. I haven't eaten anything real in two days, and I knew I wasn't—"

I put my hand up, stopping his words, and handed him a bowl. "You're welcome. Just be careful today. There are lots of people. That's not always a good thing."

He shoved half of the scrambled eggs in his mouth and raised his eyebrows. "I'll be fine."

I nodded as I sat down next to him and piled my eggs on the piece of toast. I folded the strips of bacon on top. I hadn't eaten anything real in longer than two days, so I knew I should eat slower to avoid getting sick.

We ate in silence, so I watched the crowd for any new dance partners. As I finished my last piece of food, my eyes found a man in a grey collared shirt and dark jeans, walking down the sidewalk.

His clothes didn't scream "high-end," but he dressed well enough that he had money. His hair was well kempt, slicked back, and clean. He looked like the man in charge, exuding the energy of someone who lived above the rest.

And I needed what he had more than he did.

"I'll see you back in the Caves," I said, keeping my eyes on the man as he neared the center of the market.

"Mmm-hmm" was Dregg's response as I stood up and began to follow my new mark.

I studied the man's path as he made his way across the square, veering in, out, and around different vendors. I kept my distance, stopping intermittently to look at random items and ask about pricing. I slowly meandered closer to him as he moved.

A funnel of people clustered at the end of a walkway. It would force us all closer by default. I used my short stature to blend in with the crowd and reached the funnel first. I waited as the man paused at a nearby tent with household tools.

He eventually purchased something and continued on his path, passing me without a glance. I stepped out, half hiding behind the other shoppers, and slipped my hand into his back pocket.

I began to turn with his wallet when a hand grabbed me, crushing my grip and pulling me back. I tried to pull away, but his hand held mine in a vise. A black tattoo adorned the top of his wrist—a black triangle with a bold B inside.

My heart dropped. B was for Barrios. The leaders in each faction marked themselves with their own letter inside the triangle. I just stole from a Barrios sentry.

My face drained of color as I glanced back up at his face. And then he laughed. He actually laughed at me.

Time slowed as he stared at me. His sharp features blurred as the sounds of the market dropped away and disappeared into silence.

A sentry was an elite guardsman. They were trained to protect their faction, their people, their territory, and their Duke. They were trained to follow orders—like the one that killed my sister.

I knew pulling to release my arm again would yield nothing. So I waited, waited for him to say something, waited for my punishment.

Staring back into his cold, dark eyes, I held my breath as he finally spoke.

"Not many can get their hands near my pockets, never mind in my pocket." He smiled. "Nicely done." My face scrunched in confusion. "What's your name, thief?"

I raised my chin. "What does it matter?"

"When I introduce you to Duke Klintone, he'll be able to call you something other than thief."

I spoke before my mind could stop me. "Well, you can tell Duke Klintone that I have other things to do today."

He smiled again, still holding my wrist. "Oh, he's going to like you."

I looked around and realized the crowd had moved back to give us space. Strangers formed a circle around us, watching.

I raised my head a little higher. "And what if I don't want to meet your Duke?"

He chuckled in reply, flashing me a smile. He leaned closer, his nose inches from mine. "I'm sorry. You think I was giving you a choice, little thief?"

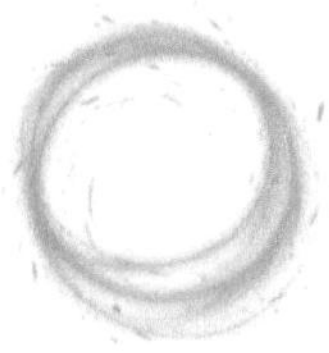

The journey doesn't end here.

or visit
miscelleana.com

ACKNOWLEDGMENTS

Since the nights my father read me bedtime stories, books have been a source of joy and inspiration. As I grew older, they provided an emotional escape during difficult times, taking me to places that no other medium could. As an author, it brings even more fulfillment to know that others may experience something similar within the pages of my own books. Connecting with readers on such a level is a gift like nothing else.

Without the dedicated support of those closest to me, I would have never made it through this incredible journey from concept to publication. My story could not be told without every single person who stood by my side.

My Tanis, I wouldn't be where I am today without your immense and unwavering faith in me. You have always believed in me and because of that belief, that love, I can finally share my creativity–my art, my joy–through my words. We have already written so many chapters in our life together, and this one is just another filled with long nights and days chasing our dreams. This time, it just happens to be mine. Thank you for pouring yourself into this chapter as much as I have.

Samantha, Anastasia, Kristopher, Konstantine, and Emily. Thank you for being my biggest supporters and for listening to me rattle off a thousand thoughts for my many scenes. Your own ideas have sparked plot points and character traits throughout this series and others to come. You helped bring magic to my words in more ways than you all know.

Papa, what can I say other than I am who I am because of you? I am a writer because of you. You pushed me to follow every single creative aspect of myself and taught me to never stop chasing my dreams. Our Workshop nights are still my most treasured growing up, and I have never felt more creative than I did in those days. Thank you for instilling in me the power to never give up and to pursue my passion for writing no matter how many trees are in the forest. ...And back.

Sending appreciation and love to my west and east coast family and all of my family in between. You all have believed in me throughout the years, supported me, and now as I changed from a writer to an author, you are all still by my side, cheering from the sidelines. Your unshakeable support keeps me pushing every day.

To my most incredible and talented editor, Heather, you took my draft and breathed life into every piece of this book. It went from a story in my head to a novel on the pages with your guidance. Thank you for being able to stay true to me and my vision and for always challenging me to follow my gut–the best piece of advice I've received throughout this entire process. I'll take that with me forever through every novel, every series, everything.

My amazing marketing duo–Abbey Ryan and Charlotte Zang–Thank you for answering my millions and millions of questions with the same spirit and passion that I feel every day adding words to a page. Your true dedication and joy helped me lay out an incredible marketing foundation for my entire series. For that, I will always be grateful.

To the rest of my publishing team–Stefanie Gilmour, M.A. Hinkle, Brandy Lay, Megan Buttaro, and last but absolutely not least, Amanda Bronson–who kept the process moving smoothly from beginning to end–I'm sending my own special thank you to each one of you for your part in making this book (and my next two in the series) completely magical. From refined details, beautiful layouts, and constant support, encouragement, and knowledge, you all are truly the dream team. Thank you with all my creative heart.

www.ingramcontent.com/pod-product-compliance
Lightning Source LLC
Chambersburg PA
CBHW020504310726
48979CB00016B/2781/J

* 9 7 9 8 9 8 8 1 0 6 1 1 1 *